Praise for *Side Effect*

"In this page-turning courtroom drama, Essay provides an informative and sober look at Big Pharma, and the deadly consequences of the opioid crisis facing America today."

—SUZANNE SIMONETTI, *USA Today* best-selling author of *The Sound of Wings*

"Compellingly readable and brutally insightful. . . . *Side Effects Are Minimal* dives into the layers of greed and deceit surrounding the opioid crisis in America. A riveting fictional tale that will keep you on the edge of your seat."

—LARRY WIDMAN, MD, psychiatrist and author of *Max Out Mindset*

"If you want to understand the overdose crisis in all its multifaceted angles, this is the book for you. Essay uses this captivating and engrossing narrative to explain what few policymakers can articulate. A heartbreaking and illuminating story."

—DR. JAY K. JOSHI, author of *Burden of Pain*

"Laura Essay's debut novel transports you inside the opioid crisis while exposing the pharma giants in a thrilling courtroom drama. With a memorable cast of characters, crisp writing, and page-turning suspense, this novel is a time-worthy and important read!"

—ANGELA PISEL, author of *With Love from the Inside*

SIDE EFFECTS ARE MINIMAL

A NOVEL

LAURA ESSAY

SHE WRITES PRESS

Published 2024
Printed in the United States of America

Print ISBN: 978-1-64742-704-7
E-ISBN: 978-1-64742-705-4
Library of Congress Control Number: 2023924188

For information, address:
She Writes Press
1569 Solano Ave #546
Berkeley, CA 94707

Interior design and typeset by Katherine Lloyd, The DESK

She Writes Press is a division of SparkPoint Studio, LLC.

To Raymond Woodbury Pence
1885–1978

*My great-grandfather, my inspiration, and an author
who showed me the value of the written word.
Still looking up to you, Pa.*

CONTENTS

1 FIRST CHAIR...1

2 PREVIOUS BAD ACTS.................................5

3 DINING ON LOMBARD..............................10

4 BACK SCRATCH......................................35

5 BELIEVE ME, YOU DON'T 45

6 ELUSIVE ANSWERS...............................55

7 SMOLDERING EMBERS..........................66

8 NOT SO FAST..82

9 RECREATION FOR ARISTOCRATS 96

10 THE SECRET ROOM..............................101

11 DECEPTIVE CHARADE.........................117

12 SILVER BULLET..................................129

13 NO! NO! NO!......................................142

14 LET IT GO..153

15 PAPER CUTS.......................................158

16 OPIOPHILIA..171

17 MUDDIED WATERS..............................181

18 SIX DEGREES OF SEPARATION.............192

19 PRIZE MONEY 199

20 IATROGENIC ADDICTION......................208

21 OVERPROMOTED AND OVERPRESCRIBED........213

22 RED BLOSSOMS.................................224

23 RANDOM ACT 233

24 NO FRIEND OF MINE.........................240

25 POPPY..251

26 FISHING HATS AND PLUSH TOYS 275

27 MARGO'S TEARS 293

28 DEFIANT SCHOOLGIRL.........................313

29 SWEET BABY GIRL 319

    OPIOIDS: WHAT WE SHOULD KNOW.............329

    ACKNOWLEDGMENTS 333

    ABOUT THE AUTHOR..........................335

1

FIRST CHAIR

The door flew open, and there she stood, right hand gripping the frame. She licked the sweetness from her lips, unsure if it was sugar or the taste of victory. Unfazed by the frigid air, Claire dashed out the door of the café and skidded through two inches of white powder. Airy flakes clung to her fur-lined boots. The newly fallen snow offered gaiety, rather than annoyance, to her walk to Blackman & Bradford law firm. She was invigorated by the respect and deference she'd received from other partners. Mostly the deference. Her eyes gleamed, and her walk looked more like a skip.

Claire paused at the corner and pulled her smartphone from her coat pocket. She tapped the screen several times. She swiped to the left to check her calendar and grinned at the blank pages. Returning the phone to her pocket, Claire strolled down Chestnut Street, breathing in the cold air and warm comfort of familiarity. The greater Philadelphia area had groomed Claire for almost forty years, and her legal career was blossoming with commensurate recognition for her hard work.

Claire flipped the hood of her coat over her head as she admired the storefront of Black Threads Boutique. While she leaned in closer to examine the deconstructed jeans cinched onto the faceless mannequin, the brass bell jingled against the glass door as it swung open.

"Damn girl, it's freezing out here," chirped the slight redhead propping a sale sign against the front window.

"I'm warm-blooded. I don't even feel it."

"Don't give me that. You've been shopping here for years. I know what sweaters you own. Get your butt in here where it's warm. You need to check out the laser-cut dress that just arrived. The purple will ignite you, and I only have a handful of sizes."

"Maybe later. I'm running a bit late."

Claire chuckled and resumed her pace. Turning the corner, she stopped to stare at the commanding building ahead. Her shoulders dropped as she walked past the glass-block waterfall adorning the entrance of Blackman & Bradford. She paused again at the foot of the gold-embossed entrance mat. Before continuing through the revolving door, Claire took several deep breaths, straightened the collar on her wool coat, and stomped the snow from her boots. She then reached forward and pushed.

The receptionist's boisterous greeting startled Claire but brought a smile to her face. Madalyn perched behind the front desk wearing a skintight leopard-print turtleneck and an excited grin.

"Good morning, Ms. Hewitt. The quarterly meeting? It was at Southside Café this morning, was it not?"

"Six o'clock sharp."

"Your face says it all. You killed it."

"I dominated."

"I knew you would. Girl power," snickered Madalyn.

"I guess." Claire smiled at Madalyn's casual familiarity as she continued to the elevator and stepped inside.

When the elevator bounced to a stop on the twelfth floor, Claire leapt into the hallway with the energy she carried from the café. She smiled at the morning activity and exchanged mutual pleasantries with other attorneys. She then grabbed a hot cup of coffee from the break room and hummed her way down the hall. Balancing both her briefcase and her coffee, she unlocked her office door and entered. A corrugated box with a bright yellow Post-it Note had been left on her desk. Claire walked to the note. *Satori—First Chair.*

"Oh God." A slow smile creased Claire's face as she set her briefcase by her feet. She reached inside the box, grabbed the top folder, and flew to her office door. With both hands grabbing the frame, she peered out. Her head whipped back and forth. When Morgan emerged from the break room, Claire's left hand flapped in the air. Morgan nodded and headed Claire's way.

"Do you know about this?" asked Claire, grabbing Morgan and pulling her inside.

"About what?"

"The Satori case."

Morgan shook her head.

"Everyone knows about it," said Claire. "A dead teenage girl. Doctor-inflicted? Maybe. Drug-induced? Definitely. And God knows how many counts of criminal wrongdoing by one of the largest pharmaceutical companies in the nation. This has class-action written all over it."

Morgan grabbed the folder from Claire's hand. *Clifford and Margo Satori vs. Novo Analgesic Systems, Inc.* She licked the index finger of her right hand and swiped pages as she skimmed the contents.

"I do remember hearing about this," said Morgan. "Lord, woman. They gave you the Satoris."

"Against Novo Analgesic Systems. This will make my career."

"Speaks volumes about the trust Walter and David have in you." Morgan dropped the folder onto Claire's desk. "There's no one bigger than Clifford Satori. All of Philadelphia listens to what he says and watches what he does."

"I know. And it's about time they let me in. I've earned this case."

"You know there'll be naysayers who lose their shit over you representing the Satoris."

"Screw them. Walter Blackman wouldn't risk losing a class-action, and he assigned this case to me." Claire reached inside the box for more material.

"Clever choice of words. That's how they'll say you landed the assignment. How else would a woman get a case this big?" Morgan ran her fingers through her hair. "Tits and ass."

"Who cares?" A contagious grin brightened Claire's face. "Let their jealousies eat 'em alive while I take my tits and ass into that courtroom and bring NAS to their knees."

2

PREVIOUS BAD ACTS

"I'm sorry, Your Honor, but you don't understand." Claire's words echoed across the courtroom. "Every element of medical negligence is present. Dr. Delaney had a duty to Emma Satori as his patient. There was a dereliction of this duty the moment he prescribed the deadly drug Deprexone. Therefore, Dr. Delaney is the direct cause of Emma Satori's death, and her death has caused serious and permanent injury to the Satori family. This is medical negligence resulting in death, plain and simple."

"Plain and simple, my ass," Landon mumbled as he shifted in his seat and straightened the crease of his Armani pants.

"Dr. Delaney has shown reckless disregard for his patients," Claire continued. "The purpose of this hearing is to determine if the material evidence presented today substantiates the plaintiffs' claim that Dr. Delaney is liable for the wrongful death of their daughter and should be held accountable in a court of law. I believe it does."

Claire took a deep breath and adjusted a bobby pin tucked into the loose bun at the base of her neck. She looked up at

Judge Connor with skeptical but unwavering eyes. Her heart fluttered under her blouse while she watched the judge ignore her pleas.

"To find otherwise would gravely endanger innocent lives in the state of Pennsylvania." Claire returned to her seat.

"Objection!" Landon jumped to his feet and wiped beads of sweat from his thinning hairline. "The evidence presented today shows no such thing. Ms. Hewitt has made unfounded accusations that fail to support medical negligence resulting in death. Pennsylvania law mandates that the evidence presented be sufficient to raise a legitimate question of liability appropriate for judicial inquiry and not simply an unfortunate medical result."

Landon's volume rose as his words slowed. He locked eyes with Claire, who leaned back in her chair as she listened to his rebuke. Her hands were clasped in her lap, and her heart still fluttered. She looked like a schoolgirl nervously awaiting the results of a recent exam. With visible unease, she broke eye contact, and Landon continued addressing Judge Connor.

"Sometimes unfortunate results occur. Sometimes patients are unhappy with these results. We can't jump to medical negligence every time we don't like the outcome. These people expected miracles only God could provide."

Landon sat down as Judge Connor looked from defense counsel to the prosecuting attorney. His eyes continued to ricochet as he cleared his throat and addressed them both with a deep grumble.

"Ms. Hewitt, you need not inform me of the purpose of this hearing nor the extent of your personal beliefs. I'm well aware of one and find no relevance for the other. Mr. Sims, there is no problem with the acoustics in this courtroom. I suggest you adjust your volume."

"Yes, sir," came the united reply.

While Landon returned to his seat, the courtroom door creaked open. In rushed Jack Freeman. As CEO of Novo Analgesic Systems, Inc., Jack moved with the swift elegance of supremacy. His thin nose and high cheekbones accentuated his narrow face. He hustled up the aisle with no regard to the ongoing proceedings and bent down to Landon's ear. The two men conversed in hushed tones. Jack then gave Landon a pat on the back as he turned and strolled out. Landon glanced over at Claire, who ignored the brief encounter. She wouldn't give Landon the benefit of her curiosity but wondered if it was a genuine issue or staged theatrics.

While Judge Connor had the reputation of being a tough but fair judge, he also was known to enjoy the power his black robe bestowed. He savored the control that came with deliberating from the bench while everyone waited. Today was no different. Judge Connor reviewed each piece of evidence as his salt-and-pepper hair glistened under the fluorescent lighting. His stern expression then landed on Claire.

"Although you've enumerated upon circumstances in which Dr. Delaney prescribed opioids for his young patients, you've failed to show serious injury sustained by these patients. Nor have you shown a motive or intended plan. Previous bad acts are not admissible, Ms. Hewitt. And you've presented no evidence that would mandate an exception to this rule." Judge Connor looked down at the papers he held as Claire's shoulders sank and she puffed air into her cheeks.

Afternoon sunlight cast oblong shadows through the narrow windows, creating an ominous glow in the courtroom. Law clerks fiddled with documents while both attorneys waited. Landon Sims's faint hum displayed smug confidence as the bitterness of defeat hung over Claire's downcast face.

"Having Freeman show up is bush league." Claire glared across the aisle. "Doesn't intimidate me a bit."

"I'm not trying to intimidate anybody," claimed Landon.

"Like hell. But we're closing Delaney's doors and NAS is going to write a big fat check."

"Doubt that, Ms. Hewitt. Doesn't look like this will even make it to trial."

Claire turned back to the paper she held as a signal she was finished with Landon. The fingers of her right hand nervously drummed the table as her left hand tried to steady the paper she pretended to read. The toe of her red pump rapidly tapped the floor beneath her chair. Landon watched her with a tight smile that flattened his pointy chin. He crossed his ankles and leaned back in his chair.

Judge Connor looked up with serious eyes and a loud clearing of his throat. Claire tried to read the expression on his blank face as she stopped drumming her fingers. She took several deep breaths, anticipating either a favorable ruling to proceed or the humiliating failure of a dismissal. She felt Landon's eyes upon her.

"Ms. Hewitt, while the evidence you presented today has failed to show a correlation between previous opioid prescriptions written by Dr. Delaney and the allegations presented in this case, you have established a question of liability concerning the prescriptions given Emma Satori."

Claire's eyes closed as she exhaled the breath she'd been holding. Judge Connor rose from his chair and left the courtroom with no further comment. Claire watched the door close as Landon smacked the table in front of him.

"Looks like we're getting back into NAS's offices after all." Claire sprung from her seat to face Landon with cautious glee. She watched and waited.

Ignoring Claire's zeal, Landon gathered folders spread across the defense table. He stacked them into a single pile and tapped the edges. Claire shifted on her feet with impatience. Her cheeks were flushed as her heart raced with excited prudence. She had attained the small victory expected of her, but Judge Connor's comments spoke to the uncertainty of the complaint.

"I'd rather our visit to the NAS office be sooner than later. And we're opening every door in the place," said Claire.

"Fine by me." Landon shrugged one shoulder.

"We're going to expose everything hidden in that building. And I think the court will be very interested in the secrets we discover."

"I'm afraid you're going to be disappointed. But you're welcome to try."

Landon stood and squared his shoulders as he faced Claire. His strong arms were folded across his chest. Claire stepped into the aisle and raised her chin.

"Not sure what your shtick is, Landon. But your maneuvering is getting tedious."

"Then stop looking for what doesn't exist. Judge Connor omitted the previous opioid scripts the same way he omitted Novo Analgesic Systems' previous Deprexone testing. Connor's making my job easier one hearing at a time."

"Don't kid yourself." Claire adjusted another bobby pin in an attempt to look unruffled. She turned from Landon and scooped up the last of the files. She tossed them into her open briefcase and slammed the lid shut. With fictitious certainty, she grabbed her jacket from the chair and draped it over one shoulder before turning back to Landon's voice.

"You know this isn't my first battle with Blackman & Bradford," said Landon. "I know the intimidation of sitting on this side of the table. But that's all it is. You're a declawed cat who's more scared than scary."

"Think so?" Claire tilted her head.

"Prove me wrong."

3

DINING
ON LOMBARD

A handful of manila folders skidded across the desk, scattering several memorandums and dozens of medical records onto the plush carpet. Claire walked through the door seconds behind the folders she had thrown. She ignored the mess and collapsed into her thick leather chair. She slapped the glass nameplate facedown on her desk and spun her chair to face the skyline outside her window. Her knees swayed as she swiveled the chair left to right.

"How'd it go?" Morgan popped her head into the office.

Claire jumped from her chair and spun to face Morgan. She stood motionless as her chest rose and fell. Her eyes filled but no tears spilled over.

"Uh oh, not so well." Morgan entered the room.

"I worked my ass off for this case, but I can't control it," said Claire.

"That bad?"

"That bad. I feel like my hand is plunged into an aquarium trying to grab a guppy. Every time I know I have a firm grip, it pops out the other side, leaving me empty-handed."

Claire turned back to the six-foot plate of glass framed by the wall behind her. The city below was swarming with life. People scurried in and out of buildings as cars started and stopped to let them pass.

"Today's small victory is smothered in red flags." Claire's eyes bounced around the activity on the street below.

"What red flags?" asked Morgan.

"Connor didn't dismiss it. But I think he's gunning for an implosion at trial."

"Don't get all crazy about it." Morgan opened Claire's top drawer and grabbed a mint. She popped it in her mouth and dropped the wrapper in the trash.

"Crazy? I'm scared shitless," said Claire. "I'm still proving myself in a man's world."

"In what decade do you live? 'A man's world'?"

"Lead counsel for the Satoris? I overheard voices in David's office questioning whether I'm up for the job. Male voices."

"Of course they were male voices," said Morgan. "There aren't too many of us around here. But don't underestimate yourself. I've been following in your tailwind since I sat in that auditorium as a diddly freshman watching you accept one graduation honor after another. It sure as hell wasn't a man's world that day. And today isn't either."

"That doesn't help."

"You don't need help. You're fine."

"I will be," Claire flattened her palms against the cool glass. "But this should be a cakewalk. You know what people think of doctors."

"They're rich and egotistical?" Morgan joined Claire by the window.

"And powerful. Doctors sit in the captains' chairs circulating the quick-fix drug manufacturers provide. And everybody wants a quick fix."

"I know. Believe me, I know."

"You'd second-guess yourself if you were in my shoes." Claire turned from the window and leaned against the counter next to Morgan. She glanced at the folders spread across her desk but let her eyes rest on the mounds of envelopes piled in her inbox. "If anyone questions Walter, he'll be pissed. It'll force him to question his decision placing me as first chair. He'll think the case is too big for a new partner."

"Is your pity party over?"

"I'm just getting started." Claire looked sideways at Morgan.

"The opioid crisis is on the front page of every newspaper in America." Morgan lifted her hips onto the counter and crossed her dangling ankles. "Connor fears reversal on this one. He's covering his ass."

"Yeah, while he's kicking mine."

Claire sprang forward and raced from the office, leaving a dumbfounded Morgan perched behind her desk. The door bounced off the file cabinet as Claire ran down the hall. She came to an abrupt stop as she grabbed the recessed doorframe of the elevator. She poked the small button and looked up. Too impatient to wait, she ran to the adjacent stairwell. Landing on every other step, she felt juvenile pride at beating the elevator to the eleventh floor.

Two law clerks idled in the far corner of the library when she entered. They both looked up before opening books as if consumed with work. Claire ignored the feeble attempt to feign busyness and found an available computer on an empty table. Her fingers rapidly tapped the keys while the nearby printer waited. After several moments, Claire paused and blew air into her cheeks. As was a frequent habit, she swished the air back and forth in her closed mouth. She then resumed typing as the printer began humming.

Warm papers filled the output tray as the two law clerks whispered to themselves. As if coming to agreement, one clerk approached Claire. He stood silently as Claire's fingers raced across the keyboard. Without looking up, her fingers slowed.

"Is there something you need?" asked Claire.

"No, ma'am. Is there anything you need, Ms. Hewitt? Any research you'd like me to do?" The clerk rocked on his heels with both fists shoved deep into his pants pockets.

Surprised the clerk knew her name, Claire smiled. "Thank you, but no. I have everything I need."

Claire resumed typing as the clerk hurried back to his friend. The two flipped through magazines while Claire continued her search and the printer continued to print. When assured her mission was accomplished, Claire put her screen to sleep and grabbed the papers from the tray. The two clerks looked up and watched her leave with the same urgency they had seen when she arrived.

Claire again took the stairs and didn't slow down when she pushed through the stairway door. As she rushed past the break room, she overheard Morgan's voice. Claire reversed her steps and stuck her head inside the bright room. Without a word, she motioned for Morgan to follow. Morgan finished her conversation as Claire continued to her office, clutching the cooling papers to her chest. She was stapling related reports when Morgan entered and closed the door.

"We're going to play 'Capture the Flag?'" said Claire.

"What?"

"I'm going to play it with Connor. These additional occurrences give me what I need to capture every damn one of those red flags he was waving. Police reports, news briefings, magazine articles, obituaries. All individuals lost to opioids."

"Oh shit . . ."

"You're right, oh shit. The opioid crisis is too immense for him to ignore or make light of. These are tragedies that force everyone to acknowledge that people taking opioids are dying. Every hour, eleven souls leave this earth because of some drug."

"The big man in the black robe has no idea."

"America has no idea." Claire dropped into her chair and cupped her face with both hands. She leaned forward with a deep breath and then fell back with her fingers over her eyes. A bead of sweat dripped in front of her ear and traveled down her neck into her blouse.

"Don't take this case personally." Morgan reached over and jostled Claire's chair.

"It is personal, Morgan. You can call it a professional privilege. I call it a personal battle." Claire dropped her arms toward the floor without lifting her head and looked over at Morgan.

"It's both." Morgan walked behind Claire's chair and gripped the thick cushioned sides. She rocked it as she spoke. "NAS became a powerhouse when they shifted their marketing from drugs for the treatment of acute pain to drugs for the treatment of chronic pain."

"The drugs didn't change. They're the same damn opioids."

"For decades, society worshipped them for helping Dad make it through his back surgery, and for giving the little chemo girl a chance to play soccer. But they've gone too far, and you've been given the chance to prove it."

"Prove that your chronic pain won't kill you, but your opioids will?"

"Exactly." Morgan gave Claire's chair a final nudge as she walked away. "The truth about their marketing scheme. The truth that their dynasty is built on the backs of opioid addicts."

Morgan sat down in front of Claire's desk as Claire shot up and reached for a news report. She gripped it tightly, crumpling the edge as her eyes scanned the page. Without looking up, she handed it to Morgan and grabbed the next. She continued for several moments as her breathing became unsteady and her handoffs aggressive.

"Look at this." Claire shoved another report at Morgan. "In 2021 alone, 107,000 Americans died of drug overdoses. That's a 16 percent increase in one year." Claire read another obituary, crumpled it, and dropped it on her desk.

"Don't wallow in the misfortune of the unknowns." Morgan stood up and looked down at the same obituary. "Find out who they are and let a jury force NAS to pay for the lives they destroyed."

"That's what I intend to do." Claire stood and rolled her chair back with her calves. "NAS will discover how expensive it is to deceive physicians into prescribing opioids for every bump and bruise. Before I'm finished, they'll see how much aggressive campaigns cost when innocent people are hurt. When athletes crumble and teenagers die."

Claire leaned onto her desk with straight arms. A single tear escaped down her cheek. With slow, methodical movements, she straightened the research into tidy piles and centered the nameplate on her desk. She slid the lamp to the right corner, and the stapler and several pens were swept into the top drawer. She then looked at Morgan with a sad smile.

"They'll pay for treating hospitals like carnivals and opioids like candy, sending everyone home with their basket full."

"That's a noble battle but a steep hill to climb while people are screaming for their sweets." Morgan walked around the desk and brushed her thumb across Claire's cheek.

"Yeah, well. I have the endurance."

"You've always been a tough one," said Morgan as she walked over to the couch and dropped back onto the cushions.

She swung both legs onto the coffee table and wiggled her toes. "But be ready for the onslaught. *Pain* is a dirty word, and Oxycodone is the answer."

"Oxycodone, hydrocodone, Deprexone, oxymorphone. They all are. But real answers come in small doses, not by the hundreds. It's a game-changer when you leave the hospital with hundreds of opioids in your pocket."

"Tell me about it. I left the hospital with 120 oxycodone after my surgery last October. I could be an addict right now had I not chosen ibuprofen instead. Not that I don't have other addictions," laughed Morgan as she smoothed her skirt and wiggled her toes again.

"Opioids aren't the answer the drug manufacturers claim." Claire wiped her fingers underneath both eyes and looked over at Morgan. "A patient taking an opioid longer than three months has a 1,500 percent greater chance of becoming addicted."

"It's a cluster." Morgan wiggled to the edge of the couch. She scooted up onto the side arm and balanced the balls of her feet on the table. "Show Connor, show that jury, how NAS makes millions while doctors use opioids like Band-Aids."

"Sometimes the most obvious transgressions are the hardest to prove." Claire stepped back from her desk and hoisted herself onto the counter. She gripped the edge with both hands and tapped her feet in the air as they dangled. "Connor kept spouting off about the inadmissibility of previous bad acts. Classified every previous script written by that old man as inadmissible."

"For fuck's sake, Claire. Find a pattern, an intent, or the absence of a mistake. All three of those create an exception to the inadmissibility rule."

"Listen to your mouth." Claire grabbed a handful of papers and walked over to where Morgan was balanced. She dropped onto the couch and jabbed Morgan with her pointy elbow.

"What the hell?" said Morgan. "I'm trying to help you."

"Thought you said I don't need it?"

"You don't. So stop acting like a little bitch because of one hearing. Find the missing piece of evidence that develops your pattern or forms an intent. Professor McDaniel barked about the MP for three years. Act like you learned something."

"That stupid acronym won't change anything. Clifford Satori will crush my career if I can't find an answer for his daughter's death."

"The MP will be your answer." Morgan stood to leave. "Satori wants revenge, and so do you."

"A new revenge. A revenge called justice." Claire watched Morgan slip back into her shoes.

"MP? Is there a missing person?" Alec breezed into Claire's office and looked back and forth between both women.

Morgan rolled her eyes and headed for the door. She nudged Alec in the ribs as she passed and smiled to herself. Alec stumbled sideways, exaggerating the force. Claire enjoyed the exchange and repositioned on the couch, tucking one foot underneath her outstretched leg.

"Your virtuoso has arrived. From what I hear, no MP can escape him." Morgan's voice became faint as she continued down the hall. "Best new hire the firm has."

Claire watched Alec redirect his attention to the floor around her desk. With raised eyebrows that formed deep wrinkles across his forehead, he picked up a handful of papers and added them to an existing stack. He then turned to face Claire.

"Who's missing?" he asked.

"Well, Mr. Marshall, evidence the defendants don't want us to find," answered Claire.

"What's the MP you were jabbering about?"

"I don't jabber. Missing piece. Our evidence professor thrived on sending us in search of the missing piece of evidence. We always missed something. I can hear him saying 'The MP is out there just waiting to be found.' He was a demanding bastard."

"Weren't they all?" Alec grabbed another handful of folders from the floor. "These must have slipped from your hands." He smiled and then reached under the chair and grabbed two more.

Claire untangled her legs and stood in front of the couch. She repositioned the lavender-scented candle by the glossy coffee table books and picked up the research behind her. With simmering enthusiasm, she walked back to her large leather chair while Alec chose a smaller cushioned chair in front of her desk. She examined Alec with tenacious eyes as she handed him the news briefs and several obituaries. While Alec read the papers he held, Claire pressed the call button on her phone. There was no need for words. The buzz was enough to let Ellen know she was needed.

Ellen was the perfect legal assistant. She was a dynamic woman in her late fifties who possessed the appearance and energy of a much younger woman. Very few gray hairs were seen among the dark brown strands that fell to her shoulders. And although she swore to the contrary, she could have been the poster child for Botox.

Ellen arrived but stopped short of entering when she saw the floor covered in paper. Most had landed around Claire's desk. But several had made it as far as the door, and one was under Ellen's foot.

"Can you please grab the Satori depositions?" asked Claire.
"Of course."

Ellen lifted her foot and picked up the paper. She softly set it on Claire's desk and scurried off to fulfill the request.

Claire gathered the remaining folders from the floor as Alec skimmed the material he'd been given. She placed several in the file cabinet behind the door and flipped around to face Alec. With a crease in her brows, she gripped her hips and watched him read.

"What do you make of that?" she asked.

"Horrifying."

"No kidding," said Claire. "Every state in the nation has an opioid death rate, yet nobody sees it."

"Oh, they see it. These articles were written by someone. These police reports were filed by someone. Somebody attended these funerals."

Claire stacked several reports on top of each other and then piled those reports on top of others. She scooped the large stack into her arms and rushed out the door. Alec followed. Claire brushed past Ellen in the hallway. Without stopping, she grabbed the depositions.

"We'll be in the conference room," said Claire.

Claire tossed the documents onto the table upon entering the room. Alec again followed but stopped at the door and leaned one forearm against the frame. An air of confidence lingered around him. Although he possessed an intellect he revealed only at his pleasure, his physical attributes could not be ignored. He was six foot two with his blond hair kept in a short military style, and his ready, gleaming smile accentuated his olive skin. Claire looked him up and down until their eyes met.

"Thank God you weren't in that courtroom today." Claire broke eye contact and dropped into the closest chair. She busied herself separating research material from depositions.

"Why's that?" Alec continued through the door and stood behind Claire. He scanned the documents she sorted with an intrigued expression. "Connor an ass?"

"With a capital *A*," said Claire. "I've done this a thousand times. You push a bit; some evidence is inadmissible. But Connor threw out everything."

"Sounds like last week with NAS drug testing."

"Close enough. He ruled Delaney's previous opioid prescriptions inadmissible as previous bad acts."

Claire scanned the first deposition, flipped it closed, and grabbed the next. She flipped through the pages of the second one in the same manner.

"What are you doing now?"

"Searching for a pattern that'll force Connor to admit the evidence we need." Claire held her breath as she looked up at the evergreen eyes staring back. Alec shrugged both shoulders and walked to the end of the long table. In a laissez-faire manner, he placed his hand alongside a tall stack of folders and slid them to Claire.

"Establishing a pattern with Delaney won't be difficult. He's been handing out scripts for decades." Alec dropped into the chair next to Claire. "But a company like NAS knows how to cover its ass. They had a class-action lawsuit in the nineties that taught them the safest way to hide information they didn't want found. And the doctors were more than happy to assist. Didn't want to lose their supplier."

Claire pushed away from the table, mumbling about liability, and walked to the file cabinet behind the door. As she pulled open the bottom drawer, several brightly colored brochures dropped to the floor. She scooped up the pamphlets and fanned them in the air.

"Supplier or not, doctors won't assume blame for deceptive promotional campaigns. In the beginning, the campaigns were aimed solely at them, and doctors believed that opioids carried a low risk of addiction." Claire tossed the propaganda to Alec.

"Looks like they learned the truth the hard way," said Alec as he leafed through the multicolored publications.

"Not as hard as the patients who lost their lives."

"Isn't that the truth. But doctors will protect themselves before they promote a drug or protect any drug manufacturer. They'll abandon NAS if affiliation would jeopardize their reputations."

"Then let's rattle some cages." Claire collected the pamphlets as she detailed her plan. "We request a warrant to examine every test NAS has conducted on every drug they've released. From the beginning. If they cut the slightest corner, we expose it. If enough corners were cut, we have a pattern of negligent drug testing." Claire lifted the brochures as if they were her trophy and smiled at Alec.

"They'll know we're coming, so they'll be prepared."

"But they'll never guess we want access to everything from the first day Daddy hung out his shingle. They'll lose their shit over that."

"Can't wait." Alec tossed the pamphlet he held to Claire and walked to the small refrigerator underneath the counter. He grabbed a bottle of water and turned back. "As a judicial clerk for the Second Circuit, I witnessed some dramatic meltdowns in the courtroom. This might be the next."

"But you're not sitting up with the judge this round. You're going to be down in the trenches with the rest of us."

"That's what I'm looking forward to most." Alec drank the bottle in three gulps.

Alec sat across the table from Claire and began reading depositions and memorandums. He scanned each one looking for key words and set it aside. After forty-five minutes of silence, Alec rocked back with a loud groan. He stretched his arms out to the side before reaching across to swap new documents for ones he had read. Claire continued her search.

As the hour approached 6:00 p.m., the office began clearing out. For two more hours, Claire and Alec continued their inventory. At 8:00 p.m., with Claire consumed in HIPAA requirements and Alec sifting through drug data, Walter Blackman burst into the room. His dark gray suit was strapped to his assless body with a thick black belt cinched below a protruding belly. He clung to a leather briefcase worn slick.

"No rest for the weary," Walter bellowed. His voice was an octave lower than most men's and his volume several decibels higher.

"No, sir," said Alec.

Claire's expressionless face tilted toward Walter.

"I wasn't in that courtroom today, but perhaps I should have been. Clifford has paid for the best representation this city has to offer. I have no intention of letting him down."

Claire's face hardened at the patronization.

"I've studied this case, Ms. Hewitt. It's routine medical negligence." Walter's eyebrows raised as he looked over the rim of his glasses. "And I do mean routine. You're not searching for a needle in a haystack."

"No one has ever put a needle in a haystack." Claire's face was as inexpressive as her tone. "So a needle will never be found there."

"That's a disappointing attitude. Not only has Clifford invested in this firm, this firm has invested in one of Stanford's best. As his mentor, make sure he sees yours." Walter looked from Claire to Alec and back. "We'll talk in the morning. I expect to be enlightened."

Walter walked out, leaving the door behind him open. Claire stared into the empty hallway. She leaned forward on her forearms as her right foot tapped the carpet. Her bruised ego covered her face.

"Let's call it a night and grab something to eat," suggested Alec.

"Sure." Claire watched the hallway.

"We can stop by Luigi's Corner. You need a drink."

"Yes, I do."

Claire shivered as she stepped out the front door of the Blackman & Bradford building. It was cooler than normal for an August evening, and there was a slight mist in the air.

"I hate evenings like this," Claire sighed.

"Evenings like what?"

"Ones where you can't tell if it's actually raining or if it's so humid that you feel like it is. You can't tell if raindrops are hitting the ground, or if they're trapped in the heavy air unable to break loose."

"It's better if they don't break loose. I don't want to get drenched walking to dinner."

"That's my point," said Claire. "We get wet either way. You don't feel like it's raining but your suit will show rain spots when you step inside. It's called a meteorological cluster bomb. It's a real thing."

"Right." Alec smirked at Claire.

"It is. Google it." Claire's spirit was beginning to lift. She picked up the pace as her stomach growled. She glanced sideways at Alec, hoping he hadn't heard. "Did you make a reservation?"

"I probably should've. You sound hungry," laughed Alec.

Claire nudged Alec. She continued to smile as her steps quickened. "We're going to miss the dinner crowd at this hour. So I think we're fine."

Moments later, as Alec swung open the ornate green door, a fragrant array of basil and oregano engulfed them. At the first sight of his new guests, Dino Luigi rushed forward with infectious energy. His long hair was strikingly white and swept back into a short ponytail. He greeted them both with affectionate hugs. He kissed Claire on the cheek and wrapped his thick arm around her waist as he escorted her to a quaint table in the front window. Alec followed.

"I'd love a glass of your Tignanello Cabernet," Claire requested as Dino pulled out her chair.

"Scotch on the rocks for me," said Alec.

Claire picked up her menu and peered over the top at Alec. Her hidden smile widened as she listened to Alec's animated exchange with the host. Dino laughed with boisterous pleasure and motioned for Alec to sit. He then bid them an Italian farewell as a slender waiter approached.

"Ah, signorina. Buonasera e benvenuti. Mi chiamo Lazzaro e vi servero stasera. Avete gia deciso cosa desiderate mangiare?"

Claire lifted her face to Lazzaro as he spoke.

"I'll have the special with a side Caesar."

Lazzaro clasped both hands together. His unexplained delight was apparent as he turned his attention to Alec.

"E per lei signore?"

"Io prenderei gli gnoochi al pesto," Alec replied in his best Italian.

Lazzaro lifted his chin with a broad smile and waltzed away.

"I didn't know you spoke Italian," said Claire.

"I don't, signorina. I studied in Rome for a semester and remember very little."

"*Signorina*? Seriously?" Claire fluttered her eyelashes in jest.

"Just repeating Lazzaro." Alec shrugged.

"An old Italian can call me that. But that's where I draw the line."

Claire smiled and kept her eyes on Alec as he folded his napkin in his lap. He folded it and unfolded it and folded it again. She enjoyed his nervous demeanor and the deference he gave her. When he looked up, Claire's glass was tilted toward him.

"You can call me that too if you want," said Claire. "Cheers."

Claire's cheeks flushed as the corners of Alec's lips turned upward. His head nodded, and he lifted his glass. The conversation paused at the next table as diners glanced over at the sound of the light clink.

"To the end of a rough day."

"And the start of a nightmare." Claire quickly sipped her Cabernet. "We're in a shit-storm."

"Judge Connor didn't hurt us." Alec swirled the ice around his glass. "He expects us to expose the marketing scam at NAS and put an end to the sideshow in Delaney's office. We can do both."

"Hope you're caught up on your sleep. Sounds like a lot of late nights."

"I don't need much."

Alec turned to the kitchen door. A pungent aroma of garlic escaped as Lazzaro walked out with a large tray. He gently set the tray on a stand beside Claire, and Alec requested another scotch. With a soft tone, Claire ordered a second glass of wine. She finished the last sips in the glass she held as waiters performed their duties with a formality requisite to the finest Italian piazzas. She enjoyed the finesse that swirled around them as they waited for their drinks and took their first bites.

"NAS will fight us every step of the way, so we need to be ruthless," said Claire in between mouthfuls of romaine. "Tomorrow morning, let's take another shot at the Deprexone test results."

"The ones we got from Shaggy?" asked Alec.

"You need to stop calling him that. You're going to do that in front of Connor, and I doubt he'll think it's funny."

"I bet he does. He strikes me as a Scooby-Doo kind of guy. And who doesn't love Shaggy?"

"You have a point," admitted Claire.

"Not sure his personality matches up, though. He has a sinister side behind that sappy surface. He engages in endless conversations with anything that breathes. But he gets that look on his face that says he's up to something."

"I don't know. But I hope that sappy surface becomes our secret weapon. We need to convince him to talk to us. About the lab, the stupid monkeys, and that nut-job Westcott."

A little before midnight, Alec held the door for Claire as she stepped into the clammy night air. With a cautious step onto the wet sidewalk, Claire balanced herself on Alec's arm. He hesitantly placed his hand on top of hers as they started down the street.

A few steps past the ornate green entrance, Claire's free arm shot forward with a loud pop. The violent force threw her against Alec's shoulder and onto the ground. Her briefcase was ripped from her fist. Alec stumbled over her, his foot landing on her flattened hand. The light moisture on the concrete diluted the dabs of blood Claire's cheek left behind.

A black-hooded sweatshirt hid the face of the culprit who bolted toward the parking garage, Claire's briefcase tightly tucked under one arm. Alec recovered his footing and sprinted in pursuit. Claire lay collapsed on the ground. As she lifted her head and touched her cheek, she winced when her fingers brushed her torn skin. She licked the blood from her hand. A blotchy road rash spread down the left side of her face and chin. She pulled her knees in closer and rested her head back on the damp ground.

"Prick," growled Alec, sprinting up the steep ramp.

Several yards beyond the first curve, the hooded runner slid across the hood of a green sedan and leapt over the three-foot wall. Alec ran into the wall while the small figure disappeared into the dark. Alec watched.

Claire remained on the ground with her legs pulled up to her chest when Alec returned. He knelt beside her and turned her chin.

"You okay? You were hit hard."

"I'm fine." Claire straightened her twisted bloody sleeve. "You didn't catch him?"

"No. He did some Starsky and Hutch stunt off the second level. Otherwise I would have. He ran like a girl."

"A speedy girl," said Claire.

"Obviously. I'll call the police." Alec pulled his phone from his pocket.

"I already did."

Alec returned his phone without comment. He scooted around Claire in his squatted position and placed his hands on her bent knees. Claire dropped her bleeding face in the palms of her hands and held her breath.

"Are you sure you're all right?"

"I said I was fine."

Alec rubbed her back as it shook when she gasped for air.

"You can cry. Let it out."

"I don't want to feel weak."

"You're one of the strongest women I know," said Alec as he continued to rub Claire's wet back.

Alec looked up at the sound of loud sirens piercing the air. The volume increased as flashing lights approached. A blue squad car and a white ambulance were racing toward them. Both vehicles slammed to a stop by the curb. Alec stepped back as three EMTs approached. He watched them surround Claire and seized the opportunity to retrieve his car.

Two of the EMTs were large men and repositioned Claire in

between them. The third was a smaller woman who looked into her eyes with a small beam of light. She then pinched Clare's chin and slowly moved her head from side to side.

"State your name," said the female EMT.

"Claire Hewitt."

"Do you know where you are?"

"Sitting on the ground."

"In what city, ma'am?"

"Philadelphia."

"Do you know how you got here?"

"Yeah, some dick threw me down."

"Aside from this elbow, I don't believe you've sustained any serious injuries," said the woman. "Let's immobilize it. Take some Tylenol for discomfort and try to relax for a few days."

The EMT snapped her bag shut and returned to the ambulance as a heavyset Black woman climbed out of the squad car. She sauntered over with a mixed expression of annoyance and fatigue.

"Are you Ms. Hewitt?" the officer asked.

"Yes." Claire stood up with an equal look of annoyance.

"Did you get a good look at who attacked you?"

"No."

"I saw him," said Alec as he jumped out of his cardinal-red Camaro. "I chased him into the garage."

"And then what?"

"He jumped over the wall."

"You didn't follow him?" asked the officer.

"For God's sake, no."

"That's good. I've seen men go crazy when someone comes near their dates."

"He's not my date," snapped Claire, causing the officer's eyes to dart between her and Alec.

"Are you sure you're okay? I don't need someone flipping out on me. My day's been hard enough already." Thick Black hands squeezed the sides of a round belly as Officer Powell tilted her head.

"Yes, for the third time, I'm fine. I just need to go home."

"In due time, Ms. Hewitt. After you come down to the station and file an official report." Powell lowered her voice and pointed her index finger at Claire as if at a child. "It's best to take care of this immediately following the occurrence. We need documentation of what happened, what was taken, and a description of the assailant."

"I told you I didn't see him."

"You may start to remember details on your drive to the station."

"I need to be at work in a few hours."

Officer Powell puffed at the remark and placed her large hand on Claire's right shoulder. Her fatigued expression softened.

"Look, I understand you want all of this behind you, but you need to come to the station. You need to help us if you want us to help you. And if you need to be at work in a few hours, we better get going."

"Fine."

"You want to ride in the squad car or with your date?"

"He's not my date," Claire snapped again.

"She can ride with me," said Alec.

The officer responded with a dismissive wave as she walked away. "It's faster if you take Sixth Street south."

Alec stepped closer to Claire and held on to her forearm as she took her first step. She winced as she moved.

"I can't believe in the matter of seconds, some jerk reached muscles I haven't touched in twenty years." Claire watched the ground as she walked. "How am I going to face everyone at work? I can hear all the questions now."

"Don't worry about that." Alec reached around Claire and opened the passenger door.

"None of this was in your recruitment brochure, but I appreciate your help. You've gone above and beyond." Claire stepped down from the curb.

"Just being a decent person, I guess."

Claire pinched her lips as she lowered herself into the car. "We better get a move on before Powell gets her panties in a wad and issues a warrant." She swung her legs inside.

Alec pushed the door closed. Claire leaned her head back, her eyes squeezed shut. Her chest rose and fell with slow deep breaths. Her hands lay in her lap as she picked at the chipped polish on one of her nails.

"Are you okay?" asked Alec as he climbed into the Camaro.

"Stop asking me that. My back hurts and my head's throbbing."

"The station won't take long. I promise."

"You can't promise that," said Claire. "You don't know. And how can I face Clifford looking like this?"

"I can meet with them. You stay home."

"They'll eat you alive."

"I can handle the Satoris," Alec assured Claire. "I'm tougher than Clifford, and Margo won't be able to resist my charm."

"You're not that charming, and I'm not staying home."

The dark commotion at the station was to be expected. Disheveled young men leaned on benches next to drunken old men and disheveled old men leaned on benches next to young drunks. The place was packed.

Alec maneuvered his way to the information desk with Claire trudging behind. A muscular middle-aged man lifted his eyes from his assortment of paperwork and magazines. He stared at Alec but offered no greeting. Alec placed the business card the officer had left with him on the dirty counter in front of the clerk and reiterated her instructions.

"Powell!" the information clerk yelled into the stale air behind him.

Claire flinched at the aggressive outburst and pinched the bridge of her nose. Alec gave no reaction as he assessed his surroundings. Heated arguments between police officers and handcuffed suspects ensued around them while obscenities flew through the air mixed with tears and pleas of innocence.

"Wait over there." The clerk pointed to a row of folding chairs lined along a stucco wall.

There were two vacant chairs, but a sleeping Asian man separated them, and splashes of dried vomit clung to his leg and the chair to his right. Alec motioned for Claire to sit in the empty seat at the end of the row. He stood beside her.

"Oh God, what is happening?" Claire dropped into the chair. "We'll be fine."

"You'll be fine," said Claire. "You're the firm's prodigy. Stanford's best. I'm a new partner. A female partner who's not quite ready to run with the big boys."

"Nobody thinks that."

"They will when they discover the Deprexone results are gone. They'll jump all over Walter for trusting a dumb broad."

"Gone where?"

"If I knew, they wouldn't be gone," snapped Claire. "Maybe you can tell me. You chased them." Claire watched her shoe tap on the dirty tile. Alec bit the inside of his cheek as his eyes slowly blinked. They looked like two adolescents resisting the urge to fight.

"The Deprexone test results are in your briefcase?" asked Alec.

"Of course they are. My day isn't finished when I leave the office."

"Oh I realize that," said Alec. "Are there copies at the office?"

"We pay people to make copies, but I didn't request that with the results we just got. I was going to take care of that in the morning." Claire looked up at Alec. "That's not going to work out so well, now is it?"

Alec scanned the station theatrics as his clenched jaw pulsed. He ignored Claire's rhetorical question.

"All I could think about was getting out of that damn office. We had spent too many hours trapped in that stuffy room." Claire rested one elbow on each thigh and propped her chin on her clenched fists. "By this time next week, you'll be placed on a different case."

Claire dropped her forehead to her fists as tears dropped onto her shoes. Alec resumed biting his cheek and watched his boss struggle.

"Don't overreact." Alec placed his hand on Claire's shoulder. "We'll request replacements."

"Don't underreact." Claire swiped her index finger underneath both eyes and looked up at Alec. "Those NAS bastards don't fight fair."

"Then we won't fight fair. And we'll fight harder."

After twenty long minutes, Officer Powell sauntered over to Claire. She offered her a single sheet of paper and a puckered scowl.

"Fill out the front and back and make sure you sign it. Then leave it with the clerk." Officer Powell turned and disappeared into one of the side offices.

"What the hell!" Claire shrieked at the door Powell slipped behind. "We drove all the way down here to answer the same damn questions. This is ridiculous. A total waste of taxpayer dollars."

Alec cringed at Claire's increased volume. He glanced around, noticing it caught nobody's attention. Claire filled out the form, returned it to the disinterested clerk, and stormed out the front doors. Alec followed behind.

Repeated weather reports and highlights of the day's news played on the radio as Alec drove back to Blackman & Bradford. No conversation was exchanged. Alec watched the road ahead as Claire fogged the passenger window beside her. As soon as Alec pulled up to the back door of Blackman & Bradford, Claire jumped out of the Camaro.

"Thanks. I'll see you in a few." She hustled to her car without looking back. A few steps from the driver's door, Claire stopped. She turned around. "I do mean thank you."

Alec nodded with both hands gripping the wheel. "You're welcome. And I can take care of the Satoris if you think it's best to stay home tomorrow."

"Not a chance. I need to be here when they fire me."

Claire turned to her car and fumbled her keys. Alec gave a double honk and pulled away. Still favoring her injured shoulder, Claire tried unlocking the door with her right hand. Having grown up left-handed in a right-handed world, she was accustomed to making the forced accommodation. But today the keys dropped to the ground.

"What the . . . ?" groaned Claire.

Dropping her head against the driver's side door, Claire squeezed her eyes shut. She let her right arm dangle from its socket as her left arm hung in its sling. She held her breath. After a few short moments, she forcefully exhaled and opened her eyes. A scuffed pair of men's shoes stood beside her. Claire screamed. She jumped from the car. Two hands grabbed her by the arms.

"I couldn't leave you alone in a vacant lot."

Claire's head dropped onto Alec's chest. Her body was stiff

and her breathing jagged. Alec looked at the lone streetlight a few yards away.

"Let me take you home."

"No." Claire pushed back from Alec as he picked up the keys and opened her door. She slid into the driver's seat.

With a disconcerting frown, he pushed the door closed and stood back. Claire drove away as Alec watched her go. She glanced in her rear-view mirror and watched him watch her leave. She shook her head and pulled her eyes back to Lombard Street.

"He couldn't leave me alone in a vacant lot," she whispered to herself. "He is Stanford's best."

4

·········●●●●●●●●●●●●·····

BACK SCRATCH

Claire pulled between the lines of her designated spot as the vibration of her watch announced the early hour. An amber hue beaming from the twelfth floor of Blackman & Bradford caught her attention. She grumbled across the empty lot. Claire was always the first to arrive.

As she leaned against the back wall in the dimly lit elevator, Claire pulled a hand mirror from her purse. She smoothed the makeup around her eyes and added more blush. The lighter shade was an excellent choice for hiding the ruddy bruise on her cheek. She then tussled the hair from behind her ears to amplify her intentionally messy style.

When the elevator doors opened to the dark hallway, Claire took a deep breath and headed toward the conference room lights. She stopped outside the open door and watched. Alec tilted his chair back, let it fall forward, then tilted it again. She thought his restless movements looked like those of a highschooler trying to overcome boredom. He guzzled coffee, picked up the newspaper, and tilted his chair again. He then looked up at the clock and compared it to his watch.

"Good morning, hot shot," said Claire as she entered the room.

"Oh, hi." A startled Alec grabbed the table as he lost balance of his chair.

"Did you go home or come straight here?" asked Claire as she dropped her backpack on the chair opposite Alec.

"I went home. But I told you I don't need much sleep."

"You did, and I know I should be pleased with your punctuality. But I don't like pulling in and seeing a light coming from that window." Claire nodded at the window adjacent the counter.

"Why not?" asked Alec.

"I like to be first. And I'm in a shitty mood."

"After last night, I understand the mood."

"You understand my mood? I doubt that. I was mugged last night. Do you have any idea how demoralizing that is? How humiliating?" Claire dropped into the closest chair and let her bag fall to the floor.

"I don't know what to say. You're right. I don't know how you feel."

"Vulnerable. That's how I feel. I've jeopardized the reputation of this firm and the relationship we have with one of the most powerful men in Philadelphia because I didn't take time to use the damn copy machine. Walter gave me a chance. He acknowledged my capabilities in front of every other partner in this firm by placing me as first chair in a class-action lawsuit. And I fucked it up. That's how I feel."

Alec folded the newspaper he was holding. He dropped it on the chair beside him as he walked to the small refrigerator underneath the coffee pot. He grabbed a water bottle from the top shelf and walked it to Claire. He opened it and set the bottle and the cap beside her. He then returned to his seat and rested his forearms on the table and folded his hands.

"Nothing that has happened in the last twenty-four hours sheds a poor light on you or your abilities as an attorney. If anything, the fact that you're here today illustrates your commitment to the Satoris and this lawsuit. That's what Mr. Blackman and Mr. Satori want."

"Satori wants compensation for the death of his daughter. And no number is too big." Claire kept her eyes on Alec as she grabbed documents from her backpack and drank the cool water. "Most are too small."

"Then let's shoot high."

"We're in what's known as a public health emergency with NAS at the helm," said Claire. "The CDC has defined the problem. All we need do is label the players."

Claire set a stack of documents next to the research Alec was reviewing. She separated them into smaller piles and slid those piles around the table as if constructing a diagram. When confident with the formation, she walked to the coffee pot and poured a hot cup.

"According to the CDC, the opioid epidemic came in three waves." Claire turned back to Alec as she detailed the development of opioid use for chronic pain. She sipped coffee in between sentences.

"The first wave began in the early nineties when the Joint Commission promoted pain as the fifth vital sign." Claire picked up the *Joint Commission Journal on Quality and Patient Safety* and held it up. "There were four vital signs prior to this new designation. That sound familiar?" Claire dropped the journal and traced her index finger along the table as she walked past Alec.

"Yep." Alec leaned back and rested his hands on his thighs as his eyes followed Claire.

"This inventive designation induced physicians and pharmaceutical companies to find solutions for patients with chronic pain."

"Acute pain was covered," said Alec. "But physicians were now offered a new market if they focused on chronic pain?"

"Yep. Chronic pain was a brand-new playing field. Pharmaceutical companies began spitting out drug after drug to alleviate chronic pain." Claire rifled through papers in the corner stack and tossed a report to Alec. "Zylodone was a big one. Released in 1994. It flew off the shelves from the get-go."

"I read about Zylodone when I started researching. But didn't realize it started the whole mess."

"It didn't. The beginning of the opioid epidemic was a decade earlier." Claire moved to another stack of documents and pulled a news article from the pile. She walked toward Alec and dropped it on top of the Zylodone report. "In 1980, a letter published in a respected medical journal challenged the belief that opioids have addictive properties. That letter served as the starting gun."

"Seriously?" mumbled Alec as he picked up the article and began reading.

Claire was pleased with the intensity she saw in Alec's facial expression as he studied the material. She feared that, as a new associate, he would either go on a rampage trying to prove himself or become lackadaisical, feeling as if he had made it simply by being hired at Blackman & Bradford. Alec did neither.

"That letter pushed for more liberal use of opioids in pain management. And guess whose opinion that was?" asked Claire.

"How would I know?" Alec flipped to the cover of the article. "Oh shit. Phil Westcott?"

"Phil Westcott. He was young when he wrote it." Claire pulled additional papers from the second stack and sat down next to Alec. "And I think he was either too naïve or too power-hungry." Claire handed the papers to Alec.

With a pinched crease between his eyebrows, Alec looked

from the papers to Claire and back. He scooted his chair closer to the table and leaned on his forearms as he scanned the data.

"That's the clinical study that inspired the infamous letter that changed pain management," said Claire. "When Westcott first began working for NAS, he followed a handful of patients who were prescribed opioids while in the hospital. Had nothing to do with chronic pain yet went viral. Physicians from around the world point to that letter as being the true start of the opioid crisis."

"These are some of the most educated people in the world," said Alec. "They jump on Westcott's bandwagon because of one letter?"

Claire stood up and resumed tracing the table's edge as she explained the details to Alec. The information was committed to memory, so there was no need to reference the data displayed on the table. She spoke slowly and with a tone of disbelief.

"Westcott described opioid use as nonaddictive and doctors from everywhere saw the doors fly open. That statement was seen as support for prescribing opioids for chronic pain."

"Patient support or an ego trip and money maker?" said Alec.

"We'll never know, but the prestige empowered Westcott. He continued playing with monkeys and pumping them full of who knows what."

"He'd established himself as the opioid boss. Why didn't he sit back on his laurels and enjoy the notoriety?" asked Alec.

"Opioids don't all work the same way. A few years later, Westcott became obsessed with the extended-release formulation. He claimed this formulation was more effective and had even fewer addictive properties than the immediate-release formulations he'd previously released. Thus, the birth of Deprexone."

"This is better than fiction. Has movie written all over it."

"Horror movie maybe. NAS fell in love with Deprexone.

After a few more years, they went public with an enormous marketing campaign."

Claire froze midstep as her jaw dropped open. After a few short seconds, it closed with a wide smile. A rush of adrenaline thrust her to a stack of NAS marketing materials. She grabbed the latest campaign and flipped through the pages as she turned to Alec.

"Deprexone was marketed as the safest and most effective treatment for chronic pain because of this new extended-release formulation. FDA approval was used as validation of safety, and additional brochures, audiotapes, and other propaganda were created. Everything claimed Deprexone was the greatest treatment. But they ignored federal mandates and jumped too soon."

Alec stood as Claire sat down. He ran his hand through his short hair and reached for a brochure that had dropped to the floor. Tossing it back onto the table, he began pacing as Claire had done.

"Every new drug must be compared to the safest and most effective product on the market before it's released. That's a no-brainer in drug manufacturing." Claire's tongue swept across her lower lip as she typed and stared at the screen of her tablet.

"Our first discovery when our investigation began was that Deprexone research was insufficient due to the omission of data concerning addiction," said Alec as he stood across from Claire. "If NAS never made the effort to compare their shitty data to the best available treatments, what the hell did they base their marketing campaigns on?"

"They make shit up."

"How'd they pull that off when there's FDA oversight to prevent bad drugs from getting into bad hands?" asked Alec.

"Smoke and mirrors. Was there minimal research or was there ample research but only positive outcomes submitted to the FDA? We're onto something, Alec. NAS is the real shit show, and they're going to hand us our pattern of deficient drug testing."

Claire rose and returned to the coffee pot while Alec sat down. A black drip sizzled on the hotplate when she poured a second cup and resumed pacing. Their movements looked choreographed as they continued peeling back the many layers of deceitful drug development at Novo Analgesic Systems, Inc.

"We know there's ghost data by the fact that we were given different compilations of information from different scientists." Alec reached for the separate sets of data and set them side by side to his left. "It's up to us to decipher which results are accurate and what was submitted to the FDA. I do love a puzzle."

"Westcott will claim his results are the accurate test results because he doesn't make mistakes and because they were the results submitted to the FDA."

"Then what did we get from Shaggy?"

"Test results that reveal the addictive properties of Deprexone. Test results the FDA never saw."

"Shaggy has a conscience," said Alec. "Not so much for Westcott. What did he do with the negative results showing Deprexone's addictive properties? Where are they?"

"Hidden."

"Where?"

"That's why we're getting back into that lab." Claire tossed a folder to Alec. "That's Delaney crap. Years of scripts will give us our pattern of negligence."

"We've got more than a single pattern," said Alec, ignoring the folder. "The FDA requires due diligence in patient monitoring. I see no evidence of it in Delaney's office."

Alec handed Claire a case study he had been reviewing before she arrived. Claire leaned against the table as she read.

"There's our guilty verdict," said Alec. "In *Pierce vs. Whitacre*, the Pierce family sued Whitacre for prescribing hydrocodone for their son and never scheduling subsequent visits."

"No parent liability?" asked Claire.

"Federal law requires a follow-up when a physician writes an opioid prescription. It's considered malpractice to drug 'em and turn 'em loose."

"Yikes, Delaney's been shuffling patients in and out of his office for years with no more than a pat on the back and a script with their name."

Claire sat down next to Alec. She tucked the Whitacre case inside Delaney's folder and secured it with the attached plastic band. There was an inquisitive look attached to her silent demeanor. With her arms folded across her chest, she leaned back in her chair and dropped her head to the side.

"Delaney will use NAS as his defense," said Claire. Her eyes squinted as she spoke.

"How's that going to work?"

"The aggressive marketing campaigns NAS used were intended to entice medical professionals to prescribe their opioids for chronic pain."

"That's a defense?" asked Alec.

"He'll try to make it one."

Claire jumped up from her chair and grabbed her coffee cup and a new folder from the end of the table. She walked to the counter with both and filled her cup for a third time. She opened the folder on the counter beside her and turned to face Alec as she brought the cup to her mouth.

"From 1996 to 2018, Novo Analgesic Systems funded more than fifty thousand educational pain programs and launched a multifaceted campaign to promote using opioid medication for chronic non-cancer pain in patients of all ages. As part of this campaign, NAS contributed large sums of money to support the agendas of the American Society of Pain Specialists, the Academy of Advanced Pain Medicine, and numerous other physician organizations. As a result, these organizations recommended vigorous treatment of chronic pain with opioid medications."

"Man, that's a lot of back-scratching," said Alec.

"Excuse me?" Claire raised her eyebrows at Alec.

"You scratch my back, I'll scratch yours. NAS offers extravagant programs to promote NAS opioids. Doctors accept this offer and pay to attend these events. NAS thanks the attendees by using the profit from these events to contribute large sums back to the physicians' organizations. And the physicians show their gratitude by promoting NAS opioids. Everyone's back is scratched." A pleased smile spread across Alec's face.

"It's a vicious circle. But it solidifies our guilty verdict. Whitacre proves that even if Delaney shows that the NAS marketing scheme influenced his prescribing habits, he's still required to prove he had no knowledge of Deprexone's addictive properties. If he were monitoring his patients, he would have known."

Alec relaxed his shoulders and crumpled the random notes scattered around him. "That's the evidence Connor wants to see, and the evidence Satoris need."

"Oh, geez." Claire dropped her chin and looked at the floor as she returned to her chair. Reaching as far across the table as she could, she used her forearm to consolidate her piles. With deep, slow breaths, she pulled one folder at a time from the haphazard stack and returned it to her bag.

"You agree?" asked Alec.

"Need isn't always what you want. Delaney pumped that poor girl full of opioids and never gave it a second thought. They lost their daughter. Nothing can change that. Nothing can fill the hole Emma left."

"It'll give the Satoris closure."

"It won't bring Emma back."

"It's not meant to bring Emma back." Alec scooted more case studies toward Claire. "It's an understanding that allows them to accept what happened and move on."

"Move on to what? A life that's no longer there?"

"The new life they've been given."

"What good is that?" Claire squeezed the overstuffed backpack against her ribs. Frustration controlled her breathing as she struggled to zip it shut.

"Are you okay, Ms. Hewitt?" asked Alec. "The EMTs last night said you should rest."

"They exaggerate, Mr. Marshall. I'm fine." Claire lifted the heavy bag to her good shoulder. "I can relate to the Satoris. I understand how events change you and how you hide the hole in your heart. You hide the hole so others can move on and don't suffer."

"I'm not sure what that means. But I have a feeling it involves more than last night or this case. I don't mean to overstep, but I've sensed it for days. The expression on your face when we talk about Emma? The tone of your voice? You're struggling with something."

"I'm not struggling," said Claire. "And I don't need rest. If they're going to can me, they're doing it to my face."

"Nobody's getting canned. Walter and David may consider it with your new college-girl image. Not sure the urban backpack is the look they're going for." Alec smirked at his own humor.

"Smart-ass." Claire smirked back as she left.

5

BELIEVE ME, YOU DON'T

C laire chewed the tip of her pen as she calculated billable hours. She drank coffee from a mug she received when she completed her last 10K and added numbers. She then pressed the call button on her phone. Within seconds, Ellen stood readily at the door.

"Is everything set for the meeting?"

"Yes, ma'am. I have coffee and iced tea on the buffet and had Simon's deliver deli sandwiches with ham, turkey, and beef."

"If we can't eliminate his anger, we'll eliminate his hunger," mumbled Claire as she slid the ledger inside her top drawer. "I'll be in the small library. Have Alec join me with the evidence we presented at the hearing last week. He'll know what I want."

Clutching several folders to her chest with one hand and balancing cold coffee with the other, Claire rushed past Ellen. She caught a glimpse of Morgan leaving the breakroom and motioned for her to follow.

"You look a little off this morning." Hot steam swirled from Morgan's mug.

"Tell me about it." Claire's hair fell across her face as she used her hip to push open the door to the small room. Black coffee splashed from her cup and dripped down her leg. "Damn it."

Claire fumbled the folders as she continued into the room dropping two onto the floor and skidding a few more down the middle of a round table. She continued to the window as she wiped coffee from her leg. She kept her back to Morgan and stared through strands of hair at the building across the street.

"What's up with you?" asked Morgan. "I've never seen you this unnerved. The Satoris are big, but they're not that big."

"You have no idea," said Claire.

Claire continued looking out the window and let the mug hang loosely in her hand. She kept her back to Morgan, unsure of what to say. The surreal events of the night before swept through her mind as if taunting and belittling her.

"Hey, big shot, I think I have some idea."

"I thought I did too. I was mugged last night." Claire turned to face Morgan.

"What?"

"Outside Luigi's."

"Oh my God." Morgan rushed to Claire. She grabbed her face and turned it toward the bright window. She lightly touched the sanguine smudge spreading from Claire's ear down to her chin. "What happened?"

"God only knows." Claire brushed Morgan's hand from her face and walked away. She swept one folder from the floor as she approached the table. She slid it by the others and stared at the shelves holding antiquated federal reporters. She felt her heart pounding in her chest. She folded her arms around her waist as she faced the shelves and spoke to Morgan. "Some ass-wipe ran past Alec and me as we left Luigi's. Ripped my briefcase from my hand and threw me to the ground."

"Oh geez. That's supposed to be a safe part of town."

"Safe until the Satoris arrive."

"Clifford Satori attacked you?" Morgan's eyes widened as did her open mouth.

"Not personally. But I was attacked because I represent them." Claire stepped sideways to a framed picture hanging between the two mahogany shelves. She shifted her head to adjust her reflection in the glass. She ran her fingers through her hair, grabbing a handful and twirling it into a bun. She loosened a small section in front of her right ear to help conceal her deepening bruise.

"What did Alec do?" asked Morgan as she watched Claire fiddle with her face and hair.

"Chased him. But not fast enough."

"Tell me this, why are you here today?"

Morgan reached for Claire as Claire ducked around her and swept her arm across the table to corral the folders she'd thrown. She picked up the last file from the floor and added it to the stack. She then pulled her cellphone from her pocket and checked the time. She felt Morgan's eyes on her but couldn't let her emotions escape. It would be a flood with no dam to stop the damage. Claire struggled as she felt her chin quiver.

"Did you hear me? You should be home getting some rest. Clearing your head."

"I'm rested enough and clear as crystal." Claire swallowed hard.

"You don't sound rested. You sound agitated."

"I've earned agitated." Claire slipped past Morgan to shut the door. "You have no idea what's on my plate." Claire whispered as if it were a secret.

"Oh, I have some idea."

"Satoris are demanding, in-house counsel for NAS is my worst enemy, I spent most of the night at the police station, my head has been throbbing since midnight, and I had to get the cake in the oven."

Claire returned to the picture to recheck her appearance. She brushed her loose hair behind her ear and then pulled it forward again, convinced that neither look was better. She turned back to Morgan as her eyes bounced around the room in search of nothing but needing answers. She looked like a lost child waiting to be found.

"Look, Claire, I've known you a long time and see it every year. This day shows up, and you relive it like it was yesterday. You pile it on with everything else. Your plate's a little full this year. Can you cut yourself a break?"

"My alarm blared 'Dancing Queen' before sunup this morning. It was the music for her floor routine." Claire walked to the window as if Morgan had said nothing. "I stared at the ceiling watching Molly flip across that mat. Not an ounce of fear and a perfect landing every time." Claire placed her palm on the cool glass. "Until there wasn't."

"Stop. Don't do this to yourself," said Morgan. "It was unfortunate, but nothing good comes from this."

"Unfortunate? How about devastating? A split second changed everything. A fraction of an inch stole her dream. It stole her life."

Claire spun around and dropped back against the wall. She looked down at her fingernails and pulled at the hangnail on her thumb. She then looked up at Morgan. Her heart leapt from her chest when their eyes met. Morgan had become the sister Claire had lost. Claire relied on her for guidance, for strength, for love. In her mind, Claire cried the tears that dulled the pain. But only in her mind.

"This anniversary arrives every year like a dark storm cloud for you to wallow under." Morgan walked over to Claire. "I know it was devasting, but you can't focus on that and represent the Satoris. It's too much. Go home."

"Go home?" Claire pushed off the wall. "I'm not going anywhere."

"Then change the song on your alarm clock so you start your day on a more positive note," said Morgan.

"Maybe I will." Claire stepped past Morgan and peered out the door.

"Did you get the cake finished?" asked Morgan.

"Of course I did." Claire turned back to Morgan as a subtle smile toyed with her downturned lips.

"I don't see dragging yourself out of bed to bake a cake as a positive start to your day. It's pulling you down a rabbit hole."

"How can baking a cake for my sister not be positive?"

"Because your sister is gone." Morgan inhaled deeply and held her breath, waiting for Claire's reaction.

Claire dropped her eyes to the floor as she spoke. "I began baking the birthday cake when that fall stole Molly's purpose in life. I wanted to give her something that made her happy. And it did. I can still see her laughing as she licked frosting off her fingers. There's no rabbit hole."

"Why keep baking it?"

"Because it makes me happy."

"You don't look happy." Morgan stepped toward Claire with outstretched arms but again was pushed aside. Claire returned to the round table.

"I'm facing the Satoris in an hour," said Claire. "Wish me luck."

"Speaking of rabbit holes."

"I said wish me luck." Claire's eyes widened as her eyebrows shot up. A hesitant smile replaced the melancholy. "The whole cake is in my office."

"Watch out for rabbits. I'm heading for cake." Morgan flipped around and left.

Claire was circling the perimeter of the small room when Alec walked in. Her hands fanned the air as she pleaded with an invisible jury. Although her movements were stiff, she portrayed a skilled litigator. She spoke with assertive passion and her attire completed the picture. Her crisp navy suit that touched just above the knee offered a refreshing alternative to the usual mid-calf courtroom attire. It added a feminine touch to her powerful image. And her choice of heels as opposed to flats spoke to her confidence.

Claire's steps and voice both stopped. Her hands fell to her sides as her head dropped back and she looked up at the ceiling. She faced the far wall and stood motionless.

"Opioids are a distinct class of addictive drugs," said Alec as he continued through the door. "They're effective for treating acute pain but most often inappropriate for treating chronic pain. Clinical guidelines urge physicians to prescribe opioids for chronic pain only when safer alternatives are not feasible." Alec held his laptop and dropped relevant caselaw onto the chair by his side.

Claire spun around. Her appreciation showed in her eyes, and Alec continued.

"The cost and potency of opioids have gained them extreme popularity in the United States. In 2020, there were 51.4 prescriptions written for every 100 people. That's equivalent to more than 168 million opioid prescriptions."

"Nice work."

"But out of the 168 million trips to the pharmacy, the high risk of misuse, addiction, and overdose was seldom disclosed or discussed."

"I was getting to that crossroads in my argument right before you got here," said Claire. "This past year, over ten million people misused their opioid medications, and 47,600 of them died from an overdose. Emma was one of them. Big pharma makes money and doctors are complacent."

"Yeah, she got fucked by both," said Alec.

"When describing the situation to Cliff, you might want to choose a less brutal vernacular." Claire smirked and sat down.

Alec shrugged and glanced out the door. "No sign of the Satoris."

"I dread facing them."

"Don't. You've got this," said Alec.

"I hope. I'm starting with Delaney and may not address NAS fabricating the Deprexone studies at all."

"That's wise."

"It's straightforward," said Claire. "I won't make excuses for yesterday, but I'll explain how it won't change the verdict. At trial, I'll show a pattern of negligence with irrefutable evidence and get a conviction. They need to trust me."

A slamming door echoed throughout Blackman & Bradford. Claire's eyes shot to the door. She tugged on the front of her long jacket and ran her hands down the front of her skirt. Alec peered into the hallway.

"Conference room is open," said Alec.

"Here we go."

Clifford Satori was pacing back and forth, rebuking everyone within hearing range when Claire walked into the room. She caught the tail end of a rampage about his real estate empire sustaining Blackman & Bradford for decades. Obscenities flew out the open window to pedestrians passing below.

Walter was listening from the far end of the table. His pinched face and wrinkled chin displayed his unmistakable anger. Next to Margo Satori sat David Bradford, whose rigid posture expressed similar resentment. Margo's swollen eyes stared at nothing.

Clifford Satori stopped speaking midsentence when Claire placed her material on the small podium at the end of the table opposite the three enraged men. Walter and Clifford were both standing, so Claire stood as well. She rested the tips of her fingers on the table on either side of her notes. Her silent composure and focused eyes grabbed control of the room and the situation. There were no cordial greetings.

"Mr. Satori, Judge Connor did nothing yesterday that will jeopardize our case." Claire's eyes bounced from Clifford to Margo and back. "We have strong evidence that will withstand the scrutiny of defense counsel. We're in a very promising position."

"Promising!" Clifford Satori threw his thick hair-covered arms in the air. "I don't want any fucking promises! How dare you make promises to me. What are promises when I've lost my daughter?"

Acknowledging her underestimation of Clifford Satori's vernacular sensibilities, Claire glanced over at Alec. Margo dropped her chin and sniffed, dabbing her nose with the back of her hand.

"I understand, Mr. Satori. Believe me, I do."

"No, Ms. Hewitt. Believe me, you don't."

Claire shifted her weight with intent yet sympathetic eyes on Clifford Satori. When Clifford turned to the window, Claire shot a desperate glance at Walter and then David. Receiving no help, she whispered to Alec.

"Go get the opioid binder. I need data."

Alec ducked out, and Claire turned back to the hostility. She looked from Walter to David to Clifford and took a deep breath before resuming.

"I understand this is painful, Mr. Satori. I understand that nothing I do will bring back your daughter. I understand more than you will ever know, and I am doing everything I can to find justice for you and Mrs. Satori."

Alec returned as Walter drummed his fingers on the back wall. Claire walked over to David and Margo with the large binder outlining the history of opioid use in the United States. The expression on Walter's face softened as Claire placed her hand on Margo's back and spoke in a tender, authentic tone.

"Pain medications have been prescribed in the United States since the 1800s. Morphine was used to relieve pain during the American Civil War. Although it's hard to believe, Bayer was selling heroin as a pain reliever in 1898."

Margo's breathing slowed as she looked up at her husband. He furrowed his dark eyebrows and squinted as he listened to Claire and shook his head. Walter and David's expressions were stern as they watched their new partner perform.

"Around 1920, the addictiveness of these types of medications became evident, and doctors became more guarded with writing prescriptions. Heroin was classified as an illegal drug in 1924, although it was still common among musicians throughout the sixties and servicemen during the Vietnam War."

"Emma was not on heroin!" Clifford slammed both hands onto the table.

"I understand that, Mr. Satori. But it's important for you to understand the connection between legal opioids and illegal opioids."

"Why the hell would that matter to me?" growled Clifford as his face contorted. "Emma was a gymnast. An international champion. She never so much as let a tater tot contaminate her body, let alone an illicit drug."

"I'm not saying Emma took illegal drugs," said Claire. "But

we need to be prepared for defense counsel to claim that. The binder in front of you contains decades of studies involving opioid use in the United States. And I can guarantee you that NAS and Dr. Delaney are going to use that data to accuse Emma of misusing Deprexone."

"What the hell! How is that even possible?" Clifford clenched his fists as his bloodshot eyes darted back and forth between Walter and David. His nostrils flared and his chest heaved.

"I can't change the facts, Mr. Satori," said Claire. "Regardless of whether an overdose occurred from a prescribed opioid, heroin, or some other illegal drug, more than half of those addictions began with a legally prescribed opioid. I know this is overwhelming, and I understand how helpless you feel."

"You have no idea, Ms. Hewitt. The last thing I am is helpless. They poisoned my sweet Emma, and they're going to pay for it. They both are. I won't stand for it! I won't!"

Clifford pounded the table with both hands as he yelled these final words. He dropped his head as Walter gripped his shoulder, and Margo quivered as only a mother would. Claire noticed Margo's silent tears dripping from her downturned face and handed her a tissue as she collected the data she had shared with the Satoris. Her thin eyebrows were deeply furrowed as she handed the large binder to Alec. She grabbed her notebook as she walked past David and continued to the small podium where she first addressed her clients. With her shoulder blades pressed back and her chin lifted, she watched the medley of power and emotion in the room.

"Mr. and Mrs. Satori, no words can express my sorrow, and I cannot bring back Emma. But I know your pain, and I understand the dark hole Emma left inside of you. I can't tell you it will go away. I can't tell you how long until it softens. But I can tell you justice will be had." Claire turned and walked out.

6

ELUSIVE
ANSWERS

"This is not everything." Landon Sims slapped the test results onto the high lab table in front of Phil.

"What do you mean it's not everything? Do you realize who I am?" Phil gazed over the rim of his readers.

"We all do, Dr. Westcott. That's why I expected a hell of a lot more."

"I began this research when you were still in diapers." Phil jumped from the chair as his cheeks flushed. "I traveled to the poppy farms of Turkey and blistered my hands so that others might know the pain relief of morphine. I made sacrifices of biblical nature."

Phil held out the palms of his hands in the same manner as seen in depictions of Jesus Christ. Landon threw his sport coat on the chair in response to the absurd display. Phil's vanity had risen to a new height.

"Because of my endless efforts to help distressed individuals, I was the first to provide the relief that oxycodone and hydrocodone offer. And I am one of the few who has explored the addictive nature of the semisynthetic opioid heroin. Yet you come in here and question my research?" Phil hopped back into his elevated chair, causing it to roll several feet.

"I have no doubt you've spent hundreds of hours testing the addictive nature of your opioids," said Landon. "And I'd bet money that personal testing was part of the process."

"How dare you." Phil again jumped to his feet, sending the chair spinning backward. His posture was rigid. "You have no basis for that insidious slander."

"I know all about your research, Westcott. And your 1980 letter that changed the world. 'Addiction Rare with Opioids.'" Landon made air quotes with his fingers. "I know it's been cited over six hundred times as authority that addiction is rare. But I also know that seldom was it mentioned that your research was conducted in a hospital and did not consider chronic pain patients using opioids. Yet doctors wary of opioids were thrilled with the news and pulled out their prescription pads."

Phil huffed at Landon's accusations and rolled his chair back to the table. He riffled through charts and looked into nearby cages as his nostrils flared with each deep breath. Landon leaned against the table on one elbow and watched the theatrics.

"Why did you waste time vetting me when all the answers lie within these walls?" Phil asked. "Instead of being hung up on the overview of one letter, focus on the major advancements I've brought to medicine. In 1994, when the number of people fatally overdosing on fentanyl and methadone doubled, I used the very primates you see in this lab to develop the immediate-release synthetic opioid Zylodone."

"Disappointing it was so short-lived," said Landon. "I don't think you should hang your hat on an opioid that was pulled from pharmacy shelves shortly after its release."

Phil huffed again and turned to another cage. He reached

inside and wrestled with an unseen animal. Landon picked up the test results with an exasperated sigh, thumbed through the pages, and tossed them back down.

"How can you be so shortsighted?" asked Phil. "I mean, does being narrow-minded come naturally? People misunderstood the proper use of Zylodone, the same as they misunderstood my letter. My Zylodone studies led to the extended-release formulation and the phenomenal development of Deprexone." Phil stood with a beaker in one hand, a water bottle in the other, and a wet grin on his face.

"Ah yes, the development of Deprexone." Landon nodded with an exhausted smile. "The reason I'm here today."

"What do you need that I haven't given you?" asked Phil.

"Valid test results." Landon slid the papers toward Phil. "I expect to see an increase in participants between Phase One and Phase Two, monitored doses, and randomization. This is a bunch of crap. I hold Novo Analgesic Systems to a much higher standard."

"You need to relax."

"No, I need to defend you against a very powerful man who thinks you killed his daughter. And he's hell-bent on proving it."

"I didn't kill anybody."

"Prove it with valid research. They aren't going to rely on your word. The court needs to see evidence of what goes on in this lab."

"That's valid research you shoved back at me."

"That's chicken scratch."

"You have no idea." Phil dropped his chin and stared at Landon with unblinking eyes. "I don't need you or some fat cat challenging my work."

"No challenge. A simple request. I need evidence to substantiate your claim."

"I have reams of supporting scientific data for every claim I make. I've made amazing advancements in the management of acute and chronic pain. I developed a risk evaluation and mitigation strategy to provide safeguards against abuse and ensure benefits outweigh risks. The FDA loves me." Phil slid the research back toward Landon.

"If it's so amazing, where is this research?" asked Landon.

"In front of you."

"I'm not amazed."

"We thoroughly test every drug that leaves this building with our name on it. We test it, we obtain definitive results, and we release it. We have neither the funding nor the time for needless repetition."

Landon slammed his briefcase shut without noticing his sport coat fall to the floor. Several cages rattled at the noise, and Phil scowled as he wiggled his fingers through the metal bars beside him. An agitated marmoset grabbed a finger and sucked.

"Montgomery & Sims has defended dozens of lawsuits involving pharmaceutical companies. You've given me monkey tests due to limited funding." Landon scanned his surroundings with a sarcastic chuckle.

"This lab has more than adequate funding," said Phil. "We simply don't waste that funding."

Phil shoved his way past Landon and thrust his hand into another cage. He stroked the paw of a timid tamarin as he reached underneath for a small box. He then shook the box as a signal of an impending surprise. Throughout the lab, cage doors rattled as fingers wrapped around the metal bars and noses poked through.

"We follow proper protocol," said Phil as he sneered back at Landon. "We conduct extensive preclinical testing on every one of these sweet animals before moving onto damaged humans.

The primates in these cages give up their lives so that humans can improve theirs." Phil dropped morsels into the cages he passed. "I refuse to waste research dollars retesting a drug that has shown success. Once we know a medication will provide better relief than anything else on the market, we move on. It's that simple."

"It's not that simple." Landon slapped the table in front of him. "Animals aren't humans. You won't go to prison if some distraught monkey overdoses." Landon folded his arms as he watched Phil reach into cages and grab the paws of several primates as if shaking their hands.

Phil's commanding demeanor vanished. His chin jutted forward as his fingers formed a fist around the metal bar of a nearby cage. As if injured by the insult, he kept his back to Landon and watched his knuckles turn white.

"You've not shown adequate human testing," said Landon. "Nor have you compared Deprexone to the best available alternatives on the market."

"Enough!" Several primates slunk to the back of their cages at the sound of the harsh response while Phil turned to face Landon. "The opioid receptors in primates are similar to ours, and my years studying primates in the field has made me an expert on both primates and humans. Look around you." Phil swung his arms full circle. "This laboratory has experienced exponential growth due to my diligence and expertise. It's federally funded research supported by the CDC. If miserable human beings need help, Phil Westcott will provide it."

Phil returned to the table and patted the results into a neat pile. Landon pushed several folders across the table and grinned as they knocked Phil's pen to the floor. Phil's eyes followed the pen without moving his head.

"I need all test results from the Deprexone you gave human

volunteers." Landon gripped the edge of the table. "That includes accurate numbers showing Deprexone's extended-release formulation controlled pain for twelve hours without creating withdrawal symptoms or signs of addiction. Nowhere does your research reveal any risk of addiction when taking Deprexone. I know it's there. You know it's there. And the prosecution is waiting to shove it down our throats."

"Let them try," said Phil. "Deprexone is a triumph touted by doctors worldwide. In the last five years, it's brought over two billion dollars in revenue to NAS."

Phil darted between cages, filling food dishes and water bottles. His wet lips were spread into a stern grin. Landon took a deep breath in through his nose and blew the air out his mouth as he watched Phil's misguided pleasure.

"We need to justify that revenue, Phil."

"That's the beauty of Deprexone." Phil flipped around with empty food dishes in each hand. "Deprexone justifies itself. Palliative care is different with every individual, yet Deprexone makes pain relief imminent in every case."

Phil dumped beakers into a drawer, then meticulously repositioned them into straight lines. He admired his arrangement before pushing the drawer shut. He again flipped around to face Landon, placing both hands on his narrow hips. He tilted his head sideways and shot one skinny arm toward Landon.

"Look at that wall to your left, Mr. Sims. That's proof spread all over it. Those framed documents are awards I've received for advancements I've made in the study of palliative care. People are in pain, and I can make it stop."

"Your awards mean nothing," said Landon. "They don't matter to me. They won't matter to the court. A dead teenage girl is what matters now. Why was she given Deprexone?"

"It's the best medication for postsurgical pain."

"Why was she sent home with a prescription for over two hundred more tablets?"

"You'd have to ask the doctor. But refills can be a real bitch. Have you ever stood in line at the pharmacy wondering what was happening at the counter?" Phil brushed past Landon.

"Pain medication isn't prescribed to avoid long lines," said Landon. "Our defense can't be that we didn't want to inconvenience the Satoris."

"I gave you the same data I gave the FDA," said Phil. "If they didn't question it, why are you?"

"I stood in front of a judge yesterday and painted a pretty little picture to cover your ass." Landon used the back of his hand to wipe the sweat from in front of his ear.

"That shouldn't have been difficult. My work does all the heavy lifting," Phil snickered.

"Judge Connor doesn't care about your awards, your status, or your monkeys. His only concern is Deprexone. Who developed it, who put it on the market, and what it did to that girl."

Showing no concern for Landon's pleas, Phil picked up his clipboard with an exaggerated display of looking for a pen. He saw the one Landon had pushed to the floor, picked it up, and jotted notes onto the paper.

"Hewitt will destroy you," said Landon.

Phil's pen stopped. His lashes fluttered at his writing before raising his face in dramatic slow motion. "Bring it on."

Landon grabbed his sport coat off the floor and his briefcase from the table. The pounding of his shoes on the tile reverberated in the basement as he stormed out of the lab. He continued to the elevator and jabbed the round lit button on the wall. His chest rose and fell with angry breath. When the doors opened, he stepped inside and jabbed again.

On the fourth floor, he resumed his angry march down

a brighter carpeted hallway. He turned the corner once and stopped in front of Jack Freeman's enormous double doors. He stared at the doors as laughter escaped from the other side. After two taps on the hard wood, Landon walked into an animated conversation between Jack Freeman and someone on the other end of his cellphone. Jack motioned for Landon to continue in.

"Great to see you again, counselor," Jack whispered as he pulled the phone from his mouth.

"Not so sure about that."

With only forty-two years under his belt, a Princeton degree, and innumerable Ivy League connections, Jack Freeman had the success and the wrinkles of a much older man. Deep creases formed at the corner of his eyes when he smiled. The pressure and prestige of running the pharmaceutical empire his father opened in 1970 showed on his face but not in his demeanor.

Waiting for Jack to conclude his conversation, Landon roamed the office, ogling at the black flat screens attached to the ivory walls. Three were turned off, but a fourth displayed a data-flow diagram showing the success rate of a newly released NAS drug. Jack's glass desktop was another monitor with numerous reports streaming on the screen. With polite haste, Jack sent his love to someone on the other end of the phone and reached for Landon's hand.

"To what do I owe this honor?" asked Jack.

"Random battle cry."

"I was under the impression everything was running smoothly."

"Nothing runs smoothly with Westcott," said Landon.

"Oh, geez. What now?"

"That bastard is digging his grave, and I'm expected to save him."

"Dana assured me everything was fine," said Jack.

"Of course she did. She's half of the problem."

"She's in an advisory position only. Nothing more."

"Not according to Dana," said Landon. "She challenges every move I make. As in-house counsel for NAS, she thinks she can do a better job at deciphering a course of action."

"She's a guard dog," chuckled Jack.

"She's not guarding. She's meddling. She questions our strategy and disputes our decisions. She's a conflict of interest."

Jack ignored the flashing red light on his desk phone and stared at the mail stacked in his inbox. His large hands rested on his thighs. The intensity between the two men was accentuated by the darkness of Jack's squint. Landon watched Jack but said nothing.

"Dana can be aggressive," said Jack as he shifted his eyes to Landon. "But she knows her involvement in the development of Deprexone places her in the defendant's chair with the rest of us. She'll recuse herself. I'll speak to her."

"Will that make a difference?" asked Landon.

"I'm still her boss."

"Does that make a difference?"

"I believe it does. You have to understand Dana. She manipulates people like chess pieces, always looking for the right move and anticipating the next. But I'm the better player, and I'm in charge."

"If you say so," said Landon.

"The hearing worked in our favor, didn't it?" asked Jack. "Connor found most of their arguments inadmissible."

"The prosecution is out for blood," said Landon. "They claim we didn't thoroughly test Deprexone in accordance with FDA requirements and fraudulently minimized its addictive nature. They want it pulled off the market and us held liable for every incident of opioid use disorder and overdose."

"Regardless of the treating physician?"

"Yep. They allege inadequate testing exposes a pattern of negligence that's been occurring for decades. If they connect any procedures that show a pattern, it's all admissible."

"Unbelievable." Jack leaned back in his chair and pushed away from his desk.

"Is it possible that something suspect has been going on?" asked Landon. "In the lab?"

"Are you kidding me?"

"No. A lot of opioid development occurred before you took over the company, and careless researchers could have ignored the severity of addictive properties or not disclosed them when marketing. There might be skeletons in closets that are just now showing up."

"My father would have never tolerated that."

"He may not have known. And Hewitt is on a witch hunt," said Landon.

"Get rid of her before the publicity kills us. Get rid of this whole mess." Jack squeezed his thighs as he leaned forward in his chair.

"I intend to," said Landon. "But we're paddling upstream. From 1990 to 1999, the total number of opioid prescriptions grew from 76 million to 116 million."

"It's 2022, Landon."

"That growth hasn't slowed."

"That's why we're a success," said Jack.

"It makes opioids the most prescribed class of medication in the United States. But it shines a beacon on who's responsible for negative outcomes. That's where our battle lies."

"We're not responsible for that girl," said Jack. "This case is bullshit. Do whatever it takes to get it dismissed."

"As lead pharmacologist in the development of Deprexone, could Phil Westcott be the problem?" asked Landon.

"Phil follows protocol. At least I thought so."

Jack turned off the glass screen in front of him. He then walked over to his file cabinet that was as much a toy as it was office equipment. He pushed a button on the upper right corner, and a keyboard lowered from the top edge. As Jack typed in the proper code for Deprexone, the cabinet drawer slid forward, and the requested files lifted. Jack took the files from the cabinet and placed the large stack in front of Landon. He then pressed three buttons on his desk phone.

"Carol, I need you to make copies for Mr. Sims."

The top folder read DEPREXONE 2000. Landon looked from the folder to Jack.

"Is that where I'll find your skeletons?"

7

SMOLDERING EMBERS

Claire rounded the corner for the third time. The sun shone on her sweat-glistened face. Her steps were more relaxed, but tension showed in her clenching hands and the words she mumbled to herself. She dropped against the wall beside a brightly lit pharmacy and watched cars speed past. Buried in thoughts of Margo's tears and David's rebuke, she stared at the sidewalk beneath her feet. She continued to mumble.

Claire jumped when a peppy jingle broke through the mundane sound of engines. She glanced to her left and saw the manager of Black Threads Boutique balancing a sign in the front window. Their eyes met, and Stephanie planted both fists onto her hips with playful eyes.

"Girl, it's been forever. I almost called. We missed you for drinks last week."

"I've been crazy busy."

"You always are. Now get in here and check out these dresses. They're on sale, and there's one left in your size. Just one." Stephanie walked back into the store as if knowing Claire would follow. And she did.

When the tall blonde spun around with a deep purple dress hanging from her outstretched hand, Claire's mouth dropped open. She stood frozen as Dana Massetti glided from mirror to mirror admiring herself. Claire didn't acknowledge the salesclerk or the dress.

"Claire Hewitt," Dana blurted as she caught Claire's reflection behind her. "I haven't seen you in months, maybe years."

"Years." Claire's forced grin looked more like a sneer.

"Well, look at you. That fancy firm must be treating you like a princess. I see no bags under those baby blues."

"It's fine. That's a stunning dress. It reminds me of my sister."

"You always chirped about Molly having a sense of fashion. Wish I would've met her."

Dana turned sideways and ran both hands down her flat stomach. She then arched her back to take a second look at the curve of her butt in the tight-fitting dress. She stood motionless as if enjoying the view.

"Take this and get behind that curtain," the salesclerk insisted as she nudged the small of Claire's back. "You're going to regret it if you don't grab this dress. Trust me. Purple is the new black."

"Oh, I trust you," said Claire, slipping to the side. "I'll stop in after work. I should wear more purple and more dresses."

"Don't let how I look in this dress influence you, Claire." Dana spun full circle in front of the mirror. "It's not like we run in the same circles anymore."

"You don't influence me." Claire lifted a trendy pair of plaid pants up to her waist.

"Whatever." Dana coddled her breasts, increasing the exposed cleavage. "Geez, I can hardly keep these girls from jumping out. I'm not sure you could risk wearing a dress like this. It might mar your lofty legal career."

"Lofty?" Claire raised her eyebrows at Dana.

"Lofty? Snooty? You get what I mean." Dana scooted behind the curtain.

"Boy, do I," said Claire.

"Is she being sarcastic or did I miss something?" asked the confused clerk.

"God no. The woman's a feral cat."

"You know her? How did I not know that?"

"We were close friends in law school," said Claire.

"I've known you forever. I've never seen you together."

"Pseudo-friends. That is until my valedictorian medal smacked her in the face and revealed our unspoken rivalry."

"Shit, girl. I forgot all about you being valedictorian. That was one crazy day. I remember that much."

"I only mention it so you understand what I'm dealing with when it comes to her. My medal forced little Miss Competitive to accept second-place success. She didn't take it very well. Not then and not now."

"No wonder I've never seen her with you. She's a frenemy."

"I guess. I'm surprised to see her in here today."

"She's in here all the time. Calls herself a clothes whore."

"She's half right." Claire glanced at her watch. "Gotta run. I'll stop in later and try on a few things. That blazer in the window is to die for. It would rock the office paired with the cheetah boots."

The salesclerk flashed her brilliant white teeth behind her thick ruby lips.

"Bye, Dana." Claire returned the clerk's smile, ignoring the loud silence behind the curtain.

•••••

Claire tucked her feet between the couch cushions and flipped the page. She licked her fingers and flipped three more without pausing on any. Her eyes looked at the elegant photos of *Modern Design*, while her mind saw Molly arranging trophies on her shelves.

"I wish I could bring you back, sweet sister of mine," mumbled Claire.

Without warning, the door flew open and in wandered Alec. Claire jumped out of her memory unnoticed by Alec. He swapped jury questions for medical charts on Claire's desk. He flipped through several pages of the first chart, dropped it, and moved onto the second. And then the third. He mumbled over each one as Claire watched from the couch.

"Unbelievable." Alec read further. "Lying prick."

"Couldn't have said it better."

"What the—!" Alec flipped around. "What are you doing here?"

"It is my office." Claire hugged a throw pillow on her lap.

"After that meeting with the Satoris, I thought you'd cut out early."

"Blow off an afternoon because my feelings got hurt? I treated myself to some retail therapy instead. It's the least I deserve after the ass-chewing I got from David."

Claire swung her feet to the floor and nestled the throw pillow by the corner cushion. She straightened other pillows around it and tossed the magazine onto the coffee table.

"Let's get back to Delaney and establish our pattern. We have dozens of patient charts to scour. I don't want that joker surprising us."

"Joker or genius?" asked Alec. "He has people opening their wallets for nothing more than his charm."

"People see 'MD' and don't ask questions." Claire divided the charts into two piles. "I'm surprised Satori hasn't gone after him. He seems like the kind of guy who has people who take care of people."

Alec laughed and sat down in front of Claire's desk and pulled the stack of charts closer. He reviewed the top chart, jumped up, and headed to the coffee pot on the counter.

"It's a big job. Need some of this?" Alec held up his mug, and Claire shook her head.

After too many hours of reading about sprained ankles, jammed fingers, and injured joints, Claire spun her chair to the window and lifted her face to feel the bright sun. Alec continued to read.

"It doesn't seem that long ago," said Claire.

"What?"

"That February morning I found the Satori file on my desk."

"Six months wasn't that long ago."

"Snow covered the ground. I had a breakfast meeting that morning and felt invincible." Claire swiveled her chair as the sun's warmth touched her closed eyes. "In the beginning, I was ecstatic over this case. I devoured every piece of information I could find. I could rattle off facts like a pharmacy-school professor."

Claire swiveled her chair a moment longer and then jumped up, banging her chair into her desk. She meandered around her office with her hands clasped behind her back. Her face was tilted upward as she ran her hand along a shelf displaying *Law Reviews* from years past. Alec stopped reading and watched.

"I uncovered everything there is to know about the opioid epidemic," said Claire. "I was ready to be Emma Satori's knight in shining armor. But not now, not anymore."

"Why not?"

"I don't know. I feel like a campfire the following morning. Smoldering embers." Claire kept her hands clasped as she returned to her window and looked at the dynamic street below.

"Smoldering embers can still burn down a forest."

"Not if they don't reignite."

"Use these medical records to incinerate the entire courtroom," said Alec. "They're proof that Novo Analgesic Systems provides the opioids Delaney needs to shuffle patients in and out of his office with naïve trust and a ticket for addiction."

"I guess that counts as a spark." Claire returned to her chair and flipped open her laptop. "I've scheduled the nation's top three experts in pain management to testify. I emailed you the dates of their depositions."

"Already on my calendar."

"They'll testify that the opioid epidemic is a problem unique to America, with 40 percent more opioid prescriptions written each year than any other country," said Claire.

"Makes us look like a nation of dopeheads. I hate that when most of the poppy farms are in other countries." Alec tilted back on his chair.

"It's American insurance companies. They favor drugs over expensive therapies, and pharmaceutical companies provide easy access to drugs. It's a straight line. From 2000 to 2010 opioid scripts soared while non-opioid scripts decreased at the same rate. And there was no change in reported pain."

"If opioids are so plentiful, what led to the increased heroin use of the second wave? I know I've seen it in our research." Alec returned to the counter and thumbed through research material.

"The almighty buck," said Claire. "People addicted to opioids switched to heroin because it was cheaper. But in 2013, this second wave of heroin use was surpassed by overdoses from synthetic opioids created in labs all over the country. Welcome third wave." Claire directed Alec's attention to material in the last pile.

"From prescription opioids to heroin to synthetic opioids. Once you're on the ride, you can never get off." Alec frowned as he leafed through the research.

"People have no idea how powerful opioids are," said Claire. "Eighty percent of heroin addicts began with prescription opioids. That shows aggressive opioid prescription practices, like Dr. Delaney's, played the biggest role in creating the opioid epidemic."

"If people only knew how screwed up the American medical system is."

"I don't think the American medical system realizes it either." Claire returned to her laptop. "Clinical guidelines only suggest opioids be prescribed for chronic pain when safer alternatives aren't feasible. There's no mandate. And the Prescription Drug Monitoring Program only monitors a patient's prescription history if someone cares to look. It doesn't monitor the number of prescriptions a physician writes. There are no laws governing the free flow of opioids."

"Maybe the court will change that," said Alec. "The jury will see Delaney overprescribing and NAS overproviding."

"You head back to NAS and request replacement test results." Claire grabbed Alec by the arm. "Explain what happened, but don't tell the truth. Make something up."

"Shaggy might show sympathy if he knows you were injured in the line of duty."

"Stop already. Do you call him that to his face?"

"No. But I could. He'd take it as a compliment. It'd make him famous."

"Do what you need to and get him to talk," said Claire. "Find the start of Deprexone. I'll head back to Delaney's office and see what opioids he's been handing out since Emma died."

"Good luck with that. I can't imagine what you'll find behind those doors."

Alec walked to the couch and reached down to stretch his legs before sitting. Claire pushed on his back as she passed. With fluid movement, she dropped back on the couch and swung both legs onto the table. She also leaned forward to stretch her legs.

"Too many hours sitting in a chair makes me feel like an old man," said Alec. "My legs don't want to move."

"There are so many unanswered questions swirling around one girl's death," said Claire as she held on to her ankles, ignoring Alec's remark.

"Like what?" asked Alec.

"How many heroin users are there because their opioids got too expensive? How many scripts did they get before turning to heroin? How many opioid deaths have been reported? How many unreported?"

"Sounds like you want to take down the whole industry."

"Maybe it's time," said Claire. "Wish I could file assault charges."

"Against whom?"

"Whoever attacked me. Was it someone from NAS or a random thug? Can you answer that?"

"Do I need to?"

"You can't." Claire pointed to Alec as a challenge. "Nor can you tell me why."

"You think it's tied to NAS in some way?"

"Sure do." Claire swung her feet to the floor. "Lombard Street is too sleepy for a money heist. And they didn't go for my purse. Someone from NAS wanted what I had in that briefcase."

"How would they know what was in your briefcase?" asked Alec.

"Common sense. I'm an attorney, and they're the defendants. Anything in my briefcase could be beneficial."

"That's a stretch."

"Who else could it have been?"

"Any of the hundreds of thugs prowling the streets of Philly."

"Before we go after hundreds of unknowns, why don't we look into the one we do know?"

"Exactly. In a court of law. Not with some accusation of a street crime," said Alec.

"Is a street crime that different from what we know they've done? The aggression is upfront, but the danger is the same. Addiction kills."

"Listen to yourself, Claire."

"Drug manufacturers are no more than drug dealers. Just like the street dealers, they're in possession with intent to deliver. They deliver to doctors who then deliver to patients. Pretty soon everyone is caught in the web, and everyone's addicted to something."

Alec walked over and sat beside Claire on the couch. He shifted onto his hip as he turned Claire's direction. Claire scooted to the opposite end. She positioned two pillows between them with a pouty expression.

"Emma's death isn't the isolated event you want it to be," said Claire. "NAS gave us the test results under court order. They didn't want us to have the results, so they stole them back."

"Why wouldn't they want us to have those results?"

"Liability for a deficiently tested opioid. They're a drug dealer protecting their turf."

"Stealing them would make no difference." said Alec. "Although not everyone uses them, there are copy machines in every office building in the United States."

"Ouch."

"I'm kidding, but this conversation is irrelevant."

"Copies are irrelevant," said Claire. "They won't stand up in court because there's no chain of custody. Without the proof those test results provided, NAS can contradict everything we say. It's a long shot, but one I think they took."

"I'll grovel when I get there and hope they're generous." Alec held his crossed fingers up to Claire.

"If not, I hate to think how many butts you'll have to smooch."

"I'm not worried."

"Where did you grow up?" Claire asked as she picked up another small pillow and hugged it to her stomach. "I know it's random, but when you were younger, wasn't there some kid in your class put on an arbitrary drug for some unknown reason?"

"I remember kids getting passes to see the school nurse. But I never really thought about it," said Alec.

"I guarantee you had friends taking drugs the family doctor prescribed. Complaining paid off if you whined long enough. And even if you didn't, parents, teachers, coaches, any adult could decide you needed to take something."

"I guess so. Let's get back to work."

Claire scooted off the couch and headed to her desk as her thoughts continued to bounce from one topic to another. She gripped the desk's edge and stared at the piles of paperwork covering the deep brown wood. She grabbed a pen, dropped into her chair, and picked up the top file.

After making some progress, Claire looked up at the sound of a soft tap. Ellen cleared her throat as she pushed the door open. She looked minuscule next to a tall, balding man wearing a well-pressed uniform. The stern expression on his face depicted his sour mood. He held Claire's briefcase by his side.

"Oh my God!" Claire shot up.

"I apologize for interrupting, Ms. Hewitt, but Sergeant Jones insisted on seeing you. He said he has a very tight schedule and is in need of answers."

"That's fine." Claire motioned for Sergeant Jones to continue in as Ellen slipped away.

"Please have a seat." Claire pointed to the sitting area by the couch as she spoke. Jones ignored the gesture and seated himself in front of Claire's desk, scooting in until his knees hit the back panel. He looked sideways at Alec, then back to Claire. Claire sat down across from him.

"Ms. Hewitt, I'm Sergeant Jones. We found the briefcase you allege was stolen."

"Allege?" asked Claire.

"Have you thought through what happened on Lombard Street? It concerns the Philadelphia Police Department." Jones kept his serious eyes on Claire.

"It happened a day ago, Sergeant Jones. I haven't stopped thinking about it."

"You can call me Jay."

"Well, Jay, it's been on my mind."

"Ms. Hewitt, the police department is apprehensive about the attack. The briefcase was recovered completely intact within a block of the incident."

"Why does that cause apprehension?"

"Stolen items are seldom found intact with the contents undisturbed. That's troubling."

"Troubling?" asked Claire.

"It looks suspicious," said Sergeant Jones. "The location of the attack and the time of its occurrence seem unlikely. Lombard Street is not a high-crime area."

"What are you insinuating? Whether it happened? Do you want to see my bruises?"

"No, ma'am."

Claire remained seated while Sergeant Jones stood and walked around the office with his arms folded across his chest. He spoke slowly.

"I realize this is one of Philadelphia's most prominent law firms. But in any environment, the work can become mundane, and individuals can desire more activity and attention."

"Excuse me?"

"Have you found a need to spice up things in your work environment?"

"Spice up things? Are you kidding me?" Claire shot up, sending her chair banging against the counter.

Sergeant Jones stopped directly in front of Claire. He closed his eyes for several seconds, then opened them. Alec remained seated and watched the exchange.

"Ms. Hewitt, we need to consider all the possibilities."

"What possibilities?" asked Claire. "I was attacked. My brief-case was stolen. Are you suggesting otherwise?" Claire looked to Alec as if wondering what he thought of this awkward exchange.

"I'm not suggesting anything. I'm looking for answers."

"I represent some of the largest real estate developers in this state. I have neither the time nor the desire to 'spice up things,'" said Claire.

"I'm investigating a crime, Ms. Hewitt, and looking at the whole picture. I must eliminate the possibility that this incident was contrived. That evidence was planted."

"By whom?"

"You tell me. Your briefcase was unopened." Sergeant Jones raised his eyebrows.

"Did I purposely bruise my shoulder and scrape chunks of skin off my hands and face?"

"I don't have that answer."

"Common sense gives you that answer. It's no."

"I hope that's correct."

"It is. And your fishing expedition is over."

"I didn't mean to offend you." Sergeant Jones placed one hand on his chest. "I am required by law to conduct a thorough investigation. I must question everyone involved."

"I understand," said Claire. "But accusing me of fabricating a crime is not required by law. You didn't come here to investigate an attack on Lombard Street nor to speak with a victim. You came here to interrogate a suspect."

"That was not my intent," said Sergeant Jones. "But I would be remiss to ignore any possible evidence."

"I'm the victim, Jay! If you don't want to see the scrapes and bruises, you can talk to my witness." Claire glanced over at Alec.

Sergeant Jones scowled and grabbed his notepad from Claire's desk. With his eyes drawn to the carpet, he walked out and left the door open. Claire slammed it shut.

"What in the hell? He disregarded everything in that police report and questioned my integrity!"

"Maybe you are right." Alec walked to the window and looked at the street below. "I thought last night was a random act, but maybe NAS is involved."

"Can I say I told you so?"

"Not yet. I have doubts. Common sense says the aggression alone would preclude their involvement. Camouflaging fraud seems more the NAS style."

"Do we even know their style?" Claire leaned against the edge of her desk. "We've hit a closed door with every discovery attempt."

"I know. We've spent hours waiting for researchers who never showed and received stacks of useless documents irrelevant to the case. But physical aggression?"

"Physical aggression to retrieve evidence," said Claire. "You head to the police station and see what leads they have on last night's attack. I'll make a few calls to see if anyone has heard anything. You never know what you'll find if you ask the right questions of the right people."

"I hope that's true," said Alec.

Claire and Alec left the office together, ignoring the looks from coworkers as they took the elevator to the lobby, walked out the front doors, and parted ways.

"Catch ya later," Alec said as he headed south.

"Good luck." Claire stood for a moment and watched Alec walk away. She thought again of his protective comment when leaving the station.

"He couldn't leave me alone in an empty lot," she mumbled to herself.

Alec walked into the police station for the second time in as many days. He bypassed the information desk. A young woman with small features and ebony skin had replaced the muscular middle-aged man he dealt with the previous night. Alec gave her a polite nod as he walked up to the first counter and stood in line behind two others. The tumultuous atmosphere from the night before had disappeared.

The two gentlemen in front of Alec had minor questions. A short woman with a gray pageboy haircut gave them each an answer and sent them away. She then turned to Alec with an irritated expression.

"What do you need?"

As soon as he uttered the word *evidence*, she shook her head with a belittling smirk.

"You're in the wrong place, honey. This is the police station."

"I'm aware."

"I'm sure you are, sweetheart." The smirk returned. "But instead of interrupting my day, you should be bothering someone at the courthouse. That's where you'll find court documents."

"The evidence I need will be in the police reports," said Alec. "I believe I pick those up here."

"Well, you should have started with that."

The unpleasant woman trudged to a bank of computers and began typing. She pounded the keys as she yelled over her shoulder.

"What date do you want?"

"The past two weeks."

"Are you kidding me?"

Rolling her head on her neck, the woman resumed typing. She continued banging the keys until the printer spit out the last report.

"Total waste of more than a few trees." She smacked the copies onto the counter.

"Thank you." Alec grabbed the papers and hurried out of the station.

Claire walked into the Bar Association office with an irritated expression. She ignored an old acquaintance reading a newspaper by the window and headed for a corner table. She dropped into a chair, opened a paper calendar, and placed a call.

"Can you check a date on my calendar? The Brotherly Love Fundraiser."

"Am I your secretary now?" asked Morgan.

"Go to my office. Check for me. I'm at the Bar Association and need to know. I need to turn in the list of volunteers."

"You sound bitchy."

"It's not that. I'm still pissed that Sergeant Jones confronted me the way he did. I don't need my integrity questioned. He thinks I fabricated the attack."

"He's an ass. Did he see your bruises?"

"I offered to show him. I'm hoping he's a crazy old man. Text me that date. We'll talk later." Claire disconnected and placed her next call. She leaned back in the chair with her legs stretched out and ankles crossed. She feigned a serene composure as she white-knuckled the armrest.

"Hello."

"Hey, Dana, it's Claire."

"Claire Hewitt?"

"What other Claire do you know?"

"Great to hear from you. I think. What's up?"

"We need to get together," said Claire. "Really get together. Not just small talk at some boutique. We need to catch up."

"Catch up on what?"

"Our lives. Our professions. Our loves."

"Busy. Attorney. Have none," said Dana.

"We all are. I know. And I doubt that. Can you be free Wednesday after work, say 5:30?"

"Sure. Meet you at Bin 402. You do know where that is, don't you?"

"Not funny. Of course I do. See you there."

Claire disconnected and pressed Google Maps on her phone.

8

NOT
SO FAST

Landon and Jack ended their meeting on friendly terms despite impending misfortune. It was Landon's job to prevent it, but Jack would be held accountable if he failed.

"There's a lot of research to tread through," said Landon. "But I think it'll reveal what's happening in your labs."

"I don't mind it. The last time I was involved in research was in Pharmacology 430 my senior year." Jack chuckled.

"Was that the start of your interest in drug development?" asked Landon.

"That whole semester was. As an ambitious wannabe, I scheduled trips to Virginia and Vermont poppy farms to see firsthand the advancements in opium production in the United States. I planned on furthering my pharmacology education with graduate work when Dad announced his retirement. What could I do?"

"Good point," said Landon.

"Thanks for the update. I'll give this data a full review." Jack rested his hand on the thick binder.

"Are you going to call Westcott?"

"I don't think so. We need a face-to-face. We've had a tense relationship from the start. A phone call would simply add to any bad blood he may be harboring."

"If there are any discrepancies with Deprexone that could threaten the stability of this company, Phil Westcott is involved."

"I'm well aware," said Jack.

Although Jack wasn't a daily presence in the lab at Novo Analgesic Systems, Inc., he was conversant with the research it conducted. He understood the FDA regulatory process for prescription drugs and its application to opioids. Jack didn't need to wear a lab coat to run his business.

"This research will show if there's a problem with Deprexone or if Mom and Dad just don't like the outcome," said Jack. "From Westcott's initial formulation to nationwide distribution, I'm going to know who played what role in Deprexone development, everyone's subsequent involvement with its release, and who I can trust. I'm going to find out if the problem is with the people or the process." Jack patted the binder.

"When production increased to cover the national opioid demand, Dana assured me she was monitoring the procedures," said Landon with his hand gripping the doorframe. "She claimed she scrutinized the progression between the three obligatory phases of testing and evaluated the extent of randomization and the number of participants involved. She guaranteed that everything was bona fide."

"Guess we'll find out."

Landon nodded and walked out. As he pulled the door closed, a light above the door caught his attention. A lustrous white Do Not Disturb illuminated the hallway.

"More gadgets," Landon mumbled to himself.

Jack opened the binder with pen in hand. He read page after

page of data on Westcott's extended-release formulation, jotting notes in the margins and intermittently mumbling with intrigue.

Landon pressed the green button on his phone as he looked back at the illuminated sign above Jack's door. The reception was weak, but the call connected.

"I'm leaving Jack's office now. Can you meet me in thirty?"

"Yep."

"Does Solid Grounds work for you? It's on this side of town."

"Sure does."

One hour later, Dana Massetti pushed into the crowded coffee shop. She overreacted to the rich aromas swirling through the narrow room as she lifted her face and breathed deeply through her nose. She looked around. Book clubs and study groups consumed most of the space, but a small table against the back wall sat empty except for a brown leather briefcase. Dana weaved past hushed conversations and approached the table. The familiar initials *LDS* on the briefcase indicated she had chosen the right spot. She set her briefcase on the floor and sat opposite a scattering of notes and a yellow highlighter.

"What can you tell me about Deprexone?" asked Landon, approaching Dana with a large macchiato and a black coffee.

"What would you like to know?" Dana raised her eyebrows with a look of innocence as she accepted the cup.

"Don't be cute. The Satori lawsuit should worry you. Whether it's a suicide or a homicide, everyone is under scrutiny. I need to know everything there is to know. And how did Westcott get Jack on board?"

"Where do you want me to start?" asked Dana. "Westcott was there long before I arrived. He was cooking opium back in the eighties, and America loved it. He came up with some new concoction and tested it on his little monkeys. Jack went apeshit over it." Dana giggled.

"Not funny. I told Jack you guaranteed everything is legit."

"It is."

"It looks like this extended-release formulation isn't much more than a marketing scheme," said Landon. "Ingenuity is great. Ineptitude is not."

"There's nothing inept about relieving pain."

"It's inept to shove a shitty drug down peoples' throats. The test results are unrealistic for a new drug. It smells like corruption."

"It smells like success, Landon."

"Not so fast, Dana. No investigational new drug is an overnight success. INDs take hundreds of tests and hundreds of random volunteers to progress to this magnitude."

"Or an experienced pharmacologist who knows what he's doing," said Dana. "The medical community has faith in him. He finagled his way onto the AMA's Task Force to Reduce Opioid Abuse."

"Is he advancing the purpose of the task force and helping physicians combat the opioid epidemic, or is he concealing the problem?"

"What are you so hyped up about?" asked Dana.

"The overdose rate from opioid use is rising, and 74 percent of those overdoses are from legal opioid prescriptions."

Landon drank his black coffee and watched Dana shift her position and tug on her short skirt. She avoided eye contact as she bit the side of her cheek and watched other patrons throughout the shop. When she had her solution, she flipped her head to Landon.

"Westcott isn't responsible for every doctor," said Dana. "Mercedes-Benz makes an amazing automobile. It ranks as one of the highest in automobile safety. The manufacturer isn't responsible for the idiots who crash these cars and kill innocent people."

"Not even close. We aren't in a car-crash crisis." Landon rolled his eyes and his head at the same time. Exasperated with her childish analogies, he looked around the room as if in search of an escape. He was losing traction with Dana, as often occurred when she needed to spin an argument another direction.

"We kind of are," said Dana. "Every day hundreds of people die on our interstates."

"People make informed decisions about buying cars," said Landon as he looked back at Dana. "They decide what they want, what they can afford, and then shop the dealerships."

Landon grabbed material from the pocket of his briefcase and slapped it on the table in front of Dana. He shuffled through additional papers as sweat glistened on both temples and his breathing quickened. With his irritation evident, he highlighted the first paragraph of an additional report and slid it in Dana's direction.

"People don't shop for opioids," said Landon. "They're given opioids in difficult, often tragic, situations. Sometimes these opioids come with guidance, often not." Landon slid the papers closer to Dana. "As those reports show, in 2018, there were more than fifty thousand overdose deaths from drugs. A lot more than car accidents on American roadways."

"Statistics don't change the facts." Dana scooted the material back to Landon.

"Statistics are the facts."

"No, Landon. Statistics are surface numbers. NAS isn't liable for every adverse outcome because some doctor was irresponsible. Westcott's extended-release formulation carries less risk of addiction and was approved by the FDA."

"FDA approval doesn't negate responsibility once the opioid hits the market. If anything, that responsibility increases." Landon gulped his black coffee.

"Westcott's lived up to his responsibilities," said Dana. "Since the release of Deprexone, he's submitted every required report under the FDA's Adverse Event Reporting System. He also developed a risk evaluation and mitigation strategy."

Dana stood as she completed her sentence and walked away. She shimmied through the crowd and headed toward the barista. She kicked a backpack when squeezing past a small group of students but said nothing and continued to the counter. The student retrieved the backpack, glanced up at Dana, and commented to others at the table. Landon watched as Dana ordered another beverage and returned to the table blowing the hot steam.

"The REMS report only disseminates methods of educating prescribers about the drug," said Landon. "More education equals more sales. It's NAS self-promotion."

"An opioid can only survive in the competitive market if it provides what it promises. Successful pain relief equals more sales." Dana blew the steam from her cup before taking a sip of the hot beverage.

"Speaking of sales, tell me about Deprexone marketing," said Landon.

"The marketing department can give you details, but suffice it to say it's creative and provides widespread visibility."

"The campaigns I've seen emphasize a low risk of addiction. Where's the supporting research?" asked Landon.

"The pharmacologists are responsible for the storage of research they've conducted." Dana closed her eyes and pinched the bridge of her nose.

"Is someone toying with Deprexone in order to make unsubstantiated claims that increase sales?" asked Landon.

"Toying? That's called research."

"Deprexone needs solid, irrefutable research to support the claims made. It's your responsibility to ensure that happens." Landon's tone became less inquisitive and more critical. His eyes narrowed as he looked from the marketing materials to Dana.

"I'm aware of my responsibilities," said Dana.

Landon silenced further dialogue with his raised palm. Dana's eyes darted back and forth between Landon's face and his hand. She leaned back in her chair and kept her eyes on his face.

"Someone needs to oversee that crazy bastard," said Landon. "If he didn't follow every regulation, Novo Analgesic Systems is going to pay, and dead teenagers are expensive."

"NAS isn't going to pay a damn penny," said Dana as she grabbed the table's edge. "I've been in that lab. There are no irregularities with the Deprexone research. Are you questioning Westcott, or are you questioning me?"

"I'm questioning everyone." Landon shoved a Pendaflex folder at Dana. "Look at those results. After the preliminary monkey tests, Westcott acts like he won the lottery. Press releases, seminars, educational courses, speakers. The marketing outweighed the data."

"Why do you question his research?"

"I'm simply the first one in line," said Landon. "This is a class-action lawsuit. The prosecution will challenge every experiment and interrogate every person."

"Let them," said Dana.

"That's easy to say before it happens. Westcott needed to do a lot more research to support the aggressive marketing of Deprexone as a less addictive opioid. All his research proves is that he's damn lucky."

"What do you want me to do about it?" asked Dana. "Question a respected pharmacologist who's developed opioids for decades? I need specifics, and you need to be realistic about your expectations."

"Verify the increase in the number of participants between each phase of testing," said Landon. "Establish that there was a similar pain diagnosis between those receiving Deprexone and those receiving the placebo. Ensure that no known addictions were deleted from the data. Is that specific enough?"

"That's white noise, Landon. Read the research. It's all there." Dana stood. Her tall frame towered over Landon.

"Look again." Landon leaned back and looked up at Dana. "We're screwed if Hewitt finds anything."

"There are no discrepancies with Deprexone. It's different and less addictive. You should be delighted."

"Delighted we're being sued?"

"Delighted Deprexone is putting millions of dollars in NAS coffers," said Dana.

"If Westcott took shortcuts to camouflage his results or if he marketed this product without supporting data, his success will become a debacle," said Landon. "If he's hiding anything, the money will go straight to the Satoris. And to every other addict in this suit."

"Westcott may be crazy, but he got approval from the FDA. He's good."

"He's not that good." Landon grabbed the reports and stuffed them in his briefcase.

"He is that good."

"Then how did we end up here?"

"We're here because wealthy people expect fairy-tale endings," said Dana. "When they can't buy one, they blame someone."

Dana drank the last of her second macchiato. She threw her bag over her shoulder and pushed the Pendaflex toward Landon. She remained standing and looked down at Landon as he spoke.

"Transparency in that lab is your gig, Dana. If they lose, you lose."

Dana turned and walked away. Landon watched her toss her crumpled cup in the trash can and meander through the crowd. The door jingled as she left.

Jack studied Deprexone data in the quiet of his office for two hours before shutting the binder and rushing out. He brushed past Carol outside his door but didn't stop.

"I'll be down in the lab and would prefer not to be bothered."

"Oh." Carol jumped. "I need to confirm—"

"Later."

Jack stepped onto the elevator and stood in the middle of the cab with his arms folded and his hands balled into fists. He looked up at the decreasing number until the doors opened.

"Westcott?" Jack yelled.

"I'm right here," snapped a distant angry voice. "Do you feel as though you're above my request for silence, or do you simply choose to ignore my sign? Unexpected noises are disruptive."

"I didn't see your sign," said Jack.

"You had it printed for me."

"Well, I missed it. Where the hell are you?" Jack walked past mailboxes and a small podium, ignoring the entry log. He peered down the first row of cages, looking for the source of the voice. He turned to the right and came upon a pair of long legs in dirty tasseled loafers jutting out from beneath a large wire cage and pointing to the ceiling. Jack bent down and saw the lengthy torso of Phil Westcott lying on his back with a screwdriver in hand.

"I have questions," said Jack. "Deprexone looks like a science fair project. An incomplete fucked-up project."

"Here we go again."

"I have enraged parents crawling up my ass," said Jack.

"They'll get over it. My research is solid. A lot more solid than this damn cage with its flimsy hinges." The shoes flipped over as Phil crawled out from under the cage. He stood and brushed himself off.

"They'll get over their dead daughter?" asked Jack.

"I got FDA approval for the first extended-release opioid available."

Jack stepped sideways to block Phil from walking past. The flustered pharmacologist vacillated as he opened an adjacent cage and reached inside. With flushed cheeks, he turned to Jack, cradling a small marmoset. He stroked its belly.

"Do you see what your intrusion has done?" Phil's nostrils flared as he continued to stroke the animal.

"My intrusion is the least of your worries. How about the number of patients addicted to Deprexone? Will they soon outnumber the ridiculous seminars we've sponsored across the country?"

"My seminars are the lifeblood of Deprexone." Phil uncharacteristically threw the marmoset back into its cage. He slammed the door and stepped closer to Jack. "Physicians need to be educated on the multitude of benefits Deprexone provides. My educational courses and seminars launched Deprexone into the pain-management ring."

"What pain-management ring?" asked Jack.

Jack stood less than two feet from Phil. Although they were both close to six foot two, Jack's broad shoulders and strong stature made him appear taller. His dominance was discernible as Phil attempted to stumble by him again.

"There is no ring, Dr. Westcott," said Jack. "There's a dead teenage girl with very rich parents."

Jack looked down at the cage beside him while Phil stepped back. He then ran his hand along the top as he stood before the flustered scientist. He examined the adjoining cages and then directed his anger and his questions back to Phil.

"Does Deprexone have the same addictive qualities as other opioids?" asked Jack. "Can you ensure that this dead girl isn't the first in a long line?"

"I can assure you we need only show proper procedures were followed." Phil squirmed past Jack and stopped at the edge of the next cage. He looked inside and turned back to Jack. "I can assure you that after Deprexone leaves our building, it's up to the dispensing physician to make sure appropriate monitoring is provided. My drug didn't kill that girl. A neglectful doctor killed that girl."

"But our marketing campaign touts that Deprexone is appropriate for chronic pain," said Jack. "And we're marketing the hell out of this drug to convince doctors across America that it's the ideal medication for all types of chronic pain. Can we support that?"

"I don't know. I'm not in your marketing department," said Phil.

"For Pete's sake, Westcott!" Jack slammed both fists onto the cage beside him. "We're being sued."

"As I'm constantly reminded." Phil raced to the cage and shoved Jack aside. He opened the door and leaned inside as far as he could, mumbling in soft tones. Jack stepped back and muttered obscenities to himself.

"Why are you not accepting the severity of this lawsuit?" asked Jack.

"Information regarding Deprexone is on every bottle," said Phil with a muffled voice. "Full disclosure comes from the treating physicians. We thoroughly tested Deprexone, noted that it may not agree with every individual, and placed a label on every bottle. We're covered."

"'May not agree with every individual'?" Jack repeated.

"That's not the exact wording, but it's close." Phil faced Jack. "Elaborating on every imaginable outcome isn't what's mandated. Deprexone is an excellent medication for pain. No two people experience the same pain, so we can't tell a physician how patients will react. We paint with broad strokes. We give every prescribing physician an array of possibilities."

"What does that gibberish mean?" Jack walked down the aisle of cages, tapping the bobber on several water bottles as he passed.

"It means I've shielded you from greedy people looking for a deep pocket. You should thank me."

"That shield is full of holes," said Jack.

"Like what?" Phil cocked his head to the side like a child challenging a parent and stuck out the opposite hip.

"Unrealistic success rates that look suspicious," said Jack.

"That's why it's different."

"Different or dangerous?"

"Opioids are complex." Phil shook his head and shoved both hands into the pockets of his apron. "They have been around since 3400 BC for medicinal purposes. While people have become addicted throughout the centuries, opioids have given new life to millions."

"How does that history help us?" asked Jack.

"I've developed the first extended-release formulation that alleviates pain with minimal risk of addiction. It's that simple."

"It's not that simple," said Jack with his tone deflated, his expression weary.

"Yes, it is. Other opioids blast into the human system and cause addiction. You knew Deprexone was different when I submitted my proposal. I told you people would be skeptical. That it was bound to raise concerns although supported with solid research."

"It raises the hairs on the back of my neck." Jack paused at the end of the aisle and squatted to see the animal inside. He wiggled his fingers inside the cage.

"It shouldn't. I've spent thousands of hours developing, testing, and refining this landmark discovery," said Phil.

"And I've spent thousands of dollars funding it." Jack stood and rubbed the back of his neck. "The federal grant was no more than seed money. When it was gone, you guaranteed that with more research Deprexone would change the world."

"It has changed the world," yelled Phil, his arms suddenly stiffening as if by electric shock.

"It sure has for the Satoris." Jack's eyes narrowed as he walked toward Phil. "I gave my stamp of approval but am questioning that decision."

"What is there to question?" asked Phil.

"Everything," said Jack. "Its success rate is inflated. Is that artificial inflation? I'm concerned something illegal or unethical is happening in the NAS lab."

"I guarantee you are mistaken." Phil flapped the front of his apron as he licked his thin lips. "You need to crawl off me and talk with your marketing department. They're the ones who released the propaganda that started this Deprexone mess."

"The propaganda came after the research." Jack's tone deepened as his face tightened. "Dana Massetti is going to take a closer look at what goes on in this lab, and she's going to report back to me."

"Send her up to marketing," suggested Phil.

"She'll talk to them, but we need additional eyes in here as a guarantee."

"A guarantee of what?" asked Phil. "Someone looking over my shoulder changes nothing."

"But it could expose everything." Jack tilted head as if it were obvious. "I trust Dana to protect this company at all costs."

Jack Freeman turned on his heels and walked out. An enraged Phil Westcott didn't move as he spoke to the small animal he was still holding.

"That meddling bitch has caused enough trouble. She's not looking over my shoulder. Not for one minute."

9

RECREATION
FOR ARISTOCRATS

D ana pushed on the door to the NAS lab. She ignored the loud creak and the incessant chatter of primates.

"Westcott?"

Phil groaned at the sound of the door and the female voice as he squatted behind a black wire cage. Although there were several feet of unused space between cages, it was an awkward fit for Phil's six-foot frame.

"Westcott?"

"I'm right here."

Dana jumped at the harsh whisper as her eyes followed the sound. A scuffed wingtip protruded from behind the cage as Phil knelt on one knee and extended the other leg. She stepped back and watched the monkey inside the cage grab the bars and shake its body back and forth.

"Am I interrupting, or do you have a minute?" asked Dana.

"Yes."

Phil scribbled on the back of the cage, looked at his clipboard, and made a second notation. He then crawled from behind the cage. He tugged on his lab coat as he glared down at Dana's defiant eyes.

"What in God's name? Are you pleased with yourself? Do you see what you did to this poor animal? Look at him ricochet around his home."

"Of course he is. You were behind his cage." said Dana.

"It was the door that terrified him. You pushed too forcefully."

"Buy WD-40. Can we talk? I'm in a hurry."

"If you're in a hurry, send an email." Phil turned his back to Dana and slipped behind another cage. The primate inside ran to the back and stretched its thin arm between the bars. It grabbed on to Phil's hair and pulled with a firm grip and open mouth. A pinched grin spread on Phil's face as he gently removed the hand and wrapped the fingers around the cage bar.

"Give me the information I need, and I'll oil your damn door," said Dana.

"Oiling my damn door won't compensate for your intrusion or your unreasonable demands." Phil stepped to the front of the cage as the primate followed.

"Do we have to go through this every time?" asked Dana.

"Only when you burst in like a tornado disrupting this fragile environment. These animals are like family to me. This laboratory is my home."

Dana winced at the bad breath of the man berating her. She took a step back and watched Phil walk from cage to cage talking to his primates. She wondered if his breath was as offensive to them. She reasoned it didn't matter since theirs was equally repugnant.

Phil stopped in front of a protruding tuft of bright orange fur. The lethargic animal lay pressed against the front bars. Phil slowly opened the door and gathered the fur into his arms. He then turned to face Dana as his eyes scrolled up and down her body.

"You seem to have your arms full. Let me hurry," said Dana. "I need data verifying similar pain diagnoses between those receiving Deprexone and those receiving the placebo. I want verification from the FDA's Center for Drug Evaluation and Research that the health benefits outweigh the risks."

"What the hell is wrong with you, woman?" Phil's grip on the primate visibly tightened.

"Excuse me?"

"Don't waltz in here spewing demands like you're new to the game. You've been here from the start. You know the diagnoses, and you've seen the risk/benefit analysis."

"But compiling, updating, and filing the data is your job."

"Don't tell me what my job is, missy. I'm sick and tired of adolescent know-it-alls harassing me with unreasonable demands. You're the third one today."

"Who else was here?" asked Dana.

"Sims and Freeman."

"Not Claire Hewitt?"

"I said Sims and Freeman. Doesn't look like either of them have faith in you. I'm sure Hewitt isn't far behind. It's been Grand Central Station."

"Faith is irrelevant. What's up with Jack?"

Phil grabbed on to the orange fur with a tight fist. He used his other hand to feel for its face and gently turn its chin. He blew the fur back and stroked the animal as he spoke with a calming voice and closed eyes.

"Jack Freeman graced me with his presence to illustrate his ignorance of my contributions and his arrogance pertaining to drug development. I'm not sure whose side he thinks I'm on."

"This lawsuit worries him." Dana looked at the literature spread across the table to her right. Without scooting anything aside, she set her briefcase on top.

"Worries him why?" Phil's eyes popped open. He looked from Dana to the table. He shifted the primate to one arm and pulled a handful of letters from underneath the case. He tossed them into the mail bin at the end of the table and readjusted the sleeping primate. He then turned his frustration to Dana. "One young girl misuses the drug, and everybody freaks. Nobody knows what other recreational drugs she was enjoying. We can't second-guess Deprexone based on angry parents with a lot of money and big egos. This lawsuit is recreation for an aristocrat."

"This lawsuit is not recreation. The Satoris want to fight. And like you said, they have the money to do it."

"So do we. Are you going to let some blueblood with a tight sphincter make unreasonable demands?" asked Phil.

"What do you think?"

"I think that's what it looks like when you harass me about the results I've obtained with my research."

"This is nowhere near harassment," said Dana. "I'm the one who threw money at you when you claimed the extended-release formulation had fewer addictive properties. And I threw more money at you when you weren't getting results as quickly as you hoped. I threw money at you based on a theory."

"You didn't give me a dime. I work for Novo Analgesic Systems."

"I am Novo Analgesic Systems." Dana stepped closer to Phil. "I pled your case to Jack. I begged for money on your behalf. And what do I get? Your lab rat handing out test results like campaign flyers, and Claire Hewitt grabbing everything she can get her sticky little fingers on."

"That's Ethan's screwup. Not mine," said Phil.

"It happened in your lab."

"Is that why you're riding me? I get that you're angry at Ethan and scared of Hewitt. But Ethan is a lab tech who doesn't know shit. None of that can be blamed on me."

"Ethan is your responsibility," said Dana. "Backroom files are NAS property that shouldn't be shared with anyone outside the NAS family. Not competing manufacturers nor incompetent attorneys."

"Too late," said Phil.

"Better not be. You and Ethan clean up your acts."

"I'm spotless," said Phil.

"Then take care of Ethan. He's not. Discredit him as inexperienced and the information he disseminated as erroneous. I'll take care of Hewitt. When she shows up, which she will, keep me out of it. We have a past, so to speak."

Dana grabbed her briefcase and turned for the door. Several envelopes and two journals fell to the floor. Phil gave no reaction as he unloaded the large bundle of orange fur back into its cage. Dana paused when she reached the heavy steel door wondering if she had gained any traction with Phil. She looked back at the angry pinched face watching her leave.

"Collect the information I need," said Dana. "I'll stop by later. And I better not find you or Ethan sharing backroom information with anyone who doesn't work in this lab. I don't want to be blindsided by some rich family looking for revenge or pity. Are we clear?"

"Crystal."

10

THE SECRET ROOM

A strong wind swept the door open as Alec stepped out of his building. A friendly neighbor caught it, so Alec said thanks and kept walking. He kept pace with the early morning crowd for half a block, then leaned against a brick building to place his call.

"Good morning," said Alec. "Giving you a heads-up on the police reports I picked up the other day. They tell us nothing. The PPD follows format with their investigations."

Alec pushed away from the wall and weaved around slow-moving pedestrians. His pace increased, as did his dialogue with Claire.

"We can relax about Jones too," continued Alec. "He's a little nuts, but the NAS lab is the answer. They have the evidence we need to expose what they did and what Delaney failed to do when Emma was still alive."

Alec's brisk movement increased to a jog as he listened to Claire's advice on the other end of the line. He nodded to fellow pedestrians who stepped out of his way and dodged those rushing faster than him.

"I'm heading to the lab now. If I hurry, I'll catch the early train. And once I'm there, I'll schmooze anyone who needs schmoozing. You've seen my masculine charm open doors."

Alec stood at the crosswalk staring at the red light and smiling at his humor. When the light turned, he sprinted off the curb. A small man in a tailored suit stepped out of his path, and Alec picked up his pace. He ran up Washington Avenue. He cut down an adjacent alley filled with potholes, rats, and overstuffed trash bags. Focused on getting to Thirtieth Street Station in time for the next train, he tripped over a bearded man sleeping underneath a pile of dirty blankets. The man rolled over unfazed, and Alec continued running.

A frenzied rush whirled throughout the train station. Alec purchased a ticket, ran through the turnstile, and narrowly slipped through the sliding train doors. His eyes scanned the confined area. Within moments, he found a vacant aisle seat next to an obese gentleman with folded arms and searching eyes.

The gentleman scowled as Alec sat down and placed his briefcase between his feet. When Alec was no longer perceived as a threat, the large man resumed scrutinizing other passengers until the train departed with a jolt. Standing passengers grabbed seatbacks and neighboring shoulders for balance.

As the train settled into a smooth rhythm, Alec let the lids of his eyes fall shut. He dozed until a firm grip on his shoulder awoke him, and his eyes flew open.

"Alec?"

"Patrick." Alec stood up and offered his right hand. Patrick returned the gesture.

"Man, I haven't seen you in ages."

"Not since ballfields and big dreams," said Alec.

"Too long." Patrick punched Alec's arm as Alec laughed and scanned the surrounding seats.

"I'm sitting a few rows back," said Patrick. "Come join me."

Alec picked up his briefcase and followed Patrick. The suspicious heavyset man nodded approval as if he had arranged the encounter. He then placed his jacket on the empty seat. Patrick strolled to the back of the train car with Alec in tow. He stepped past his row to let Alec slide in first.

"How have you been?" Patrick sat down. "Can't believe we didn't stay in touch."

"I'm good," said Alec. "I survived undergrad. Made it through Stanford Law."

"They gave you a law degree?"

"They didn't kick me out." Alec shrugged. "How about you?"

"Stayed in the city and did the same. Cardozo Law. Guess I'm lucky they didn't kick me out either. If they had, Novo Analgesic Systems would be missing out on my incredible legal acuity." Patrick dropped his head back with a puff of air and watched for Alec's response.

Alec disguised his surprise as a cough, a hard cough. He covered his mouth and looked out the side window. Patrick leaned forward and grabbed Alec's bicep.

"You okay, man?" asked Patrick.

"I'm fine," Alec cleared his throat. "You work for Novo Analgesic Systems?"

"You've heard of them? The big pharm company?"

"Sure have. You must know your shit."

"Just lucky," said Patrick. "But I'm glad I suffered through those awful undergraduate science classes. Keeps me from embarrassing myself at company meetings."

"I'm sure you still manage to embarrass yourself." Alec laughed again, a camouflaged cover.

"You're not funny."

"I kind of am. Tell me about this job of yours. Are you one of their litigators?" Alec knew he wasn't.

"No, I spend most of my time in business development. I assist Jack Freeman in negotiating contracts for joint ventures with other drug manufacturers."

"The competition must be fierce," said Alec.

"It boils down to the marketing. A company has no problem jumping on board if they see a persuasive campaign. Every one of those crazy bastards wants to create a cure for something, and every company wants to dominate the market."

"Do you have much contact with the pharmacologists?"

"I know who they are." Patrick smiled at a tall woman as she leaned onto his seat to let another passenger squeeze past. "But they're more concerned with having the funding than where it comes from. I don't get involved in their pissing matches."

"Probably a smart move. So it boils down to marketing. I don't remember you being all that creative." Alec continued to probe.

"Our marketing department is top-notch. Awards up the ying-yang. They begin working on a campaign when a drug is in phase one. By the time FDA approval is granted, they're ready to run." Patrick smiled at Alec. "They don't let me near the department."

"Can you blame them?" Alec returned the smile. "Tell me about Jack Freeman. What's he like?"

"Decent guy. People like working for him. He delegates authority and doesn't hover. He trusts a select few and then condones anything they throw his way."

With no interruption from Alec, Patrick highlighted dozens of drugs released by Novo Analgesic Systems, Inc. and emphasized the financial windfalls each provided. He dropped names and used scientific terms he had picked up on the job. Alec's questions kept the information flowing while revealing no motive.

"Sounds like you're climbing the ladder at a decent click."

"Nah, I'm a peon. The facility is impressive though. You should stop by and check it out."

"How about today?" Alec smirked.

"You don't need to change your schedule for me."

"I'm not. Have you heard of *Satori vs. Novo Analgesic Systems*?"

"Are you shitting me?" Patrick's face dropped.

Patrick grabbed both knees with straight arms. He looked out the window across the aisle as his chest rose and fell with deep slow breaths. The hum of the train coalesced with their silence. Alec waited until Patrick looked back.

"You ass." Patrick turned to face Alec. "I hope our little reunion doesn't cost me my job."

"Be serious, Patrick. You didn't tell me anything I didn't already know. I was being friendly."

"We're on opposing sides of a case that could have a major impact on drug manufacturing. Not friendly."

Heavy silence engulfed both men again. Surrounding passengers were reading, sleeping, or conversing with others and offered no convenient distraction.

"I would have said something had I seen your name on any filings," said Alec. "But this fight isn't between us."

"You're right," Patrick admitted in a softer tone. "But you're damn lucky I'm not litigating this case."

"Why is that?"

"I'd kick your ass." Patrick elbowed his old friend.

The mood lightened, but both men joked in guarded generalities. When the train screeched to a halt in Penn Station, briefcases were retrieved from underneath seats and magazines tossed aside. Patrick wedged his newspaper in between the cushions.

"Ironic running into each other," said Alec as he slid to the edge of his seat.

"Irony can be a real bitch."

"Why don't we share a cab?" asked Alec. "We're headed the same way."

"Sure."

The cab ride to Novo Analgesic Systems, Inc. was the longest thirty minutes of the day for both men. Streams of sweat dripped down the back of hot necks as each man fidgeted to release the stickiness gluing him to the seat. The cab driver pushed buttons to increase fan speed but with no noticeable improvement in temperature.

After numerous red lights and incessant honking, the cab pulled up to the impressive NAS building. The cascading sound of the glass-block waterfall could be heard through the closed windows of the cab. The cab driver flipped down his visor to block the sun as it glistened off the arched glass façade.

Alec jumped out of the cab before Patrick and walked around the front of the car. He waited with a strained smile. Patrick joined him with an equally contrived expression and motioned for Alec to follow. Alec studied the imposing building as both men approached the front doors.

Patrick began a tour of the facility without inquiring as to Alec's interest. He escorted him down pristine white hallways and noted the contemporary details on each floor.

"I'm no architect. But as a member of the NAS family, I'm expected to share the spectacular details of our architectural masterpiece." Patrick made air quotes around his final two words.

"It is impressive."

"Drama was the goal," said Patrick. "They didn't want it to

look like a laboratory or appear too sterile. They put hundreds of thousands of dollars into porcelain tile flooring throughout the building and white limestone fireplaces on the end of every floor."

"I'm glad none are lit. I'm sweating like a dog." Alec jostled the front of his shirt.

"They'll turn them on in about a month and run them through May. They don't put out much heat. Aesthetic value only."

Patrick continued his tour as if Alec were a potential investor. He noted the uniqueness of the angled walls and translucent cornices that divided meeting rooms. He expounded on architectural details, as he had been trained, revealing a required fondness for the priceless artwork adorning the walls.

"Jack has a real thing for Van Gogh. He got *The Night Café* on loan from Yale."

"Seriously?" asked Alec.

"He paid big money to have it shipped from Connecticut. It's here through April."

"And Yale agreed to that?"

"Even the Ivy League has a price tag," said Patrick. "Jack was giddy."

"Bet his insurance company was too."

"The man bleeds money."

Patrick led Alec down a long, narrow hallway. When they reached the end, he pulled open a heavy steel door revealing a new array of sights, smells, and sounds. Accosted by the change in surroundings, both men stopped as the door shut behind them. The spectacular architectural designs seen throughout the building had vanished. There were no porcelain tiles, no priceless artwork, and no beautiful designer pieces. These luxuries had been replaced with cold gray steel.

"This is the infamous lab," said Patrick. The men continued

walking. "There's a distinct aroma, but it could be worse. NAS elegance is left upstairs."

The room contained wire cages of varying sizes intermixed with glass boxes illuminated with heat lamps. Larger marmosets, tamarins, and spider monkeys scurried around the cages while babies of all varieties slept under the lamps. Cubicles containing computer monitors ended each row.

"I've never seen so many monkeys," said Alec as he peered down the long row of cages. "What's up with those? They can't be sleeping. They look dead."

"Depends on which opioid is being tested. Behavior changes can be erratic."

Alec nodded as he squatted to get a better look inside a cage. He stuck his fingers in between the bars and jiggled the furry animal. He got no reaction. The screeching was unremitting. Distress calls intermixed with what sounded like laughter. Climbing and jumping in one cage didn't appear to faze the dazed or sleeping in the next.

"I have a meeting upstairs," said Patrick as he smiled at his friend's curiosity. "Where can I take you?"

"I'm meeting Westcott."

"Of course you are," said Patrick. "I'm surprised we haven't seen him. I didn't think he ever left the lab." Patrick took several quick steps forward and looked down another row of cages. He looked behind two nearby cages and then back at Alec. "Do you mind waiting? I can't be late."

"I'm fine. Get out of here. And thanks for the tour."

"You're welcome. Good luck, and let's get together. I mean outside of work."

The men shook hands. Patrick pushed on the door but glanced over his shoulder as if questioning his decision to leave.

"Go." Alec pointed to the door.

• • • • •

Alec wandered farther into the lab. He ran his hand along stacks of books, reading each cover, and thumbed through folders discarded on tables.

"Dr. Westcott?" he said, his voice a little more than a whisper.

As he rounded the corner of the third row of cages, he found a computer monitor and an empty chair. The screen displayed information in an indistinguishable language. Alec glanced at the screen but continued past additional cages housing primates in fluctuating stages of glee and distress. Metal feeding dishes were wedged into corners and water bottles attached to the side of each cage. Several startled monkeys ceased masturbating when Alec's entrance caught their attention.

"Dr. Westcott?" Alec again whispered.

No human voice echoed over the chorus of screeching monkeys. As Alec wandered deeper into the room, he examined everything around him. He read the labels on medicine bottles, the headings on compilations of data, and the covers on every book he passed. He ignored the monitors displaying a language of their own.

As Alec turned the next corner, he stopped short. Absorbed in the material he was reading, a disheveled Ethan rambled toward him. Alec stood and waited for Ethan to look up.

"Geez, man!" The scraggily blond head popped up. "I thought I was the only one in here."

"Sorry. I'm waiting on Westcott."

"He's in here somewhere. Always is." Ethan stretched his neck to look down nearby aisles. "Likes to watch over my busy-work and demand repeats if not completed to his standards."

"Sounds like a drill sergeant," said Alec.

"More of a drill general." Ethan continued looking down

aisles and behind cages. "Has been for years. When the joint commissioner promoted pain as the fifth vital sign, Dr. Westcott went crazy. He and his monkeys rose to the status he felt they both deserved."

"What status can monkeys reach?" asked Alec. "They're monkeys."

"Maybe not the monkeys. But Westcott sure did. He amplified his opioid production and demanded praise for every new development."

Ethan dropped the book he was reading and several folders onto a nearby cage. The primate inside twisted its neck and rolled its eyeballs to the top of his lids to see what Ethan was doing. Ethan ran his fingers across the front of the books shelved above the cage. He swapped the one on the cage for a new one and looked back to Alec.

"Between you and me, he's a maniac. I've caught him more than once playing with his methadone tablets and three or four tamarins. And his fentanyl transdermal system about put his ego over the edge. There's no stopping him."

"Is there a need? To stop him, I mean."

"I guess not," admitted Ethan. "His pace seems haphazard, but he's successful. Zylodone propelled him to the top."

"I've heard of Zylodone."

"Zylodone was a synthetic immediate-release opioid that was marketed as powerful on pain yet nonaddictive to the sap who popped the pill. The national mania was nuts. Dr. Westcott was a rock star."

"I thought that craze was short-lived," said Alec. "Didn't opioid use disorder become commonplace with Zylodone?"

"Sure did. Overdoses quickly followed, and Zylodone disappeared. But that didn't stop Westcott. He turned his obsession to the extended-release formulation. A few dozen marmosets and spider monkeys turned into hundreds of primates."

"Westcott never owned up to the dark side of Zylodone?" asked Alec.

"Westcott lives on the dark side. He was determined to eliminate chronic pain and the risk of addiction. He knew there'd be casualties. And Jack Freeman had been hovering over the lab waiting for a new breakthrough drug."

"That's big pharma for you." Alec resumed walking toward the back of the lab, looking into the cages he passed.

Ethan grabbed another book from the shelf and followed Alec. "I better get back to filing, or he'll can my ass."

"I thought I passed file cabinets up front?" asked Alec with a puzzled expression.

"They're all over the place." Ethan circled his head in all directions. "The important stuff is behind the wall."

"Behind what wall?"

"Right there." Ethan pointed to the recessed door in front of them. "Westcott's paranoid. Thinks people are scheming to steal his life-altering discoveries. But he'll swear he's not hiding them. He's protecting them."

"From whom?"

"Monsters?" Ethan contorted his face. "I've told him it's not necessary. I've told everyone it's a waste of space. Nobody listens to me, so I shut up and do my work."

"Who's everybody?"

"Westcott, some of the other techs, that bitchy lawyer. But I always keep my eyes open when she's around." Ethan dropped the book to his side. "Since Westcott isn't here, can I help you?"

"That'd be great," said Alec. "Remember the Satori lawsuit?"

Ethan nodded.

"Our firm has a strict policy of document shredding to protect confidentiality. We let nothing slip into the wrong hands." Alec put his plan into action. "Somebody was a little too zealous with our Deprexone files. When I showed up at the office, I found thousands of shreds."

Ethan offered a knowing smile. "Hard to scold someone for trying."

"There was a little scolding. But it's hard representing our client without that information. Any chance I can get replacements?"

Alec watched Ethan as he looked around the room with intermittent pauses. It didn't strike Alec as a search for Westcott but more of a decision-making tactic.

"I should have called ahead, but I didn't think of that until I was on the train," said Alec. "And like an idiot, I left the list of what we need at the office." The act continued.

"I can make replacement copies if that'll help." Ethan's smile returned.

"You have no idea."

Ethan slipped past Alec and pressed his palm against the recessed square in the wall. The door slid open as Alec's mouth did the same. Without looking back, Ethan waved for Alec to follow.

"Looks like the set of a sci-fi movie." Alec made light of the peculiar entrance.

"Security. Westcott demands several layers of security protecting our research. His research. It's annoying, unnecessary, and a waste of money. Why are copies of copies necessary when we have digital copies of everything?"

"Copies of copies?"

"Dr. Westcott is convinced he'll be the victim of a cyber-attack, and his research will fall into the wrong hands."

"Whose hands might those be?" asked Alec.

"Any hands that aren't his."

Ethan redirected his commentary to the advanced technology at Novo Analgesic Systems, Inc. Alec feigned interest in what Ethan was saying with fervent nods and brief comments of encouragement.

"A lot of trees have given their lives for Westcott's research. I thought this place would be greener," Alec noted aloud.

"The environment is only important in the public eye," said Ethan. "Pharmaceutical companies do lots of things that aren't great for the environment. It's all in the name of science. And in the advancement of Westcott's career."

"Does Dr. Westcott call all the shots around here?" asked Alec as he read the labeling on cabinets he passed.

"Sure does."

"Does anyone challenge him?"

"Not if they want to keep their jobs."

Ethan led Alec deeper into the narrow room, stopping in front of a tall cabinet labeled DEPREXONE. Ethan pressed his thumb onto the pad next to the cabinet and the top drawer slid open. Long rows of thumb drives were embedded inside.

"What files do you need?" asked Ethan.

"I'm not sure."

Ethan grabbed the first drive and slid it into the slot located on the adjacent panel. A document appeared on the screen. Ethan flipped his head and looked at Alec.

"Shreds."

Ethan typed the required password, pressed the print button, and removed the drive. He slipped a second drive into the slot and again looked to Alec. Alec nodded, Ethan typed, and the printer hummed. The routine continued with each drive located in the top drawer.

"I feel like I've struck gold." Alec dropped back against an adjacent table and crossed his right foot over his left. "You're really saving my ass."

"It's no big deal."

When the data on the last thumb drive slid into the printer drawer, Ethan scooted the entire stack of warm papers toward Alec.

"Your gold, Mr. Marshall."

Ethan then returned the last drive to the drawer as Alec tucked the papers inside his briefcase and snapped the lid shut.

"You're lucky you ran into me today," said Ethan. "This went a lot smoother than if you would've found Westcott. Even though it's the same information, he holds a death grip on his research."

"Big egos do that," said Alec. "I appreciate your help. I'm carrying answers some powerful people are waiting to hear."

The two men continued their small talk while Ethan left his prints everywhere needed to secure the room. As the men shook hands in a final farewell, loud footsteps reverberated in the lab.

"What in God's name is going on in here?" bellowed Phil Westcott as he stormed in their direction.

Ethan stopped in a wide stance. He dropped his shoulders with a deep inhale and looked sideways at Alec. He then turned his attention to the angry man approaching them.

"This is Mr. Marshall," said Ethan in a deep voice unfamiliar to Alec.

"I know who he is." Phil's razor-sharp eyes scanned Alec. "But nobody should be in this lab when I'm not here. Who thinks they have the authority to grant that permission?"

"No permission was granted. Mr. Marshall was inquiring as to—"

"I know exactly what he wants," Phil interrupted. "That

doesn't mean he's allowed into this lab requesting my property without my knowledge."

Ethan stepped toward Phil. The two men stood face-to-face locked in a combative glare. Ethan's unexpected defiance challenged Phil's need for control.

"I was working on the oxymorphone tests when Mr. Marshall arrived." Ethan's voice was low and direct. "He expressed a need—"

"I know very well what he wants," Phil interrupted again. "It has nothing to do with need. His camouflaged request involves valuable research you don't hand over to every shmuck who waltzes in here. Have you lost your godforsaken mind?"

Westcott turned his back on both men. His edge was gone. He marched toward the front of the lab with his hands clenched by his sides. Alec couldn't help but smile at the tantrum as he and Ethan followed.

"I understand your concern, Dr. Westcott," said Alec. "I've made no request for new information."

Westcott grunted at Alec's attempt at cordiality. He continued his silent march until he reached the last cabinet in the front of the lab. He typed several numbers onto the attached keypad, and the top drawer slid open. Alec rolled his eyes at yet another exaggerated security procedure. Phil grabbed the front folder and shoved it at Alec.

"Your replacement copies, Mr. Marshall."

Alec grabbed the folders Phil shoved against his chest as Phil placed his hand in the middle of Alec's back and pushed him toward the door. Ethan stood to the side witnessing the hostile exchange.

"I've gone out of my way to accommodate Blackman & Bradford in this nonsensical lawsuit," said Phil. "I'll submit a bill for this additional time and expense."

"Of course you will," said Alec.

Neither Ethan nor Alec disclosed what had transpired prior to Phil's arrival. Alec looked down at his briefcase full of answers and then to Ethan's pulsing jaw. Alec had a feeling that the battle between the two scientists wasn't over. Both men looked as though they were preparing their next move. Ethan's demeanor had a foreboding force that seemed more powerful than Phil's awkward authority.

"I suggest there be no further intrusions, Mr. Marshall." Phil pushed the door and held it with his outstretched arm. "Sneaking in here without my authorization amounts to trespassing. I will be speaking to Ms. Hewitt. Now go."

Alec stepped toward Phil. His face was relaxed and his breathing slow. He dropped a Blackman & Bradford business card into Phil's pocket.

"In case you don't have her number." Alec walked out.

11

DECEPTIVE
CHARADE

C laire sat by the front window sipping Chardonnay. Her preferred choice was Cabernet, but it was a hot day and the crisp
chill felt delicious on her tongue. Her fingers slid the pendant
along the delicate chain around her neck as her rehearsed lines
spun through her mind. She knew it made her look nervous, but
Claire didn't care. Her main concern was handling Dana.

As if the strong wind offered no option, Dana Massetti ran
toward Bin 402. Her stiletto heels clicked on the concrete as she
kept perfect balance. She looked as if she would blow past the
door but grabbed the long handle. Claire watched through the
window as a knowing smile spread on her face. Dana's arrival
was as it always had been, theatrical and apropos.

"Well, look at you lurking in the window," said Dana, making
a rapid U-turn as she entered the bar. "Just like a black panther."

"Black panther?"

"Sleek killer instinct radiates from you." Dana flipped her
hair as she spoke, overplaying her effort to look chic. "Your prey
has arrived."

"I must have whiskers or a tail, because that's the second feline reference directed at me this week."

"Are you serious? Don't tell me you lost a case and some egotistical prick called you a pussy. I'd file a complaint." Dana pulled out the chair across from Claire and sat down. She placed both hands on the table, glanced down at her purple nails, and stood. She slid the chair under the table and sidestepped over to Claire. She eased into the new chair and patted the table.

"Much better." Dana glanced at Claire.

Claire smiled as Dana picked up the drink menu and feigned indecision. Familiar with the façade, Claire chose to watch out the window as businessmen in sober discussions approached Bin 402. Some meandered down the sidewalk while others scurried in haste. Once inside the door, heads flipped back and forth in search of available seats. Arms shot up and voices called out as spontaneous groups were formed.

"Hendrick's martini, dirty and straight up," barked Dana to a scrambling waiter. As he waived an affirmative hand and looked back, Claire ordered as well.

"Manhattan, please."

Dana scooted closer to Claire as if anticipating copious gossip. She lowered her chin while her wide eyes focused on Claire. Claire took a deep breath and let the air puff her cheeks as it left her mouth. It would be a battle of give and take, and Claire needed Dana to give more than she took. Dana continued her stare behind thick long lashes as the bustling waiter returned with two drinks. His staged jocularity briefly eased the tension.

"Finally. Thought I would die of thirst." Dana lifted her glass and let the bitter fluid flow into her mouth.

"You seem more stressed today than at the boutique," said Claire. "What's up?"

Dana leaned back in her chair and crossed her tan legs. She took another lingering sip as she gazed at Claire over the rim of her glass.

"Hump day. Need I say more?"

"I get it. I try to think of halfway as almost there." Claire enjoyed Dana's fervor. She had witnessed only a moment of it at Black Threads Boutique and knew she might get a full production today.

"Half is half." Dana thumped both elbows on the table as she leaned forward. "I put in a lot of hours; word games don't change the length of my days nor the work that needs to be done."

"Optimism feels better."

"More word games." Dana pointed her long finger at Claire. "You know that's why I'm compelled to ignore some of your phone calls. They're incessant, and I don't have the time for chitchat and needless babble."

"What are you talking about?"

"Every time I turn around, I'm getting another call from Claire Hewitt. My purse is a vibrator. In the middle of a meeting, Claire Hewitt. I walk into court, Claire Hewitt."

"Not by choice," interrupted Claire. "As vice chair of ABL, I'm required to contact every attorney when an event is scheduled. Take your name off the list if you don't want my calls."

"It's not you, doll. Attorneys for Brotherly Love needs me. Needs my money anyway." Dana lifted her glass but didn't drink. Her dark brown eyes followed several men entering the bar as the rim rested on her full lips.

"We're not looking for money."

"Of course you are," said Dana, flipping her eyes back to Claire. "But you should consider the email option. It won't score you as much, but it is an option."

"Could I possibly be calling as a friend?" asked Claire.

"Yes, yes, yes. Don't get all huffy. It warms my heart when I hear the ring and see that 215 area code."

"215? How about 445."

"You used to be 215. I know you were." Dana leaned in closer to Claire. "Remember how we talked all the time? Inseparable for three years?"

"Back in the day." Claire leaned away. She knew her cool indifference would expose the impetuous Dana Massetti.

"Great memories," said Dana. "But I couldn't keep up with you. You ate, drank, and breathed everything law. And talk about competitive."

"I don't know about that," said Claire.

"Oh, come on. You know how you are." Dana squeezed Claire's forearm. "Or at least how you were."

Claire turned to the crowded bar as an escape. Exposure to Dana's passive aggression was exhausting but a small price to pay for entrance into her trove of knowledge. A contentious rebuttal would end the meeting. So Claire kept her silence.

"The boutique encounter was odd. But we're good." Dana squeezed Claire's arm again. "And I bought the purple dress. It works wonders. I mean if that's what you want, it'll do the trick."

Claire laughed and picked up her glass. "To old friends and purple dresses." She tapped Dana's glass with her highball and a look of doubt.

Dana dropped her eyes to her scarlet Prada pumps without taking a drink. She wiped a smudge off the toe with her thumb as the other hand kept her martini glass tipped toward Claire. She controlled the tense moment.

"To frenemies." Dana looked back, still in command.

Claire dropped her head onto her right shoulder and gave Dana a blank stare. She set her glass on the table and folded her hands as an indication that she would not be toasting.

"Frenemies?"

"Do you want to tell me the real reason I'm here? Is it the Satoris?" asked Dana.

"How do you know about the Satoris?" Claire's suspicions were confirmed.

"Everybody knows about the Satoris."

"I doubt that," said Claire.

"Girl, are you kidding me? Wake up. People are starting to notice. When you jump into the ring with the big boys, people can't wait for an implosion. What do you need? Dirt on Clifford?"

"I can't discuss an open case with you."

"Don't pretend that's not why I'm here," said Dana. "I've always been your go-to when you need intel, evidence, or excuses. Which is it?"

"I don't need anything," said Claire. "Especially not with the Satoris. What do you know about an attack on Lombard Street?"

"There it is." Dana flashed her bleached teeth.

"What do you know?"

"Just what I heard on the news," said Dana.

"I doubt that too."

"You and your doubt. Why do you ask me something and then question my answer?" asked Dana as her body slumped in an exaggerated pout.

"Because I'm looking for truth."

"Stop right there." Dana again pointed her long finger at Claire. "You called me under the pretense of friendship when all you wanted was information you thought I might have."

"I thought you might know something," said Claire. "But that's what friends do. They share information they may have heard."

"Fine. I can share. Give me a few details, and I'll be a first-rate sleuth."

"Damn it, Dana." Claire slammed her drink, causing drops of dark booze to splash onto the napkin. "You know about the attack. And not just from the news."

"Where do you get these ideas?" asked Dana. "I'm no ambulance chaser."

"No need to be. You're an insatiable snoop."

"Is name-calling part of sharing?" Dana continued her pout.

"Am I wrong?"

"I pay attention to what happens in my city," said Dana. "KMTV blasted a headline about a female attorney being attacked on Lombard Street. That kind of news catches the attention of everyone who owns a television. But that's all I know. Why don't you fill in the blanks?"

"I have nothing," said Claire.

"How can you have nothing? You were there." Frustration crept into Dana's voice.

"It's a blur."

"You were drunk!" Dana jumped from her seat and grabbed Claire's shoulder. Her face lit up as she panted with excitement. "Too drunk to remember."

Claire grabbed Dana's hand and pushed it away. She stood from her chair to shove Dana back into hers. Claire's hip hit the table, causing more brown booze to splash out of the glass.

"I was not drunk, you crazy bitch." Claire glanced around to see if their antics were noticed.

"You can admit it to me. I totally understand."

"What is wrong with you?" asked Claire.

"Nothing's wrong with me. I get it." Dana grabbed Claire's hand with both of hers. Claire watched the purple nails squeeze around her fingers. "I've been drunk before and don't remember everything. On more occasions than I'll ever admit."

"That isn't what happened," said Claire. "I was attacked

walking home from dinner. I did a face-plant on the sidewalk. I need time to process what happened. It takes time."

"Not that much. Try to remember as much as you can while you process. Or do whatever it is you feel you need to do."

"This isn't funny." Claire pulled her hand away and finished her Manhattan.

"It is a little funny. 'Random attack on drunk attorney.'" Dana made air quotes around the fictitious headline.

"I can't believe I thought this would get me anywhere. If you knew this from a news report, concern would have been your initial reaction. You're giddy. You've heard something, and now you're getting to peek behind the curtain at the real actors."

Dana tucked both feet under her chair and leaned into the accusations. She whispered with freshly created compassion. Her words and her blinks were slow and deliberate.

"The real actor in this case happens to be my friend, and I want to help. I can help if you'll let me. But it starts with facing the facts, admitting unnecessary risks you may have taken, and paying attention to details. Let's start with what you could have done to prevent this."

"Whoa. Slow down." Claire patted the air.

"Why would we slow down? We can't do that. We'll lose evidence."

"We?" Claire scooted her chair several feet back and turned it directly toward Dana.

"Yes, *we*. Do the police have any leads? You must be an active player in this investigation, Claire. You need to be vigilant."

"I need to go home."

"You can't leave yet." Dana gave Claire an exaggerated finger wave like a schoolteacher scolding a child.

"Why not?" asked Claire. "This is getting us nowhere."

"That's because you're not trying. What can you remember? What did you see? Do you have any enemies?"

"Damn, woman. I don't know."

"How can you not know?" Dana looked up and scowled at two women when one bumped into her chair in passing. They each glanced down with innocent smiles as they hurried past. "I don't get you." Dana turned back to Claire. "You call me for help and then slam the door in my face."

"I'm not slamming anything. But I sure as hell don't get the sudden concern."

"We've been friends a long time." Dana brushed the side of Claire's cheek with the back of her fingers. "I'm here to help."

"Feels more like an inquisition," said Claire as she pulled away.

"I don't mean to sound harsh. I care. I want you to know I've got your back."

"You've got my back, or want to stab me in it?"

"Oh, Claire." Dana threw herself back in her chair.

"You've never had anyone's back," said Claire. "In any show you're not running, you assess your surroundings, define your objectives, and reposition to gain control."

"You overestimate me."

"Do I?" asked Claire.

Dana finished her martini as Claire drummed her fingers on the table beside her empty glass. Their meeting proved fruitless, and Claire would leave with new concerns about Dana.

"I have neither the desire nor the energy for this charade," said Claire.

"What charade? My concern is no act. And I have no modus operandi, regardless of your irrational suspicions."

"Call it intuition," said Claire.

"Word games again. What could I possibly know?" asked Dana. "You and your boytoy were the only ones there."

Dana surveyed additional prospects walking through the door while Claire checked the time on her phone. As if the revelation had entered with the dark-haired man wearing horn-rimmed glasses propped on the bridge of his nose, Dana slapped the table, and her spine shot straight. She nodded at Claire with the silly grin of a child discovering a secret.

"That's it. He saw everything. He saw what happened. He saw who it was. He chased him. He knows everything."

"Who's *he*?" asked Claire.

"Your boytoy. Your associate. Whatever his name is." Dana fluttered jazz hands at Claire.

"What gives you the idea he was there?" asked Claire. "Or that there was a chase?"

"Oh geez." Dana rolled her eyes with a snarky smirk. "KMTV gave some details behind their headline. They referred to a couple. I know other people in your office."

"And the chase?"

"Common sense, Claire. A real man would chase anyone who attacked his woman." Duplicity brushed across Dana's face. She lifted her empty glass out of habit. She looked at the few drops left in the bottom and not over the rim at Claire. "Your handsome assistant knows," Dana whispered to her glass.

"Knows what?" asked Claire.

"Who attacked you."

"You don't know when to give up," mumbled Claire.

"You mean stop caring?" Dana brought back her innocent blinks.

"Dishonesty looks good on no one."

"Listen to yourself. I don't have a dishonest bone in my body."

Dana tugged on her neatly pressed cuffs. "We're at a stalemate because you're being a bitch."

"I'm a bitch? I'm not the one with all the secrets."

"Secrets? I'm trying to help a friend," said Dana.

"I didn't see his face. Alec said he ran like a girl." Claire leaned onto the table.

"A girl?"

"Guys always say that. Means nothing."

Dana swirled her empty glass on the table. She watched a few drops of the leftover liquid spin in the bottom as she mumbled in response. "Ran like a girl."

Claire glanced around the bar desperate to leave.

Dana sat upright and lifted her glass. Her finger rapidly tapped on the edge as impatience grabbed hold. "What is up with the service in here?" snapped Dana, waving her glass in the air.

Dana yelled for another round as a frazzled waiter hurried past. He nodded and looked to Claire, who smiled. Both women repositioned in their chairs as if starting anew. When their drinks arrived, Dana's exuberance resumed.

"If you can't talk about the Satoris, tell me about Novo Analgesic Systems. I mean in general." Dana crossed her legs as she took a long sip of the dry, olivey Hendrick's.

"What do you already know?" asked Claire. She gripped her Manhattan with both hands but didn't drink.

"I know nothing," Dana lied. "I know nothing about the stupid attack. I know nothing about the lawsuit. I know they exist. That's all. Cut me a break."

"Sure," said Claire. "What do you want to know?"

"Any hot scientists? I guess I'm on the market."

"None that would interest you," chuckled Claire.

"Never hurts to ask. I could use a tall, dark, and handsome."

"We all could. But you won't find him there," said Claire

as she crossed her ankles and leaned back. She watched Dana fidget with her necklace and her blouse.

"If there are no hotties running around, are there dealers? I mean it is a drug-testing facility." Dana let her head drop back as if letting Claire in on a joke.

"I know very little about what goes on there. I'm sure there are plenty of drug seekers. You on the market for one of them too?"

Dana cocked her head without answering and scanned the bar. Both women remained trapped in their deceptive charade. Their conversation slowed as they fabricated interest in the growing crowd. Bin 402 was the perfect host to whiskey-induced decisions and a hot spot for the up-and-coming. As a nearby political discussion spiraled into a heated debate, Dana dropped her forehead into the palm of her hand.

"Oh. My. God! I have tickets to the Kimmel Center tonight."

"Of course. And you forgot," said Claire with an expectant tone. "What are you seeing?"

"No clue. I'm attending as a guest. But my dress is at the cleaners. I have no gift for the host. And look at this hair." Dana tousled her hair.

Claire picked up her Manhattan and settled back in her chair. With childlike enthusiasm, Dana threw her arm in the air and waved. Familiar with Dana's demands, a waiter rushed over.

"I need a bottle of your best Cab to go. And I needed it an hour ago. Please grab me something, anything." Dana spoke with her voice and her hands as she begged for fast service. Her tone was deep, and her head tilted forward. She then fluttered her fingers to hurry the waiter along. "It's the perfect gift. Don't you think?" asked Dana, turning her attention to Claire.

Moments later, Dana was holding a bottle of Far Niente

Cabernet and the afternoon's bill. She placed money in the waiter's palm and shot a demure look to Claire.

"This one's on me."

The waiter thanked both women as Dana jumped from her chair and dashed to the door. Claire shifted in her seat with her Manhattan in hand.

"Talk soon," Dana yelled as she waved in the air without looking back.

"Some things never change." A sagacious smirk grew on Claire's face as she watched Dana leave.

12

●●●●●●●●●●●●●●

SILVER
BULLET

Alec rushed out of Novo Analgesic Systems, Inc. with a briefcase full of answers. An astute doorman opened the door of the nearest cab, and Alec thanked him with a crisp twenty.

"Penn Station." Alec set his briefcase next to him and popped both metal tabs. He wedged his cellphone between his chin and shoulder as he listened to the faint ring.

"That place is a zoo." Alec thumbed through the still-warm papers. "Westcott controls the underlings, but it's not with a firm grip. Somebody's got a tighter hold on him."

Alec looked at the driver. "Penn Station?"

"Waiting on that delivery truck. He's in no hurry."

Alec returned to his papers and his conversation. He flipped through pages skimming the content as excitement bounced in his eyes. When the cab pulled away from the pretentious entrance, Alec glanced out his side window for one final look at Novo Analgesic Systems, Inc.

"I saw a new side of Shaggy, Claire. He's no hapless buffoon, more like a double agent. Gave me everything we wanted and put Westcott in his place. I'll fill you in when I get back."

Alec disconnected but held his cellphone as he watched the city speed past. He snapped his briefcase shut when the station came into view and swiped his credit card before jumping out. He hurried into the station, looked up at the ticker tape, and stepped into a coffee shop line for much-needed caffeine.

"I'll have a Venti Sumatra with an extra shot of espresso."

Alec returned the barista's buoyant smile and walked away gripping the warm cup. He watched a commuter train depart as he gulped the beverage and paced the station. After finishing the last drop, he tossed his cup into a trash and joined the rushing crowd heading to Gate 12E. He brushed past a young couple entwined in a farewell embrace as he darted through the train doors. He slid into the first available seat and placed his briefcase in the middle. A vivid cue he preferred nobody join him.

The evening train was less crowded than the earlier one had been. With a surplus of available seats, most passengers chose ones unconnected to others. As the train pulled out of the station, Alec grabbed the top Deprexone folder and began reviewing Westcott's work. Frequent nods accompanied his right hand as it slid down the side column.

As the train pulled into the Thirtieth Street Station, passengers edged to the still-closed doors. Alec grabbed his jacket from the adjoining seat and stepped into the aisle. People were beginning to push. The train stopped with a jolt, and the doors slid open. Passengers escaped like trapped animals and scurried in all directions.

Alec stepped into the bustling crowd. He exited the station and filed into the closest line. Honking horns and shouting men directed passengers to open cabs. Progress was swift, and Alec ducked into an empty cab within moments.

"Blackman & Bradford."

"They're open at this hour?"

"Unfortunately, yes," chuckled Alec. "But I won't be working alone."

As Alec predicted, Claire was squinting into the glow of her computer with only her desk lamp to ease the strain. Alec leaned against the doorframe, watching. His ankles were crossed, and his posture relaxed. After a few short moments, Claire looked up.

"What the hell? Creeper."

"No creeping. Didn't want to interrupt." Alec pushed off the doorframe and headed toward the full moon shining through the window behind Claire. He leaned on the counter and gazed out at the nightly display. Claire remained seated facing her computer screen.

A long dark cloud slowly drifted in front of the moon, darkening half of it. Alec turned back to Claire and dropped his briefcase beside her desk. He leaned his folded forearms on the back of her chair as he looked over her head at a divided screen covered with news reports.

"Looks like you had a shitty day." Alec walked to the front of Claire's desk and dropped into a chair.

"Why do you say that?"

"You're sitting in a dark office in the middle of the night reading news reports.

"Research a law clerk sent me. But I did have a shitty day. Met with Massetti."

"Sounds awful."

"Claimed she saw a news headline about an attack on Lombard Street, then accused me of being drunk."

"Are you serious?"

"The control freak grilled me about what I remembered. It was an inquisition, and she wanted answers."

"What made you think you'd get anything from her?" asked Alec.

"Wishful thinking? I don't know. It was worth a shot. She's hiding something. When she realized she wasn't getting anything out of me, it was game over. Pretended she forgot an engagement, jumped up, and ran out. I mean literally jumped up and ran out."

"Your day sounds awful, whereas my day was awesome." Alec reached both arms out to his side in an exaggerated stretch and then sat tall with his chin held high. "I deserve the Academy Award."

"For what?" asked Claire as she scooted her laptop aside and leaned forward on her desk.

Alec pulled the first set of Deprexone documents from his briefcase and placed them into separate piles. Preclinical data was placed on the far edge followed by the IND application. Alec gently closed Claire's laptop and watched for her reaction. With silent confusion, she placed it on the counter behind her. When she turned back, Alec was arranging the separate phases of testing into rows in front of her. Claire rolled her chair in closer.

"Ethan gave you the preclinical data used for the IND app? All the precious monkey tests?" Claire leafed through the data. "You do get the Academy Award."

"I told you my charm is irresistible. You didn't believe me." Alec walked back to the window and leaned against the counter, watching Claire read.

"Yeah, I didn't buy that sales pitch of yours." Claire traded the preclinical data for a closer look at the application. "That kind of charm doesn't work with guys. I can flirt my way in, but if you try it, you're a pervert."

"Not so. Shaggy and I were a team. I was indecisive, and he took control. I shrugged my shoulders, and he pressed buttons. It was magic."

Claire flipped back and forth between the preclinical data and the application. Her clenched jaw softened as her index finger traced the answers on the application and compared them to the data. She nodded with quick small movements as she read.

"I ran into an old friend on my way into the city. He's an attorney with NAS."

Claire's head popped up. "Why'd you wait to drop that bomb?"

"Wanted you to see the extent of the research first."

"Okay, I see it. What happened?"

"It was a chance encounter. Exchanged a few pleasantries before he went into a monologue about drug development and recent releases at NAS. But it all went south the moment I mentioned the Satori case."

Alec hoisted himself onto the counter and shimmied closer to the window. Claire swiveled her chair to face him with curiosity and clasped hands. She battled impatience as she listened to Alec's unnecessary details.

"My connection to NAS pissed him off at first. But he simmered down once he realized it was no big deal."

"Is he involved with the case?" asked Claire.

"Unfortunately, no. We shared a cab to their headquarters, and he was dropping names and flaunting their financial gains like Mr. Big Shot the whole way. But became a turncoat the moment we walked into that building. Gave me an elaborate tour reciting nothing but his scripted lines."

Alec hopped off the counter as Claire swiveled her chair back toward her desk. He pulled the second set of Deprexone test results from his briefcase and arranged them on top of the first. Claire tilted her head with narrowed eyes. Alec set down the last document and bent forward with one arm bent across his waist in an exaggerated bow.

"Signed, sealed, and delivered."

Claire picked up the material. She opened the top folder, thumbed through the data, and set it down. She did the same with the next folder and the same with the third.

"Ethan is our lifeline," said Alec. "The more I empathized with his drivel, the more information he offered."

"Duplicates?" asked Claire with palms flipped upward.

"Ethan gave me everything we need. I was leaving when Westcott stormed in. He threw a tantrum like you wouldn't believe."

"Because Ethan gave you copies?"

"For allowing me in the lab when he wasn't there." said Alec. "He lost his shit. But Ethan stood up to him. He wasn't backing down."

"I didn't think he had it in him."

"I told you, Ethan's no idiot. Westcott lost control, so he gave up. He marched me to the front of the lab, handed me a preassembled set of replacements and shoved me out the door. Said he was going to call you to report my trespassing."

"Oh my God. I told you they stole them. Have you compared the results Ethan gave you with the results you got from Westcott?"

"I did a cursory review on the train. The preclinical data, IND application, and the first two phases are identical." Alec grabbed the referenced material and tossed them onto the chair beside him. "Phase Three is where things get dicey. They aren't additional copies as Ethan claimed."

"There are no issues the first two phases?" asked Claire.

"They don't justify moving onto Phase Three, but they sufficed. They tested too few individuals, didn't compare pain diagnoses between those receiving Deprexone and those receiving a placebo, and there's no mention of reduced reaction or drug desensitization."

"Doesn't sound like it adds up to much."

"The NAS marketing department seemed to think so. Marketing is their lifeline. They make the most flaccid researchers look like inventive geniuses."

"Based upon what?" asked Claire.

"Dollar signs."

Alec walked to the opposite side of the desk and separated Ethan's Phase Three test results from Westcott's. Claire picked up the data as Alec stood back. He again looked over her shoulder as she leafed through the stapled pages.

"Phase Three is where everything changes," said Alec. "Ethan's Phase Three results, from the back file room, show no comparison of Deprexone to any current pain medications and revealed the same level of addiction as seen with immediate-release opioids. Westcott's Phase Three results compare his miracle pill to every opioid on the market. It surpasses each one and reveals minimal risk of addiction. That's how they got their approval."

"And how they killed Emma."

Alec dropped his hand onto Claire's shoulder. She glanced over at the tan fingers as a moment of silence engulfed them. Needing to escape the sorrow, Claire grabbed both sets of data with one hand and her briefcase with the other. She hurried to the couch and placed the research on the coffee table as it had been on her desk. She placed her briefcase on top. Her rapid movements halted as she licked her thumb and rubbed at a deep scratch in the leather. She then brushed it with her fingers and clicked the metal tabs.

"You haven't opened that yet?" asked Alec, walking to the couch.

"Didn't think we'd be doing a comparison."

Claire lifted the lid. Four folders lay on top secured with

a large black clip, and six pens, two red and four black, were clipped to the edge pockets. A sticky note reminding Claire of a lunch date was still stuck on the top page of a legal pad and several rubber bands were wedged along the left side.

"Nobody touched anything. Even my scheduling worksheet is still on the bottom," said Claire as she lifted the files to check underneath.

Claire ran both hands along the side of the leather case as she kept her eyes on its organized content. She peeked inside the lid pocket to ensure it was still empty and collected the rubber bands. She felt the knot in her stomach tighten as she wrapped the bands around her hand. She knew something wasn't right. But she didn't know what.

"It's a scare tactic," said Alec, balanced on the arm of the couch.

"Why? I'm no timid little girl."

Claire flipped the briefcase back on its lid throwing the folders onto the floor. She tossed a pen at the open case and dropped against the back cushions.

"They're hoping you might be," said Alec. "Let's ignore their desperate efforts and use the evidence we have to bring them down. We can compare backroom results to Westcott's results and discover every dirty little secret they have."

Alec straightened the contents of Claire's briefcase and closed the lid. He leaned it against the couch on the floor beside her. Claire looked up at him with an embarrassed smile.

"Any chance you'll overlook my meltdown and we can move on?"

Alec patted Claire's knee and realigned the two sets of results in the middle of the oval table. Claire pulled the table closer to the couch. Alec joined her with erect posture and excited eyes.

"This could be an all-nighter. Are we up for it?" Claire glanced at her watch.

"I am, if you are."

Claire picked up the IND application and the preclinical data. She reread what she already knew and handed them to Alec. Both reviews revealed the same answers as Alec had discovered on the train in his cursory review. No discrepancies.

"Never dreamed I'd spend this much time learning about monkeys," said Claire.

"Same."

Alec tossed the applications and preclinical data onto the armchair. He threw the Phase One and Phase Two results on top. As Claire's hand followed the results, Alec grabbed hold. He forced her hand back to her side as he spoke.

"Let's not waste our time on those. It's all in Phase Three. Westcott's study skyrockets with dozens of unaddicted participants while backroom results struggle with a handful of addicts."

"I argued that to Judge Connor." Claire reached for the briefcase and dragged it to her lap. "I can show you the evidence Ethan gave me."

There was a slight softening to her anger as it turned into frustration. She mumbled to herself like an indignant child as she threw open the lid, reached under the legal pad with the sticky note, and easily found the results she'd presented at trial.

"There were seven volunteers . . ." Claire stopped midsentence with her lips parted and her eyes glued to the paper she held. "This isn't the evidence I took to trial."

With bewildered haste, Claire pulled everything from the brown leather case. She tossed the legal pad aside and pulled the documents from the top folder. She read them and tossed them aside. She grabbed the information from the second folder and did the same. And then the third and then the fourth. A red glow rose to her cheeks as she searched for information that wasn't there. When every folder was empty, her hands dropped to her sides, and her defeated eyes turned to Alec.

"I argued that inadequate Deprexone testing and contentious marketing were a direct cause of Emma Satori's death. Ethan's data proved that. These documents are not the information I had in that courtroom."

"Damn, you've been right all along. NAS did steal your briefcase. But they didn't steal the research in it. They switched it." Alec picked up the documents Claire tossed on the couch and scanned the pages. "Someone took the research Ethan gave you and replaced it with the research Westcott submitted to the FDA."

Claire felt oddly reassured that her suspicions were correct. She was beginning to doubt herself but found a nugget of success in knowing she had accurately interpreted the situation and the players. She ignored the pit in her stomach as she arranged the test results into three columns instead of two.

"NAS insinuates that Westcott's research is all there is," said Claire. "Test results showing minimal risk of addiction."

"Of course they do," said Alec. "If that research were the full extent of their testing, it would eradicate their guilt for every addiction that occurred from taking Deprexone."

"That's why those results are stored in the front file cabinets. But eradication doesn't come that easy. You came back with two sets of test results, and I have a third set." Claire pointed to the three piles sitting on the table. "We'll finish our comparison and find the truth behind Deprexone. Will Ethan help?"

"I couldn't get him to shut up today. And he's no friend of Westcott's."

"He could be our silver bullet." Claire walked to the window and leaned her head onto the cool glass. She closed her eyes, ignoring the busy street below. "He'll be priceless on the stand."

"I think he's hoping we ask."

"Westcott, on the other hand, is bat-shit crazy. Do we dare put him on the stand?" Claire twisted her head to look over at Alec without lifting it from the glass.

"It's a big gamble," answered Alec. "He's unpredictable and will do anything to protect his monkeys."

"Fucking monkeys."

Alec walked over and stood beside Claire, who closed her eyes again. He leaned on the counter and watched the activity below. It was minimal at this time of night.

"You should've seen Landon at that hearing, gloating like a little boy," said Claire.

"How do you gloat with a dead girl on your hands?"

"By counting the zeros on your paycheck."

Claire pushed off the window and returned to the coffee table. She collected the piles and straightened the books. Alec gathered the preclinical data, IND applications, and first two phases of testing. They returned each item to the correct folder, and Claire shoved them into the top drawer of the cabinet by the door. She pushed down on the bulk so the drawer would slide smoothly.

"Damn, it's about bedtime." Alec propped against the counter again.

"Past my bedtime."

"We've had a breakthrough. Let's grab a drink to celebrate."

"It's past midnight." Claire compared the wall clock to her watch as she returned to the couch.

"There's plenty of time."

"I need some sleep."

"Sleep is overrated," said Alec. "Let's stop by the End Zone and have a quick one."

"Sleep is not overrated. And I need more of it." Claire settled into the couch.

"If Westcott's getting under your skin, a nightcap may help." Alec moved over to Claire.

"He's not."

"Then what is it?" asked Alec.

"It's a long story."

"I have time."

"You have no idea," said Claire.

"Then give me one."

Claire squeezed a pillow to her stomach and looked around the quiet room. "I've been having the same nightmare since I was a teenager. My parents were told it was due to anxiety and would subside. It hasn't subsided."

"You were an anxious teenager?"

"Not always. They called it anxiety transference. I think they made up that diagnosis."

"What happened?" asked Alec.

"I'd been out all night on a school night rebelling against my strict parents. When I snuck home at the crack of dawn, my sister wanted to talk. She did that a lot after her accident. But I couldn't stay awake. Tried, but couldn't."

"What accident?" asked Alec.

"Molly was a gymnast who competed internationally. An Olympic prospect. She took a bad fall and her life crumbled."

"She recovered though?"

"From the fall, yes. But the pain meds after surgery ruined her life."

"Oh man."

"Zylodone."

Alec dropped his hand onto Claire's knee as he leaned forward, trying to read the expression on her face. Claire turned away and blinked back painful tears, wanting the moment to end.

"I don't want to discuss it," said Claire. "Molly needed me. To this day I blame myself."

"Why?"

"For not being there. For not staying awake." Claire's tone was sharp and growing louder.

"You fell asleep. For what, like a few hours? That doesn't sound nightmare-inducing."

"I can't get into this tonight, Alec. I need to head home. Maybe I'll be too tired to dream."

Alec stood and walked back to the desk for his jacket. He looked over to Claire as he headed to the door. Claire offered a feeble smile but was glad Alec was leaving. The day had been too emotional to relive Molly's torturous path tonight.

"Are you sure? A stiff drink may take the edge off."

"I'm sure."

"If you change your mind, I'm right down the street."

"I'm good. You go."

As the office door closed halfway, Claire opened her laptop. She heard the elevator chime as she began typing. After a few short moments, her eyelids drooped, and her head bobbed forward. She jerked it up and shook it. She toyed with the thought of meeting Alec. She preferred that to the tumultuous ride of a nightmare. She resumed typing, but only until her eyelids closed again.

13

NO! NO! NO!

Dew splattered the glass. Cold drops sprinkled my face as I pounded louder. Molly had to wake up. The sun was peeking over the pines by the driveway, and panic was creeping up my spine. If Dad backed out of the garage and saw me tapping on my window, no story would save me. I knocked louder.

"Settle down." Molly closed the bedroom door and hurried over. "What is wrong with you, Claire?" She slid the window open. "You know you're going to get caught."

"Because I can't rely on you." I lifted my hips to the window and swung my right leg over the sill. "I've been banging on this stupid window forever. What if Dad pulled out and saw me?"

"He'd see an idiot."

"How hard is it to open one window?" I slid down the wall and hugged my knees to my chest. I closed my eyes to block the throbbing in my head.

"I was downstairs getting my leo from the laundry room." Molly threw an armful of clothes onto her bed. "How was I to know when you'd be home? Does Princess expect me to sit by the window waiting?"

"Princess expects nothing." I laughed and opened one eye at

Molly. "You should come with me next time. You're not competing until next year. You should have a little fun before they regulate the hell out of you again."

"I regulate myself," said Molly. "And I may compete sooner."

As I watched Molly stare into the mirror, I saw a reflection of myself. The fourteen months that separated us felt more like fourteen minutes. Our side-by-side cribs were replaced with twin beds the moment we both could walk and one king bed in junior high. We shared a room. We shared a closet. We shared dreams.

Molly examined herself from different angles, running her hands down the pleats of her short skirt. With a dramatic drop forward, she began her stretches. One leg straight. One leg bent. Teeth clenched.

"Damn, girl. With as hard as you push it, you'll be out on that mat sooner than later." I moved to the edge of our bed and watched.

"I have to push it. If I don't, the pain will destroy me."

Molly shook her head so her ponytail swept the floor. After one sweep left and one sweep right, her body went limp, and she flopped on the floor next to me. Her eyes were closed and she breathed through her nose. I wasn't sure if she was joking or groggy. When she took too many pills, grogginess took over. After a few quiet moments, a smile spread on her face, and her body shook with laughter.

"Damn you!" I grabbed the stuffed bear and smacked Molly. "What?"

"Get that shit-eating-grin off your face. You scared me."

"I did not," said Molly as her grin widened.

"You kind of did. You act all weird when you take too many of those pills, and I never know what to think."

"My Z-done? I never take too many. I always take just

enough. I'm going to beat this friggin' pain, and I'm going to beat it on my own terms."

"Zylodone has its own terms. You be careful."

I unbuttoned my blouse as I eased off the edge of the bed and unsnapped my bra. I tossed both onto the floor and slid into a soft cotton tee. My head was pounding. As I unzipped my jeans, Molly pushed from the floor and stood with one hand serving as a kickstand on the mattress. Her high ponytail in its bright blue bow swung behind her. She smiled with dazed approval as she caught her reflection in the mirror. She had that drug-induced lethargy that was becoming all too common. She gripped the Zylodone bottle in her hand.

"I'm rocking this pony, don't ya think?"

"You look great." I kicked off my shoes.

"Where were you last night?" Molly squinted into the mirror as she applied the correct blend of Trixie Taupe and Bashful Blue eye shadow. "What story did you invent to get past Mom?"

"I told her I was studying at Rachel's."

"And she bought that? She may seem smart, but that woman is a few colors short of a rainbow. Or you're her favorite."

"She's a full rainbow. And I'm her favorite." I flashed my teeth in cocky reply.

"The baby always is. When I was a junior, school nights were sacred. I didn't dare leave the house."

Molly finished her final touches and turned toward me. She clung to the dresser as she waited for my verdict. Her eyes focused with a deadpan stare. "Aren't you going to tell me how I look?" she asked.

Before I could answer, Mom's voice rang up the stairs. Breakfast was ready. Molly's face dropped at the commanding sound of our mother's voice. Fear lurked behind her round blue eyes, and she held her breath. Familiar with these unexplained meltdowns, I rushed to her and slid my arms under both of hers as she wobbled. She still held the Zylodone in her hand.

"What happened last night?" I whispered as I lowered her to her bed.

"Nothing."

"Nothing? Why are you so unsteady?"

"I don't know," said Molly. "Don't let Mom come up here. She gets crazy if I don't wake up with bells on. She suspects. She always suspects."

"Suspects what?"

"I don't know," whimpered Molly.

"Okay, calm down. You can handle this. Go downstairs and be yourself."

"She'll suspect something," said Molly. "She'll question me and stare at me. She'll act like she's cleaning the kitchen, but she'll be watching me."

"What is there to suspect? Did you take too many?"

"No."

"Are you sure?" I asked.

"I promise."

"Then you're fine," I said as I climbed into bed.

"You can't go to bed! You have to go down with me."

"I didn't get any sleep last night, and I don't have class. I'm going to sleep this headache away." I tried to focus on Molly's frightened eyes as I pulled the covers up to my chin. "You've got this, Molly. If you didn't take too many Zylodone, you have nothing to worry about. Now go eat."

I collapsed into my pillow as Molly's voice grew faint. I convinced myself that sleep would ease the hangover gripping my every nerve. Molly would be fine.

· · · · ·

As afternoon clouds cast shadows in my room, my eyes shot open. I sat up in bed and looked at the clock. The day was half gone. Running my hands through my moist hair released a malodorous smell. I crawled from under the blanket as my damp T-shirt clung to my body. We both needed washing.

As I stepped away from the bed, a dull pain pulsed behind my eyes. I stopped and rubbed both temples. I massaged small circles into both sides of my face, but to no avail. I crawled to the bathroom to find something for the pain. I opened the top drawer only to find toothpaste, skinny combs, and hairbands. The second drawer was stuffed with extra washcloths and a random bottle of sunscreen. I opened the third to an assortment of Zylodone bottles. I shook several to ensure they were empty and slammed the drawer shut. Mom and Dad had to know. Or did they cling to the hope of Molly healing and ignore the cost?

After unsuccessfully rummaging through every other drawer and both cabinets, I put on a loose-fitting pair of jeans and headed out the front door. It was a short walk. Hunger was joining my discomfort, and the Eastside Market carried the giant candy bar I craved.

It took less than ten minutes to find the ibuprofen, pass through the candy aisle, and make my purchase. As I walked through the sliding glass doors and shimmied through the first row of cars, my mind hit replay on the party the night before. I shook my head to scatter my thoughts. Rapid relief from the ibuprofen was not an option, and the pain in my head forced me to shuffle with elderly steps.

As I reached the hill to my neighborhood, I remembered my beer-stained clothes. They had to be washed before they were discovered. Mom would zero in on the smell if I dared to drop them in the hamper. I hoped Dad was fighting traffic on the Schuylkill Expressway, and Mom was stuck in another unexpected meeting. That would give me plenty of time to clean up the mess and maybe sneak in a short nap.

The view from the top of the hill erased it all. Gray smoke puffed from the tailpipe of an ambulance in front of my red brick house. A black police car with white letters on the side door was parked by the edge of the driveway. Random cars lined both sides of the street. I stared at the cars and, in my mind's eye, played who's who with the owners. Although several looked familiar, I couldn't be sure about any except the few I sometimes drove.

My mother's car was parked four down from the mailbox, and my father's car was tightly wedged between the police car and the ambulance. But I didn't see Molly's car. It wasn't in the driveway, and it wasn't in the street. There were so many cars, but none were Molly's. I tried to run. I stumbled. I caught my balance and took off again. I stumbled again. My body couldn't get to my house as fast as my mind demanded. I imagined what I would find as I tried my best not to vomit. I tasted the regurgitation of the medicine and felt the nausea.

"Where is it?" Small pebbles scattered under my feet. "Where is it?"

And then I froze. My eyes locked onto a muted shade of green with blotches of rust, and my heart jumped. Molly's Volkswagen was the last car parked by the curb. It was Molly's favorite spot, in the shade under the large oak tree sheltered from the sap of the surrounding pines. I emptied my lungs as tears flowed down my cheeks. I staggered toward the red brick façade, foreboding as it now was.

I lifted the garage door enough to duck under to the other side but collapsed onto my knees. Pain shot through my head and ran down my spine. It took my breath away. I let the door lower and struggled to my feet. I needed to see Molly.

I continued into the laundry room hearing hushed voices mingle in the kitchen. As I entered, the quiet conversations stopped. Everyone turned to me. I stared back, struggling to breathe in the thick silence.

My father stood rigid by the oven talking with a heavyset uniformed officer. The sudden silence caused him to look my way. He hurried over and wrapped me in his arms. His shoulders shook as he pulled me in and led me to the den. He sat beside me on the couch and looked into my eyes as tears fell from his. I watched his Adam's apple vibrate on his throat as he tried to form words and force them from his mouth. Whatever it was, the words would not come.

"What is it, Dad?" I swallowed my fear. "Tell me."

Empowered by my torment, I slipped from under my father's arms. Without looking back, I ran from the den to search for my mother and Molly. As I hurried through the kitchen gate, confused faces turned to stare.

"Stop looking at me," I mumbled to them all.

I scoured the room for round blue eyes among the unfamiliar faces. I saw neighbors staring back at me with pity. A familiar face that I couldn't give a name was shaking his head as if I had done something and they all knew what it was. I looked away from his judgmental glare and caught sight of my mother sitting at the end of the kitchen table crying with Father Michael. He cupped her hands in his, their heads tilted inches apart. I saw his lips moving and my mother's eyes closed. I knew he was extending spiritual peace. He was offering an explanation that made no sense and gave no comfort.

I turned and ran from the kitchen, the malaise too oppressive to bear. I needed to find Molly. Her car was in its special spot, so she had to be close by. I bolted through our bedroom door, but Molly wasn't there. I stared at our disheveled bed as a stale odor wafted to my nose. It brought the nausea back. I ran from the room.

"Molly?" I begged as I stumbled down the hallway. "Where are you, girl? Damn it, Molly. I thought you were all right. Molly? Please be all right. Please."

I leaned into the mirrored wall at the end of the hall and examined my face. I struggled to recognize the girl looking back. The dark oily shine on my hair flattened each strand against my head. My skin had the hue of dirty white glue, and my eyes were wet and vacant. Dark empty tunnels looking back at me.

I turned and leaned against the mirror and slid down onto the carpet. I pulled my knees up to my chest and closed my eyes to stop my frightened tears. The nightmare was growing too dark, and I was growing too weak. I wanted to be strong but couldn't find the drive behind the desire. I needed Molly. I needed Molly to be all right.

"Claire?" A male voice echoed up the stairs.

My eyes shot open for the second time that day. I jumped up.

"Coming," I yelled. "Please don't come up here," I whispered.

I gazed into the mirror one last time. I wanted to see a hero. To see the girl who helped Molly keep it together. The anchor that kept her from drifting and the safety net that always broke the fall. But I didn't know where Molly was. I ran my fingers through my hair and headed back toward the stairs.

On the fifth step from the bottom, I looked straight into the eyes of Principal Ward. I froze as unfamiliar anguish squeezed the air from my lungs. There was no reason to see Mr. Ward. He shouldn't be in my home. Panic engulfed me as sounds of heartache stung my ears. I remained in a locked gaze with Mr. Ward. He reached for me.

"Claire," he whispered.

"NO!" I yelled. "NO! NO! NO!"

I jumped off the stairs and pushed past Principal Ward. I uttered "No" with every step. I ran into the kitchen, searching for Molly. As I stood at the entrance, I tried to focus on the blurred faces that stared back at me. I didn't see Molly. I looked and looked and didn't see Molly. I covered my face with my hands.

I was back on the couch in the den when my eyes opened to my father's gentle gaze. I watched the whiskers on his chin quiver as he looked down at me. I opened my mouth but found no words. The heavy air was suffocating. I bolted up. My father gripped my shoulders and sat me down again.

"Where is she, Dad? Where's Molly?"

The look in my father's eyes gave me the answer I didn't want to hear. His eyes gave me the answer I wouldn't accept.

"No, no, no, no, no." I collapsed in my father's arms, my tears drenching his shirt.

Dad squeezed me against his chest and buried his nose into my dark blond hair. I knew he wanted to be strong. I knew he was searching for the words. But he couldn't find them. There was nothing either of us could say. It wasn't something any parent ever thought would happen, and yet it was the one thing every parent feared.

After several moments in my father's embrace, I lifted my face to his. Puddles of sorrow gazed at him, wanting to know but not wanting to know. My broken heart silently asked him to make it go away. I knew he wished he could.

"Molly's gone, baby."

"No." I collapsed onto his lap. "Please, no, please."

Dad cradled me as he rocked back and forth. He rubbed my back and turned his face away. I felt him wipe away his tears to keep them from falling onto the shoulders of the only daughter he had left. This awful moment held us both as we struggled to find comfort in each other. Dad was finding his strength by holding me, and I was finding mine by being held. But nothing eased the pain.

I curled up in my father's arms while the police officers finished their work and neighbors said their goodbyes. I watched Father Michael walk people to the door and offer what comfort he could. My Mom was gone. I didn't know where.

"It's tragic when we lose a child," a giant but gentle officer explained to Father Michael. "And suicides are the worst. The Hewitts will need your guidance as they suffer, and no answers are found."

"Perhaps some answers will be found." Father Michael placed his hand on the kind man's shoulder as he spoke. "I didn't think she would choose this path. I don't believe anybody did. But she's in our Lord's hands now."

The officer nodded as I squeezed my eyes closed to block the lies. Molly didn't choose a path.

"Dad, where is Molly now? Where did they take her?"

"Oh, baby, she's in the ambulance."

"Molly didn't want to die, Dad."

"I want to believe that. I really do."

"Then believe it. She didn't take those pills to end her life. She took them to fight the pain. To live again. If I had stayed awake, I could have stopped her."

"There was nothing you could have done, sweetheart."

"Yes, there was. I could have taken those pills from her. I should have taken those pills from her."

"Like you said, baby girl, she needed those pills for the pain. The Zylodone got her back in the gym."

"Zylodone took her from us." I buried deeper into my father's lap. My tears soaked his thighs. He rubbed my back, and his warm fingers slid the hair from my damp neck.

I felt safe with him yet so alone. Why didn't they see the power of the pills? The pills made a mean bargain. A bargain Molly could only pay one way. The opioids erased her pain, but those wicked pills stole her dreams, her fight, and her very last breath. They stole our Molly while nobody was looking.

Dad looked down at me and ran his thumb across my cheek. "Oh, baby girl, there was nothing you could do. There was nothing any of us could do."

After a torturous and fitful night, my eyes began to blink. I pulled the covers over my head and fought against the morning sun invading my room with its bright new day. The morning had come too soon, and the night was gone. I cried into my pillow. The night was gone, and so was Molly.

"No. No. No. Please come back. Please don't leave me. Please don't take that pill."

My blinks were long and slow. I was falling back to sleep.

"I'm so sorry, Molly. I wasn't there for you." My eyelids grew too heavy. They stayed closed, and I fell asleep again. I dreamt of Molly.

14

LET IT GO

As the morning cleaning crew pushed vacuums along the carpeted hallway, Claire hit the floor with a heavy thud. Her eyes flew open. She glanced around as her fingers caressed the crease that ran down the side of her cheek. She struggled to roll over in the tight space.

"What the hell," she whispered.

Reaching behind her, Claire lifted herself back onto the couch. She grabbed a bobby pin from the cushion and slipped it onto the end of her sleeve. She wiped her damp cheeks with the back of her hands. She then glared at her laptop propped on the floor like a tent. She snapped it shut and set it on the table.

"Damn it." Claire slipped her feet into her Weitzman pumps. "I can't deal with this today."

The office door creaked open several inches. Claire quickly wiped the smeared mascara she knew was under her eyes and fluttered her eyelids. Her fingertips then felt the lashes.

"Oh my gosh." Morgan poked her head inside. "You never went home."

"I fell asleep."

"That sucks. You look like hell."

"Thanks."

"You've been crying," said Morgan as she continued into Claire's office. "Molly's birthday?"

"Every year." Claire's eyes dropped to the floor as she felt Morgan's scorn.

"Why do you do that to yourself?" asked Morgan.

"I'm not doing anything to myself. I get ambushed."

"It's like you're lying in wait expecting it to happen."

"I expect a restless night or two. But nothing a few glasses of wine can't conquer."

"There must be a trigger. Something triggers these memories."

"Emma Satori."

"Of course Emma Satori." Morgan leaned against Claire's desk. "She was about the same age as your sister. A teenager, no longer a kid yet not grown up. How's that going for you?"

"Another nightmare. Parents are devastated. Dad wants revenge."

"Lovely."

"Why are you here so early?" asked Claire.

"Reviewing for a deposition in a few hours. Are you going to be all right? Your makeup is a mess."

"I'm fine."

"Stop baking her a damn birthday cake every year. That's your trigger." Morgan lifted herself up onto the edge of Claire's desk. Several papers drifted to the floor. "However, this year's Scandinavian fantasy was the best you've made. And I've tasted them all."

"It's therapy. I bake her a cake to make up for falling asleep and not saving her."

"That's shitty therapy." Morgan propped her feet on the chair in front of Claire's desk. "Thinking you could have made a difference is ridiculous."

"You don't know that I couldn't have."

"You don't know that you could have. People make their own choices and must live with the consequences."

"Even teenagers?" mumbled Claire.

"Especially teenagers."

Claire looked at Morgan with piercing eyes. She knew it was the truth but hated that Morgan knew it too. After several moments, she let it go and looked up to the black clock that hung above her door. Morgan followed her eyes.

"Is that my signal to leave?"

"Not at all," said Claire. "That clock cheers me up. It was a gift from an old boyfriend when I graduated from law school. After a couple of years, I got rid of the boyfriend but kept the clock. I liked it better."

"There was nothing you could do, Claire."

"What's wrong with me? I'm almost forty years old."

"Nothing. You need more time."

"Time doesn't heal all wounds." Claire grabbed a pillow from the floor and leaned it against the armrest. "It's a cliché people use to comfort others. Some grief never leaves. It latches on and makes itself at home."

"But it softens and becomes bearable."

"I'm still waiting for that."

"It begins with forgiveness," said Morgan.

"Forgiveness? I never blamed her."

"Not Molly. The doctors, your parents, yourself."

"Not sure that'll happen. After her surgery, she clung to the only thing she knew, her Olympic dream. They gave her opioids and told her that dream would come true. They lied to her."

"Let it go."

Claire grabbed the pillow and squeezed it with both hands. She sucked in deep breaths of air and blew them out her mouth.

She stared down at the pillow as she felt Morgan's eye on her.

"Everyone jumped on the opioid bandwagon. The doctors, my parents, our pastor, teachers. Every one of them shared opinions. But none of them had the facts."

"They did the best they could. Let it go."

"I was a kid and saw the cravings she had after one week of Zylodone. Yet they drove her to the gym with a pill bottle in her hand. The more opioids she took, the more opioids she needed. It was a vicious cycle that she didn't start."

"Did her doctor up her script whenever she wanted?" asked Morgan.

"I have no idea. All I know is that she never ran out."

"That proves none of it was your fault."

"Bullshit. If I was the only one who saw it and did nothing, I'm the only one to blame."

Morgan hopped off the desk and walked over to the couch. She grabbed a pillow for herself and nestled in next to Claire. "Now you're talking nonsense. You were a kid."

"Molly was sucked into a whirlwind with nothing to hang on to." Tears puddled in Claire's eyes. "They threw her in with phony promises and false hope."

"Not intentionally."

"The prescriptions weren't written by accident." Claire stood up in front of Morgan with feet apart and arms folded. "Her doctor drank the Kool-Aid the drug manufacturers were serving and promised Molly wouldn't become an addict."

"Then blame them. Not yourself. Let them lose sleep."

"They don't sleep."

"Okay. But you need to let it go. Let go of Zylodone and Molly. Focus on your job."

Claire dropped her arms by her sides and looked up to the clock. With unexplained vigor in her movements, she picked up her laptop and the Satori depositions that lay on the table. She walked them to her desk and gathered opioid articles from the side table and two chairs along the way. With the precision of a librarian, she straightened the Martindale-Hubbells displayed on the bookshelf and made a pile of court decisions to return to the law library at the end of the hall. Her movements were swift and her cheeks ruddy.

"What is happening?" asked Morgan as she witnessed the unexpected frenzy from the couch.

"I'm letting go."

"You won't regret it. Your firsthand knowledge of this devastating crisis gives you power. It gives you motive and incentive to win and stop the deaths."

Claire used her forearm to sweep pens, notepads, and old mail inside her desk drawer. She shuffled them to push it shut.

"I'll get to those later. I'm supposed to be at Delaney's office in a few hours." Claire looked at Morgan and at the clock a third time.

"Fix your makeup." Morgan headed for the door. "I have some in my office."

15

PAPER CUTS

At 7:00 a.m., Claire parked her black BMW in the first visitor stall by the front doors. The large windows facing the parking lot were still dark. Her phone rang, and Claire smiled at the name on the caller ID.

"I fixed my makeup. And my hair." Claire smiled into the rearview mirror as she held the phone to her ear. "Hoping my early arrival shakes up the old goat. He's an arrogant prick."

Dr. Delaney pulled into the lot, and Claire hung up. She watched his agitated sneer through her rearview mirror when he noticed her car parked by the door.

"Good morning, Richard," Claire mumbled as she remained in her car and watched him park his.

As Dr. Delaney's gray Buick pulled in between the white lines several stalls away, Claire stepped out of her car and strode over to greet him. She stood several feet back from the driver-side door watching as he gathered his things and crawled out.

"Good morning, Dr. Delaney."

"Is it?" An irritable expression accompanied the curt reply.

With no further discourse, they both shuffled toward his

office. Dr. Delaney held the door open for Claire and nodded for her to proceed.

"Where would you like me to go?" Claire looked sideways at Delaney. "I can only imagine your preferred reply."

"You can work in the conference room after my office manager gets here. Ann will assist with whatever you need. Wait here until she arrives."

"Thank you."

Claire sat down on a sturdy wooden chair with a soiled tweed cushion. She squinted at the dark room around her. It was an unremarkable office. It provided the requisite reading material and toys to pacify waiting parents and comfort restless children. There was a marred box in the shape of a truck sitting under the window. It was filled with smaller trucks and bright colored blocks. Several plastic heads and one lone foot poked up between the blocks. Claire looked down at the brown side table next to her and assessed the magazines with curled corners and moisture rings. She rested her hands in her lap and waited.

Dr. Delaney flipped light switches as he proceeded through the door to the receptionist's station. He plugged in equipment and reviewed the day's schedule before heading into his office and shutting the door.

At 7:30 a.m., a bell chimed as the front door swung open. An attractive, middle-aged woman strolled in, fidgeting with the clasp on her purse. The light from the front office reflected off her dark chestnut hair that dropped just inches below her shoulders. Her black pencil skirt and red silk blouse accentuated her figure and spoke to her confidence. Claire rose from her chair.

Claire had spoken with Ann Meyers on previous occasions and knew her to be an impressive woman who knew her role and played it well. Ann seldom confronted problems she couldn't resolve and never created reckless ones that accomplished little. The management of a lucrative medical practice offered personal, financial, and legal challenges on a daily basis. Ann handled everything from insurance reimbursements to patient grievances to staff jealousies.

"Hi, Claire Hewitt. We've spoken on the phone." Claire offered her right hand.

"Yes. Good morning. I'm sorry to have kept you waiting." Ann shook Claire's hand as she continued walking.

Claire and Ann shared small talk about the typical August weather as Ann led the way to a small room. She also held the door open and nodded for Claire to enter. It was another chalk-colored room as commonplace as the waiting room had been. There was a large, rectangular table in the middle encircled by black low-backed chairs. Cheap artwork hung on the walls in addition to a short row of certificates lining the side of a single window. Ann followed Claire through the door and continued to the far side of the room.

"These cabinets contain patient records. We're not up to date with our electronic system. Not yet." Ann made light of the absence of paperless records as she unlocked a row of file cabinets lining the back wall. "Conversion to electronic records is time-consuming. We're getting there. But I'm afraid your day will involve paper files, paper copies, and perhaps a few paper cuts."

"I garden. My hands can take it."

"Let me know if you need anything," said Ann. "My extension is 246." Ann pointed to the landline on the counter. "Band-Aids are under the sink." She laughed and left.

Claire walked to the counter and picked up a colorful drug brochure. She read the front, flipped it over, and saw it was addressed to Michelle Moss. Dozens of other multicolored brochures were scattered across the counter. Each displayed the elaborate marketing tools used by Novo Analgesic Systems, Inc. in the promotion of opioids.

With a deep frown displaying her concern, Claire grabbed duplicates, tossed them onto the large table, and walked to the first file cabinet. She pulled open the heavy top drawer. She ran her fingers along the tabs, reading the labels before grabbing an armful of charts. She walked them to the table, sat down on one of the hard chairs, and dialed Alec's number.

"I'm sitting in the most antiquated office east of the Mississippi. Hundreds of paper files. Nothing's electronic. The office manager warned of paper cuts." Claire flipped through the brochures as she spoke. "I also found propaganda left by drug reps for Michelle Moss. Most are glossy sales pamphlets from NAS. I'll bring duplicates back to the office."

Claire wagered with Alec on the number of cases needed to establish a pattern of negligence and hung up. She opened the first chart. She scanned the pages, jotted notes on her legal pad, and reached for the next. Chart by chart, Claire documented who made the medical diagnosis, who prescribed medication, and what monitoring occurred.

Jacob Castle; body aches & fever, Oseltamivir, MM. Morgan Parker; coughing & fever, Topaprofen, MM. Katie Imani; torn labrum, Deprexone, MM. Megan Jones; fracture radius repair, Deprexone, MM.

After four hours of documenting one inconsequential infirmity after another and jotting the initials *MM* beside each patient name, Claire peeked her head into the hallway. Dr. Delaney's nurse practitioner, Michelle Moss, had just stepped out of Delaney's office. She glanced in Claire's direction.

"Do you need something?" Her agitation was evident.

"I'm heading to lunch. I'll be back in an hour."

Without response, Ms. Moss disappeared behind another door.

Claire rushed out the back entrance to a restaurant nearby. She ate lightly so as not to induce the need for an afternoon nap and slipped back into the office unnoticed. Energized from the short break, Claire zipped through the remaining charts and solidified the pattern of negligence she needed.

Leslie McBride; joint pain, Deprexone, MM. Susan Patterson; knee surgery, Deprexone, MM. Laura Landry; fractured fibula repair, Zylodone, MM. Heidi Selling; appendectomy, Deprexone, MM.

Claire closed the final chart. She leaned back with a deep sigh as the deafening blast penetrated both ears. A single shot. Claire froze as if struck by the bullet. The vociferous sound flooded the small room. Her jaw went slack, but her dry lips sealed her mouth closed. She stared at the table and listened to the silence that came next. She waited. Muffled sounds grew louder. Claire pushed back from the table. She walked to the door and gripped the knob. She listened. Screams ricocheted down the hallway. Claire twisted the knob and inched the door open. Two women ran past. Claire's eyes followed them to the back door as they both glared into the parking lot, stretching their necks as if they could see around the stone corner. Finding nothing to detain them, they raced back toward Claire as Dr. Delaney ran to the front desk. Claire tiptoed behind.

"Oh no, oh no, oh no," Ann repeated as she eased Michelle Moss into a chair.

"What the hell was that?" asked Delaney, his eyes scanning the surroundings.

"A woman walked in," said a young receptionist with a top knot and alluring green eyes. "I thought she was lost. She looked around for like one second and then pointed a gun at Michelle. She shot her." The receptionist burst into tears.

"Oh, Michelle." Ann began crying too.

"Who was she? Does anyone know?" asked Delaney.

"Couldn't see," mumbled Michelle. "Silver hair?" Her eyes closed.

Claire watched the chaos continue despite Delaney's weak efforts to remain calm. He ran to the front door and peered through the glass as sirens filled the air. Ms. Moss slumped in a rolling office chair behind the desk. A white towel with a growing red smudge was pressed to her sternum.

Dr. Delaney jumped to the side as three EMTs bolted through the door. A muscular police officer followed. Two additional officers remained outside in front of the large plate-glass window. All had guns drawn.

"She's gone." Dr. Delaney said to the officer.

"The gunman was a woman?" the officer asked as he rushed around the waiting room, opening two closed doors and looking down a hallway.

"I guess."

"Do you know her identity?"

"Our receptionist saw her, but this is her first week here," answered Delaney. "We have hundreds of people coming through this office every week. Could have been anyone. A patient, a family member of a patient."

"You don't appear to be alarmed." The officer rested his gun on his hip.

"More dismayed. We get threats from pain patients and their disillusioned family members all the time. You become immune. But nobody has ever returned to follow through."

"Until today." The officer looked from the tearful staff to Delaney.

"Until today." Delaney walked away from the officer's damning glare.

Having witnessed enough trauma, Claire snuck back into the conference room. She slipped marketing brochures into her bag and glanced at the clock on the wall. The hands silently ticked as the hour neared 5:00 p.m. Moments later, there was a light tap on the door. Not waiting for a response, Dr. Delaney walked into the room. In slow motion, he eased the door closed and looked over to Claire, who was propped on the edge of her chair.

"I apologize for the commotion today. I'm glad you were back here when it occurred."

"Thank you."

"Pain pushes some people over the edge."

"What happened?" asked Claire.

"An angry woman with a gun waltzed right through the front door." Delaney looked down at his feet. "I've received personal threats before, but my gut tells me this woman wasn't looking for me."

"It was a woman?"

"Rage isn't sexist."

"Who was she looking for?" asked Claire. "Was anyone hurt?"

"Ms. Moss was shot."

"Oh my God. Is she okay?"

"She was taken to the hospital. The police are questioning our receptionist."

"Moss was the target?"

"I don't know. Violence against medical professionals is off the charts. Mounting regulatory pressure requires us to search for alternatives and taper patients off addictive painkillers. This opioid crisis has put every doctor in danger."

"Patients don't want alternatives or tapering?"

Delaney shook his head at Claire's rhetorical question and walked along the counter covered in opioid brochures. He glanced down at the haphazard assortment but ignored the mess and the irony. As he approached the gray metal file cabinets, he turned back to Claire with hands clenched tightly in front of his round stomach.

"If not closely monitored, opioids can literally hijack the brains of patients and convince them there is no addiction. Even with monitoring, it can happen."

"Then why prescribe opioids?" asked Claire.

"Because they're often the best option. The problem multiplies when irrational family members expect miracles. When you don't fulfill their fantasies, they want revenge. I've had disgruntled people waiting for me in the parking lot. Ms. Moss and I both have."

"If it's that risky, is it worth it?"

"It's the cost of doing business."

"That's a high price," said Claire.

"Perhaps. But depriving patients of proper pain management would be a higher price. Not providing the best possible care would amount to malpractice."

Claire glanced down at an opioid brochure protruding from her bag. She looked at the variety of pills printed on the cover depicting the true power they possessed. While they eased the suffering of those in need, they controlled the doctors who prescribed them. And they terrified the friends and family on the sidelines.

"I could refer my patients to a pain specialist. But they made an appointment to see me, and I see no reason to pass the buck if I can help." Dr. Delaney walked to Claire and stood beside her chair. He looked at her with new empathy. Claire felt his fatherly desire to comfort.

"That puts you in a difficult situation," said Claire.

"We're all in a difficult situation. But there's never been a follow-through prior to today. We have alarm systems and panic buttons to help address suspect situations." Delaney turned from Claire and walked around the table, tracing the edge with his index finger. "But I need to do more to ensure the safety of my staff." Dr. Delaney stopped and leaned onto the table with both hands. He looked over at Claire and spoke in a whisper. "I can never let this happen again. That silver-haired woman reminded me of how fragile life is."

Claire nodded as she watched the anguish in Delaney's eyes. She rested on her forearms and tapped her fingertips together, unnerved by the torment gripping him.

"You would think I would have understood the fragility of life in medical school," Dr. Delaney commented as he headed toward the door. "Guess I'm a slow learner."

"Doubt that," said Claire. "You know Pennsylvania has a 'shall issue' gun law that waives the permit requirement to carry a gun in a place of business."

"I'm aware." Dr. Delaney lifted the back of his shirt to reveal the black ribbed handle protruding from his waistband. "But I wasn't by the front desk today."

Dr. Delaney walked out, and Claire sat for several moments, swishing air back and forth inside her mouth. She then grabbed the table with both hands and pushed. The chair rolled, and Claire jumped to her feet. Leaving patient charts and a few remaining brochures on the table, she hurried out of the drab room. She glanced down the hallway, pleased that it was empty, and let the back door slam shut.

By 6:00 p.m., Claire cruised along the Delaware Expressway, gripping the wheel with sweaty palms. Wet smudges glistened on either side of her hands. Her eyes dropped to the radio dial when a perky voice mentioned an incident at a local medical office earlier that afternoon. Claire groaned and then glanced at her speedometer. She tapped the brake.

The elevator ride to the twelfth floor of Blackman & Bradford made no stops, and Claire bumped into Alec's chest when the doors opened. Her purse slipped from her shoulder as she fumbled the patient charts in her arms. She dropped none, and Alec placed the strap back on her shoulder.

"Don't leave yet." Claire motioned for Alec to follow. Alec turned as commanded and took charts from Claire's full arms so she could unlock her office door. With unmasked pleasure, she admired the tidy result of her earlier frenzy as she retreated to the sitting area. She took the copies of patient charts from Alec and tossed opioid brochures onto the couch. As reality sunk in, she patted the couch for Alec to sit.

"Did you catch the news?" asked Claire.

"No, I've been here."

"There was a shooting at Delaney's office today."

"While you were there?" Alec sat down.

"I was in the conference room but heard it all."

"Thank God you're okay." Alec placed his hand on Claire's shoulder. "Was anyone hurt?"

"A nurse was taken to the hospital with a gunshot wound. It was mayhem."

"Who did it?" asked Alec.

"They don't know. Maybe an angry patient or an angry family member of a patient. Some crazy old lady with a gun."

"A woman?" asked Alec.

"Yeah, it was a woman. That surprises me. It shouldn't, but it does."

"The opioid crisis is an ironic mess," said Alec. "Addiction changes everything. It makes the doctor-patient relationship even more tenuous. When patients were unhappy with their doctor in the past, the worst that would happen was nonpayment. Welcome to 2022. When the patient is unhappy, the doctor gets a bullet."

"It doesn't take addiction for an opioid prescriber to run into trouble. When a family member doesn't see the relief they expected, revenge takes over. Michelle Moss got caught in that line of fire today."

"Because she prescribes opioids." Alec shifted sideways to face Claire.

"That's why Delaney felt guilty," said Claire. "He lets her do his job, and then she's the one taken out."

"You're not serious."

"I am," said Claire. "She sees every patient, overprescribes, and struts around that office with an ego the size of Texas."

Alec winced and picked up a patient chart. He thumbed through it as he walked to the window. His steps were slow. Claire leaned back on the couch and swung one foot onto the adjacent chair.

"Are they all like this?" Alec spun around and held the chart up in the air. "Do we have our pattern?"

"We do. Delaney and Moss run quite a business. The only thing Moss isn't doing is forging Delaney's signature. Of course, I have no proof that she isn't doing that as well."

"What does Delaney do?"

"How would I know? Nap?" Claire sat upright and propped her feet against the base of the couch as she sifted through the charts. "He sees a lot of patients with insignificant ailments. Coughs, fevers, crap like that." Claire separated the piles as she continued describing the process. "But there's an alarming number of patients seeing him for postoperative care and an equal number of pain issues stemming from sports injuries."

"What a bunch of pansies. My generation never ran to the doctor. We ran to the freezer." Alec returned to the couch and swapped his chart for two others.

"Ice won't do the trick for postoperative pain," said Claire. "But Delaney doesn't want to refer anyone to a pain specialist."

"Doesn't want to gift his payday to a competitor?"

"Said he doesn't want to pass the buck to someone else if he can solve the problem. So he and Moss set up a direct line to Deprexone."

"Perfect."

"For whom?" snapped Claire.

"Satoris and our case."

"I guess." Claire wrapped her arms across her waist in a hug as her right knee bounced. She stared at the charts. Her jaw muscles pulsed as she grit her teeth.

Alec leaned back with his elbow on the armrest and crossed his legs. He watched Claire glued to the charts with her knee bouncing. The silence in the room begged to be broken.

"Delaney and Moss have shuffled people in and out of that office for years," said Alec. "Do you think NAS was their supplier from the beginning?"

"Probably," blurted Claire, emerging from her trance. "We know they are now."

Claire tossed the pamphlets from Delaney's office to Alec. She then scooted back on the couch and wedged one foot under the cushion. Alec scoured the brochures.

"There's no evidence NAS provided Delaney with opioids when he first opened his office," said Claire. "But my money is on them. They're too aggressive and too controlling to let anyone else through the door."

"Let's head there tomorrow and find out," said Alec as he dropped the propaganda back on the couch.

"Good idea."

Claire glanced at Alec as she picked up her purse and threw it over one shoulder. They both headed into the hallway and stood in front of the elevator doors watching the numbers above. A comfortable silence surrounded them as the elevator descended to the lobby, and they headed out the front entry. Before turning toward her car, Claire thanked Alec for his long hours. He returned the praise with a hug.

16

OPIOPHILIA

Claire leaned against the wall beside an electronic message board waiting for Alec. She sipped her caramel latte as hurried commuters rushed by. Countless people ran past with desperate looks of urgency while others lingered, trying but failing to look at ease.

Alec startled Claire as he jumped from the rushing crowd. He slid in by the message board with a rolled newspaper in hand. Claire glanced over, then turned back to the hectic crowd.

"For you." Alec offered the paper.

"What's this?"

"Headline caught my eye."

Claire unrolled the paper and read the bold print. FATAL OVERDOSES CLIMB TO RECORD HIGH.

"There were 70,699 overdose deaths in 2019." Alec pointed to the accompanying chart like a student showing his work. "That number grew to 107,000 in 2021. Most of those started with a legal opioid prescription."

Alec looked around the station as Claire continued to read. With restless energy, he turned back and followed along, pointing to Deprexone in several paragraphs.

"They name NAS as the manufacturer of numerous popular pain meds," said Alec. "No accusations are made. But they point to them as a major contributor."

"With drug overdoses skyrocketing, all eyes are on pharmaceutical companies." Claire folded the paper. "The problem is they're boarding up their doors. I don't doubt, for one minute, Westcott's desire and ability to shut us out today."

"He doesn't know we're coming this time. We get in and head straight for Shaggy. He'll give us what we need."

"One can only hope."

Claire glanced up at the arrivals board as she grabbed her briefcase and joined the rush. She moved through the crowd and boarded the train as if it were her daily routine. She slid into the middle seat of the third row. Alec sat on the aisle. They watched as other passengers scrambled for the last available seats.

"We're going to face obstacles with Westcott regardless of whether he expects us or not," said Claire. "He'll exaggerate his involvement in opioid development while hiding any mistakes that were made."

"That's where Ethan comes in. He'll help us before helping Westcott."

"I hope so. We need to see how NAS perpetuated the opioid pendulum."

"Opioid pendulum?" asked Alec.

"That's how physicians refer to it. In the 1980s, there was opiophobia, an overzealous fear of opioids. Opioids were prescribed only for surgery, hospitalized post-op, and end-of-life cancer pain. Drug manufacturers saw that fear as a perfect opportunity."

"Opportunity for what?" Alec rolled the newspaper into a tube as he spoke.

"Developing new opioids and marketing them as safe for chronic pain," said Claire.

"They were right. The market's flooded."

"And people are drowning." Resting her hand on the seat in front of her, Claire turned sideways to face Alec. "The pendulum swung the other direction in the '90s and created opiophilia. Opioids previously used for acute or cancer pain became the perfect answer for anything that hurts."

"Oh shit."

"That's why we are where we are in 2022."

Claire's brief nap ended with the gradual slowing of the train. She opened her eyes to the yellow glow of the New York terminal walls. Passengers rustled, shutting laptops and returning magazines into seat-back pockets. Alec perched on the edge of his seat.

"You can't relax at all," said Claire.

"I'm combat-ready."

"Oh, Lord."

When the train pulled to a stop, Alec jumped from his seat and raced off. Claire grabbed her briefcase and weaved through the crowd in pursuit. A distant Alec bolted through the front entrance and was standing by a cab as Claire hurried toward him.

"Your chariot, madam."

Claire climbed in and scooted across the seat.

"Novo Analgesic Systems," said Alec.

The driver pulled from the line of taxis and maneuvered through the sounding horns. Alec stretched his neck to look out the front window.

"What is up with you?" asked Claire.

"It's like we're on a scavenger hunt."

"We are on a scavenger hunt."

"That's why I'm amped up to get there. I can't wait to see Ethan give us their research while Westcott tries to stop him.

Ethan's tougher than he appears." Alec leaned back with anticipation in his eyes.

"You keep saying that. I hope it's true."

With flawless timing, the cab driver pulled in front of Novo Analgesic System's pretentious façade and glanced into the back seat.

"Traffic was on your side today."

"Yes, thank you." Alec swiped his credit card before following Claire down the etched walkway. They pushed through the gold-paned doors and entered the lobby. Familiar with his surroundings, Alec dashed to the front desk.

"Jack Freeman, please."

The preoccupied brunette flipping through a *Cosmopolitan* magazine ignored him for a moment and then glanced up. She raised her eyebrows and stared.

"Jack Freeman."

"Do you have an appointment?"

"10:00 a.m."

A deep inhale enlarged the young woman's large chest as she dropped her magazine and picked up the phone. Her eyeroll revealed her displeasure.

"Hi, Carol. Can you let Jack know he has visitors in the lobby. I don't know. They just showed up."

Overestimating the authority of her position, she replaced the receiver and turned her annoyance toward Alec. She then looked back and forth between Alec and Claire as if deciding whom to scold.

"Jack has a full schedule and will see you when he can. I'm not at liberty to say how long that may be. I suppose I could get you some coffee while you wait." She stood up from her chair but moved no further.

"No, thank you," replied Alec.

"I'll take mine black," said Claire.

The receptionist's shoulders dropped. Another deep breath. As she trudged to fulfill her duty, Claire and Alec stepped into a sitting area for the indeterminable wait.

For less than ten minutes they leafed through NAS propaganda until Jack Freeman waltzed toward them followed by the coffee-carrying receptionist. Jack offered amiable handshakes to both and passed the hot coffee to Claire.

"I'll trade you." Claire took the coffee and handed the search warrant to Jack.

"I've been expecting this. Let's go." Jack ignored the warrant.

Claire and Alec followed Jack to the elevators located behind the lobby desk. They assessed their surroundings as Jack's uncompromising eyes focused ahead. When the elevator doors opened, he bowed in jest with an extended arm.

"Phil Westcott lives in his laboratory and will be happy to assist you." Jack offered a goodwill smile to his guests.

"That would be wonderful." Claire returned the gesture.

"I want you both to know that Novo Analgesic Systems will be as compliant as possible with your requests. We are more than willing to cooperate."

"We'd appreciate that." Claire's tone questioned his candor. "How we proceed will depend upon what we encounter with Dr. Westcott."

"I understand. I guarantee he will assist you in every way he can."

Claire's raised eyebrows again questioned the sincerity of Jack's promise. With no further small talk, the doors opened to a narrow hallway on the lower level. Bright beams of sunlight streamed in through large windows on the west side and reflected off the metallic artwork hanging on the opposite white wall. The effect was startling.

Jack led them to a small room adjacent to an oversized gray metal door. The room was as lavish as all other areas had been. Four textured walls were a dark forest green with metallic artwork similar to that seen in the hallway. It had a rustic chic motif, and there was the warm aroma of pine in the air.

One dozen thick folders were placed at the edge of a long walnut table next to a small dish of peppermints. Claire looked at Jack with a puzzled expression. Answering her unspoken concern, Jack offered a flimsy response.

"Those are files relevant to the Satori claim. They should give you everything you need. The mints prevent dry mouth. My idea." Jack smiled.

"Everything we need?" asked Claire.

"This is a large laboratory that's been in operation for decades. Locating all research conducted on every opioid is a daunting task. If we can supply what's needed for trial in a less cumbersome manner, we think that would be best for everyone."

"I don't think so," said Claire.

"The mandate you've given us is quite possibly insurmountable, Ms. Hewitt."

"I'm sure you're up for it, Mr. Freeman."

"You may not appreciate the time frame required." His tone hardened.

"You'll need to discuss that with Judge Connor. The warrant gives us access to all opioid research and development conducted by your company. It includes your poppy farms in Turkey if we're inclined to make the trip."

"Begin with the results in front of you," snapped Jack. "Dr. Westcott assures me those are the strongest results relevant to the Deprexone claim. If you need additional research, you can contact him."

"Where will we find him?" asked Claire.

"Like I told you, in the lab. It's right through those doors." Jack pointed through the wall to the lab next door.

Claire's eyes followed the complaisant gesture as Alec reached around her and picked up the top file. Claire then looked back to the diminutive challenge placed in front of them and thumbed through the second.

"If we encounter obstacles along the way, where might we find you?" Alec lifted his chin as Jack shifted on his feet.

"I'm upstairs."

"Good enough. We'll start with these."

With a relieved exhale and forced smile, Jack turned. He offered no encouragement and no parting words. He walked out of the small room, pulling the door shut behind him.

"He doesn't give a rat's ass about any of this." Claire threw the file.

"Maybe he has too much trust in too few people and thinks those individuals can protect his company." Alec perused more data.

"That's about to change," said Claire. "Westcott may be an obstacle, but not an invincible one."

Claire left Alec and marched into the laboratory. Once inside the strange environment, she stood by the door and looked around. A chorus of screeching monkeys welcomed her. Most were pacing in their cages and began shaking the bars when they saw her approach.

"Dr. Westcott?"

No answer. More screeching. She wandered further into the lab.

"Dr. Westcott?"

"He's not here." Ethan shoved white towels into a drawer and then whipped around the corner to greet the new voice.

"Hi, I've met you."

"Yes, Claire Hewitt."

"I remember."

"You provided us with Deprexone research for the Satori lawsuit. We need additional information."

"Sure."

"We have a warrant granting us access to all research pertaining to the development of opioids marketed under the NAS name."

"From like when?"

"The beginning."

"Oh man, the very beginning? There was some insane experimentation going on long before I arrived. It's going to take me forever to decipher who was doing what."

"Better get cracking." Claire clapped at Ethan.

"That warrant says to give you everything? Westcott lost his shit the last time I did that."

"Everything," said Claire. "Jack Freeman has the warrant upstairs."

"Don't you have everything you need for that case?" Ethan grabbed another stack of ratty towels.

"We have a smattering of Deprexone test results, but we need documentation of every volunteer who took the stuff. We also need to see how it originated and the testing of other opioids released under the NAS name."

"That's insane. Why do you need info on every drug if your issue is with Deprexone?" Ethan concentrated on Claire as he absentmindedly bit on the edge of a lab towel he was holding.

"Yes, we have an issue with Deprexone. Do we have an issue with you?"

"Not with me," said Ethan. "But you may with Dr. Westcott. Every time you ask for more information, he has a meltdown. This is going to push him over the edge."

"If Westcott can't handle this, he can talk to Jack or the judge."

Claire looked inside the cage next to her. As she leaned in closer, sharp black nails reached through the bars for her arm. She jumped back. Ethan chuckled and guided the hand back into the cage.

"I'll start grabbing boxes as soon as I'm finished here." Ethan picked up the basket of towels. "But it's going to be a lot of boxes. Hope you brought help."

Claire returned to the small room empty-handed. Alec was seated at the far end. She leaned one hip against the large table and tucked both hands under opposite arms.

"I told him to pull everything," said Claire. "He reiterated Freeman's concerns."

"Patterns of negligence can take years to unfold." Alec looked up at Claire. "The longer it takes, the stronger the pattern."

Claire picked up a file and reviewed the contents. She then examined another. After thirty minutes of wasted time, she and Alec left the small room and pushed open the heavy gray door. Loud chatter echoed through the lab. In the back of the room, Ethan was struggling with the weight of a full metal cart. Boxes towered above him, and he used his body to maneuver around tight corners.

"Decades of test results demonstrating NAS success." Ethan stopped pushing when the cart reached the front of the lab.

Alec took hold of the end handle as Claire grabbed the other side. Ethan slid his palms into his lab coat pockets. He bounced on the balls of his feet as he watched the two take over.

The front wheels of the cart spun before realigning and rolling forward. Ethan scurried around them to open the door. Beads of sweat glistened on his upper lip and beside the veins spider-webbing his nostrils. He grunted as he pushed. A silent Phil

Westcott stood waiting on the other side with his arm extended, ready to pull. Four pairs of eyes ricocheted from one speechless face to another.

"Well now, what do we have here?" Phil asked of no one in particular.

Claire met Westcott's bewildered face with challenging eyes. Her fingers tightened on the cart as his opened and clenched by his side. Ethan looked back and forth between the two.

"Ethan, my office."

"Okay," Ethan said to the floor.

"I said now." Phil stormed through the door that Ethan held.

"I said okay."

Claire and Alec rolled NAS boxes across the hall. Ethan let the lab door shut.

17

MUDDIED WATERS

Alec rocked back and forth on his chair in the small room as he stared at the test result in front of him. He bit the middle knuckle of his tight fist.

"What leads them to making such disastrous decisions?" asked Alec.

"They don't start out disastrous," said Claire. "You've been a runner your whole life. Never had an injury?"

"I didn't let an injury control me. I never let opioids ruin my life. I never let opioids in the door."

"You're one of the lucky ones." Claire leaned in and pushed a stack of folders to the end of the long table. "No surgeries?"

"No surgeries."

"That's all it takes for the less fortunate. Hospitals use opioids. Doctors use opioids. A few pills is all it takes for some people to never turn back."

"The hundreds of pages of research documenting NAS opioid testing are a bunch of crap," said Alec. "It doesn't add up."

"Of course it adds up. It's all about the money. No test eliminates the risk of addiction. They test to cover their asses." Claire grabbed three brochures and a black glossy binder from the box next to her and slid them toward Alec. "Look at the amount of promotional material they circulate. The cornerstone of the opioid crisis in America is pharmaceutical sales. Bottom line. And NAS is no different than the other big names."

"The doctors do the prescribing."

"But they must first make the decision that an opioid is the best treatment and have an opioid readily available. Pharmaceutical companies use sophisticated marketing data to influence physician prescribing. That binder and those brochures are from NAS."

"How sophisticated is this marketing that it influences prescribing?" Alec leafed through the binder.

"They compile profiles on medical professionals detailing their prescribing patterns. They identify the highest and lowest prescribers of a particular drug in a single zip code. They evaluate that information and zero in on the highest prescribers of the drug they're promoting."

"Sounds like a violation of privacy." Alec looked up at Claire. "Must be a violation of the Consumer Fraud and Deceptive Business Practices Act."

"Could be both. There's data in that binder on Deprexone, Delaney, and Michelle Moss. The database showed a lot of chronic-pain patients walking into that office and an equal number of Deprexone scripts walking out. NAS wants to keep that ball rolling."

"I'm sure they do. But how?"

"Oh, let me count the ways." Claire picked up another folder and rifled through the contents. "On March 22, 2021, Ms. Moss was visited by Jason Weber. On April 10, 2021, Ms. Moss met with Douglas Jones. In May of 2021, William Bartlett paid a visit. July was Conrad Cooper. They're all NAS salesmen."

Alec continued turning pages as he shook his head. His left hand touched the dates of office visits as his other followed the corresponding Deprexone orders. He glanced at Claire in disbelief when the order seemed excessive or the dates too frequent.

"NAS has a lucrative bonus system to increase sales of Deprexone," continued Claire. "The bonuses paid for increased visits to prescribers with high rates of writing Deprexone prescriptions are huge. Last year, the annual bonuses to sales reps averaged over $75,000. NAS paid over $40 million to spread the word on Deprexone."

"Did nobody look at the overdose numbers?" asked Alec. "That comparison would raise a few eyebrows. Patients shouldn't blindly accept prescriptions. They should take ownership of their treatment before an overdose occurs or a lawsuit is filed. They should take some of the responsibility to stop the opioid parade."

Alec grabbed a pen and jotted numbers on a legal pad as he counted on the fingers of his other hand. Claire leaned back in her chair and stretched her legs out straight. She laced her fingers behind her neck and swiveled her chair as she watched Alec's frantic calculations.

"Your naïveté baffles me," said Claire.

"Naïveté?"

"Naïveté. I've lived the opioid reality. The inactions of a family can't be judged."

"I'm not judging. I'm just saying people need to pay attention when they accept these prescriptions."

"Who are you to insinuate they aren't paying attention? You have no idea how much more complicated it is than that."

Claire scooted to the table and leaned onto her elbows. She teepeed her index fingers and leaned into her hands. Her eyes shifted to the metallic artwork displayed on the wall. She stared at the artwork as Alec stared at her.

"The opioid crisis is like a Magic Eye picture," said Claire. "The truth lies underneath. And if you stare long enough, it may be revealed." Claire didn't blink. "This picture is a paradigm of NAS research. Hundreds of patients blur into a hazy mass of names, pains, and opioids. You must fixate on what you see before anything emerges. But you must be prepared because you may not get the truth, and you might not like what appears." Claire fluttered her eyes to hold back her tears.

Alec walked over, sat next to Claire, and took her hand in his. She let him without moving her eyes from the art.

"Are you okay?"

No answer.

Alec leaned into her line of vision. "Do you need to take a break? This case is messing with your head."

"I can't do that." Claire broke her gaze. "It's not the case. I'm getting ambushed by memories."

"What memories?"

"The past."

"All memories are of the past," said Alec. "That's what makes them memories."

"But mine don't want to stay in the past."

"Focus on today. NAS is a morally bankrupt drug manufacturer, and Moss is their dealer. Don't let it get personal."

"It is personal, Alec. We assess their lives, gauge their decisions, measure their progress. Every volunteer who tested Deprexone is judged by us. That's personal."

"That's not what I mean," said Alec.

"I know what you mean. You want to find a pattern of negligence in NAS drug testing, but it makes you uncomfortable if the volunteers get too close."

"We can't let them get close at all."

"They become a part of our lives the moment we walk through those doors. Six degrees of separation, Alec."

"You can't be serious." Alec turned his back to Claire as he read the name listed on an open file.

"I'm more than serious. It's true. Everyone is six, or fewer, social connections away from everyone else."

"You're making it closer than six degrees." Alec flipped back to Claire. "These test subjects aren't your family. Their issues aren't yours."

"They could be. It all comes down to the hand you've been dealt," said Claire. "One trip over a shoelace could've changed your luck, and you'd be in the battle of your life along with them."

Alec moved to a new stack of folders as he and Claire resumed working in silence. Claire's movements revealed the sorrow she felt. Her fingers glided along each line as she read. She whispered their names. She grimaced and smiled and often looked to the ceiling for a break. She squeezed her eyes shut when a break wasn't enough.

While Alec read in haste, Claire gently closed the cover of one file and replaced it with the next. There was precision to her movements and sincere empathy for each patient. She treated every file the same, and every file looked the same. Until one did not.

"Oh, God!" Claire collapsed into the crux of her arm. Her head lay on top of the chart as her chest heaved and her eyes soaked the pages beneath. Alec shot up and rushed to Claire.

"What just happened? What is it?"

"I knew it'd be them," Claire sputtered without lifting her head.

"Who?"

"NAS. They gave her the Zylodone that killed her. I didn't want to think it. But I did. I wanted to be wrong. But I'm not."

Claire slid off the table and wiped her eyes, smearing her mascara. She bit her bottom lip and tasted blood as she slid the damp chart toward Alec. He whispered the words on the smeared page.

"Molly Marie Hewitt." Alec's eyes met Claire's.

"My sister." Claire held her breath as she grabbed the chart from Alec. Salty tears flowed down her cheeks and seeped onto her tongue.

"I'm so sorry," said Alec. "I had no idea." Alec leaned in closer. He wrapped his arm around Claire's shoulder and pulled her to him.

Her labored breathing continued, as did the tears.

"I understand why this is personal for you," said Alec.

"Molly was a world-class gymnast until Zylodone stole it all. It stole everything. It stole Molly." Claire sobbed.

"I'm so sorry."

"They put her on Zylodone in the hospital after her surgery," said Claire. "When she was discharged, they sent it home with her like a new puppy."

"God, that sounds awful." Alec continued rubbing Claire's back as she relived her nightmare with slow sentences and tears.

"Molly was in a lot of pain, and the Zylodone helped in the beginning." Claire pushed away from Alec. "But after a few weeks, Zylodone grew, and Molly shrank. Zylodone kept growing, and Molly kept shrinking. It got bigger and stronger while Molly kept getting smaller and smaller. One day when I looked at Molly, all I saw was Zylodone. The bottle in her hand, the blur in her eyes, the drop in her shoulders. We had lost Molly."

"I have no words," said Alec. "I can't imagine what facing Emma must be like."

"Emma is different," said Claire. "I know that. But in some ways she's not. It's so hard to understand."

"We never understand some things. We accept them."

"I can't do that. The memory of that day ambushes me. It sneaks in to remind me of my mistakes."

"You were a kid when Molly died," said Alec.

"I was there when Molly died."

"There how?"

"There like right there. She needed me. I could have taken those pills from her if I hadn't snuck out, if I hadn't been stupid enough to get drunk, if I hadn't fallen asleep."

Claire placed both hands over her face and let her head drop back. She blinked her eyes through the spaces between her fingers while tears dripped into her ears. She sniveled as moisture puddled above her lip.

"There was nothing you could do, Claire. You were a teenager who knew nothing about the Zylodone Molly was taking."

"I knew Zylodone was the carrot they dangled in front of her when she dreamed of returning to the gym."

"What could you have done? You weren't the one dangling the carrot."

"Why does everyone keep saying that? I saw what Zylodone was doing to her and didn't say anything. If I hadn't crawled into bed, it would all be different. She would be here." Claire leaned forward and cried into her lap.

"Stop." Alec reached for Claire's chin and turned her face toward him. "It was no fault of her own, but Molly became an addict. And addicts are unpredictable. Interventions require a lot of time and a lot of people. Not one afternoon with one sister."

Claire looked down at Molly's chart. She ran her fingers across her name and rubbed each letter. She scratched the word *Zylodone* as if she could scrape it from the page.

"I still can see the look on Molly's face and hear her voice as I crawled into bed. Her eyes begged me not to shut mine. And the fear in her voice still echoes in my ears."

Alec squeezed Claire's shoulder and stood. He collected files and returned them to the proper boxes. He then stacked boxes onto the cart. Claire tucked Molly's chart inside her bag.

"Let's get out of here," said Alec.

"Let's." Claire fluttered her eyes to dry them. "We have all we need to make them pay for killing Emma."

Alec stood behind the cart propped against the open door. Claire walked over to the lab door and pulled. Alec maneuvered the loaded cart through both. They entered the lab amid the familiar mewling of monkeys. Phil Westcott was engaged in menial cage maintenance and talking to the animal inside.

"I don't want those," snapped Phil as he slammed the cage door and turned to Claire.

Alec pushed the cart a few feet farther before Claire pushed back as a signal to stop. She turned to Phil's uplifted chin.

"Take them to Ethan," said Phil. "He's the one who gave them to you."

"We'll leave them right here." Claire let go of the cart.

"Wait one minute! You're not leaving them here!"

"That's exactly where I'm leaving them."

"Oh, no, you're not. I'll call security."

"Call anyone you want." Claire took a step closer to Phil. "You've always rubbed me the wrong way, and today, you're on my last raw nerve."

"I see no reason for your cantankerous attitude, Ms. Hewitt. We've met every one of your unreasonable demands."

Claire's dark stare deepened. "Want to know why I have my cantankerous attitude, Dr. Westcott? Negligent drug testing, hiding test results, and malicious marketing all make me can-tankerous. And dead teenagers make me a real bitch. I'm leaving your damn cart right where it's sitting."

Claire's face was inches from Phil's when Ethan raced in. Phil's lips were spread into a thin, wet line as he stared back at Claire. She didn't blink.

"Stop. Everyone calm down," Ethan begged as he rushed to Phil's side. "This is simply a misunderstanding."

Ethan looked to Alec but received no response. Alec continued watching the confrontation between Claire and Phil. His relaxed expression showed no desire for it to end.

"Enough!" Phil's chest rose and fell. "There is no misunderstanding. You people need to mind your own business and stay out of my laboratory."

Phil stepped back from Claire and jerked his apron straight. With unmasked aggression, he snapped his head toward Ethan. Ethan cowered.

"And you need to stop giving NAS property to every busybody who waltzes in here. There are a lot of people who want to confiscate our discoveries. We must not allow that. We are scientists who conduct research under the strictest of guidelines."

"They had a warrant." Ethan wrapped his arms around his waist. "I had no choice."

"No choice?" said Phil. "The file cabinets in front of you comply with any warrant that comes through that door. Deprex-one research is securely stored in those drawers."

Claire and Alec watched as the showdown shifted to new players. Both men were immersed in a battle over NAS power inside the lab. The old regime was encountering a young, new force.

"I think we're right about Ethan," Claire whispered to Alec. "He helped us in spite of Westcott."

The battle continued with neither man inclined to back down. Ethan had found his voice. And Phil was fighting for the only control he knew.

"That warrant includes everything within these walls, Dr. Westcott."

"Stop talking." Phil stepped within inches of Ethan's face. "The law does not require us to lie down with exposed bellies. We are scientists. And it's our job to protect our priceless discoveries from collusive thieves."

"There are no thieves," said Ethan. "As scientists, we need to protect the people as well as the medications we create. We need to ensure safety before releasing anything. We must have clear sight of what ramifications may occur."

"There is no crystal ball that can predict every consequence," said Phil. "You expect us to continue testing until the same medications have been released by other companies. That equates to bankruptcy for Novo Analgesic Systems."

"Lawsuits equate to bankruptcy. We need to continue testing until safety has been verified."

"Wishful verbiage, young man. Has Mr. Safety developed an extended-release opioid? Has Mr. Safety been published in a scientific journal for releasing a new opioid? Has Mr. Safety had his name attached to any opioid that has helped thousands of people? I think not."

Claire looked over at Alec and motioned with her head. They tiptoed toward the front of the lab while Phil and Ethan spit accusations at each other.

"We just had a front-row seat to the animosity surrounding Deprexone and this lab," said Claire.

"The water is a whole lot clearer. That's for sure." Alec stepped in front of Claire and straight-armed the heavy door. It slammed into an agitated woman attempting to enter.

"Sorry, excuse us." Alec brushed past.

Claire followed Alec as her eyes landed on an agitated Dana Massetti. Claire's shoulders dropped as Dana lifted her chin, and they silently passed. The waters muddied again.

18

Six Degrees of Separation

Alec hustled to the first available cab, oblivious to the tense exchange. He dropped a small box into the trunk and held the door open for Claire.

"Nice work today," said Claire. Her voice was sharp.

Alec stood to the side as Claire climbed into the cab. She scooted across the seat and looked out the front window as the driver adjusted his meter. Her hands gripped the edge of the seat on either side of her thighs.

"I guess we now know NAS isn't as rock solid as Freeman pretends." Alec climbed in and pulled his door closed.

"I guess."

The chilly response silenced Alec. He leaned back and looked out the side window. Fast-moving pedestrians darted between slow-moving cars, and a bicycle raced past with its bell ringing. The driver pulled into traffic.

When they boarded the train back to Philly, Claire grabbed the first available seat. She ignored other passengers and leaned back with closed eyes. Alec settled into the aisle seat across from her.

"There is no scenario that would place that woman in that lab other than the Satori lawsuit." Claire spoke without opening her eyes. "I can't bear the thought."

"I'm not following," said Alec.

Claire responded with silence and closed eyes. Alec looked down at the veins protruding in her hand as she clenched the edge of the black vinyl seat. He watched the rapid movement of her closed eyes.

"There you are," whispered Dana, pausing in the doorway of the law library. Her shrewd eyes were glued to her nemesis. A cunning grin showed on her face as she sauntered up to Claire.

"Well, aren't you a professor's dream. Starting your research already?"

"I'm reading," said Claire. "Do you need something?"

"Then you haven't seen the list."

"Oh shit. Are you kidding me?"

Claire jumped up and slipped through the library to join other law students in front of the white concrete wall. A yellow piece of paper with MOOT COURT in black letters hung next to the door. The competition was listed with two columns of student names. Claire's mouth fell open when she saw hers in vivid letters to the right of Dana Massetti's. Claire slid her hands inside her front pockets and stared at her name as other students cheered or moaned at the position they held. She then weaved back through the crowd, dreading the upcoming exchange.

"Was I right?" chirped Dana.

"It's moot court," said Claire. "Like it matters. It's another hoop to jump through before graduation."

"Moot court with benefits. The winner will compete nationally, and scouts from the big firms will be watching. I plan on dominating that courtroom."

"Go for it." Claire returned to her reading.

"Don't be bitter, Claire. After the first round, we'll both advance. Just in separate brackets. Scouts will be watching both of us."

"Do you need something? Or are you overthinking this for my benefit?"

"I'm being friendly," said Dana.

"Friendly, my ass."

"We both know the moot court competition is rigged." Dana perched on the end of the couch opposite Claire. "The faculty who judge us already have their minds made up. And the practicing attorneys who judge the appellate round don't care who wins. They consider it first-round interviews in disguise."

"What's your point?" asked Claire.

"Winning brings optimal job opportunities. So you better have something extra to offer, if you know what I mean."

"The world's oldest profession." Claire laughed at her own comment.

"Don't kid yourself. You play the game as much as I do. I saw you talking, or should I say flirting, with Dylan Henley in the commons the other day. You know he's a judge."

"I was talking about their first-year internship program."

"Sure you were. He's a partner in my dad's firm and has known me since I was a little girl. He probably thought your flirting was cute."

Claire closed her book and looked out the window adjacent the shelves on her right. Students were walking past or sitting on the edge of the fountain. She bit on her bottom lip, as was her habit when she was nervous or agitated. It was usually the latter with Dana. But Claire didn't want to give Dana the satisfaction of knowing she'd gotten under her skin. She decided leaving was her best option and unzipped her backpack.

"You're leaving?" asked Dana. "Class doesn't start for twenty minutes. We have time to hang. We can discuss other attorneys who can sway the results in our favor. I had a date with Anthony DeMarco last Thursday. This is his first year as a judge."

"A date?" Claire slid her book and a highlighter into her bag.

"Kind of. He graduated from here two years ago, and we were introduced at the Hayes & Hayes open house. He gave me a ride home, and I guess we kind of hooked up." Dana giggled.

"Does he pay well?"

"Grow up, Claire." Dana shot up and towered over Claire. She flipped her hair, as was her habit when provoked. "Women don't have the same opportunities as men. Your A+ on the refrigerator won't land you a great job. Won't land you any job."

"There are different ways to land a job." Claire stood to join Dana. "My skill set is a little different from yours."

"Bullshit. We're all taught from the beginning to create our own opportunities, to set goals and design a path for getting there."

"Is bed-hopping the first path that comes to mind?"

"Nobody's hopping anywhere," said Dana. "And don't act like you've never taken the path of least resistance."

"Are there a lot of partners from daddy's firm on that path with you?"

"Screw you." Dana's arms swung wide in her dramatic turn from Claire. "You do what you want. I always land on my feet."

"On your feet or on your back?"

Papers slipped from Claire's wet palm. Her eyes shot open when the pages slid down her shin. She grabbed them off her shoe as she looked over to see if Alec had noticed. He did and laughed.

"You were talking in your sleep."

"I was not."

"Were too. Mumbled something about confetti."

"Oh shit." Claire rolled her eyes. "More like *Massetti*. She was the woman we passed leaving the lab."

"That was her? Why didn't you say something?"

"What was there to say?"

"Alec, let me introduce you to Ms. Massetti?"

"You don't want to meet that woman." Claire rolled her eyes again.

"Does she work there?"

"What do you think? She was visiting a friend? That's what she's been hiding. I can't get over the way she played me. Peeled back layers of my career the other night without revealing anything about hers. Asked if there are any hot scientists in the lab."

"You didn't ask her about where she works?"

"Of course I did. But she was evasive. I didn't suspect anything. I was curious. No, I was being polite. I couldn't have cared less about her job. But she couldn't get enough of mine."

"Imagine that." Alec shared his boyish grin. "Now we both have friends at NAS."

"That woman is not my friend."

"Do you think she's in Westcott's pocket like the rest of them?"

"Or he's in hers. She has a PhD in physics or neurology or something like that. Had it when she came to law school."

"Why law school?"

"She was a professional student. Needed another degree on her wall. She must be their in-house counsel. No other explanation."

"Can we maneuver her to our benefit, like Shaggy?" asked Alec.

"Not a chance. She helps no one, especially not me."

"Not a Claire Hewitt fan?"

"The opposite. That woman despises me." Claire flipped

through the NAS documents she held. "She omitted her damn name from these documents."

"That's a whole new level of bizarre. A handful of people with curious connections meandering around a couple of dead teenagers. From different generations."

"Six degrees of separation," said Claire. "It's a thing."

"Urban myth.'"

"Myth or not, it went viral. Three students at Albright College got ahold of it and invented the game 'Six Degrees of Kevin Bacon.' Google jumped in, making it possible to find your 'Bacon number' through their search engine. I'm serious."

"I know you are," said Alec. "I have a bacon number, but it deals more with the pig than the actor."

"We all have that number." Claire returned the documents to her bag.

"I admit that most people have a connection to someone else," said Alec as he shifted on his hip toward Claire. "It's called the fabric of life. Threads of different colors."

"Molly was the brightest thread in my fabric. I think about her every day but never thought I'd find her in that lab."

"I bet not." Alec reached across and placed his hand on Claire's forearm. She looked down at his hand and placed hers on top.

"Or run into Massetti," said Claire. "She shows up from out of nowhere and meanders in and out of everywhere. You never get a clear picture with her. I feel like I'm playing *Where's Waldo*, and if I look long enough, I'll find Dana hiding in the details."

"They say the devil's in the details," laughed Alec.

Claire looked out the window beside her. Tall brick buildings and simple wooden houses passed by under the rhythmic hum of the train. Busy streets, crowded playgrounds, and a few stray cats going about their lives as hundreds of strangers caught a brief glimpse of the activity. Children rode bicycles or threw balls as playful dogs chased anything that moved.

Claire leaned back and closed her eyes for the remainder of the ride. She needed to be prepared for Dana Massetti yet not distracted by her presence. There was a reason for Dana's deception about her involvement with NAS, and Claire feared when it might be revealed.

19

PRIZE
MONEY

"What is it you don't get?" asked Ethan. "Boundaries are crucial."

"Science has no boundaries. I'm disappointed you're not aware of that by now." Phil wiped the paw pads of the capuchin he held.

"Jail cells have boundaries. Thick iron boundaries." Ethan ran his hand through his unkempt hair and waited for Phil to react.

"Don't be an alarmist." Phil closed his eyes and dipped his chin.

"I'm more than alarmed," said Ethan. "We've been hashing this out for months. Every stage needs to test a specific number of randomly selected volunteers before the drug progresses. That's Science 101."

"That's your problem. This lab isn't Science 101. Novo Analgesic Systems far exceeds 101, 201, or whatever *01* you want to give it."

"Is that your moral code? Addiction is the ugly stepchild. So let's hide her in the attic. It's not right, and I'll put an end to it."

"You won't put an end to anything except your career," snapped Phil. "Is that what you want? When I went to Jack Freeman, I was under the impression I was hiring a precocious young scientist. Not a timid coward."

"My research is far from timid."

"What research?" said Phil. "You're hanging on my shirttail and puffing your chest because those attorneys have been stroking your ego since August. This is a clean lab."

"A clean lab with a corpse in the corner?"

"That reckless teenager doesn't sully this lab."

"Rushing an opioid to market sullies this lab," said Ethan.

"Listen to yourself. Because we don't run needless tests on successful medications searching for adverse reactions, you call it rushing? You've seen the results. They're solid."

"A handful of randoms. Other results show Deprexone needs more testing."

"When do we stop?" asked Phil as he tossed the capuchin back into its cage.

The small animal landed on top of another drinking from an attached water bottle. The two tussled over the nozzle until the first one resumed drinking. Phil watched the exchange with little concern.

"We stop testing when it proves safe," said Ethan. "I'm not jeopardizing my reputation and my career because some egomaniac wants to make a name for himself."

"I already have a name for myself," said Phil. "You have neither a name nor a reputation. And you certainly don't have a career."

Phil opened an adjacent cage door and thrust his hand inside. He flapped his hand around, searching for the animal, and then bent down to look. A small tamarin was pressed to the back wall with wide eyes and an open mouth. Phil slammed the cage door, grabbed the journals that sat on top, and turned back to Ethan.

"I won't stand for insubordination in my lab. Hundreds of pharmacology techs would love to be in your shoes, and I can make that happen. After all the opportunities I've given you, this is how you repay me?"

"Repay you? If I owe my job to anyone, it's Jack Freeman. It's his name on my paycheck."

"Jack knows nothing about how this laboratory operates," said Phil.

"Perhaps he should be enlightened?"

Phil dropped his arms, and several copies of *Advanced Drug Therapy* slipped from his grip. His eyes watered as he faced Ethan's unbridled challenge to his authority.

"I will not allow your immature ideology to jeopardize my research and sabotage this company." Phil spoke slowly. "I don't know what your intent is, but I can *guar-an-damn-tee* you that nobody is going to stand by and watch you make a mockery of this lab. I refuse to let that happen."

"My intent is to hold this lab to a higher standard," said Ethan.

"There is no higher standard. I'm a pharmacology icon. My research has been published internationally for over a decade."

"I'm well aware of that. Your name is plastered all over the journals. But it's appeared in a few federal judgments as well." Ethan shoved both hands into his pockets and took one step closer to Phil. "You've flooded the market with controversial medications in the past, and there are people waiting for you to do it again. Perhaps Deprexone is the icon's next big mistake?"

"I don't make big mistakes. I find cures in places others haven't considered looking." Phil straightened the collar of his lab coat as sweat beaded in the gray hair at his temples.

"Are those cures worth the risk?" asked Ethan.

"Everything in life involves risk." Phil stepped closer to Ethan and stopped within inches of his florid face. Ethan's eyes watered as he inhaled the foul breath.

"What in the hell is happening!"

Both men jumped as a deafening voice shot into the lab.

"Someone had better enlighten me. How is it that we've spent months building a defense and now that we're in the middle of October with a trial in a matter of days, I'm being sabotaged? I want answers!"

Dana threw her briefcase onto an empty table as she marched toward Ethan and Phil. Phil picked up the journals that lay at his feet and turned to face Dana. He clutched the journals to his chest and waited. Ethan stood behind him with silent worry on his face.

"I'm hauled into court and challenged at every turn while you two pass out NAS research like candy at a carnival," said Dana. "Can either of you explain that to me?"

"I handed out nothing," said Phil.

"Interesting. Last time I checked, you were in charge of this lab."

"I'm in charge of medical research. Others sneak around in the shadows searching for false praise." Phil scowled at Ethan. "You don't see their true colors until it's too late."

Phil placed the pharmacology journals on the file cart next to him. With Dana's eyes following his every move, Phil continued with his work. He slipped past Ethan to grab a clipboard and several charts. He reviewed the charts and added them to the top of the clipboard.

"Someone has dillydallied long enough. There's work to be done." Phil flipped his head to Ethan.

"One of you had better tell me what information Hewitt has," said Dana over the sound of her phone ringing. "Excuse me. I need to get this."

Dana turned from the men with her phone pressed against her ear. She mostly listened but spat salacious rebuttals in between long pauses. Ethan turned his head to Phil, who shrugged his shoulders in response.

"Sounds like she's on someone's bad side," said Phil.

"Maybe it's Freeman."

"Why would she be on Freeman's bad side?"

"She's not as honest as she looks, and maybe he found out."

"Found out what?"

"That she's been submitting receipts for research projects that haven't been funded or conducted."

"And you know this how?" asked Phil.

"I have friends in accounting. I was in the elevator and was asked about a project and a receipt for a large order. Typical stuff we frequently request, so they didn't question it."

"How big?"

"To the tune of ten grand."

Phil kept his eyes on Ethan as he unlocked the cage beside him and reached inside. His hand tapped around the floor of the cage before pulling out a gray pygmy mouse lemur. He brought the two inches of fur to his cheek and rubbed it against his face. He continued to shake his head as if trying to understand.

"I acted surprised that they were familiar with the research," said Ethan. "That opened the door for them to gush about knowing how research is funded in this lab. She's been submitting fake receipts for some time."

"I'm not leaving until I get answers!"

Both men fell silent at the sound of the repeated demand.

As Dana returned to her underlings, Phil bent toward the open cage and opened the palm of his hand. The small gray puff of fur scurried out. Once inside its familiar home, the lemur stopped, and two large eyes looked back at Phil. Ethan stepped to a new cabinet and resumed filing.

"Hewitt barged in here sometime last winter, barked about a lawsuit, and we gave her Deprexone crap." Ethan spoke quietly. "What we gave her wasn't enough. Last Wednesday, or whenever it was, she showed up with her sidekick and a warrant requesting access to every opioid developed."

"What did you give them?"

"The warrant required—"

"I know what a warrant requires," interrupted Dana. "But I also know what they don't require. Warrants are narrowly drawn, requesting specific information. What did you give them?"

"We gave them information on opioid development, as requested." Ethan glanced at Phil in a plea for help.

"I gave them nothing." Phil grabbed the end of the cart and shoved Ethan. "I had nothing to do with it."

"I gave them what's required by law." Ethan didn't shove back.

"You showered them with confidential information. I can trust no one!" Phil shoved Ethan again.

"You released Deprexone too early," said Ethan. "And don't take out your trust issues on me. I'm the only honest one in here."

Dana's eyes glowed with repressed anger as Ethan gripped the metal bars of the cart. Phil's wrath was more fervent, and he shoved the cart a third time. Ethan staggered back.

"I understand your zealous desire for perfection." Dana walked to her briefcase while she lectured. Her steps were more relaxed than they had been. And her tone softened. She swung the briefcase onto the end of the cart. "But you must understand that competition in the pharmaceutical industry is fierce. It's imperative that marketing departments create unique strategies to promote newly developed medications. Creativity is a must." She clicked the locks.

"Creativity or lies?" asked Ethan as he walked away from Dana and the cart.

"The release of new medications is like a Thoroughbred race," said Dana. "There's minimal prize money for second place and a negligible return for showing."

"How much prize money is there for dead?"

Phil's anger reared its head again as he listened to Ethan's remarks. He slammed the clipboard onto the top of a nearby cage, then winced at his own actions. He bent over and peeked inside as the tamarins huddled together.

"It doesn't work like that," said Dana, frustration growing in her voice. "The FDA supports the development of new medications. The positive results in the file cabinets in the front of the lab indicate Deprexone is successful."

"Successful doesn't mean safe," said Ethan. "The FDA wouldn't find it safe if they reviewed the research stored in the back room. And the marketing is a blatant lie."

"There are no lies," Dana shot back. "Positive outcomes occur when using Deprexone as prescribed."

"Oh, geez," said Ethan. "We're pill pushers. More pills equals more money. Other companies have faced huge fines from the FDA for doing the same thing."

Phil's head dropped back with a muffled gasp. Squeezing the rolled journals in his fist, his head shot up, and he slapped Ethan. Dana's jaw dropped as Ethan turned around and shoved Phil with both hands. Phil stumbled back into a cage. A series of high-pitched squeals responded.

"You have no idea, you ignorant moron," said Phil. "Deprexone is administered under strict protocol."

Dana stepped in between the two men. Phil stood in front of the squealing cage while Ethan held on to the cart. Dana gripped each of them by their biceps and pressed her long nails into their pale skin. She glared at them angrily through squinted eyes as her lips turned upward with amusement.

"You two are ridiculous," said Dana. "We're not facing FDA fines; we're being sued by a vindictive millionaire who can't accept his daughter's mistakes. Deprexone is a safe opioid and your concerns are irrational." Dana threw their arms out of her hands.

"I don't think the Satoris would find my concerns irrational." Ethan rubbed the redness on his arm.

"The Satoris are looking for a scapegoat." Dana reached into her briefcase. "These are the medical records that girl brought with her. She was a mess. You can't blame Deprexone."

"I don't want those," said Ethan as he turned away from Dana. "Send them over to marketing. Let them put a new spin on them."

"There's no spin." Dana slipped off her jacket and tossed it over the cart. Light patches of sweat showed under each arm and down the middle of her back. "Emma chose not to follow the instructions she was given. That doesn't shift the blame to us."

"Our marketing propaganda creates delusions that Deprexone will eliminate pain without addiction. We've shoved it down every throat we could find. Those misrepresentations shift the blame to us." Ethan lifted Dana's jacket and grabbed the charts underneath. "You can't argue with that."

"That's a trendy bandwagon," said Dana. "Make sure you see the big picture before jumping on. Every shitty practitioner wants to blame someone else. We've done our job and protected ourselves. The financial buffer we have from releasing Deprexone when we did is a lifeline when someone doesn't like the outcome because of their own misjudgments."

"Emma lost her life to be a lifeline?" Ethan's skeptical eyes bounced between Dana and Phil as hostility weaved around them. At a loss for words, he dropped his eyes in defeat while Dana glared and Phil gloated.

20

· · · · · · ●●● ● ●●●● · · · · ·

IATROGENIC
ADDICTION

Standing motionless with hands cupping her hips, Claire examined the elaborate display board as Alec stumbled in like a discombobulated librarian.

"According to the CDC, the number of people who died from opioid overdoses from 1999 to 2021 was over half a million," said Claire as she glanced over but paid little attention to Alec's balancing act. "With Novo Analgesic Systems at the helm."

Alec dropped the awkward stack of books onto the table and collapsed into a chair. With closed eyes, he dropped his forehead onto his folded arms.

"They advocate for the use of Deprexone in the nonmalignant pain market," Claire continued. "This promotion contributed to a nearly tenfold increase in Deprexone prescriptions for chronic pain. Prescriptions jumped from 670,000 to 6.2 million."

"I'm surprised the increase wasn't larger." Alec didn't look up. "Their marketing department initiated a patient coupon program to increase the number of prescriptions. It's the first time a drug manufacturer offered patients a free limited-time prescription for a seven-day to thirty-day supply."

"I'm surprised it's legal to hand out free opioids with the intention of persuading people to purchase more of them." Claire turned to the sound of Alec's muffled voice. "What's wrong with you?"

"I feel awful."

"Then why are you here? You should've stayed home."

"Couldn't. Boss would've had my head."

"Funny. Go home. Nobody wants to breathe your contagions."

"I don't have any contagions, and that's not a real word."

"You do, and it is. Several people are home with the flu. Get out of here."

"I'll be fine."

Alec crawled out of his seat and approached the display board. He braced himself against the table's edge as he glanced at the pages outlining Claire's argument. The front of his shirt stuck to his sweaty chest. Claire grabbed the papers and took several steps back.

"The commercial success wasn't dependent upon the merits of the drug compared with other available opioids." Alec pinched the bridge of his nose. "In evaluating the efficacy of Deprexone in the IND application, the FDA's medical review officer concluded that Deprexone had not been shown to have a significant advantage over conventional, immediate-release opioids other than frequency in dosing."

"That was NAS's initial hook and the first point of my argument." Claire walked around the table to put more distance between Alec and herself. "Frequency in dosing makes all the difference. People feel less dependent upon a drug if they aren't opening the bottle as often."

"Second hook is the guarantee that the extended-release

formulation decreased the addiction rate to less than 1 percent." Alec returned to his seat and dropped his head back onto his folded arms. "When we win the Freeman case, that verdict will magnify Delaney's obligation to monitor his patients."

Claire rifled through a thick manila folder and returned to the board. She stapled two new documents beside the existing material and stood back again. Alec looked up but didn't stand.

"Drug Delivery Resulting in Death," said Claire. "We prosecute Delaney under that statute. It's the climax of my argument."

"Pennsylvania leads the nation in prosecuting overdose deaths as homicides under the DDRD law. I submitted briefs to the Second Circuit on that issue." Alec placed his forearms on the table. "But most cases dealt with low-level drug dealers. A doctor?"

"Why not?" said Claire. "Over a quarter of the drug-induced homicide cases nationwide are filed right here in the commonwealth, and 3 percent of those cases were against doctors. The door is wide open."

Claire studied the evidence. She used a yellow highlighter to emphasize points of interest and a black Sharpie to chronologize her argument. She stood back to study the board and rearranged supporting evidence to better align with the numbers she had written. She mumbled to herself, paying little attention to Alec.

"I understand wanting to be a trailblazer," said Alec. "But won't the jury be inclined to give Delaney leeway because he possesses a medical degree?"

"That's where iatrogenic addiction comes into play. It's another branch to hang a guilty verdict on and will erase any inclination to cut the good doctor some slack. It'll shine a spotlight directly on him."

"What the hell is iatro-whatever you said?"

"Emma died from it." Claire tossed research from the *Journal of Pain* to Alec and turned back to her displayed evidence. "Iatrogenic addiction is addiction caused by the medical treatment itself. She wasn't a street addict taking illicit drugs. She made a doctor's appointment for postoperative care and was prescribed the opioids that caused her addiction and her death."

"Defense won't buy it," said Alec. "Sims will claim Emma's addictive behavior was the cause of her addiction. He'll point to her personality and poor decisions as the reason Delaney can't be held accountable. He'll compare it to prosecuting the gun in a murder trial."

Alec read the research Claire tossed him as he tugged on his damp shirt to loosen it from his hot skin. His cheeks were flushed. Claire looked back and forth between the argument she held and the evidence stapled to the board.

"You could be right, but the Satoris will strike a nerve with every juror harboring a negative medical outcome. Malpractice insurance shows how quickly patients turn on their doctors." Claire turned to face Alec. "Did you take your temperature before you trudged in here? I can't afford to get sick."

"You're not going to get sick." Alec drank from the water bottle he'd brought in with the books and wiped the back of his hand across his mouth. "Malpractice claims signify patient disapproval when monetary compensation is a possibility. The jury will have no monetary investment. Will they be willing to stand up against the almighty MD?"

"If they empathize more with the Satoris than Delaney." Claire dropped into a chair.

"We can build a moral chasm between the two," said Alec. "One the jury couldn't justify crossing."

"Not until the succubus paints the Satoris as neglectful parents and Delaney as an altruistic hero trying to save the poor girl."

"Who?"

"Dana Massetti."

"Why would Massetti be at the trial?" asked Alec as he wiped the sweat from his temples with his fingertips.

"Because she's in-house counsel for NAS."

"But she recused herself from this case because of her involvement in the development of Deprexone."

"She'll be there," said Claire. "Sims may be leading the litigation. But she'll have a front-row seat."

"Since she has some connection to the lab, maybe she'll be a witness? We could dismantle her on cross-examination."

"There's no dismantling of Dana Massetti. She'll be batting her eyes, flipping her hair, performing for the entire courtroom. I've seen it before. She's quite good."

"I've seen the likes of her also. More concerned with how she comes across than telling the truth, the whole truth, and nothing but the truth." Alec laughed.

"It's all image with her. And she'll destroy anyone who tries to tarnish it."

"Poor Landon."

"Poor everyone."

21

●∘●∘●∘●●●●◉●●●●∘●∘●∘●

OVERPROMOTED AND OVERPRESCRIBED

D ana pressed her palm onto the black square. As the blue beam swept across the screen, the pocket door slid open. Ethan followed with a mixed assortment of research material. He stopped at the first file cabinet and did a balancing act with one arm. Dana placed her laptop on an adjacent table and flipped it open. The two worked in silent tolerance until the door slid open a second time.

"Nice try." A manila folder flew into the room followed by an indignant Phil Westcott. The folder struck Ethan's shoulder, fell to the floor, and spilled its contents.

"What the hell?" Ethan looked down at the folder.

"Don't play innocent with me. That research belongs in this room, as do the rest of these." Phil slapped several more folders against Ethan's chest. They all fell to the floor.

"Who's going to pick those up?" Ethan looked down at the scattered papers.

"You are. You're the careless one who left them lying around. I'm guessing in hopes that Hewitt would stumble upon them."

"I have no time to play guessing games around some attorney," said Ethan. "And as you can see, I was filing updated research when you stormed in all crazy."

"All crazy? It's called protecting my research," snapped Phil.

"From big scary Hewitt?" Ethan contorted his face.

"For the love, will you two knock it off?" Dana slammed her laptop shut. "I don't give a damn about who left what where. Confidential information was leaked, and we need to get it back."

"You can't just ask for it back." Phil picked up the folders he threw at Ethan.

"I'm not going to ask for anything. I know what I'm doing, but I had better not find either of you playing both sides."

Dana and Phil both looked at Ethan. Phil raised his eyebrows in accusation, while Dana's face was expressionless. Ethan continued cramming files into overstuffed drawers as he ignored his two companions.

"We've been through this before." Dana spoke directly to Phil. "I've protected NAS from jealous manufacturers and skeptical physicians. We've always remained on top. Why is it that the Satoris' legal posse waltzes in and every opioid is being second-guessed?"

"Ask Ethan."

Dana glanced at Ethan but stepped closer to Phil. She slid her reading glasses off her nose and held them loosely by her side. Phil shoved both hands into his lab coat pockets. The front of the coat vibrated from Phil's fluttering fingers.

"That bitch sticks her nose into every research decision made. She disputes the validity of processes she doesn't understand and questions the integrity of everyone involved. You're in charge of this lab. She better not find so much as a monkey in the wrong cage."

Dana walked out. Phil watched the door slide shut as the

clicking of her heels echoed through the laboratory. The sharp clicks coincided with the opening and closing of cabinets and drawers. Phil dropped into Dana's warm chair and examined the work she left behind. Ethan continued filing.

"The FDA's Center for Drug Evaluation and Research determined that the health benefits of Deprexone outweigh any known risks." Dana burst back through the door with a deep frown and full arms. She emptied her arms but held on to the frown. "They evaluated Phil's monkeys, our human test subjects, and the current treatment landscape. No other treatment options were found to be superior."

Phil's jaw dropped. "I tested many species of primates before moving onto human subjects. They evaluated more than the monkeys."

"Stay with me. Both of you." Dana tapped her fingertips together and waited for the undivided attention of both men. "Ethan."

Phil nudged Ethan in the ribs as he kept his wide eyes on Dana. Ethan took in a deep breath and pushed the last drawer shut. Letting a loud puff of air escape from his mouth, he turned to face his opposition.

"Although health benefits outweigh the risks, the potential for abuse is still present," said Dana. "The Satoris claim that potential increases because Deprexone is overpromoted and overprescribed."

"It's not overprescribed," said Phil. "It's often prescribed because it's effective. I developed a thorough risk evaluation and mitigation strategy to identify and manage known risks. We're fine."

"The hell we are," said Dana. "The FDA's risk-benefit assessment found that the benefits and risks with Deprexone are difficult to predict when used for chronic pain."

"The risks are spelled out on every label," said Phil.

"They're overshadowed by the marketing."

Dana and Phil argued the merits of the REMS implementation versus the robust advertising that thrust Deprexone into the national spotlight. Ethan leaned against the file cabinet with annoyance lingering behind his bloodshot eyes. He added nothing to their debate and reached around Phil to pick up a document Dana had dropped.

"That's your next project," said Dana.

She ended her debate with Phil and grabbed the paper from Ethan. Turning back to the table, she divided an assortment of publications into two piles. She slid one in front of Phil and scooted the other toward Ethan. Silence lingered in the stale air of the small room as both men looked from Dana to the publications.

"You both need to remember that while opioids have become the drug of the day, regulated medications aren't the only popular painkillers out there. The streets are rampant with illicit opioids. Heroin and fentanyl are everywhere."

"Fentanyl is not in this laboratory." Phil's slow headshake increased to a rapid vibration as his brows squeezed into a deep scowl. "I have no need for a synthetic opioid that potent."

"Doesn't need to be in this lab," said Dana. "Opioid users first jumped to heroin. It was cheaper than an opioid prescription and easier to come by. As far back as 2010, there were over 650,000 heroin addicts."

"What does fentanyl have to do with heroin addicts?" asked Phil.

"Everything. Fentanyl is fifty times more potent than heroin. So a small amount of heroin goes a long way when laced with fentanyl. It's a bigger bang for the buck."

An overwrought Phil dropped his eyes to the floor as his

head continued to shake. Ethan pushed off the file cabinet and stepped closer to the information Dana had shoved toward him. He lifted the top copy and shook his head much the same as Phil.

"The publications in front of you contain statistical data on illegal drug use in the United States," Dana continued. "According to the data you're going to read, reports on fentanyl increased from 5,400 in 2014 to over 56,500 in 2017. The borders to our south are a shit show."

"What does that have to do with us or this lawsuit?" asked Ethan.

"Let me spell it out for you. Emma was amplifying her Deprexone scrip with recreational fun. Maybe heroin. Maybe fentanyl. We aren't sure."

"What?" Phil's head popped up. "How did you come up with that?"

"Based on the statistics you'll find in the information I brought you, Emma was experimenting. We'll let defense counsel know this is new data we uncovered. It's information that can't be ignored and creates tremendous doubt as to whether Deprexone was a contributor to Emma's death."

"Oh, no." Ethan shoved his pile to the middle of the small table and stepped away. "I'm not making up shit about Emma when this room is full of research showing the addictive nature of Deprexone."

"I'm not asking you to make up anything." Dana pushed the documents back. "I'm asking that you read the publications clarifying addiction issues in the United States."

"In what way do these publications explain why we put Deprexone test results showing minimal risk of addiction in the front file cabinets and test results revealing high addiction rates in this room?" Ethan leaned on the table over the stack of publications.

"We don't need to explain our filing system. We need to acknowledge the information we already know. Illicit and legal opioids are linked."

"They are. But there has been no indication that Emma was taking illicit opioids."

"You don't know that she wasn't," said Dana. "The information I've given you shows that illicit opioids are in every high school in America. I guarantee that Emma was exposed to them. Reasonable doubt is everywhere."

"Your defense strategy is painting Emma as an illicit drug user?" Ethan walked to the sliding door and flattened both hands against the wall, resting his forehead against the hard surface.

"I'm not painting anyone," said Dana. "Mr. Sims needs reasonable doubt, and you're going to give it to him."

At the sound of the command, Ethan pushed away from the wall. He walked the short distance to Dana in four long strides. A silent Phil Westcott jumped to the side. Ethan towered over the small woman as he looked down at her full ruby lips and unblinking eyes.

"Tell me you're joking," he said.

"I don't joke, Ethan. I win."

"Winning a battle doesn't mean much if you don't win the war." Ethan lowered his menacing voice. "Sims may win this lawsuit for NAS, but I know the truth about what you're doing to this company. According to my friends in accounting, you're not the hero you pretend to be."

Dana dropped her shoulders and lifted her defiant chin. She took a deep breath and exhaled as Ethan stood solid. Phil cowered on the opposite end of the table.

"Satoris' allegations are unfounded," said Dana as she brushed past Ethan and sat down. "The court will find Deprexone is a safe opioid for chronic pain."

Dana spoke to both men as her unmoving eyes stared at the screen of her laptop. Her words and breathing were deep and slow. Ethan watched her from behind.

"I need evidence of reasonable doubt Monday," said Dana, having regained her composure.

"Monday?" asked Phil. "You do joke."

"Bring everything to my place Monday at noon. No, make that 1:00. We'll discuss how our strategy will play out and review my expectations for this lab."

"I think your defense strategy is weak," said Phil as he watched Dana watch Ethan. "Looks like we're grasping at straws."

"Grasping at straws or saving your job?"

"Saving my job?"

"All I know is that when Sims and I walk into that courtroom, he'll present evidence showing Deprexone is a safe opioid. Unfortunate outcomes can occur when taking any medication. But that in no way makes the manufacturer negligent. Are we all in agreement?"

"Not sure that's possible." Ethan's eyes were hard but his voice soft.

"You have two choices," said Dana. "Either defend the company that hired you or move on. If we can't rely on you to exonerate Novo Analgesic Systems, then we have no need for you."

"You can rely on us. Both of us." Phil scooted along the table and wrapped his arm around Ethan's shoulder. He pulled him in with a light tug as he offered Dana his signature tight-lipped grin. Ethan didn't smile.

"Today has illustrated that we're not on the same page, gentlemen. I'm fine with healthy discussions. But it's confrontation I won't tolerate. Ethan, you're an asset to this lab, but not irreplaceable." Dana looked over her shoulder as she made her way to exit the room. "The information you bring Monday will determine not only the success of this lawsuit but your future with NAS." As she continued out the pocket door, she yelled one final directive without looking back. "Don't show up early. I have a full morning."

Dana settled into the back seat of the cab, alternating between daydreaming and paging through Deprexone data. City traffic was light, so the ride time was shorter than expected. She crammed the documents into her briefcase as the cab pulled up to Penn Station. With the speed of a seasoned commuter, she rushed through the gate with her ticket in hand, jumped on board, and dropped into the first available seat. A clean-shaven businessman in the adjacent seat chuckled as she shoved her briefcase under her seat and opened a *Vogue* magazine.

"Don't judge me. You have no idea."

"No judging."

"Resting my brain before the next scene." Dana flipped past the first page.

"You're an actress?"

"Attorney."

"Heading to trial?"

"Not yet." Dana turned another page. "But this case is no more than a game, and I am a much better player. I have no intention of allowing the gumption of another woman to derail my success. The guise of gratitude from a mysterious adversary can be an amazing weapon if delivered properly." Dana gave a shoulder shrug to the acceptable stranger and ended the conversation with the turn of another page.

The train pulled into Thirtieth Street Station as Dana closed the magazine. She hurried off the train, darted to the closest cab, and settled into the back seat with a briefcase of useless information. As she jumped from the cab in front of the historic Blackman & Bradford building, two familiar attorneys walked through the revolving door. Dana ducked her head the opposite way and let them unknowingly pass. Once her fear of recognition abated, she entered the building with head held high and energy to spare.

"I have a meeting scheduled with Claire Hewitt," Dana informed the receptionist.

"I'll let her know you're here."

Dana perched on the edge of an oversized leather chair in the elegant reception area. She admired the expensive paintings adorning each wall and studied every detail of her surroundings. Claire stepped off the elevator moments later and cringed at the sight.

"Hello again. Twice in one month." Claire offered her right hand.

"Guess we're lucky." Dana reached past Claire's outstretched hand with open arms. The embrace was rigid. "And look at this place. It's exquisite."

"Thank you. Why the impromptu visit?"

"Guilt." Dana slid her hand down Claire's arm and held on to her hand. "I rushed out too quickly when we were at Bin 402. And it didn't dawn on me until I saw you leaving the NAS lab."

"What didn't dawn on you?"

"My impertinence." Dana let go of Claire's hand and slowed her delivery. "I work for Novo Analgesic Systems and never mentioned it. I hope you're not offended."

"Seriously? It would take more than impertinence to offend me," said Claire.

"I hoped so. Because I'm in-house counsel for NAS." Dana reached for Claire's hand again. "This could be fun. Like the old days when we were on opposing sides."

"Something like that." Claire stepped back in an obvious attempt to end the unpleasant visit.

"You are offended. I knew you would be. That's why I came in person. I'm taking the high road to make up for it."

"High road? This is an exaggerated production. You're taking an entire afternoon to accomplish what a simple phone call would have done."

"I'm giving you a heads-up."

"You could have done that with a phone call. Why are you here?"

"These."

Dana handed Claire a stack of folders and stepped back with a childish grin. Claire attempted to smile, but her lips formed more of a sneer.

"What are these?" asked Claire.

"Peace offering. Landon Sims missed them when he was collecting data from our lab, so I volunteered to be the delivery girl."

"Thank you. You didn't need to do that."

"It was a good excuse to make sure you weren't offended and to see your office. Are you on the corner already? If it's anything like this reception area, it's to die for. I bet—"

"You don't want to see my office." Claire cut Dana short in another futile attempt to end the forced encounter.

"Yes, I do!"

"It looks like the office of every other overworked attorney. And you better catch the next train back to the city."

"I can take the late one," said Dana. "I'm in no rush."

"The late one is a nightmare. You'll be standing the whole way."

"Don't be ridiculous." Dana grabbed Claire's arm in a forced move toward the elevator. "Which floor are you on? The top?"

"Okay, I give." Claire surrendered to Dana's demands. "You'll get your tour if it will pacify your curiosity." Claire looked down at Dana's arm wrapped around her own.

Dana displayed exaggerated interest and peeked into every open door to admire the décor. She commented on the colors, artwork, and furniture in each office.

"You must give me the name of your designer. The way she combines gray with whatever that reddish color is. It's breathtaking."

"Firestick."

"That's your designer?"

"That's the color. Blaine Drake is our designer."

"BD Interiors." Dana stuck her head into another office. "I should have known from the unique combinations. I adore that sapphire rug."

"That was Blaine's first suggestion," said Claire.

"Her progressive approach is breathtaking."

"Thanks, I probably should get back to work."

"Of course. I've taken too much of your time."

Claire accompanied Dana back to the lobby as Dana continued to survey everything she passed. She paused at open doorways and peeked around corners with overplayed curiosity. At one point, she let go of Claire's arm and scurried to a window to peer out.

"Thank you for the additional information," said Claire as they approached the front door. "Godspeed on your trip back."

"Thanks for the tour. Now I can picture where you are when we're on the phone. Talk soon, doll."

Dana embraced Claire one last time before darting out the door. She waved her hand in the air and skipped to the nearest cab. Energetic waves through the back window concluded their meeting.

22

RED
BLOSSOMS

"**N**ice!"

"Sandbagger," mumbled Claire.

"Am not. I warned you." Alec wiped his fingers across the white headband that was keeping the sweat from his eyes.

Claire bounced back and forth on the balls of her feet as Alec tossed the tennis ball in his left hand. The moment hung in the air like a starting gun. The ball shot over the net to Claire's left side. She gripped her racquet with both hands and returned the ball to the far corner. Alec sprang sideways, swung, and missed.

Alec led five games to four when the sound of a chirpy ringtone blared through the air. Claire finished the volley before running off the court. She grabbed her phone, checked the number, and tossed it back into her bag unanswered.

"Massetti." Claire stuck out her tongue as she jogged back to the court.

"Damn. She never gives up."

Claire swayed back and forth at the baseline, gripping the

yellow ball in her hand. Alec's eyes were glued to her racquet as he lightly bounced on the opposite side.

"Thirty–fifteen." Claire served.

The animated rivalry was a reassuring diversion. As pre-trial pressure increased, endorphins were best found outside the office. Claire and Alec both grabbed waters after Claire won the second set.

"We need a third set." Alec bounced a ball on his racquet as he spoke.

"That's the last thing we need," said Claire. "Our careers won't survive skipping the entire day."

"Nobody will notice."

"Everyone will notice."

"You're not that important."

"Maybe you're not." Claire threw a ball at Alec. "We need to start prepping our witnesses."

"We can prep after a third set. Mondays suck. And how many days do we get like this in October?"

"We don't have time. Massetti dropped off some dubious paperwork. Doubt it'll amount to anything, but we can't ignore it."

"Sure we can."

"It may be their backdoor attempt to get evidence into the record that we don't want in there."

"We'll look at it. One more set."

Alec continued bouncing the tennis ball as he walked back to the service line. Claire moaned and ran to the opposite side of the court. It was a grueling forty-five minutes with short rallies and no aces. Claire won the last set.

"Are there any limits to what you're willing to do?" asked Ethan. "That woman has you wrapped around her little finger." Ethan stood with his chest inflated and his feet apart. His arms were folded across his chest. He blocked Phil's path and looked intent on standing his ground.

"Do you have a better answer?" asked Phil.

"Any answer would be better."

"Do the math, young man. Seventeen million people use opioids. Over five million people admit to using heroin. And 80 percent of heroin addicts began with a legal opioid prescription." Phil nudged Ethan's shoulder as he pushed past.

"How does that involve Emma?"

Phil stopped walking and looked to his side as the tiny brown fingers of a marmoset reached through the bars and fluttered in the air. Phil let the small animal grab on to his pinky. He played tug-of-war with the small hand before pulling away and redirecting his attention to Ethan. He stood awkwardly close to his dauntless technician.

"That 80 percent gives us reasonable doubt. Let's give that to the drama queen and get her off our backs."

Phil picked up research documents from the chair beside him and patted the edges. He placed them on top of an existing pile and slid them all into an expandable binder. He grabbed his jacket from an adjacent chair and turned toward the door.

"Thanks to me, we have everything requested." Phil swung his jacket over his shoulder as he walked. "Let's go."

"I'm not going."

"You're going."

"It's unconscionable, and I won't be any part of it," said Ethan.

Phil dropped the binder against his thigh and spun around. Ethan remained sitting with his forearms on the table and hands clasped. His expressionless face made him look like a defiant child.

"There's no need to be antagonistic." Deep wrinkles formed

on Phil's forehead and between his brows as he reasoned with Ethen. "Massetti will give us a cordial reception followed by accusations about our sloppy work. She'll serve a delectable entrée with compliments and additional requests. I've been on the receiving end of this more times than you can imagine."

"Why jump through her hoops?" asked Ethan. "You can do better."

"Better? I am the best there is when it comes to opioids."

"Not when you accuse an innocent girl of being a heroin addict. Not when you place the NAS reputation on top of her dead body."

Phil's chin thrust forward as the crease between his brows deepened. His nostrils flared, and his shallow breathing was like that of a nervous dog. He leaned on the table as he addressed Ethan's brazen calm.

"I'm protecting the largest pharmaceutical company in the world," said Phil. "The pernicious decisions of a foolish teenage girl are not my concern. Gather your belongings. We're leaving."

"Don't have to." Ethan didn't move.

"Not according to the contract you signed. As an employee of this company, you'll attend the required luncheon and continue to work in this lab. If you choose otherwise, I better not find you here when I return."

Phil swung his jacket over his shoulder and headed for the large gray doors. Ethan hesitated but followed.

"Good afternoon, gentlemen. Did you bring the heroin with you?" Dana smirked and closed the front door behind them.

"We did." Phil walked past Dana, familiar with the place, and headed into the living area. He dropped his bag on the floor by the couch and nestled into the end cushion. Dana hurried in and out of the kitchen adding final touches to her table as Ethan joined Phil on the opposite end of the couch. He sat with stiff posture and a look of indifference.

"Let's see what heroin says about Emma." Dana placed a wine bottle in the chiller at the end of the table and hurried to the couch. She settled in between Ethan and Phil and grabbed a folder from Phil's hand.

Dana read through the information with quiet grunts of affirmation. In between her fervent nods, she reached across Phil to open the end table drawer. Phil stiffened as he looked down at her body sprawled across his lap with her hand riffling through the drawer. Making light of her proximity, she smirked again and grabbed a red pen. Pushing off the armrest, she wiggled back into her seat.

Dana returned her attention to the statistical data while the contemporary design of her townhome consumed Ethan. She and Phil debated probabilities as Ethen surveyed one piece of décor after another with exaggerated disinterest in the conversation. He announced his impressions and opinions as if the other two weren't talking.

"That sculpture in the corner is disturbing."

"Don't you love it?" Dana's eyes widened as she looked to the sculpture with passion.

"Gives me the creeps."

"I found it in Santorini. It was made by a wizard, or a man who claimed to be a wizard."

"The artwork by the table too? That had to be created by a wizard. Or maybe Tarzan?" said Ethan as he glanced around the open layout of the room.

Plants lined the walls and grew in ornate pots on every open surface. Vicious thorned leaves intertwined with smooth succulents as plants snuck across pot boundaries. Bright sunlight danced across the plush carpet.

"Not sure who designed that piece," Dana chuckled. "It came from the Sapo jungle in Liberia."

"Never heard of it," said Ethan.

"Most people haven't. I stumbled upon it after I spent time in the Congo Basin."

"People. What are you doing?" Phil sprang from the couch and planted both fists onto his waist. "This is a business luncheon, not a social event."

"We're finished," said Dana. "This is all we need for reasonable doubt. What material can we pass onto Hewitt? Nothing that reveals our defense."

"Why would we give her anything?" Phil pulled additional folders from his bag.

"Benevolence will shed a positive light on defense counsel as well as Novo Analgesic Systems. I showed up there with random crap the other day. Blew her away. She even gave me a tour of their offices. I scheduled a second meeting, so I need some useless paperwork to take with me."

While Phil thumbed through the material, Dana headed toward her decadent table. Four places were elegantly set with wineglasses and white linens. An arrangement of fresh aster and baby's breath was in a vase in the center, and a small silver bowl held sliced lemon. Ethan's unexpected growl served as the lunch bell.

"Excuse me. I guess I am hungry."

"Hope so," said Dana. "My crazy morning is causing us to eat later than I intended. Some things take longer than you expect."

A silver tray with chicken-filled croissants overflowing with pomegranate seeds sat in the middle of the table. A chilled bottle of French Pinot Gris was at one end and a bottle of Italian Zinfandel at the other. Salad bowls filled with fresh greens were placed at each setting.

"Come have a seat," Dana called to her guests. "Would you like Perrier or tap water?"

"Tap is fine for me." Ethan sat down.

"Sparkling. Are we expecting another guest?" Phil noticed the additional place setting as he approached the table.

"Landon Sims. We need him on board."

Phil scooted past Ethan and bumped a large plant sitting in front of the window. He grabbed a protruding stem to keep it from tipping over.

"Oops, sorry," apologized Phil.

"No worries," laughed Dana.

"What is it?" asked Phil, holding on to the stem.

"Castor bean. I love the red blossoms." Dana tilted her head as if it validated her reasoning.

"Hope you don't own any pets," said Ethan. "The ricin in castor beans is deadly."

"No pets. Castor oil is great for my skin. And I get a pop of color in my décor."

"Pillows add color." Ethan reached for one of the leaves. "And there's no morbidity in a couple of throws here and there."

"That plant offers a lot more personality than a common pillow. And it won't bother anybody unless they decide to snack on it." Dana laughed again.

Phil grabbed a croissant as Dana and Ethan bantered. Dana finished her salad while explaining her personal castor-oil concoction. Before Ethan could comment, the doorbell rang. Dana jumped from the table as the front door opened, and Landon peeked in.

"Sorry I'm late," Landon said in a serious tone.

"No problem. We just sat down."

With no further pleasantries, Landon followed Dana to the table. He scooted his plate to the side and set his briefcase in its place.

"These are copies of your depositions." He pulled two binders from the case. "You'll be asked the same questions at trial. Memorize your answers. You're going to spend a lot of time on the witness stand."

Phil and Ethan continued eating as they reviewed their answers. Ethan flipped through the pages, not appearing to read any, while Phil spent several moments rereading every word.

"My responses are genius." Phil refilled his glass, dripping red wine on the white linen.

Ethan returned his attention to the castor bean plant while Landon directed his toward Dana, and Phil kept admiring his responses. Ethan leaned in to smell a blossom as he chewed a pomegranate seed between his front teeth.

"I need copies of the release dates of previous opioids developed by NAS." Landon offered a pleading shoulder shrug.

"Seriously, Sims?" Dana bristled at Landon's demands as she picked up the serving tray and returned to the kitchen.

"I need to make sure they didn't take shortcuts," Landon yelled to the closed door.

"They took no shortcuts." Dana marched back to the dining room and stood by Landon. "I was there."

"I realize that. But we need proof."

"Focus on the marketing," said Dana. "I can take care of the lab. I have more experience at NAS than you'll ever have, and I am more devoted to them than you'll ever be."

"You're not the trial attorney here, Dana. I am. While your devotion is appreciated, it's irrelevant. Right now, we need to discuss your witness testimony. I want to depose you sometime tomorrow. Does that work for you?"

"No, that doesn't work for me."

"When would be a better time?"

"Never."

"Dana," pleaded Landon. "You have firsthand knowledge that we need in the record."

"Those two spend more time in that lab than anybody." Dana pointed at Phil and Ethan. "They can be your puppets."

"They know the pharmacology. You know the business."

"There are other people who know the business. Jack Freeman included. I'm not sitting on the witness stand regurgitating figures you've fed me."

"I understand your feelings," said Landon.

"Then don't put me on the stand."

"You'll be on the stand. Be a team player so I can save this company from bankruptcy."

"Bankruptcy?" said Dana. "The NAS bottom line is solid."

"It won't stay that way if we don't take care of the Satori problem."

"I'm well aware of that," Dana bristled again. "I'll provide everything you need without wasting time sitting in a box. Take that research." She pointed to the end of the table. "That information provides statistical data of the probability that Emma was supplementing her Deprexone scrip."

"Heroin?"

"Heroin. Fentanyl. Doesn't matter."

"Probably not. But it might. They're going to attack our Deprexone marketing, and I want them to see that Emma was on something other than Deprexone. They'll touch upon our lab protocol, but Phil can handle that. You tie up loose ends."

"I know how depositions work."

"I'll give you a call and let you know the time."

Dana returned to the kitchen while Landon saw himself out.

23

RANDOM
ACT

C laire held her unzipped jacket closed while she jogged toward
the back entrance of Blackman & Bradford. The bright sun
carried a startling north wind, and the temperature had dropped
several degrees from the morning warmth on the tennis court.
As the receptionist perched on the edge of her chair wearing
a startling bright red cardigan and equally bright smile, Claire
wiggled a fingertip greeting and rushed to the elevator. Madalyn
smiled at the greeting and returned to her work. With perfect
timing, the doors opened, and Claire stepped inside. She whispered to herself as she leaned against the back wall. Her lips
were still moving when the doors opened on the tenth floor.
Alec stepped in.

"Hello, Ms. Hewitt." Alec's smile looked more tense than
friendly.

"You made good time, but why are you down here?" Claire
didn't smile, and the doors closed.

"Associates' meeting," said Alec. "Told you nobody would
notice we weren't here. You just wanted to end the beatdown."

"Not even." Claire rolled her eyes. "I kicked your butt even with Massetti's incessant phone calls."

"If you would have answered your phone or turned it off, no more calls."

"You don't know Dana."

"I know phones."

"Everything is so simple for you."

"Not everything," said Alec. "Just the simple things."

"My life sure isn't one of them," said Claire, watching the numbers change above the door.

"You have the Satoris."

"And the memories," said Claire. "I look into Clifford's eyes and see my father's pain, and I watch my mother's tears roll down Margo's face."

"Justice may help. It won't erase the memories, but it may soften them."

Claire looked at Alec with a forced smile. "Watching Massetti try to stomach our victory will be nothing short of confetti cannons."

Alec laughed as the elevator doors opened on the twelfth floor. His eyes shifted to the number above the door as Claire locked hers with Sergeant Jones. She winced as Jones shook his head with *I-told-you-so* eyes.

"To what do I owe this pleasure?" Claire brushed past Sergeant Jones, noticing the hushed whispers around her. When she reached her office door, Alec rushed in front and slid his hand onto the knob. Claire's hand landed on top.

"What's going on?" Claire looked up at Alec.

"There's been an incident."

"I knew something was up. There was no associates' meeting on tenth."

"I didn't know what to say," said Alec.

"How about the truth?"

Alec turned the knob while Sergeant Jones rocked on his heels. Claire took a deep breath and held it in. An unusual stillness washed over the common area as conversations ended and people watched. Alec tapped open the door. Claire looked inside but didn't move.

"What in God's name?" Her body remained motionless as her eyes bounced from her desk to the countertop to furniture. As shocked disbelief covered her face, her hands grabbed onto the doorframe.

Open rectangles lined the long counter empty of its drawers, which lay on the floor. Depositions, memos, files, and folders were scattered about like haphazard rugs. Papers were stuffed between cushions and shoved under chairs. Claire released a muffled gasp as her eyes returned to her desk.

"Where's my nameplate? And the lamp?" Her tone was sharp.

The deep slash across her leather chair evoked a louder gasp. Alec placed his hand on Claire's shoulder and followed her into the room.

"What happened?"

"It's anybody's guess," said Alec.

"That's why Sergeant Jones is here." Claire looked back at the door. "He knew Luigi's was the start of something."

"We don't know that, and neither does he," said Alec. "If he did, he would have had officers watching the firm. And you."

"I locked my door," said Claire. "I always lock my door."

Alec boldly squeezed Claire's shoulders. She stiffened and pushed him away. She walked to the couch and grabbed a file wedged beneath a cushion. Two pens popped out and fell to the floor.

"My office was perfect yesterday," said Claire. "I stopped by, and it was fine. Why the hell didn't the security system work? Isn't that what we pay for?"

Claire walked past Alec and threw the file. Papers glided through the air to join the others on the furniture and floor. She leaned against the counter with her hands flattened against the cool glass and watched the animated city below. As people jumped in and out of cars, walked into buildings, or crossed the busy street, she wondered if one of them wasn't as innocent as they appeared. Had one of them snuck in here and slipped away unnoticed? Claire wrapped her arms around herself.

"I spoke with the police," said Alec, breaking the silence. "The security system wasn't triggered, and there was no damage to the locks on any doors."

"What the hell is going on?" said Claire.

"I don't know." Alec gathered files from the floor around him. "A random act."

"How many floors are in this building? How many offices? Most with easier access than mine. This is no random act."

"Nobody knows anything yet."

"Yes, we do," said Claire, her tone sharper and angrier. "There was a narrow timeframe when this could have occurred."

"What are you saying?"

"My office looked fine Sunday afternoon. Either last night or this morning while we were playing tennis, someone paid a visit. NAS is behind this. I know those bastards are."

"You think an international drug company would risk an office heist?"

"Yes, I do."

"To what advantage?" asked Alec.

"Could be anything. Desperate search for evidence."

Alec set crumpled balls of paper onto the couch and swept

his arm underneath for more. "That's a precarious move when there's no guarantee of finding anything. Makes no sense."

"It makes perfect sense!" Claire ran her hand across the slash in her chair. "Desperate people do desperate things. Thanks to Ethan, we've seen the NAS test results showing addiction with Deprexone, and we have countless brochures claiming otherwise. Brochures they published. Brochures they send to every office in the state. Trying to steal from us on Lombard Street didn't work out, so they upped their game."

"Upped their game? Listen to yourself."

"You listen to me," said Claire. "They want to prevent us from exposing the magnitude of their negligent testing and corrupt marketing scheme."

"You're grasping at thin air," said Alec. "Ethan gave us copies. Westcott gave us copies. We have so many copies, stealing them would solve nothing."

"That's the point. We have so many copies, they aren't sure what we have. Their only option is to steal evidence that needs to be replaced. And I guarantee they'll replace it with material minimizing Deprexone's addictive nature and their culpability for the marketing plan."

"That's a huge risk without knowing where evidence might be stored."

"I don't think so," said Claire. "And Massetti's involved."

"What?" Alec dropped onto the couch with an armful of papers and a dumbstruck look on his face.

"Dana Massetti's involved. She shows up here uninvited with a lame explanation for her sudden appearance. Acts like she's my long-lost friend. I don't buy it. She's involved."

"Claire."

"Don't *Claire* me. I've known that woman for years. I've seen what she's capable of doing. I've watched her weasel herself into situations with uncanny precision. She has no limits and will do anything to protect herself and her boss."

"Oh boy."

"Tell me I'm wrong," said Claire. "You can't."

Alec walked his armful of documents to the counter beneath Claire's window. He dropped them next to other folders and a book with a torn cover. He then bent down to pick up a few more. The pile of papers was sloppy and intermixed with pens, junk mail, and notepads. Claire grabbed folders from the chair in front of her desk and placed them next to Alec's chaotic mess. Nothing was returned to the empty drawers.

Claire then knelt on the floor to better reach material underneath the desk. Her hand brushed across several pens as she reached as far as her shoulder would permit. Her fingers then landed inside the decorative dish that usually sat on the corner of her desk.

"Oh my God," Claire whispered. "That evil bitch."

"Did you say something?" asked Alec.

"Massetti."

"What about her?"

"She had no reason to come here," said Claire as she climbed to her feet. "And she insisted on a tour. Scrutinized every corner of this entire place."

"Interested in architecture?"

"All part of her plan." Claire leaned against her desk and held up the decorative dish. "My extra key sits in this dish. It's always in this dish. If I think someone might need to get into my office while I'm gone, I let them take it. Where is it?"

"Probably in this mess somewhere. Let's keep looking."

Sergeant Jones tapped on Claire's door as he entered. His

face was bent toward his notepad. He offered no greeting and flipped to the next page.

"Hello, Sergeant Jones." Claire stood with her shoulders back and her fingertips resting on her desk.

"Hello, Ms. Hewitt. How are you holding up?"

"I'm fine. Am I still a suspect?"

Sergeant Jones frowned and dropped his face to the carpet. With no immediate answer, he walked to the couch and scribbled notes onto his pad. He looked behind the couch and scribbled more notes. He straightened the end cushion as he turned back to Claire. He briefly glanced at Alec.

"That attitude is unhelpful, Ms. Hewitt."

"You accused me of making a false report. You interrogated me as part of your fishing expedition."

"There was no fishing expedition. I must be thorough with my investigations so as not to be remiss. There were more questions than answers the last time we spoke. I needed—"

"Well, look around," interrupted Claire as she fanned her arms around her. "I think you have your answers now."

"And a lot more questions."

"For Pete's sake." Claire slid the top drawer closed. "And I have some solid suspicions. Ones you should pursue as you're sleuthing around."

"Sleuthing around is my job. And I happen to be quite good. Run your suspicions by me and let's put an end to this nonsense before someone gets hurt."

"We can try," said Claire. "But you have no idea who you're facing."

24

No Friend
of Mine

Dana Massetti strolled up the center aisle with her cellphone wedged between her shoulder and ear. She acknowledged no one in the courtroom as she snapped at someone's erroneous idea on the other end of the line. With fervent intensity, she grabbed journals from her black embossed briefcase and stacked them on the far end of the defense table. She followed with folders, tablets, and three black pens. The documents were aligned in front of each empty chair with a pen placed on top. She adjusted the alignment twice before rushing back down the aisle.

Claire and Alec noticed but ignored the demonstrative entrance. Claire knew she was the intended audience but thought it likely there was no one on the other end of the phoneline. Dana's preamble to the day.

"She's a piece of work," whispered Alec as he organized Exhibit A in the box behind their chairs.

Claire laughed. "A bitchy one."

"Poor Sims."

"Poor Sims? He's chosen to be one of her minions."

"You think?"

"Guaranteed," said Claire. "He's following her every command. Neither of them is as transparent as they pretend. He's lead counsel in name only."

Claire and Alec were huddled together to finalize opening remarks when the defense team arrived. It was reminiscent of a *Perry Mason* episode. In complete unison, two attorneys waltzed up the center aisle followed by their client, Jack Freeman. They each took their seats without acknowledging the prosecution. Dana reorganized the same documents she had arranged moments earlier as Landon pulled out his handkerchief and dabbed at the moisture on his damp hairline. Jack slid his hands into the pockets of his Versace wool suit and looked around the courtroom. His cheeks were drawn, accentuating his narrow face, and his intense eyes scanned every corner of the room.

With less intensity than Dana, Landon adjusted the metal tripod that held a large picture of a brain depicting the work conducted at Novo Analgesic Systems, Inc. It was the same image high-school students saw in biology class, except this one had bright-colored arrows pointing to specific areas. Claire covered her mouth to conceal her amusement. Alec laughed.

The last of the observers were settling into their seats when a bailiff entered the courtroom. Spectators silenced their smartphones and ended conversations as all eyes shifted to the formalities at the front of the room. The bailiff stood with his hands clasped behind his back as he waited for those who mumbled final goodbyes into their phones.

"All rise. The Court of Common Pleas for the First Judicial District of Pennsylvania is now in session. Judge Alexander Connor presiding."

The silent crowd stood as Judge Connor entered through the private door behind his bench. He sat down and straightened the front of his black robe while scanning the courtroom as if taking attendance. With commensurate authority, he glanced through the papers sitting before him as the bailiff officially announced the case at hand.

"*Clifford and Margo Satori vs. Novo Analgesic Systems, Inc.*"

As jury instructions were read, most jurors sat erectly and with curious expressions. Several stared at the attorneys as if additional insight might be disclosed. After a group promise to issue a just verdict in accordance with the evidence presented, Claire rose.

She smoothed the front of her navy cashmere suit as she looked from Landon Sims to the jury box. With conspicuous confidence, she approached the jury.

"Your Honor and ladies and gentlemen of the jury, my name is Claire Hewitt. I am here today with Clifford and Margo Satori. Over the next several days, you're going to see disturbing evidence of a teenage girl caught up in lies and manipulation. Lies and manipulation that lead to her death."

Jurors shifted in their seats with nervous anticipation and looked from Claire to Landon to Judge Connor. Claire shared a similar look of apprehension as she spoke.

"Clifford and Margo Satori were the parents of an elite athlete. An Olympic gymnast with her sights set on gold. Most days were filled with pride. Until the day came when they witnessed what no parents want to see. The crumpled body of their daughter lying motionless on the mat. A fraction of a second ripped Emma Satori's world apart."

Claire looked down at her feet as she walked across the room. She felt the eyes of the jurors following. Their eyes were on her, but their hearts were with poor Emma. It was exactly what Claire needed. Poor Emma.

"Nobody was going to let the miscalculation of momentum

and a fraction of a second destroy Emma's dreams." Claire turned to the jury. "Not her parents, not her coaches, and especially not Emma. Clifford and Margo Satori found the best physician in the state of Pennsylvania. They said yes to surgery. They said yes to rehab. They paid thousands of dollars and said yes to every strategy given them so that Emma would compete again."

Claire paused. As whispers of concern for the Satoris circulated in the courtroom, Claire watched Landon pretend to read the papers he held. She smiled to herself, knowing the bend in his brow was too severe and the turn of pages too swift. He exaggerated his pretense of indifference. Claire turned back to the jury.

"What began as hope became a promise before turning tragic. The surgery was successful, and Emma was given her second chance." Claire's tone intensified, and she made fists with her hands as if cheering for Emma. "This young athlete was a fighter, and she was tough. She knew pain. She had beaten it before. Postoperative pain was one more hurdle for Emma to fly over." Claire paused by the witness stand and rested her hand on the railing. Her voice slowed as she continued addressing the jury. "But Emma was no match for the answer the doctor gave. When the Satoris asked for medical help, they were given lies laced with opioids. Lies that raised more fear and opioids that transformed an elite athlete who loved her sport into a fragile girl few recognized. Lies that ended in tears and opioids that ended her life."

After nudging the collective conscience of the jury, Claire walked back to Alec. Jurors nervously squirmed in their seats as spectators whispered among themselves. Alec handed Claire a cool glass of water. She took a sip and picked up a clipboard. Holding the clipboard by her hip, she walked to the middle of the room with a relaxed stride.

"Ladies and gentlemen, in 2019, after being prescribed an opioid for chronic pain, over ten million people misused their medication and 47,600 of them died from an overdose." Claire slapped the clipboard against her thigh. "That's unacceptable. There are strict regulations governing the development of these potent drugs, not broad guidelines, as the defense will claim. They are mandatory regulations intended to prevent deaths like Emma Satori's."

A painful moan escaped from Margo Satori at the mention of her daughter's name. Every face in the jury box turned to her. She blinked tears from her eyes as she looked down at the picture she cradled in her hands. Her fingertips stroked the dark curls framing the young, placid face as she spoke to the photo. Clifford sat with his back pressed against the wooden bench.

Under the scrutiny of the jury, Clifford reached for Margo's hand and kissed the top of her head. Sweat glistened in front of each ear. His eyes locked on Judge Connor before shooting across the aisle to Jack. Jack sat rigid and compliant between his attorneys.

Claire resumed her opening remarks. She looked over her shoulder at Clifford and Margo before turning to the jury. Clifford wrapped his arm around his wife and pulled her in while keeping his expectant eyes on Claire. Anticipation cloaked the courtroom.

"When testing an investigational new drug, Novo Analgesic Systems has a fiduciary duty to the participants involved and are held to the same standard of care as physicians." Claire watched most jurors nod their heads while some took notes. "This fiduciary duty was breached when Novo Analgesic Systems focused more on the liberalization of prescribing opioids for the treatment of chronic pain than on patient care." Claire turned to face Jack. "This duty was further breached when investigational new drugs were shamelessly advertised as ideal for treating chronic pain while at the same time guaranteeing minimal risk of addiction. That guarantee was no more than a sales pitch."

Claire walked by her seat and dropped the clipboard. The jarring bang caused several people to jump. She picked up a brochure.

"The real drug problem in America begins with a marketing scheme alleging the only solution to our pain is an opioid locked away in the ominous healthcare system. A marketing scheme claiming Novo Analgesic Systems holds the key." Claire raised the brochure as she walked across the courtroom. "When pharmaceutical companies become drug lords and physicians are kingpins, we need to step back and ask why."

Claire leaned against the witness stand with certainty. She made eye contact with each juror as they waited for her to speak. Subtle nods and tightly clasped hands indicated she had touched the hearts of many.

"The evidence you will see illustrates that Novo Analgesic Systems is guilty of medical negligence resulting in death by breaching their compulsory duty to Clifford and Margo Satori. Their compulsory duty to Emma. The evidence will be difficult to see and the witnesses disturbing to hear, but a guilty verdict will not be hard to find."

Jack Freeman grabbed the edges of his lapel as his face tightened. He leaned sideways and spoke to defense counsel as jurors examined him with suspicious interest. Spectators stretched their necks for better views as their eyes darted back and forth between Jack and the jury. Landon shuffled papers, and Dana watched Claire.

"You got their attention," Alec whispered to Claire as she sat down. "Let's hope the defense can't undo what you've established."

After exchanging heated whispers with Dana, Landon stood. His expression relaxed as he picked up his trial notes and scanned the top page. With an arrogant puff, he tossed them back onto the table and offered the jury a grimace of silent reproof.

"Ms. Hewitt has painted an alarming picture. She has pulled at your heartstrings and tried to place blame. No fiduciary duty was breached. No shameless advertising occurred."

Landon grabbed the stack of journals placed in front of the empty chair. With both arms, he raised them up to the jurors. He then lowered his arms but held on to the journals.

"Ms. Hewitt ignores the incredible medical advances that have been made in the last decade. Evidence of these medical breakthroughs are right here: *International Board of Medical Research and Studies.*" Landon read the title of the first journal and then continued listing others. "*International Journal of Clinical Medicine, International Journal of Medical Sciences, International Society of Pain Management.*" Landon returned the journals to the defense table and turned back to the jury. "Ms. Hewitt would prefer we suffer in silence. Novo Analgesic Systems thanks you in advance for not letting that happen."

Landon looked at each face with his arm resting across his stomach. He walked closer to the jury as he spoke. Dana drummed her fingers as she scrutinized Landon's delivery.

"We have the best healthcare system in the world." Landon's arms circled the air as he spoke. "Don't let the unrealistic accusations of the prosecution convince you otherwise. Medical treatments can't be blamed simply because idealistic acts of God aren't obtained like the Satoris were hoping." Landon raised both open palms up by his shoulders.

Landon's extravagant hand gestures kept the attention of everyone in the courtroom while annoyance grew on the faces of Judge Connor and Claire. With a cocky gait, Landon walked over and spoke with Dana. She responded with similar arrogance before Landon turned back to the jury. Captivated by the animation, several jurors sat taller in their seats with eager expressions on their faces.

"*Success* is not a dirty word. Success shows that something is working and working well. Novo Analgesic Systems is not the monster the prosecution would like you to think." Landon softened his voice. "Over the next few days, the prosecution is going to describe chronic pain using vague medical terminology to try to place blame on Novo Analgesic Systems. They'll prance around this courtroom with a big bag of blame. They'll throw it everywhere, hoping it sticks. Sometimes there's blame to be had. Sometimes there's blame to be shared. But sometimes there is no one to blame." Landon stopped in front of the jury with both arms dropped to his sides. "No matter how hard someone searches for mistakes, no matter how hard someone throws accusations, there is no negligence."

Landon returned to his seat without looking at the prosecution or Dana. He leaned forward on his forearms and looked up to Judge Connor. Jurors continued to whisper. Judge Connor straightened the papers in front of him and issued a much-needed recess.

Claire and Alec spoke to no one as they hurried from the courthouse. Claire pushed open the heavy courthouse door, and a cool breeze swept in. Alec dashed down the stairs with his arm raised. As a cab pulled up to the curb, Alec opened the passenger door and waited for Claire.

"Blackman & Bradford law office," said Claire as she slid into the cab. "They're worried."

"They should be. You dominated."

Claire looked out the window as the cab pulled forward. She daydreamed as they headed to the office and prematurely opened the door before the cab slowed down. She held on with a tight grip until the cab pulled up to the curb. Claire and Alec both jumped out and dashed for the front doors. Adrenaline prevented a leisurely pace.

"We don't have much time. I'll head upstairs and grab the rest of the witness questions," said Claire.

"Yeah, sorry I walked off without those. I'll grab sandwiches." Alec turned toward the deli as Claire veered the opposite way.

Claire bounced on the balls of her feet in front of the closed elevator doors. Her lips were moving as she practiced her well-rehearsed lines. When the doors slid open, Claire stepped inside, still consumed with her upcoming courtroom performance.

"Ms. Hewitt! Ms. Hewitt!"

Claire shot her arm against the edge of the closing door. The door stopped before retreating to open. Claire peeked out.

"Did Ms. Massetti find you?" asked Madalyn.

"I was in court with her this morning."

"She stopped by the other day with evidence she said you needed before trial." Madalyn panted trying to catch her breath. "She's been in and out of here several times. Have you received everything you need from her?"

"In and out of here?"

"Yes."

"Did you log in the dates?"

"Yes."

Claire stepped out of the elevator and grabbed Madalyn by the arm. They hurried back to the front desk as Madalyn stumbled along and uttered excuses.

"I wasn't sure what to do. I offered to take the evidence, but she insisted on delivering it. She caught me off guard, Ms. Hewitt."

"Show me the dates she was here."

Madalyn began typing before her firm bottom hit the seat.

Claire stood behind her and watched experienced fingers breeze across the keys.

"Thursday the sixteenth, Wednesday the twenty-second, and Monday the twenty-seventh."

"Monday the twenty-seventh. Are you sure?" Claire leaned in closer to the screen.

"I checked her in. It's right here. Nine a.m." Madalyn pointed at the date and time.

"I knew it. What material did she bring?"

"I don't know. She told me she'd spoken to you and insisted on taking the files to your office herself. Since she's a friend of yours, I thought it would be okay."

"She's no friend of mine."

Claire returned to the elevator without thanking Madalyn. When the doors opened, she stepped inside and stood in the middle with both hands tapping the sides of her thighs. She stared at the numbers above the door.

On the twelfth floor, Claire stormed out of the elevator, ignored nearby attorneys, and slammed her office door. Hallway banter paused in response to the rash behavior. Inside the quiet room, Claire picked up her landline.

"Sergeant Jones, please." Claire watched the cumulus clouds passing her window as she waited on Jones. She placed the phone on speaker.

"Good afternoon, Ms. Hewitt. How may I help you?"

"Interrogate Dana Massetti. It's time."

"I can't interrogate people based upon the hunches of others."

"It's not a hunch! She was here on the twenty-seventh."

"We've looked at the entry logs. There were a lot of people in that building on the twenty-seventh. I'm conducting interviews as time allows. She's on the list."

"You don't need a list. I've found your person. She showed up first thing in the morning and tricked our receptionist into letting her come upstairs unescorted."

"How did she get into your office?"

"She snuck out with my key on a previous visit."

"That certainly sheds a new light on things. Thank you. I'll be in touch." Sergeant Jones ended the call.

Claire grabbed the Schumann file from her desk and left her office in much the same manner as she had entered. When she reached the lobby, she saw Alec leaning against an upholstered chair holding two foil-wrapped sandwiches. His arms lowered as he noticed Claire approaching red-faced and angry.

"Boy, did I underestimate her."

"Who?"

"Dana Massetti. She was here Monday morning when we were playing hooky on the tennis court."

"Who told you that?" Alec handed Claire her sandwich.

"Madalyn. Dana weaseled her way in on the pretense of being a friend dropping off evidence. She brought no evidence, and God only knows what she took."

"And used your key to open the door." Alec unwrapped his sandwich and took one bite.

"I'm above saying I told you so, but . . ." Claire dropped her sandwich into her bag with the evidence.

Claire and Alec headed out the front door in search of another cab. Claire's hair was damp, and her face flushed. Her eyes ricocheted up and down the street as Alec stepped in front of her with a raised arm. A cab pulled up to the curb, and they both climbed in.

"That bitch has my key."

25

POPPY

"Our news anchors talk about it every night. Our newspapers print it every day. They blame the opioid crisis on drug addicts." Claire rose from her chair with a thick news report in her hand and walked to the middle of the room. "You may tell yourself the opioid crisis doesn't involve you. But they're wrong, and you're wrong. The opioid crisis slips in the back door, impacts millions of us, and comes with tremendous societal and economic morbidity." Claire held the news report up to the jury as she stepped within two feet of the twelve intrigued faces. "Every hour, 11 Americans die of a drug overdose. Think about that. That's 264 people every day, and the majority of those deaths are opioid-related. That death rate exceeds the number of people in this courtroom today."

Claire turned from the jury and watched discomfort unfold throughout the room. Spectators avoided eye contact while mentally counting the bodies around them. Landon tapped his foot, and Dana picked at her cuticle as Judge Connor watched everyone with muted pleasure.

"Let's back up a bit," said Claire as she exchanged the news report for a Deprexone brochure. "Opioids are drugs that are cultivated from the poppy plant. They've been used for medicinal purposes dating back to 3400 BC. Once harvested, the dried ruminates are manufactured into morphine, opium, and heroin. While opium and morphine are naturally occurring, heroin undergoes a chemical synthesis and is a semisynthetic opioid. Deprexone, which Novo Analgesic Systems develops and aggressively markets, is derived from the same source but undergoes total synthesis and is considered a synthetic opioid. A lab-created opioid that put more than $2.8 billion in the coffers of Novo Analgesic Systems."

Groans and muted comments could be heard throughout the courtroom. Whispered opinions shot back and forth as alarmed faces looked to Jack. Dana gripped the table's edge and flipped her head toward Landon. Landon ignored the gesture although Dana leaned into his ear. Hisses could be heard while Landon appeared oblivious to the berating.

"Thousands of Deprexone prescriptions fall into the hands of innocent patients every day." Claire waved the bright-colored brochure in front of the jury. "We are inundated with propaganda about the pain relief this medication offers. But these lies camouflage the fact that the United States is drowning in opioids." Claire dropped both arms to her sides. "The rate of opioid overdoses has tripled since 1999 and continues to climb. Every year, the economic cost of prescription opioid–related abuse, dependence, and overdose exceeds $78.5 billion. That's money out of your pockets."

Claire looked over to Jack as if demanding a rationale. She delayed continuing while Jack crossed his legs and watched his black wingtips. He ran his index finger under his nose and sniffed as he avoided Claire's eyes. Claire savored the awkward moment until Judge Connor cleared his throat.

"How did this happen?" Claire raised both hands at the jury

as if someone might answer. "We all know the answer. Novo Analgesic Systems. Where did it start? Novo Analgesic Systems. Why did it start? Ego and greed."

Claire looked to Judge Connor as Alec refilled her glass with tepid water. Jurors were struggling with post-lunch fatigue and squirming in their seats. The room was getting warm.

"You may call your first witness." Judge Connor's raised eyebrows impelled Claire to hasten her pace.

"The prosecution calls Dr. Schumann to the stand."

Alec jumped from his chair and hurried down the center aisle. Moments later, a tall gentleman with the firm physique of a young man and the graying hair of someone much older followed Alec into the courtroom. Familiar with the process, he continued to the witness stand and sat down. He glanced at Judge Connor before looking to Claire.

"Dr. Schumann, what is your professional line of work?" Claire walked toward the witness, loosely swinging a folder.

"I'm senior commercial analyst with the National Society of Pharmaceutical Manufacturers. I analyze financial and operational data to monitor the competition among pharmaceutical companies."

"Has the predominance of the synthetic drug Deprexone impacted the competition?"

"Very much so. Deprexone has expanded from not only treating acute pain but becoming the most preferred option for chronic pain."

"What are the consequences of this increase in Deprexone prescriptions?"

"Consequences?"

"Yes, consequences. Has the morbidity and mortality from the use of Deprexone seen an equal surge?"

"Yes." Dr. Schumann looked from Claire to the watchful

spectators in the front row. His narrowed eyes showed concern that he might be personally judged for his answers.

"In your opinion as an analyst, what accounts for this drastic increase?"

"Modern medicine experienced a major change, in 1995, when the American Pain Society urged classifying pain as the fifth vital sign. This shifted the approach to treating chronic pain. Prior to this, there had been four vital signs monitored by medical professionals."

"Did this reclassification and emphasis on the treatment of chronic pain initiate the opioid crisis we face today?"

"Unintentionally, yes. The opioid crisis arrived in three waves. This reclassification of pain was the first wave, which began a push toward using opioid medications for chronic pain management and incited pharmaceutical companies to market their opioid medications for such. Prior to this, opioids were reserved for acute pain experienced after surgery or secondary to cancer."

"Are you telling the court that the opioid crisis began when pharmaceutical companies, such as NAS, shifted their marketing to focus on the treatment of this fifth vital sign?"

"Unfortunately, yes." Dr. Schumann shifted his eyes from the crowd to the jury. He continued scrutinizing facial expressions as reluctance slowed his answer. "Physicians were hesitant at first because there was minimal evidence supporting opioid use, concern over the addictive properties of opioids, and a fear of being investigated for liberal opioid practices."

"Despite physician hesitation, did pharmaceutical companies, such as NAS, continue to push for opioid use in chronic pain management?"

Dr. Schumann looked at Landon and shifted in his seat. He bit the side of his cheek and repositioned again. "Yes, they did. From 1990 to 1999, the total number of opioid prescriptions grew from 76 million to approximately 116 million. By 2021, the number increased to over 207 million."

Claire had a bounce in her step as she walked back to her seat. She exchanged the folder for a thin binder. After reviewing the first two pages, she turned back to her witness.

"The first wave of the opioid crisis gives us our fifth vital sign and over 207 million opioid prescriptions. What does the second wave give us?"

"The second wave involved a steep rise in heroin use." Dr. Schumann's voice became curt.

"How is heroin use connected to prescription opioids?" asked Claire as she leaned back on the table in front of her empty chair. Her crossed arms still held on to the thin binder.

"Heroin was plentiful, and heroin was cheap. Many individuals with an established tolerance and dependency on opioids transitioned toward a more concentrated and cheaper alternative. Between 2005 and 2012, the number of people who used heroin doubled, as did fatal heroin overdoses."

Claire set the binder on the table behind her as the impact of the answer hung in the air. She pushed from the table and turned to face Landon. The courtroom silently watched as Landon leaned over and whispered to Dana. Claire turned back to her witness.

"The second wave of the opioid crisis has opioid addicts rushing to heroin. What does the third wave give us?"

"Synthetic opioids." Dr. Schumann nodded as if affirming the correct answer. "They began showing up around 2013 and are rampant today." Schumann tugged on his pant legs and repositioned again. His discomfort was evident. "It's characterized by the steep rise in overdose deaths from synthetic opioids."

"Did pharmaceutical companies, such as NAS, continue to manufacture and heavily market synthetic opioids after becoming aware of the steep rise in overdose deaths from these drugs?" Claire turned to the jury as they waited for Dr. Schumann's reply.

Schumann leaned forward onto the wooden ledge. He tapped his fingertips together as if impatience were taking over. Sweat glistened on his temples as he watched Landon and Dana converse. Claire and several jurors followed his eyes to the defense table as everyone waited.

"Will the witness please answer?" Claire turned back to her witness.

"They continued promoting opioids, but I'm not privy as to what knowledge they had."

"As senior commercial analyst for the National Society of Pharmaceutical Manufacturers, are you privy as to whether these continued promotions emphasized NAS opioids as having a low potential for addiction?"

"Yes."

"Yes, you are privy to this information, or yes, NAS emphasized a low potential for addiction?"

"NAS emphasized a low potential for addiction."

"I have no more questions."

Claire returned to her seat as Dana nudged Landon. He leaned over with a quick comment before approaching the witness.

"Dr. Schumann, who made the decision to reclassify pain as the fifth vital sign in 1995?"

"The decision was made by the Joint Commission on Accreditation of Healthcare Organizations. Chronic pain had become a predominant issue in the treatment of patients across all specialties."

"Have opioids been used successfully in the treatment of this fifth vital sign?"

"Opioids have been quite successful in the treatment of chronic pain." Dr. Schumann smiled.

"Has Deprexone proved successful in the treatment of chronic pain?"

"Yes."

"Wouldn't this success be the reasoning behind the increase in the number of prescriptions written?"

"It would seem so." Dr. Schumann folded his arms as his eyes met Claire's.

Landon returned to the defense table and lowered onto the edge of his seat as Dana stood. She carried a document with her as she walked to the center of the room. With the expertise of a seasoned actress, she tilted her head at the information she read, then turned to the jury with a creased brow of confusion. She glanced back at the information before addressing her witness.

"Isn't it true that by 2015, an estimated 17 million people were using opioids, of which heroin was the most common?"

"That's correct." Dr. Schumann leaned forward again.

"I'm holding evidence which shows that over 1.6 percent of people in the United States have used or are using heroin. That's more than five million users." Dana cocked her head as if surprised. "Since evidence shows that the second wave of this opioid crisis sent prescription users to heroin, isn't it likely that Emma Satori was using heroin?"

"Objection. Heroin statistics suggest nothing about Emma Satori." Claire scowled at Dana in lieu of looking to Judge Connor.

"Sustained."

"Withdrawn. In addition to heroin, has there been an increase in the production and use of other synthetic opioids?" Dana didn't miss a beat. She skidded the information she was reading across the defense table and walked to the end of the jury box.

"According to the National Forensic Laboratory Information System, reports on fentanyl increased from nearly 5,400 in 2014 to over 56,500 in 2017. And there were 31,335 fentanyl overdose deaths in 2018," said Dr. Schumann.

"Well, there you have it." Dana threw her hands in the air. "With those numbers, Emma had to be experimenting with fentanyl."

"Objection! Move to strike!" Claire shot to her feet and looked to Judge Connor. Her cheeks were red and her hands clenched. Both from anger.

"Defense has no further cross." Dana flashed a bleach-white smile to the jury as she returned to her seat.

"The court will strike the remarks of defense counsel. And there will be no more theatrics in my courtroom. Does the prosecution have redirect?" Judge Connor scowled at both Dana and Landon.

"Yes." Claire remained standing. "The second wave ushered in heroin use because it was cheaper, stronger, and, in some cases, easier to get than an opioid prescription. Does this indicate a direct link between legal opioid prescriptions and heroin use?"

Dr. Schumann leaned back in the witness chair with his manicured hands resting on his legs. Being an unintentional character in Dana's drama had cracked his guarded nature, and he relaxed on the stand. He glanced at the jury as if in collusion and answered Claire's question in a softer tone.

"Oh, yes. Evidence shows that a large majority of heroin users today had their first exposure to opioids with a lawful opioid prescription."

"One final question. Is pain still considered the fifth vital sign?" Claire smiled at her witness.

"As concerns over the adverse effects of opioid use grew, the Joint Commission removed this designation from the accreditation standards manual in 2004."

"Thank you. I have no more questions."

Claire returned to her seat as Alec placed the prosecution's display board on a metal tripod by the jury box. There was one small picture of the human brain and a replica of the investigational new drug application. Promotional communications were hung beside the photos. When returning to his seat, he leaned into Claire.

"Ethan isn't in the witness room."

"Dana said he's home with the flu. We'll lay groundwork with Westcott. Ethan can refute it when he returns."

"Westcott on the stand?" Alec raised his eyebrows.

"He'll be in hog heaven," said Claire.

"The prosecution may call their next witness." Judge Connor looked down at his notes.

"The prosecution calls Phil Westcott to the stand."

Landon closed his eyes as Dana rolled hers. With Judge Connor's nod, Alec hurried from the room.

Moments later, Phil walked up the center aisle with fervent steps and swinging arms. He bounced on the balls of his feet in front of the wooden rail as he watched Judge Connor's down-turned head. When asked to approach the witness stand, Phil did so with his right hand held high. After repeating the bailiff's instructions to solemnly tell the truth, Phil dropped onto the edge of his seat with his excitement directed at Claire. His arched spine and wet smile resembled a child on an amusement park ride. Claire watched the jury form an opinion of the scientist waiting to speak. Several exchanged comments as they waited.

"Dr. Westcott, what is your professional line of work?"

"I am a highly accomplished research pharmacologist with Novo Analgesic Systems."

"When did you begin working for Novo Analgesic Systems?" Claire rose and rested her fingertips on the table.

"In 1980. I was twenty-eight years old. One of the youngest

in the pharmaceutical industry. I don't mean to boast." Phil wrinkled his nose above an ample grin. "I had completed both of my doctoral degrees from Temple University School of Pharmacy in Pharmaceutical Science, one with an emphasis on medicinal chemistry and one with an emphasis in pharmaceutics. My research accomplishments were attracting attention."

"What accomplishments were those?"

"Research regarding drug safety."

"Did this research involve the liberal use of opioids to treat chronic pain?"

"My research involved finding new treatments for chronic pain under monitored conditions." Phil spoke scrupulously as he scanned the jury.

"Did you write a highly publicized letter in 1980 regarding this research?" Claire held up a white piece of paper as she waited for Phil's answer.

"Yes, I did." The arch in Phil's spine increased, and his chest protruded at the recognition.

"Was this the letter that's been attributed to starting the opioid epidemic a decade earlier?"

"Misguided individuals claim that my letter became a major contributor to the opioid crisis. But they are incorrect."

Claire's question punctured Phil's ego. His deflated body sunk into the chair. He looked at his feet as he continued answering the question.

"Their interpretation was misguided, and those assertions have caused me great angst."

"What did your letter state?"

"It was a one-paragraph letter in a medical journal stating that narcotics didn't cause addiction in most hospitalized patients. Out of nearly twelve thousand patients studied, there were only four cases of documented addiction in patients who had no history of addiction. It was incredible." Phil had recovered his pride as he looked up to Judge Connor with wide eyes and raised eyebrows.

"Based upon your research, did Novo Analgesic Systems launch the start of the opioid epidemic in 1980?"

"Objection." Landon knocked his chair against the wooden rail as he stood. "The letter was written by Dr. Westcott as an independent researcher and not as a representative of Novo Analgesic Systems."

"Withdrawn." Claire looked down at her notes while Alec whispered.

"He's alienated the jury." Alec watched jurors wrinkle their noses and exchange whispers in reaction to Phil.

"Dr. Westcott, were you involved in the development of Deprexone?" asked Claire as she glanced at the jury.

"Yes, I was. I'm head of research and development at Novo Analgesic Systems and have kept them at the top of their field for decades. When Deprexone molecules cross the blood-brain barrier, they latch onto GABA neurons, which flood the system with a big dose of feel-good neurotransmitters." Phil wore his arrogance with pride. "My Deprexone replaces pain with euphoria."

"Is it this euphoria that perpetuates the high rate of addiction?"

Phil slammed back in the witness chair, grabbing the sides of his head. His eyes and nose were pinched together like a child before a tantrum. Claire watched the expected reaction.

"You are clueless when it comes to Deprexone," Phil shot back. "Deprexone produces a feeling of happiness; it also can cause drowsiness and constipation. Am I to be blamed for people dozing off at work and cramping?"

Soft chuckles spread throughout the courtroom. Alec chuckled to himself while Dana dropped her face into her hands. Claire laughed with the others as she sat down and watched Phil perform for the jury.

"Why is Deprexone an appropriate treatment for chronic pain?" asked Claire. "Your research is displayed on the board to the left of the jury. Feel free to reference it when needed."

Phil jumped from his seat and strutted to the display boards. He surveyed both before stepping closer to the large display of the defense. Judge Connor leaned forward onto both elbows, his annoyance apparent. Phil placed both hands on the small of his back and admired his own work. His chest noticeably rose and fell as he tapped his cheek with his index finger.

"The human brain rewards us when we do something plea-surable. Exercise, eating, a host of delightful activities. The dopamine it releases encourages us to keep doing what we're doing. Deprexone does the same thing."

Phil again bounced on his toes as he pointed to specific areas that depicted how Deprexone binds to opioid receptors in the brain. He used the laser pointer he pulled from his pocket for added effect as he talked down to the jury. He frequently gripped his elbows behind his back and looked for Judge Con-nor's reaction to his work. Claire leaned back in her chair as she questioned Phil. She thought it best that the spotlight remained on Phil's behavior when answering.

"When dopamine is released as the result of ingesting a drug, doesn't the brain overreact and reduce dopamine produc-tion in an attempt to normalize the sudden extreme the drug has created?" asked Claire.

"The brain works nonstop to keep everything running smoothly."

"Isn't this how the cycle of addiction begins?"

"It seldom does." Phil paced in front of the jury box as he had seen both attorneys do. With all eyes following him, he explained how pain messages are intercepted, and the pain threshold is lowered through different receptors. He spoke in slow monosyllabic detail. As he spun around by the last juror, he looked to Judge Connor for approval. With practiced conceit, he examined the crowded room before continuing his performance.

"Deprexone is a miracle!" Phil flared the fingers on both hands. "Thousands of people have rid themselves of chronic pain with this life-changing medication."

Claire ignored the burst of energy as she asked her next question. "Dr. Westcott, what is opioid use disorder?"

Phil dropped both arms to his sides and looked at the floor as he trudged back to the witness chair. He shoved the laser pointer into his pocket and sat down, his enthusiasm gone.

"OUD is a problematic pattern of opioid use leading to significant impairment of someone's ability to function."

"Can Deprexone lead to opioid use disorder?" Claire rose from her chair, watching Phil squirm on the witness stand. She rested her fingertips on the table and waited.

Dana leaned back in her chair with squinted eyes and fists tucked underneath each arm. Landon rested on his forearms with his left foot bouncing. He chewed the side of his cheek as he watched Phil's eyes scan the room but land on nothing. The topic of opioid use disorder sparked uncomfortable interest in the courtroom.

"If used inappropriately, Deprexone could lead to OUD," said Phil. "But that's the personal decision of each individual."

"When a patient undergoes surgery, does that patient personally decide what medications are used during the procedure?" asked Claire.

"Not unless they have a medical degree and can perform their own surgery while asleep." Phil looked to the jury with an indignant puff.

"When opioids are used for postoperative care, is that a personal decision or a medical decision made by the physician?"

"When they are hospitalized, the decision is made by the attending physician. You really should read the research behind my letter you were touting about. It explains all of this."

"When a patient is in the hospital for several days, does the decision shift to this patient?" asked Claire.

"I'm sure I have no idea what you're getting at."

"Can addiction begin with the very first dose of an opioid?" Claire stepped away from her chair and walked toward Phil.

"It can, but that usually occurs with someone who has previous addiction issues."

"You told us moments ago that opioid use disorder is a personal decision. Yet a patient can be given opioids for days under the direction of a physician. How is this a personal decision?" Claire held her witness questions in both hands behind her back.

"Patients don't live in the hospital forever. When they are discharged, it becomes their decision to take medications or tough it out."

"Are you saying a patient can spend several days on opioids in the hospital, be sent home with a prescription for two hundred more opioids, yet be expected to make an unadulterated decision on whether to follow medical advice or devise another method for managing pain?"

"I never said it was easy." Phil slid the glasses off the end of his nose. "Surgeries are difficult. Pain management is difficult. Every person who has undergone a serious medical event must accept the responsibility of making an informed decision as to what's best when it comes to managing pain."

"Let me clarify, Dr. Westcott." Claire walked away from Phil as she spoke. "You believe OUD is a personal decision." Claire leaned across Alec and held up a newspaper advertisement. "Despite the NAS goal of ensuring there's a bottle of Deprexone for every American adult? Those were their exact words." Claire pointed to the ad. *"A bottle for every adult."* Claire handed the paper to Alec. "Despite over 259 million bottles floating around? Despite more than 7,770,000 pills up for grabs?"

"Objection. Badgering the witness." Landon remained seated but shot a bruising look to Claire.

"Withdrawn. No further questions."

Landon rose from his seat as Claire returned to hers. He waited as he watched Phil spit on his glasses and wipe them on his shirt sleeve. He then peered through the lenses before adjusting them onto his nose. Landon picked up a Cartesian graph and walked to the front of the defense table.

"What is iatrogenic addiction?" Landon walked closer to Phil and held up the graph.

IATROGENIC was written in bold black type across the top of the page. Phil shrunk into the witness chair, shaking his head. He looked at the graph as his fingertips tapped on his thighs. He didn't answer but continued to shake and tap.

"Dr. Westcott, can you tell the court what iatrogenic addiction is?"

"Addiction to the medication prescribed by the treating physician in the management of a patient's pain."

"How often does this occur?" asked Landon.

"There have been no thorough studies addressing the issue of iatrogenic addiction during long-term opioid use for chronic pain."

"Have there been studies evaluating the use of illegal drugs in conjunction with long-term opioid use for chronic pain?"

"Innumerable!" Phil lit up with excitement. He scooted to the front of his seat and gripped the ledge.

"What have these studies found?" asked Landon.

"The consequences can be dire when an opioid interacts with recreational drugs." Phil again slid his glasses down his nose but left them perched on the tip as he looked over the rims.

"Fatalities from lack of oxygen or aspiration of stomach contents are not uncommon. And the psychoactive effects of one of the drugs may be diminished, leading someone to take dangerous amounts of the other. It's a gruesome spiral."

"Would you find the possibility that Emma died from an interaction between Deprexone and another drug inconceivable?"

"Objection."

"More than conceivable!" shouted Phil.

"Overruled." Judge Connor looked to Phil with reproachful eyes. "Please wait for my ruling before answering."

"Defense has no further questions."

"Deprexone can't be mixed with other meds!" Phil yelled again in response to no question. Several jurors jumped at the exuberance and several more laughed at the behavior. "Deprexone needs no help," continued Phil. "The misguided actions of a few shouldn't deprive others of relief." The volume of Phil's voice rose, as did his zeal. "We can't let that happen."

Phil flipped his head to the jury. He was breathless as he searched for faces of equal enthusiasm. Claire, Alec, and Landon shared questioning looks of confusion while Dana looked at a document ignoring it all.

"I guess everyone gets their fifteen minutes," Alec whispered to Claire.

"You may step down, Dr. Westcott." With palpable relief, Judge Connor adjourned for the day.

When the jury was escorted from the room, nobody hurried to leave. Spectators mingled in animated discussions while legal counsel shuffled papers and packed bags. As Alec returned trial notes to his briefcase, he watched opposing counsel conversing in terse, heated tones. Dana's nostrils flared as she spoke, while Landon spoke to the papers he held instead of the irate woman to his left.

"A long afternoon of coffee mandates a visit to the little boys' room." Alec set his briefcase on the floor and headed down the aisle.

The courtroom audience had lessened but not disappeared. Alec hurried past people meandering in the hallway, ducked into the men's room, and emerged moments later. As he stood with outstretched arms, the courtroom door flew open. Dana emerged in frenzied fashion and looked both directions before running to the far doors. It was a long hallway, and Alec froze as he watched her run the opposite way. No sooner did his eyes follow her through the courthouse doors did he race back to Claire.

"How did we miss it?" Alec panted with both hands, holding on to the back of her chair.

Claire looked down at Alec's white knuckles. "Miss what?"

"That gait. I knew it had to be a chick. She leapt over that wall like it was nothing."

"Alec, what happened in the men's room?"

"Dana."

"Dana was in the men's room?"

"No. But it was her," said Alec. "Our mysterious assailant isn't so mysterious. I chased her up the garage ramp and watched her jump over that wall. I'll never forget it. It was Dana Massetti."

"No way."

"Yes way. It was her, Claire."

"I don't know."

"I do."

"You were a Pac-12 sprinter in college. You expect me to believe she outran you?"

"Yes, I do."

"Dana's a middle-aged professional. Even she has a certain level of decorum."

"Apparently not."

Alec released the chair and hurried from the courtroom for the second time. Claire grabbed her bag and followed. He pushed the heavy courthouse door open and held it while Claire and several others passed through. With his outstretched arm still holding the door, Dana ran up the stairs.

"Well, there you are. Speedy little gal," said Alec.

The accusation in his eyes and the tone of his voice sent Dana a clear message she was no longer an unknown. Dana's shoulders sank and her jaw went slack. She rebutted with an indignant snort before speaking.

"Kind of you, Mr. Marshall. Thank you." Her tone was flippant. Her face flushed.

She brushed shoulders with Alec as she continued through the door. But it looked more like a shove than happenstance. Dana continued forward before glancing back. Alec let the door close.

"No cabs right now," said Claire as Alec descended the steps. "We can walk."

Alec puffed his cheeks with hot air and tossed it around inside his mouth as he led with a commanding pace. Claire hustled to keep up. When they arrived at the bright yellow door underneath the illuminated MEN AT WORK sign, Alec held the door open for Claire. A small Japanese man greeted them with a traditional bow and soft words. Alec and Claire returned the greeting and followed the man.

"Thank God we're not by that front window. I'm in no mood for input from meddling attorneys." Claire pulled out her chair and sat down at the small table by the kitchen.

"All I need is a stiff drink," said Alec as he scanned his surroundings.

Claire opened her menu. "Now tell me about Massetti and what you think happened."

"She mugged you." Alec lifted his menu.

"She did not."

"Yes, she did. You blame that woman for everything. Why are you struggling with this? I told you that person ran like a girl. She's a girl."

"She is." Claire leaned back and ran her hand across the menu. "But this is too much. Are there no lines she won't cross?"

"Doesn't look like it."

Claire and Alec ordered their dinner and a pair of martinis. Claire finished her first drink as they discussed Dana Massetti and Phil Westcott. With her second martini, Claire divulged current rumors and past truths about Dana and her curious morals. In more spirited moods, they again ordered drinks, finished their meals, and shared a cab back to the office. They rode in silence as the martini effects softened. When the cab slowed to a stop in front of Blackman & Bradford, Claire and Alec climbed out.

"Nice work today." Claire squeezed Alec's arm before turning toward her car.

"Thanks." Alec watched her walk away.

When the jury shuffled into the courtroom for the second day, Claire recalled Phil Westcott to the stand. With head held high, he marched to the front of the room, dropped onto the edge of the witness chair, and rubbed his palms across both thighs. Judge Connor reminded Phil that he was still under oath.

"I've handed the witness what has been marked as Exhibit C." Claire handed Phil a large red book with an illustrated cover of powders and pills. "Dr. Westcott, please tell the court what you are holding." Claire returned to her table and stood beside Alec.

"The Food and Drug Administration requirements for drug development."

"What is the purpose of these requirements?"

"Regulation of drug testing. The types of testing permitted and the environment in which this experimentation may be conducted." Phil rested the book on the ledge in front of him.

"Are these suggested FDA guidelines or strict requirements?" asked Claire.

"Suggested guidelines would create nothing but havoc in a laboratory with the expertise and success of Novo Analgesic Systems." Phil lifted his arms above his head as if the answer were obvious. "Strict requirements regulate and promote the development of extraordinary medications. We cannot choose what we do willy-nilly."

"Did you follow these requirements in the development of Deprexone?" asked Claire as she walked around the side of the table.

"Of course I did."

"Did every researcher in contact with Deprexone follow these requirements?"

"This red book is the godfather of drug development." Phil lifted the book from the ledge and held it up to the jury. "It protects everyone involved with an investigational new drug by defining the parameters in which we work. From the scientist with the initial insight to the consumer with the issue." Phil let the book drop with a heavy thud.

"What were the parameters with Deprexone?"

Claire leaned against the table's edge with crossed ankles. She was confident that Phil would magnify his expertise and his importance to the benefit of the prosecution. She hoped his arrogance would permeate his answers and alienate the jury.

"When developing an investigational new drug, there are three phases of testing with an increasing number of randomly selected participants in each phase. In Phase One, I explored the

pharmacokinetic parameters of Deprexone. Absorption, metab-
olism, elimination, things of that nature. In Phase Two, I looked
at the drug's optimal dosage in patients suffering from various
occurrences of chronic pain. This gave us our initial look at the
drug's therapeutic potential. In Phase Three, I studied hundreds
of patients suffering from chronic pain over an extended period."

"Were any red flags revealed when testing Deprexone?"
asked Claire.

"Not a one. Deprexone showed tremendous potential from
the very beginning." Phil examined the fingernails on his left
hand with the raised eyebrows of superiority.

"A copy of the investigational new drug application is posted
on the display board. Why is the risk of addiction omitted from
this application?"

Phil threw his hands up again and slapped them onto the
ledge in front of him. He dropped his head to the side without
answering. Claire remained leaning on the table's edge, waiting
for Phil to control his thoughts and his emotions. Several jurors
laughed at the dramatic reaction.

"It's insignificant," rebuked Phil. "It's negligible when assessing a benefit/risk analysis. When I began testing Deprexone in
Phase One, the results were consistent with the research I've
been conducting since 1980. The pharmacokinetics revealed that
the extended-release formulation provided relief for chronic pain
with minimal risk of addiction. My continued research determined the optimal dosage and great therapeutic potential."

"Can you define risk? One addict, two addicts, five thousand
addicts?"

"Objection." Landon spoke loudly but didn't look up. Dana
scowled at Phil.

"Less than . . ." Phil slapped his hand over his mouth and
looked to Judge Connor for reprimand.

"Overruled."

"You may answer the question," said Claire as she pushed off the table.

Phil pressed his shoulders back, lifting his chest and his face before answering. "Less than 1 percent." His signature thin grin spread across his face. "When Deprexone is taken properly by a person with no previous addiction issues, the benefits are quite astounding."

"Perhaps you should tell it to the individuals who died."

"Objection," Landon sighed. "Badgering."

"Sustained."

Claire smoothed the front of her skirt as she walked toward Phil. She stood curiously close. Phil attempted to create more space between them by scooting farther back in his seat, his discomfort apparent.

"You claim to have thoroughly completed all three phases of testing Deprexone in accordance with FDA requirements. What did you do with these test results?"

"Submitted them!" Phil jumped to his feet.

"I'm talking about the test results supporting the IND application. Did you store them in the front file cabinets in the laboratory?"

"Of course we did. Research never ends." Phil sat down.

"Did you hide the results showing a risk of addiction in the back file room of your laboratory?" asked Claire.

"Most certainly not. We hide nothing. Believe me, Ms. Hewitt, if we hid our data, you would not have found it."

"Why is the data revealing the addictive properties of Deprexone filed separately from other Deprexone data?" Claire maintained her proximity as she continued her questions.

"Each scientist decides where research is stored. We aren't in elementary school with color-coded boxes and labeled shelves.

We're highly skilled pharmacologists testing a remarkable opioid pain medication."

"Why are the test results showing the addictive nature of this remarkable opioid pain medication hidden in the NAS secret file room?"

"Objection!" yelled Landon. "Asked and answered."

"Overruled." Connor looked at Claire with an inscrutable stare.

"May I answer?" asked Phil.

Judge Connor nodded.

"We store data throughout the lab at NAS," Phil answered, oblivious to the intensity around him. "You would need to endure a laborious tour to understand the thoroughness of our filing system."

Ignoring Dana's visual reprimands, Phil dove into a detailed description of the small room with the sliding door. He elaborated on the importance of protecting research and the need for paper copies in addition to their digital data. He highlighted the intricacy of the advanced security that was shared with a select few.

"Would exposing the addictive nature of Deprexone, as opposed to keeping it secret, aid in the development of a safer opioid medication?" asked Claire.

"No!" Phil bounced forward in his seat. "The addictive nature of Deprexone is miniscule. Why would we keep it a secret?"

"Because we have a dead teenage girl." Claire's gruff response could be felt as much as heard.

Softhearted jurors murmured, watching Margo collapse onto Clifford at the reference to her daughter's demise. Her shoulders shook. Clifford watched the prosecution as he stroked Margo's head.

"Regardless of the supposedly thorough testing and low risk

of addiction, why release an opioid such as Deprexone if there is any risk that people will die?"

"Benefit/risk analysis justified release." Phil leaned back and struggled to cross his legs in the confined space. After kicking the panel in front of him twice, he placed both feet on the floor. "Drug development is a high-stakes race that pharmaceutical companies spend thousands of dollars to win."

"Why race in developing an opioid?" asked Claire.

"There are many horses on the track, Ms. Hewitt. A loss would cost us millions."

"Would not the safety of the opioid be paramount?"

"Safety always comes first." Phil leaned forward on the ledge as his tone softened. He clasped his hands and looked to the jury. "Drug development is like a racetrack, and NAS is a Thoroughbred. Placing or showing is not an option. We aim to win."

Dana dropped back in her chair and ran her fingers through her hair at the mention of her analogy between drug development and horse racing. Spectator amusement commingled with Phil's continued babble.

After too many hours of digging for answers, Claire dismissed her witness. Westcott's performance confirmed what Claire suspected, the questionable testing of an addictive opioid and the nondisclosure of addiction risks. Landon's cross-examination did little to contradict.

26

FISHING HATS
AND PLUSH TOYS

At sunrise, Claire rolled over on her pillow as brilliant hues of orange spread across the backyard. She propped her head on her forearm and watched blowing branches scratch at her window. A smile spread across her face as a familiar number lit up her phone.

"Why are you up at this hour?"

"No hello?" asked Alec

"Hello. Why are you up at this hour?"

"Reading through Shaggy questions."

"You've read them a million times. They don't change." Claire dropped back on her pillow and watched the branches battle the wind.

"Doesn't sound like I woke you. Why are you up so early?"

"You woke me." Claire smiled. "I was sound asleep. Still dreaming."

"You were not."

"Okay, trees woke me. I'm lying here watching the wind."

"You can't see the wind," said Alec.

"I can."

"Since you're up watching the wind, have you looked at the paper?"

"I'm not out of bed yet. So, no I haven't seen the paper."

"Moss died."

"Oh my God." Claire shot up from her pillow.

"It's in the paper. She passed away yesterday afternoon."

"I was there, Alec." Claire swung her feet to the floor. "Looking through charts on the other side of the wall."

"I know," said Alec. "Healthcare isn't what it used to be. You risk your life by showing up. Angry patients. Angry family members. Angry everybody."

"Delaney told me it's the risk of doing business. I wonder if he still believes that?"

At 7:00 a.m., the courtroom doors creaked open. Claire tapped the wall in search of the light while Alec walked to their empty chairs. She flipped the switch and joined him as ceiling lights flickered. The sparse conversation revealed the weight of the morning news. Bracing for continued courtroom drama, they reviewed notes from the previous day and wrote new questions as follow up.

"I hope Ethan's up to this," said Claire. "A swarm of butterflies is wreaking havoc in my stomach."

"If he has vocal cords, he'll do fine."

Twenty minutes later, a dark-suited Dana breezed into the courtroom with a provocative sway of her hips. When she reached Alec and Claire, she turned toward the defense table on the other side of the aisle and tossed a stapled stack of papers onto the table in front of Claire.

"Continuance." Dana commented over her shoulder.

"What?"

Dana pointed at the papers. Claire looked down at the bold black type. ST. LUKE'S MEDICAL CENTER—ADMITTANCE.

"What's this?" Claire stood to face Dana.

"Doesn't look like Ethan's as healthy as we thought."

"You said he was home with the flu."

"Guess I was wrong." Dana swung her briefcase onto the defense table and clicked the metal tabs.

"Continuance, my ass."

Dana looked over at Claire's incensed face. "The defense is at a severe disadvantage due to no fault of our own. A continuance is assured." Her ingenuous tone carried a twinge of deceit.

"Severe disadvantage? Ethan's nothing more than a flunky," said Claire.

"Au contraire. Ethan is a major component of our defense team."

"He's not a component of anything! When will he be available?"

"I'm sorry. I didn't bring my crystal ball," said Dana.

"I didn't think witches were caught without one."

"You'll need to find that out on your own. St. Luke's is a powerhouse when it comes to drug therapy. He probably overdosed."

"You're just making shit up."

"I don't need to make up anything," said Dana. "You can throw your tantrum, but we will get our continuance. And when we return to court, the onslaught will continue."

Dana turned back to the table and reached inside her purse. She grabbed her cell phone, tapped numbers, and sat down. She rolled the chair so that her back was to the aisle and her voice muffled.

"We need a plan B," Claire whispered to Alec. "I refuse to give satisfaction to that pretentious bitch."

"A plan B that'll erase the delusions Westcott created yesterday."

"And shed light on how that company really operates."

Claire leaned on her elbows and tapped her fingertips together. She glanced toward the whispered directives across the aisle and looked down at the revised questions in front of her. As if the answer were written on the pages, Claire bit her bottom lip and flipped her head to Alec.

"We'll call Dana Massetti to the stand."

"You've got to be kidding," said Alec. "She's as hostile as a hostile witness can be. Is she on the witness list?"

"Sure is."

Claire looked behind her. The courtroom had only a handful of vacant seats. Early arrivers tried in vain to save seats as people crowded in wherever they could.

"Looks like everybody's drawn to blood, and what's bluer than the Satoris'?" said Alec.

"My butterflies just became bats." Claire folded her arms around her stomach.

As the minute hand passed the twelve and the hour hand settled onto the eight on the analog clock on the wall, the bailiff entered the courtroom. The required formalities were followed before Judge Connor requested that counsel approach the bench. Bypassing on pleasantries, he addressed both parties.

"Ethan Hanson has been removed from the witness list. His absence is negligible. We'll proceed as scheduled."

Judge Connor then motioned for his judicial clerk. His grim expression caused spectators intoxicated with curiosity to speculate among themselves. The coolness of the room was fading as more and more people filed in. Although it was October, jackets would be removed by noon.

The obedient clerk bolted from the room as Judge Connor adjusted his robe. He surveyed the courtroom and visually addressed each attorney. Claire's animated eyes were countered by Dana's resentment.

"Counselor, you may proceed."

"The prosecution calls Dana Massetti to the stand."

Dana's jaw dropped. Her pointed tongue tapped her upper lip as her chest inflated with a long breath. She rose from her chair and turned to face the prosecution while she slowly exhaled. Claire was unwavering. She stood in the center of the courtroom with feet spread, shoulders pressed back, and hands clasped at her waist. Her unblinking eyes challenged her nemesis. The shared hostility bound them as the full courtroom watched the odd exchange. Dana turned and approached the witness stand like a model walking the runway, placing each foot directly in front of the last. She stepped onto the raised platform and slid into the chair as she looked at Claire. Her slow blinks furthered her impervious image.

Claire extended the taut moment by flipping through papers she held. She then raised her eyes to Dana's deflating composure. Dana fidgeted with her jewelry. Ethan's absence would force Dana to commit perjury or sink the company she worshipped. Watching her struggle to decide between the two was a sight long overdue for Claire. Judge Connor watched both women as his fingers drummed his desk, a signal everyone understood.

"Ms. Massetti, what is your professional line of work?" asked Claire.

"I'm in-house counsel with Novo Analgesic Systems."

"How long have you served as in-house counsel with NAS?"

"I don't know the exact date. It was after I graduated from law school in the top of my class. You already know that."

"Have you been involved with the release of investigational new drugs?"

"Are you kidding me?" Dana said. "I've been involved with the release of every IND that leaves that building."

"Then you are familiar with the federal regulations that govern the release of investigational new drugs?"

"Like the back of my hand."

"Are you familiar with Deprexone?" asked Claire as she stepped closer to the witness chair.

"Of course I am," Dana overenunciated as she rubbed her bare knees.

"Were you aware of its addictive properties prior to marketing it as an option for chronic pain?"

"I'm sure I don't know what you mean." Dana shrugged her shoulders and sucked in both cheeks as she shook her head.

Claire walked across the room, hoping Dana's eyes would follow. She wanted direct eye contact between Dana and the jurors when Dana told her lies. Claire knew the impact of lying to someone's face.

"Deprexone is an addictive opioid that has been marketed by Novo Analgesic Systems as a nonaddictive option for chronic pain." said Claire. "Does the back of your hand tell you anything about that?"

"I'm very much aware of the fact that NAS has a successful marketing department. I'm not part of the design team."

"Are you aware of research disclosing the addictive nature of Deprexone filed in the back file room and omitted from the IND application?"

Dana tugged on her too-short skirt, looking down as she spoke. "I didn't fill out the IND application. How would I know what was included and what was omitted?"

"You know federal regulations governing the release of INDs like the back of your hand, yet you don't know if the addictive qualities of Deprexone were omitted from the IND application."

"Is that a question?" smirked Dana, resting her forearms on the wooden rail.

Claire leaned onto the edge of the table with her eyes locked on Dana. Her breathing was slow as her thumb rapidly clicked the pen in her right hand. Judge Connor watched the unspoken challenge with impatience.

"Would Counsel please reword the question?"

"Ms. Massetti, what do you do with research revealing the addictive properties of an opioid?"

"I do nothing with it. It's not my job. However, all research, regardless of outcome, is placed in storage."

"Where is this storage located?"

"In the laboratory at Novo Analgesic Systems."

"Can you be more specific?" asked Claire.

"Are you serious?" Dana circled her head as she rolled her eyes in dramatic fashion before answering. "They're in file cabinets in the basement of Novo Analgesic Systems, 682 Cooper Square, New York, New York. Do you need the zip code?"

"Are these file cabinets located in the file room at the back of the laboratory, or are they located in the open area inside the front doors?"

"You've got to be kidding." Dana looked up to Judge Connor, then back to Claire. "Probably both. Dr. Westcott would have more information regarding the location of his work."

Claire stood in the center of the room, enjoying Dana's vexation. She continued questioning as Dana shifted in her seat searching for adequate answers. Dana offered creative half-truths on the complexity of the storage system and invented a mandatory NAS policy of placing discontinued research in permanent storage regardless of the stage at which it was terminated. Dana dabbed the sweat on the back of her neck as she again tugged on her too-short skirt.

"As a self-proclaimed authority on the procedures at Novo Analgesic Systems, do you have knowledge as to where Ethan

Hanson located the test results he gave attorneys at Blackman & Bradford law firm?"

"I'm no file clerk, Ms. Hewitt," answered Dana. "Nor do I babysit. I ensure that all state and federal regulations are followed. Where the data is stored is left up to the discretion of the researchers involved."

"You have no knowledge of what was on the investigational new drug application for Deprexone." Claire flipped through a file as she looked from the pages to Dana and back. "You have no knowledge of where the Deprexone test results are hidden. I mean filed. Seems as though your position with NAS is unclear."

"Is that a question?" Dana leaned forward on her thin thighs with straight arms and florid cheeks.

"Keep pushing. She'll break," Alec whispered to Claire.

"When test results revealed the addictive nature of Deprexone, what protocol governed the next step? Give clean results from the front file cabinets to the FDA? Hide the addicts in the hidden room?"

"For fuck's sake!" shrieked Dana. "I know state and federal regulations. I don't hover to see where people put their shit."

And break she did. Dana scowled at her purple nails as her ample chest rose and fell with each angry breath. Her verbal breakdown was now permanent record. Claire watched Dana and twirled a red pen in her hand.

"I have no more questions." Claire sat down.

"We have no cross," said Landon without looking up.

Dana returned to her seat next to Landon. Her runway walk was now rigid, and she looked at no one. Heated whispers shot back and forth between the two like steam hissing from old pipes. Onlookers stretched their necks to hear what was being said.

"Who needs Ethan?" Alec dropped a folder into the box behind his chair.

"Told you so." Claire rose from her seat. "Your Honor, the prosecution calls Margo Satori to the stand."

"Ouch." Alec reached for a new folder.

Margo's body stiffened at the sound of her name. She grabbed Clifford's hand as she looked from Claire to Judge Connor. Clifford leaned over and softly kissed her cheek.

Margo made the short walk from the front row to the witness stand. She promised her honesty, glanced at the jury, and sat down. Her delicate hands were still gripping a picture of Emma. She placed the picture in her lap as she looked over Claire's shoulder to her husband. Clifford gave his wife a thumbs-up.

"Mrs. Satori, can you tell us about Emma?" Claire looked at Judge Connor, knowing he would allow leeway.

"Emma was amazing." Margo looked down at the picture. Tears spilled from her eyes as she spoke of her daughter. "Gymnastics was her everything. She was our national champion four years straight. Her coaches expected big things from her at the Olympics." Margo touched Emma's face and looked up to Judge Connor. "She wanted to go to law school."

Judge Connor responded with a warm smile.

Claire and Margo continued to discuss the idealistic life of Emma Sophia Satori. Claire inquired about her training schedule, her commitment, and her occasional social life while Margo painted the colorful portrait of an elite athlete. Margo was animated when describing Emma's successes but grew sullen when discussing the changes that overtook their irreplaceable daughter.

"Mrs. Satori, do you recall what occurred on the tenth of March, 2021?"

"Emma had a qualifying meet. It was the last rotation, and she was tied for first place in three events." Margo looked down at the picture she held. Her eyes were full, and a single blink sent a stream of tears flowing down her cheeks.

Clifford folded one arm across his chest and placed his other hand across his mouth as he watched his wife struggle with her story.

"Did Emma take first place?"

"No. She got the twisties." Margo dropped her face into her hands. Her muffled tears filled the courtroom as confused strangers shared in her loss.

"Can you tell the court what 'the twisties' are?" asked Claire.

Margo's shoulders shook as she fought her tears. The courtroom watched, and Claire waited. Clifford continued to grip his chin as he watched his wife relive the worst day of her life.

"The twisties are when a gymnast becomes disoriented mid-trick by losing a sense of where she is in the air. Emma lost herself in the air. She didn't know where the ground was." Margo dropped her face into her hands again.

Claire walked back to Alec on the pretense of needing information. She knew Margo was fighting her way through the tenth of March and wanted to give her a moment to find the strength to face more questions. The courtroom was silent except for Margo's quiet weeping.

"What happened after Emma experienced the twisties?" asked Claire.

"Emma broke her femur and her fibula. She couldn't move." Margo lifted her face. She wiped her wet cheeks with the back of each hand and gently set her picture on the ledge in front of her. She looked at the picture and then up to Claire. "Dr. Kline repaired both bones in her leg. He told us rehabilitation would be long and hard. We then made an appointment with Dr. Delaney. He was my husband's closest friend and roommate in college. We know him well—or we used to."

Margo's tone became matter-of-fact. Her tears had dried,

and she no longer cowered in the witness chair. She looked to Clifford. Acquiescence showed in her eyes.

"Was Dr. Kline Emma's attending physician while she was in the hospital?" asked Claire.

"Yes."

"Was Emma given Deprexone in the hospital to manage her pain?"

"Yes. And she was given hundreds of Deprexone pills to take home. There were so many pills. Too many."

"Did Emma take Deprexone to manage her pain when she returned home?" asked Claire.

"Yes. Emma was a strong girl, but she was obedient. She did what she was told. She took the pills. She took them as prescribed on the bottle. At first."

"Did Deprexone control Emma's postsurgical pain?"

"In the beginning, it did. We were so hopeful." Margo struggled to continue. "But it didn't last. She needed more and more pills to control the pain. And then she wanted more and more pills just because she did."

Anger crept into Margo's voice and her posture. She grabbed the picture and brought it to her cheek. She looked to Clifford as she bit her tongue. She then looked back to Claire.

"She couldn't stop. She'd sneak the pills. She'd hide some to take later. It went on and on until I didn't recognize her anymore. She stopped when the Deprexone killed her." Margo collapsed with one hand gripping the wooden ledge.

"Objection. Move to strike," shouted Landon as he shot up from his seat. "The witness's last statement was inflammatory. The question before the court is what role, if any, Deprexone played in Emma Satori's death."

Silent jurors shook their heads as many wiped their tears.

Vicarious feelings of loss drifted throughout the room. Claire watched the jurors watch Landon and take sides.

"Sustained."

"What happened to Emma that prevented you from recognizing your own daughter?" Claire continued.

"She became sneaky and dishonest. Deprexone made her that way. Competing was no longer her priority. Deprexone was her priority. And because she had developed a tolerance to it, she needed more and more to alleviate her pain. More and more until it killed her."

"Objection," said Landon.

"Sustained." Judge Connor's stern expression sent a nonverbal message to Claire.

"Did Dr. Delaney continue to refill Emma's prescription for Deprexone?"

"No," muttered Margo.

"How did Emma get access to Deprexone if Dr. Delaney wasn't refilling her prescription?"

Margo bit her tongue again and looked to her husband. Clifford's angry, furrowed brows were conjoined in the middle. He folded his arms across his large chest as he watched Margo struggle. He mouthed a silent message, and Margo whispered back from the witness chair.

Thick silence covered the room as everyone witnessed the message between husband and wife. Clifford's unblinking eyes remained on his wife while Margo's eyes remained on her daughter's face. Judge Connor leaned forward with judicial concern as Claire repeated her question.

"Can you please tell the court how Emma got access to Deprexone if Dr. Delaney wasn't refilling her prescription?"

Margo looked to Clifford, and Clifford nodded.

"Michelle Moss," answered Margo.

"Did Dr. Delaney see Emma at any time?" asked Claire as she looked at Alec with the same guilt she felt upon hearing the news that morning.

"He saw her in the hospital the day she was discharged. But that was the only time. Ms. Moss said we didn't need to see Dr. Delaney in person. He reviewed Emma's chart and wanted her to continue with Deprexone." Margo's voice carried a sharp edge.

"Did you discuss Emma's behavior changes with Ms. Moss?"

"Many times. She guaranteed the pain would subside and the pill-popping would stop. She lied."

"Did you do as instructed and continue with Deprexone?"

"Of course we did. How were we to know it was a lie?" said a stronger, angrier Margo Satori.

"I have no further questions." Claire returned to her seat.

Landon rose from his seat but remained behind the defense table. "When Emma was in the hospital, was a plan devised to manage her postoperative pain?"

"Yes." Margo mimicked her husband's silent nod as he watched from the first row.

"Did this plan include other options for pain relief, such as acetaminophen and ibuprofen?"

"Yes."

"Did Dr. Delaney or Ms. Moss force you to choose Deprexone as Emma's remedy for pain relief?"

Margo's strength vanished. She dropped her chin to her chest as her shoulders shook and tears flowed from her eyes. She shook her head in answer to the question. Jurors stiffened in their seats as if accosted by the sorrow. Clifford cupped his mouth again.

"Can you state your answer for the record?"

"No," Margo whispered without lifting her face.

"Defense has no more questions."

"The witness may step down," Judge Connor muttered.

Margo rose from the witness chair. She watched Clifford as she descended the low platform. She walked to the first row and slid into her seat. Clifford whispered into her ear, and she whispered back to him.

"The prosecution calls Jack Freeman to the stand." Claire looked up at Judge Connor.

Without waiting for Connor's response, Alec bolted from the room. Claire grabbed a folder from her briefcase and pulled a small paper sack from the box behind her seat. She set both on the table.

Moments later, Jack Freeman swaggered into the courtroom with much less enthusiasm than Westcott. He wore his arrogance like a badge of honor. His indifference toward the proceedings was evident by the grunt he uttered as he followed Judge Connor's directions and took the stand. Jack promised his honesty and sat down as Claire rose.

"Please state your name and occupation for the record."

"My name is Jack Freeman Jr. I'm CEO of Novo Analgesic Systems."

"Evidence has been presented disclosing an aggressive marketing strategy used by Novo Analgesic Systems that focuses on primary care physicians with the objective of persuading them to increase their use of the opioid Deprexone. Why focus on primary care physicians?"

"Why not? Deprexone is an excellent medication for chronic pain, and primary care physicians see patients with a wide array of chronic pain." Jack propped his elbow on the wooden ledge to his right.

"Are you aware of the concern many experts have that primary care physicians are not sufficiently trained in pain management or addiction issues?"

"So-called experts are concerned about every advancement in drug manufacturing." Jack smirked at the jury.

"Of all physicians prescribing Deprexone, how many are primary care physicians?"

"I'm not sure."

"Half." Claire tapped the document on her clipboard as authority. "In the last two years, Novo Analgesic Systems has sponsored more than forty all-expenses-paid pain management and speaker-training conferences at resorts in Florida, Arizona, and California, with more than five thousand attendees. Was there a purpose for these extravagant vacations other than influencing the prescribing patterns of physicians, thus increasing the sales of Deprexone?"

"Our symposiums expose physicians to the benefits of Deprexone."

"Has this exposure lead to the overprescribing of Deprexone?"

"The safe practice of medicine is the responsibility of the physician." Jack's tone was stern. "Our job is to develop medications to assist them. Deprexone is one such medication and is a safe treatment for chronic pain."

"Does Novo Analgesic Systems use prescriber-profiling data to target physicians prescribing Deprexone?"

"We analyze the data, but we target no one."

"I see," said Claire as she walked back to her seat.

With several frequency-distribution graphs in hand, Claire walked to the front of the table and formed a small pile. She picked up the top graph and turned to Jack. He glanced at the jury and rolled up the cuffs of his sleeves as Claire spoke.

"Can you explain to the court what prescriber-profiling data is?"

"It's data we collect to analyze the need for Deprexone among physicians prescribing it."

"Isn't it more accurately described as data that details the prescribing patterns within a certain zip code so that NAS can target the highest prescribers with lucrative incentives to increase their prescribing?"

"We're meticulous about our monitoring when determining the need for Deprexone."

"When you monitor this need, do you provide lucrative incentives to the sales reps who bring NAS the most prescribers?" Claire tilted her head with a challenging grin.

"Like most successful companies, we provide bonuses for our employees. Our productivity is dependent upon it, and our success is evident of it." Jack returned the smile.

Claire reached into the paper sack and held up a stiff-brimmed tan hat. She looked from Jack to the jury. Jack's smile broadened when he saw the hat.

"Were the hundreds of Deprexone fishing hats given to your sales reps last year part of your bonus program?"

"The cost of doing business."

Claire reached into the sack again with both hands. She then held up a floppy, big-eared bunny and two music CDs.

"Are stuffed plush toys and music CDs also the cost of doing business?"

"Yes."

Claire returned the items to the paper sack and pulled out what appeared to be a yellow playing card. Alec placed the sack behind his chair as Claire walked the card to Jack.

"Were the free Deprexone starter coupons that were handed out to physicians the cost of doing business or incentives to influence prescribing practices?" Claire held up the card.

"When NAS develops medications that better serve the community, steps must be taken to encourage physicians to get these medications into the hands of those who need them." Jack's voice was curt and his cheeks red. A single stream of perspiration flowed in front of his left ear.

"Do these starter coupons encourage safe medical care, or do they promote overprescribing a controlled substance?" Claire spoke slowly. Her tone commanding.

Jack Freeman stood in response to Claire's question but quickly sat down. He crossed his arms with clenched fists, and his eyes narrowed. The courtroom was silent.

"Ms. Hewitt, my days are dictated by the aggressive competition that controls drug manufacturing." Jack dropped his hands to his thighs and leaned forward as his elbows bent outward. "As CEO of an international company, I must remain acutely aware of FDA regulations and the cost of developing medications within the confines of those regulations. I don't have the luxury nor the time to second-guess my marketing department or worry about plush toys and coupons."

"Do you have the luxury and time to worry about drug-induced homicide laws and the hundreds of pending lawsuits prosecuting opioid overdoses as homicides?" Claire stepped closer to Jack.

"DIH laws are a concern of everyone. But, as you know, they charge the supplier, not the manufacturer."

"Not yet," Claire mumbled loud enough to be heard. She dropped the graph on top of the pile and turned to Judge Connor.

"The prosecution rests."

Landon stood as Claire sat down. Intrigued jurors and Jack Freeman watched Claire leaf through the graphs. Jurors whispered to each other, and Jack's jaw pulsed.

"Mr. Freeman, what is the purpose of the educational medical conferences sponsored by Novo Analgesic Systems?" asked Landon.

"Our symposiums teach physicians how to better communicate with patients and their families to actively pursue effective pain management."

"Why is this important?"

"It's vital that patients assess their pain and communicate the status to their physician. It's only by doing this that they become part of their own healthcare team."

"Are there skilled pharmacologists and a vigorous marketing department with whom you have complete confidence?"

"Yes."

"Defense rests, Your Honor."

With a breathy voice, Judge Connor thanked the jury and both attorneys. He expressed his appreciation for their attention and joked about staying awake in a warm environment. With commensurate authority, he adjourned for the day.

27

MARGO'S TEARS

Claire entered the courthouse with a cool breeze by her side. Napkins from the top shelf of the cart blew onto the lower counter. The vendor slapped his hand onto the pile as he handed Claire her latte. She thanked him and continued to the wooden bench outside the courtroom.

Within moments, Alec emerged from the passing crowd drinking his Cuban espresso. "You and Freeman are the talk of the town. David and Goliath."

"Oh, brother." Claire rolled her eyes.

"I'm serious. Everyone's discussing Blackman & Bradford's female steamroller. You got under Mr. CEO's thin skin."

"Maybe. But I have the same pit in my stomach I took to bed with me last night."

"You killed it."

"I hope Connor sees it that way. His irritation with my incessant pushing might have painted me the antagonist in the eyes of the jury."

"You were zealous. That shows your passion for your client. Landon will have difficulty dismantling the case you built."

• • • • •

For several awkward moments after Judge Connor nodded for defense counsel to begin, Landon reviewed the papers he held as the entire courtroom waited. When Dana nudged him with childlike impatience, Landon shot up. His chair banged against the wooden rail behind him. He looked at the papers a moment longer before walking to the display board and removing the white cover sheet.

"Our society has no understanding of this research." Landon scanned the jury box as he turned to face the spectator seating. "Nor do any of us comprehend the complexity of the research taking place at Novo Analgesic Systems."

The colorful oversized brain covered with red arrows was in full view. Several of the more assiduous jurors reviewed their notes. Without referencing the large brain, Landon turned to Judge Connor.

"Defense would like to recall Dr. Westcott."

Judge Connor nodded as Dana rushed from the courtroom to find Phil. Gripping his arm and droning into his ear, Dana escorted Phil up the aisle for the third time.

With unmasked arrogance, Phil refuted all allegations of hiding the addictive properties of Deprexone and emphasized the integrity of his staff. His voice accelerated when he reiterated the ability of Deprexone molecules to flood the body with euphoric neurotransmitters and slowed when he referenced the lack of knowledge that governed his uneducated peers.

"Dr. Westcott, did randomized, controlled trials evaluating the use of Deprexone for chronic pain show significant improvement in pain relief?" asked Landon.

"Yes."

"Did you weigh the analgesic efficacy against potential problems and side effects?"

"Side effects are minimal. When people live with pain, all they want is relief. And that's what Deprexone gives." Narcissistic pride spread across Phil's face with another wet grin.

"Defense rests." Landon pulled his chair from the wooden rail and sat.

"Does the prosecution have redirect?" asked Judge Connor.

"Yes." Claire stood as Alec handed her a loose-leaf binder. She thumbed through the pages as she walked toward Phil. "In your controlled trials evaluating the use of Deprexone for chronic pain, was the improvement in pain relief extremely small?"

"You're splitting hairs."

"Is that a yes?"

"Yes."

"Did this small improvement show any consistent improvement in physical functioning?"

"What's your point?" snapped Phil.

"Is that a no?"

"No."

"One last question. Did you weigh the analgesic efficacy against the well-known opioid side effects such as respiratory depression, sedation, opioid-induced hyperalgesia, adverse hormonal and immune effects?"

"We considered all those possibilities and found the benefits far outweighed the risks."

"Prosecution rests."

Claire dashed into the courthouse deli ahead of an approaching crowd. She grabbed a Greek salad and slid a $20 bill toward the register. She didn't wait for change. She zipped out the door and down the brick path, settling onto a bench surrounded by syca-more trees. A brisk breeze rustled the leaves and her hair.

As Claire was finishing her salad, she glanced up to see Alec staggering toward her balancing a foil-wrapped sandwich, a bag of potato chips, an apple, and a large strawberry shake.

"Discombobulated seems to be your style." Claire laughed and scooted over.

"I didn't want to make two trips." Alec sat down with every-thing intact. "Ready to take another shot at Massetti?"

"I don't know. She gave us the evidence we needed, and the jury thinks she's a real bitch. Maybe we should stop with that?"

"I don't think so. Ethan would've spilled everything while all she did was paint pretty little lies."

"Hopefully not believable ones."

"Let's hit her again."

Claire picked up her briefcase and left Alec to his lunch. She meandered down the path, watching a squirrel scamper past her and race up the trunk of a nearby tree. It froze halfway up and turned its head toward her. Assessing the threat, it jerked its head back and continued its frantic race to the top.

Alec finished his lunch and dashed after Claire. As they walked toward an arched trellis, Claire froze midstep. She grabbed Alec's arm and jerked it back as her fingers dug into his skin. Racing past with arm-pumping force was Phil Westcott. Claire's eyes shot past Phil and scanned the courthouse doors. The bailiff was nowhere.

Phil sprinted up the courthouse steps while Claire and Alec walked closer and watched. He wheezed loudly as he flung his head from side to side. When a dark-haired woman walked out the courthouse door, Phil leapt. He grabbed her shoulders, yank-ing on her blouse. A white button flew off and hit Phil in the chin as he closed the space between Dana and himself. Claire tightened her grip on Alec's arm.

Dana twisted to break free, but Phil grabbed her arms with both hands and a tighter grip. He towered over her. Several passersby gawked, but no one interfered. Claire could hear their shouting, but no words could be deciphered.

The small group of onlookers increased, as did the ferocity between Dana and Phil. A large man took one step closer but was stopped when the woman he was with pulled on his shirt. After exchanging heated words, she yanked his arm, and they walked away. As the confrontation continued, Dana swung an open palm across Phil's left cheek. Phil staggered back before shaking off the sting.

A large security guard stormed out the courthouse door with a smaller man pointing in the direction of the conflict. The guard pushed through the gathering crowd as Dana shoved Phil and broke away. Phil stumbled back and watched her go. The guard did the same. He then admonished Phil and disappeared into the lingering crowd.

Phil gasped for air with his hands clenched in fists as he watched the crowd diminish. He kept his eyes in the direction of Dana's departure and grabbed the front of his shirt. With an anguished wail, he collapsed onto a nearby bench. With his head on folded arms, he sobbed.

Claire ran up the courthouse steps. Alec followed. The broken man on the bench was no longer the egocentric scientist they knew. A few stragglers lingered with nosy interest, but most had dispersed. The tumultuous encounter at the courthouse had lost its intrigue. Claire walked up to Phil and touched his arm. He groaned. Claire waited.

"She did it," cried Phil. "She did it."

"Who?" Claire stood by the bench.

"Dana!" Phil's splotchy face looked up to Claire. "It was Dana."

"What did she do?"

"She killed Ethan!" Phil flattened himself on the stone bench.

"Oh, God." Claire dropped down next to Phil.

"She couldn't have." Alec stood above them staring up at the cloudless sky.

"Are you sure?" asked Claire.

"Am I sure?" Phil rubbed his eyes, smearing tears and snot across his face. "There's no middle ground. You're either dead or you're not. And he's dead."

"Ethan was admitted to St. Luke's Medical Center. He had the flu."

"You don't think I know where he was?" Phil pushed himself up. "St. Luke's is a research hospital that experiments with ricin."

"Then you know he had the flu?"

"They have experts on ricin," Phil whimpered without hearing Claire. "Ethan wanted a miracle."

"Thousands of people die from the flu every year."

"Why are you babbling about the flu?" cried Phil. "Did you not hear me? That devil killed him. And she did it right in front of us." Phil's fingers dug into his hair and shook his head.

"In front of who, Phil?"

"All of us!" growled Phil. "At her house. We joked about her plant."

"She told you he had the flu?" Claire struggled to swallow.

"He didn't have the flu." Phil smeared more snot with the back of his hand. "He was poisoned. Poisoned with ricin as we all joked and ate our lunch. He went to the hospital with abdominal pain, and they found it in his blood. How could she do that? He never did anything to her."

Phil dropped his face into his hands and sobbed again. His

shoulders shook as Claire rubbed his sweaty back. Alec reached down and placed his hand on the wet head of the broken man.

As afternoon sunlight streamed in through the windows, Claire recalled Dana Massetti to the stand. A relaxed Dana rose from her seat and walked to the witness chair. With a trustworthy softness in her voice, she promised her honesty and dropped onto the edge of the seat.

"Miss Massetti, Novo Analgesic Systems spent six times more money on promoting Deprexone when it first hit the market than on any other drug, although it was not superior in any way. Can you explain that frivolous expenditure?"

"It wasn't frivolous at all. Deprexone showed great potential." Dana raised her eyebrows. "We needed to promote it for that very reason."

Dana answered with peculiar candor. Her poised demeanor struck Claire as odd after the earlier confrontation with Phil. She picked at the threads from her missing button as she waited for Claire's next question.

"Do you view the increase in Deprexone prescriptions an integral part of the escalating opioid abuse problem?"

"I've heard that claim, but I've seen no evidence."

"Here's the evidence you seem to have missed." Claire held up documents in each hand. "Statistics show that lifetime nonmedical use of Deprexone increased from 1.9 million to 3.1 million people between 2002 and 2004. I wouldn't think as in-house counsel you would miss millions of bottles of Deprexone leaving your facility or millions of dollars filling your pockets."

"Is that a question?"

"Can you explain the drastic increase in the nonmedical use of Deprexone?"

"Do you not understand my position?" Dana folded her arms

across her chest like a defiant child. "The marketing department focuses on increasing the numbers. The accounting department counts and balances the numbers. I ensure proper procedures are followed in the laboratory. That's my job, and I do it well."

"Thank you. We have no further questions."

Dana jumped from the witness stand before officially being dismissed. She flipped her hair with her right hand as she scurried to her seat. While half-heartedly listening to Landon, she reached into her purse and applied crimson lipstick to her lips. Claire leaned over and whispered to Alec.

"Do you believe Westcott?" asked Claire.

"Do I think Ethan is dead? Yes."

"Do you think Dana is responsible?"

"Not sure. Phil jumps to conclusions in the most mundane situations. And he loves drama. You?"

"Based on the things we know she's done, I don't put anything past her."

Dana fluttered her long false eyelashes at the jury box as she waited for Judge Connor to adjourn. A derisive smile settled onto her tight face. She sat erect in her seat and continued to ignore Landon.

Claire studied Dana's masterful act. "Murder suits you."

The following morning, Claire hid in the back pew of the courtroom and thumbed through her closing argument for the umpteenth time. Her lips moved as her eyes scrolled down the pages. Landon sat in the opposite corner doing the same while people filed in and jostled for prime seating.

Claire ignored the repeated opening and closing of the courtroom door but did stop reading when an older gentleman wearing a black Bergdorf Goodman suit and smelling of smoky vetiver and wood slid in next to her. Walter Blackman placed his hands on the wooden bench on either side of his legs and smiled at Claire. Claire set her closing argument beside her and returned the smile.

"I've been closely following this trial. I believe you've established a prima facie case of negligence." Walter turned to face Claire as he spoke. "Combining insufficient drug testing with unscrupulous marketing offers the jury several paths for finding guilt."

"I'm hoping they find their way down one of them," said Claire.

"How has Judge Connor treated you? He's a tough old bastard."

"He's demanding. But at least he treats everyone with equal harshness." Claire laughed.

"Every trial attorney should spend some time arguing in front of the old codger. His methods develop better attorneys."

"I can see that."

"He's been up on that bench about as long as we've been friends. And that's a long time." Walter nudged Claire and laughed at his own remark.

As Alec entered the courtroom, Walter stood to leave. He grabbed his lapel and turned to face the bench as Alec waited by the door. Walter's gray hair shimmered under the dim lights as he stood in observation of the room. Claire stood beside him feeling the motivation of his support.

"Good luck today, Ms. Hewitt," said Walter. "I'll be watching."

Walter slipped out the door as more spectators jostled past him to find available seats. Everyone wanted the best view of the anticipated showdown. Alec continued into the room and nodded to Landon, who also was watching the curious crowd develop.

"I got this." Claire gathered her closing argument and sat down. "There's no question in my mind that most jurors have made up theirs. If there are any doubters in that box, a small nudge will bring them to the right side."

"Some are waiting to be led," said Alec. "They want to be shown the right answer and given a guarantee they'll be able to sleep at night."

"I'll give them that guarantee. It'll come from ending Margo's tears."

Claire slid her closing argument into her briefcase, and they both headed to the front of the room. Defense counsel was conversing in terse dialog that could be seen but not heard. Everyone stood when Judge Connor entered the courtroom. As was his custom, he surveyed the room before taking command.

"The prosecution may proceed with closing arguments."

Claire stood and turned to the jury as she unbuttoned the front of her navy jacket. She ran her hand down the lapel. Anticipation brightened the faces of most jurors as they watched her walk toward them.

"In the past decade, while the rates of the leading causes of death such as heart disease and cancer have decreased substantially, the death rate associated with opioid pain medication has increased markedly. Sales of opioid pain medication have increased in parallel with opioid-related overdose deaths. Novo Analgesic Systems and Deprexone are leading players in this crisis." Claire leaned against the witness stand and looked to Landon and Dana. The eyes of many jurors followed her line of vision as the question of guilt lingered.

"What began with a letter in 1980 has grown into one of the deadliest epidemics experienced on American soil. Novo Analgesic Systems has pushed with unabated vigilance to flood the market with the addictive opioid Deprexone." Claire hurried to her table and grabbed a familiar illustrated brochure. She showed it to the jury, knowing it would spark their recall.

"While Deprexone has seen great success, and there are more Deprexone prescriptions written than any other opioid pain medication, Deprexone devastates the lives it touches. Deprexone kills."

Claire folded her hands in front of her as she looked from the floor to the curious faces watching from the jury box. Spectators squirmed in their seats as jurors sat stone still. Apprehension hung over the room waiting for Claire to continue.

"Deprexone killed an innocent girl. An elite athlete with a lifetime of success ahead of her. Deprexone isn't the silver bullet Novo Analgesic Systems claims it to be. It's an addictive synthetic opioid inappropriate for chronic pain."

Claire shook her head as she walked toward Judge Connor. She glanced up at him as he watched her with acute interest and kind eyes. She smiled before turning back to the jury.

"We live in a strange paradox in which society condemns street drugs like heroin yet condones giving the synthetic version of the same drug to teenage girls. Why do we buy into the misconception that life doesn't have pain? Because we've been fed lies and promised falsehoods. Because we've been offered a quick fix and told there are no consequences."

Claire's intensity and candor spread discomfort throughout the courtroom. Hushed jurors sat motionless as they listened to Claire's harsh truth. She then turned from the jury and faced the curious crowd. Familiar faces throughout the room watched with unease. But the dire expression of the man in the middle was unequaled. The creased forehead and flushed face of Jack Freeman exposed the fear he was trying to hide.

"Novo Analgesic Systems targets physicians not adequately trained in pain management," continued Claire. "They offer lavish all-expense-paid seminars to lure healthcare providers into their web. They hide the addictive nature of Deprexone while promoting the overprescribing of this opioid at the expense of our children. Emma would be alive today if she had not been prescribed Deprexone."

Margo Satori dropped her face with a discernible moan. Her shoulders quivered as Clifford rubbed her thigh. Jurors watched with tear-filled eyes.

"Novo Analgesic Systems sells Deprexone based on monkey research, inadequate testing, and hidden test results. They sold Deprexone in exchange for Emma's life." Claire took several steps closer to the jury. "Novo Analgesic Systems is guilty of medical negligence resulting in the death of Emma Sophia Satori."

Margo Satori climbed over Clifford and ran from the room. Jurors wiped tears as they witnessed the painful escape. Claire stared at the door as it closed. Landon's blank face rested on his clenched fists as Dana squirmed in her seat. She crossed and re-crossed her legs while she looked from the floor to Judge Connor to the witness stand, but at no faces.

Claire clasped her hands behind her back while returning to her seat. Earnest faces followed her as they found their own answers. Alec put his arm on Claire's shoulder and his mouth to her ear.

"If there were any doubters, there aren't now."

Landon ignored Dana as best he could. He leaned on his elbows as he reviewed the paper he held while Dana's sharp nail jabbed into his side. The jurors were drawn more to Dana's theatrics than Landon's deep thought. Everyone watched but no one could hear her sharp words.

"Erase everything. Hewitt spewed emotions instead of facts. I'm not losing this case because Daddy hired an overpriced woman with a personal vendetta."

Landon scooted his chair back with his calves as he stood. He put his left hand in his pocket and grabbed a pen from the table.

"Ladies and gentlemen." Landon's voice was subdued. "Ms. Hewitt has painted a devastating picture and brought tears into the courtroom in a deceptive attempt to cover the facts. We can all have our own opinions regarding the Satoris and Novo Analgesic Systems. But we don't get to have our own facts. As agonizing as this case is, it must be decided on the facts."

Landon twirled the pen between his fingers as he approached the empty witness stand. The creases of his suit coat rose and fell with each breath as he stood looking at the worn seat. With masculine poise, he turned to face the jury.

"Ms. Hewitt has trapped you in her contrived documentary about opioids and their impact on society. She'd like you to believe the science behind opioid development is black and white and pain either exists or it doesn't. But it's not that simple."

Landon walked back to the defense table and picked up the *Pain Medicine Journal*. It was the same publication he had shown them when explaining Phil Westcott's research. He held it up to the jury.

"This journal is a preeminent authority on pain management. Dr. Westcott's research is not only listed in this medical journal, but also referenced and relied upon by hundreds of premier healthcare providers. The letter referenced by the prosecution wasn't the start of a deadly epidemic but a breakthrough in the treatment of chronic pain." Landon returned the magazine to the defense table. "The misinterpretation of other physicians shouldn't be what's remembered about this letter. But instead, the fact that Dr. Westcott was the first to show the world that long-acting opioids could be used to treat chronic pain."

Landon walked over and stood in front of Claire as he continued addressing the jury. He paused and looked down at her and then back to the curious faces watching him.

"Ms. Hewitt misled you to believe that all opioids lead to

addiction and that opioids devastate lives. The truth is that sports injuries devastate lives. Twisted legs devastate lives. Opioids alleviate that devastation. Deprexone is the most prescribed opioid pain medication in the United States for one reason. It works."

Landon's enthusiasm resonated throughout the room as spirited whispers were exchanged. Alec looked to Clifford's resentful countenance and leaned over to Claire. He whispered in her ear. Claire sneered as she kept her eyes on Landon.

"Novo Analgesic Systems doesn't recklessly market Deprexone as Ms. Hewitt incorrectly stated," said Landon. "Novo Analgesic Systems strives to ensure that Deprexone is available to every medical professional treating chronic pain. NAS offers educational opportunities to educate healthcare providers on the benefits of Deprexone. Millions of people have returned to pain-free lives because of opioid pain medication. Of these medications, Deprexone is the most prescribed because it's the best."

Landon returned to the defense table and spoke with Dana. She energetically pointed to paragraphs on the document in front of her as she responded. She laughed as she patted Landon's arm. Claire watched the show as anger rose within her. She wanted to jump across the aisle and strangle them both but knew the game was best played if she appeared unaffected. Landon nodded to Dana and turned back to the jury.

"The prosecution has shown no evidence that people have succumbed to an aggressive marketing scheme. Novo Analgesic Systems provides an environment that enables Dr. Westcott to do his research. Jack Freeman doesn't need to hover, and Dana Massetti doesn't need to snoop. Every state and federal regulation is followed, and protocol in the laboratory is tight. Ms. Hewitt has used exaggerated allegations and flimsy evidence to create pity. She has taken a tragic incident and replaced facts with fear."

Margo Satori reentered the courtroom. She looked down at her feet as she walked up the aisle and slid in next to Clifford. She scooted close so their legs would touch. Clifford caressed his wife's thigh while watching Judge Connor watch him.

"Medical research does not evolve in a vacuum, and unavoidable outcomes can occur." Landon faced the Satoris. "These unfortunate outcomes are not indicative of negligence. In this case, there was no negligence."

Landon took a deep breath and looked back at the jury. He stood with feet apart in the center of the courtroom as he looked down both rows in the jury box. Most jurors watched him although a few faces were turned to the Satoris.

"You must reach over your hearts to find your sense of reason. You must reach past the pain and find the truth." Landon paused and slid his hand into his pocket. He then paced in front of the jury box as he spoke. "The prosecution scoured the Freeman laboratory in search of fault. They found none. They placed irrelevant emphasis on the location of test results and overlooked the validity behind the results. Was the testing inadequate, as the prosecution asserted? No. Were test results that reveal addictive properties hidden in the back of the laboratory? No. However, there are other unanswered questions. Was Emma taking Deprexone as directed? We don't know. Did Emma contribute to her own difficulties by supplementing with other drugs? We don't know. Doubt is everywhere, but the facts in this case remain clear. Deprexone was developed and thoroughly tested at Novo Analgesic Systems in accordance with federal regulations. Deprexone is a safe opioid pain medication that has successfully alleviated pain for thousands of individuals. And most importantly, Novo Analgesic Systems was in no way negligent."

Landon returned to his seat and Judge Connor dismissed

the jury. Little conversation ensued. Adjournment was a much-needed escape.

Claire left word with the bailiff that she would wait for the verdict outside in the courthouse gardens. As she wandered down the brick path, her navy pumps scooted orange and yellow leaves in front of her. She looked up and noticed most leaves were still clinging to the branches. A bright pink zinnia, struggling to survive in the cool fall air, caught her attention as it brushed along her calf. The faint smell was overpowered by the strong scent of the mountain mint adjacent to the path. Iron edging struggled to prevent the minty plant from crossing over the path, unsuccessfully in most areas.

Every few minutes, Claire glanced at the courthouse doors in nervous expectation. She jumped when her phone vibrated in her purse. She rifled through her bag.

"Damn it, Morgan, you made me chip a nail." Claire walked with the phone to her ear.

"I didn't make you do anything. How's the trial?"

"Massetti was classic."

"Any mention of Michelle Moss?" asked Morgan.

"Margo Satori mentioned her. She mouthed a message to her husband while being questioned on the witness stand. And got an answer. I don't know if they know she died or not."

When a courthouse door swung open, Claire jumped again. It was Alec. The bright sun highlighted his lingering tan as he held the heavy door and scanned the garden.

"I need to go. We'll chat when I get back."

Alec saw Claire and let go of the door. He sprinted down the stairs and slipped in with her casual pace. They rambled along the minty path and downplayed the anxiety of the last few days.

"The bailiff said you were waiting out here."

"More pacing than anything. I had to escape."

"Same."

"There wasn't a dry eye in the place." Claire kicked a small pile of red leaves. "In spite of wacko Westcott."

"His behavior was to our benefit, but I wonder how things might have changed if the jury had heard from Shaggy."

"You have to stop calling him that," said Claire.

"Why? Is he going to care?"

"I wonder what's happening with that," said Claire. "Phil never returned, and Dana waltzed in like the belle of the ball."

After one pass along the west side of the courthouse, Jack Freeman crept into the conversation. They debated whether he was the alter-ego of Phil Westcott or his polar opposite.

"He walked into that courtroom like a teacher on the playground." Alec reached up and plucked a lone green leaf from a branch. "He wanted everyone to play nicely but had no desire to join in the activity."

"He had an air about him," said Claire. "I don't get his naïveté in dealing with the people in his own laboratory."

"Maybe it's his way of accepting the goofballs in there. He can't question their work or their precious monkeys."

"Don't even get me started on the monkeys." Claire glanced back at the courthouse doors.

Alec chuckled as they turned the corner to circle the garden a second time. He watched the water splashing into the fountain from the open mouth of a stone fish and reached into his pocket. He grabbed a handful of coins and offered them to Claire. She took several and tossed them into the fountain.

"What'd you wish for?"

"Caffeine." Claire quickened her pace.

"At least it wasn't for the demise of the monkeys. But caffeine?"

"It's the only thing that will get me through this insidious waiting. I'm losing faith by the minute."

As Claire and Alec headed toward the arched trellis, the courthouse doors flew open and the bailiff stepped out. Alec grabbed Claire's arm and waved his hand to attract attention. The bailiff jogged toward them.

"Judge Connor is allowing the jury to read a transcription of Dana Massetti's testimony and re-examine the IND application."

"We have no objection," replied Claire.

The bailiff gave them both a thumbs-up and jogged away.

"Dana will hate that." Alec grinned.

"Who the hell does he think he is? That's impermissible."

"He's the judge, Ms. Massetti. Allowing the jury to re-examine evidence is the proper exercise of judicial discretion." The bailiff swayed on the balls of his feet.

"Well, the proper exercise of my discretion is to appeal the hell out of that. He's overstepped this time."

"Ma'am, I'm sure you're aware that it's not reversible error for the judge to allow a request for clarification if the court determines the jury is confused."

"Confused, my ass! They're not confused one bit. They're trying to pull a guilty verdict out of thin air because they feel sorry for a pathetic mother."

"Judge Connor has made his ruling."

Dana threw the paper she was holding at the conference room door as the bailiff left. The paper floated through the air in front of her while her cell phone slipped from her hand and struck the closed door.

"It's the last ruling he'll ever make!"

Dana grabbed the cracked device and threw it onto the chair. She then leaned against the window ledge and gazed at the leaves as they floated to the lawn. Phil Westcott sat on a bench outside the courthouse doors. Dana glared down.

"You have no idea how lucky you are, you big sissy."

Thick Columbian aromas engulfed Alec as he pushed open the coffee house door. Claire placed one foot inside, then spun around and walked out. She brought her phone to her ear.

"Claire Hewitt. Thank you." Claire looked back at Alec. "Verdict's in."

Alec let the door fall shut and followed Claire. Their casual walk increased to a slow jog as they headed back the way they'd come. When they reached the sidewalk leading to the courthouse steps, Alec smoothed the front of his suit and straightened his tie.

"We still have the Delaney trial ahead of us. We need to appear formidable when they read the verdict." Claire slipped into her jacket and buttoned one button.

Claire and Alec were the last to return. Clifford Satori held Margo close to his side in the first row. His exhausted expression depicted what everybody felt while Margo's presence portrayed the agony others could only imagine.

As Claire and Alec approached, Margo glanced over with a fragile smile of gratitude. Claire returned the kind gesture as Clifford Satori kept a firm watch over their return. He nodded to each of them in a veiled gesture of appreciation. It was his nature to guard his emotions until he knew where he stood. The verdict would govern his gratitude.

As soon as Claire and Alec sat down, the bailiff left. Anxious attorneys and spectators fidgeted with cell phones or idly chatted with anyone nearby. Nervous apprehension kept the activity and volume low.

"My heart jumped back to 1985 when Margo smiled." Claire leaned sideways toward Alec. "Those were my mother's eyes."

"Don't let your mind follow your heart. This is almost over."

As the jury filed in, conversations ceased, and all attention turned to the weary faces. Although a few jurors glanced at Claire and Landon, most looked at no one while finding their seat.

A dutiful silence shrouded the room when Judge Connor entered. His distinguished appearance commanded respect. He surveyed the room before sitting down.

Alec watched the jurors adjust in their seats and reached for Claire's hand. Claire glanced at his face, then at their hands, then at the jury.

"They can't even look at us. A loss will devastate Blackman & Bradford."

"Could kill our careers." Alec squeezed Claire's hand.

"Not to mention what it'll do to Clifford and Margo." Claire glanced behind her.

Sunlight streaming through the windows combined with a full room of bodies to create a comfortable warmth as whispers circulated around the room. Claire inhaled deep breaths as she waited. She had no reaction when Judge Connor issued instructions but stiffened in her chair as she watched the small piece of paper pass from the foreman. Judge Connor glanced at the paper, blinked twice, and passed it back.

"We the jury find the defendant, Novo Analgesic Systems, guilty of medical negligence resulting in death."

Alec sprang from his seat, pulling Claire's hand with him. They hugged each other and turned to the Satoris. Clifford leapt over the rail and lifted Alec to the tip of his toes with a commanding embrace. Margo's smile was no longer fragile as new tears streamed from her eyes.

28

DEFIANT
SCHOOLGIRL

The verdict spread down rows and across the aisle like a brisk breeze cooling the heat. Family, friends, and strangers hugged and cried for Emma Satori. Judge Connor left the courtroom with a rare smile.

As Claire talked and laughed with fellow attorneys, Dana Massetti sat in her chair with a stiff spine, legs pressed together, and her right foot tapping the floor. Her short skirt had slipped to the top of her thighs. She scribbled onto a yellow legal pad, scrolled on her smartphone, and scribbled again. A small group of women stood in the second row evaluating Dana's frustration with head shakes and whispers.

In contrast, Landon looked at and spoke to no one. He stuffed several files into his briefcase and left the courtroom with downcast eyes. He ignored Dana's presence and the lingering crowd.

As final handshakes and hugs were exchanged, spectators left as well. Dinner plans were finalized as people said their goodbyes and headed back to their everyday tasks.

"The Delaney pretrial conference shouldn't last long." Claire reached into the evidence box behind her seat and tossed a fishing cap to Alec. "Yours to keep."

"Thanks." He tossed it back.

Alec grabbed the Delaney documents and hurried past two uniformed officers as they walked into the courtroom. Undercurrents of excitement still bustled down hallways and in and out of office doors. A few people had returned to their duties, but most were sharing questions and opinions about the Satori verdict.

Claire snapped the tabs on her briefcase and slipped into her jacket. As she turned to leave, she noticed the few people lingering inside the courtroom had grown silent. All eyes were on the two officers approaching the women at the front. The clicking of their black shoes echoed on the tile. Being one of those women, Claire rested her hip on the table beside her and waited. She made eye contact with the first dark-haired officer as he tugged on the sleeve of his taller bald partner. The motioning of the officer's bald head veered them both toward Dana.

When the officers stopped, and as if completing a drill, squared up beside Dana, Dana snorted without looking up. Small beads of sweat pooled above her upper lip. With a haughtiness that challenged the officers to confront her, she flopped back in her seat with the folded arms of a defiant schoolgirl.

"Is there something you officers need?"

"Ms. Massetti, you're under arrest for the murder of Ethan Hanson."

The officer's blunt accusation echoed throughout the courtroom as Dana shot up from her seat. With an arrogant flip of her hair, she stepped closer to both men. Claire's eyes grew wide as her mouth dropped open. She slapped her open palm on top of her lips.

"Are you kidding me?" Dana wrapped one arm across her chest and rested her chin on the fist of the other. A crimson shade of red smeared below her lower lip.

"No, ma'am. We don't kid." The bald officer towered over Dana. "We have probable cause to believe you were involved in the murder of Ethan Hanson."

"The hell I was!" yelled Dana. "I heard the freak died of an overdose."

"Tell it to your attorney." The bald officer grabbed Dana's arm as the dark-haired officer stood beside him with both hands loosely clasped in front of him.

"You have no evidence whatsoever. You two are disgraces to your department." Dana spun sideways and slipped from the tight grip. The dark-haired officer caught her other arm and twisted it behind her back. "Get your hands off me!"

"We can add resisting arrest." The officer snapped handcuffs onto Dana's wrists.

Dana responded with another loud snort, this one producing a ball of snot at the end of her nose. She swung her head back and forth between the officers as she yelled threats about her connections in the department and filing charges. Both officers ignored the remarks.

The bald officer grabbed Dana's shoulders and nudged her forward as the bailiff strolled through the side courtroom door. He froze at the sight of Dana in handcuffs. He looked to Claire and then back at Dana as she was escorted down the aisle. Dana didn't look back to see who had entered. With her chest thrust forward and a defiant arch in her back, she continued the forced departure. The speechless bailiff turned and ran back through the door.

Alec stopped short when he entered the room and saw the well-suited legal team surrounding Delaney. Two attorneys, with whom Alec was familiar, were at the end of the table conversing in hushed tones. Two other men flanked Dr. Delaney and talked over him with zealous hand motions. A law clerk sat on the edge of the conversation taking notes.

Unthreatened by the opulent support and expensive suits, Alec headed to the adjacent table. When Judge Newburg entered the room, everyone stood. The judge casually evaluated his surroundings and took a seat in the front of the room.

"Please be seated. For the record, this is a pretrial conference in the case of *Clifford and Margo Satori vs. Dr. Richard Delaney.* Are there any questions?"

"No, Your Honor." Alec stood when he answered.

"The defense requests reconsideration of our motion in limine. Dr. Delaney's insurance provider, National Medical Protection, objects to the dissemination of private information with juvenile patients. These records are protected under HIPAA regulations."

Alec shifted on his feet. "The prosecution has presented case law confirming that HIPAA regulations do not preclude disclosure of patient information when medical negligence is at issue. These decisions have been upheld by the appellate courts."

"The motion to reconsider is denied. Is there any other discovery to address?" Judge Newburg looked back and forth between the parties.

"Yes, Your Honor." Alec glanced at the attorneys he knew. "The Court of Common Pleas for the First Judicial District of Pennsylvania, Judge Alexander Connor presiding, accepted a verdict in the case of *Clifford and Margo Satori vs. Novo Analgesic Systems, Inc.*"

"How did the jury find?" asked Judge Newburg.

"The jury found Novo Analgesic Systems guilty of medical negligence resulting in death. In the case of *Clifford and Margo*

Satori vs. Dr. Richard Delaney, the prosecution requests summary judgment in favor of Clifford and Margo Satori."

The muffled conversations among Delaney's support team could be heard but not understood. Random words jumped out and hand gestures flew back and forth as Dr. Delaney watched his fate be decided. Judge Newburg rested his chin on his folded hands, watching the fervor.

Claire battled with impatience as she waited for Alec. She stared out her window watching cirrus clouds eclipse the sun and strangers perform mundane tasks behind windows across the street. She spun her chair toward her desk and picked up the small glass dish that sat empty in the corner. She flipped it over and read the bottom. MADE IN CHINA. She flipped it back and traced the intricate design with her finger.

"Where was I when you snatched my key?" Claire talked to herself and spun the dish on her desk. "Keep it as a good luck charm. You may need it in jail."

When her office door flew open, Claire jumped as the dish spun to a stop. A breathless Alec stood in the doorway. His hands held the Delaney files.

"Someone's using the elevators to move furniture, so I took the stairs."

"Not in the shape you thought you were."

"I'm an amazing physical specimen." Alec sucked in his stomach as he strutted to the coffee table and dropped into a chair.

"Well?"

"Intimidation was their weapon of choice," said Alec. "Delaney was surrounded by attorneys and insurance executives when I arrived. I told Newburg the verdict and asked for summary judgment." Alec puffed his chest with a boyish grin.

"And?"

"Defense argued a little, but they didn't push it. They didn't want to fight a battle they weren't sure they could win. Exposure would kill them."

"So?"

"Summary judgment."

"Nice." Claire's shoulders dropped as she leaned back in her chair and smiled at the ceiling.

"How did things finish up with Landon and Massetti?"

"Oh God, Massetti." Claire's head shot up.

"What'd she do?"

"Arrested for the murder of Ethan. In the courtroom. While she was still cleaning up."

"Oh shit," mumbled Alec.

"After you left, two officers cuffed her and escorted her out. She looked like a feral cat trying to escape. Twisted and turned and hissed."

"I would've loved to see that."

"It isn't over," said Claire. "She'll deny it. Press charges against the arresting officers. She'll go after the entire Philadelphia Police Department if she thinks she can get away with it. She'll go after them even if she doesn't. Just for fun."

"Bizarre sense of fun. Bet you miss her if she goes to jail."

"Bet I don't." Claire swiveled her chair to look out the window. Large puffs of white were racing past. "I did feel a sense of satisfaction today. But I also felt sorry for the woman."

"You felt sorry for the woman who did her best to destroy you?" asked Alec.

"I caught a glimpse of the old Dana today. So consumed by her ego that she lost sight of her objective and crashed into a dead end. Albeit her crash was a lot bigger today." Claire turned back to Alec. "Enough of that. Let's talk about tonight. You have no idea what lies ahead."

29

SWEET
BABY GIRL

C laire walked over to Alec and sat on the arm of the couch. She kicked off her shoes and nestled both feet in between the flat cushions. Alec leaned on the arm of the chair watching Claire.

"The entire firm will be there tonight," said Claire. "So be prepared."

"Prepared for what?"

"Overserved attorneys and excessive toasts in recognition of the Satori verdict. Everyone will vie for attention until they're all too tipsy to care."

"I feel honored. Don't you?"

"On the surface. But you need to be careful. Handshakes and hugs will either be enthusiasm or envy. And you'll need to decipher which it is and how best to respond."

"Sounds like a game of Jenga. Be wary of a wrong move," said Alec.

"I've seen it before. There'll be a pretense of amicable support, but rivalry will be hiding behind a lot of smiles. While everyone will be proud of another B & B win, attorneys who've been here longer than you will be positioning themselves for the next big assignment."

"Can we boycott?"

"Uh, no."

"That's a lot of money wasted on interoffice contention."

"Builds morale," laughed Claire. "It'll resemble year-end evaluations mixed with excessive amounts of alcohol. You must be on your toes while making sure you don't step on others. And you'll be expected to speak."

"Why me?" asked Alec. "You won the case."

"You're the new kid on the block. There are partners who've not experienced a win of this caliber. They want to make sure they didn't waste their money buying you."

"I've been bought?"

"Bought and paid for." Claire jumped from the couch and sauntered over to the small refrigerator beneath the counter. She pulled out a bottle of sauvignon blanc and grabbed two glasses from the cabinet above.

"Are you expected to speak?" asked Alec. "You were first chair."

"A few words," said Claire. "I need to be elated with the outcome yet accustomed to success in the courtroom. Tough but not gloating. Let's start." Claire poured the wine.

"You have a right to gloat. You scored for the Satoris and kicked Massetti's ass."

"I am thrilled about that," said Claire. "But I can't reveal it. It's insinuated that those reactions are inconsistent with being a partner at Blackman & Bradford." Claire ran her fingers through her hair and took a sip of her chilled wine. "I hope I contain my delight after a few cocktails. I can hardly contain it now."

"I hope you can't." Alec slammed his wine and grabbed his jacket. "I'll pick you up at six thirty."

"You don't need to do that. Ride with the other associates."

"The celebration is in our honor. See you at six thirty."

Alec tossed the pretrial report onto Claire's desk and walked out without looking back. Claire watched the door close behind him and finished her glass of wine.

Alec watched the heat shimmering in a red haze around the streetlight above him. He reached toward his dash and pressed Claire's number. His charcoal cashmere suit resembled the cover of a *Gentlemen's Quarterly*.

"I'm a block away. I'll pull up curbside."

Claire was standing under the deep green awning when Alec turned the corner. She still wore navy but had replaced her courtroom attire with a body-skimming mini dress in navy and honey gold. She wore her hair in a formal updo that revealed diamond chandelier earrings, and her gold heels accentuated her long legs. Claire never attempted to conceal her height or her beauty by dressing down. Events that permitted fashion creativity revealed the elegant side of Claire Hewitt.

Claire approached Alec's Camaro as he pulled to a stop in front of the building. The doorman walked beside her and reached for the car door. Claire had known Norman for years and gave him a gentle kiss on the cheek before sliding in on the passenger side.

"Wow, you look amazing," said Alec.

"Thank you. As do you."

"Required attire." Alec shrugged.

Uncertainty tinged every comment on the drive to the country club. Claire and Alec wagered on who would go to the furthest extremes in hiding their jealousy and who wouldn't bother to try. They rehearsed their answers to contrived questions and practiced their spontaneous laughter. Claire reminded

Alec that the evening was as much an evaluation as it was a celebration.

"Is this commonplace with every big win?" Alec's white knuckles revealed his unease.

"No. They're making a big statement for a big client. And they're showcasing you. I told you that earlier."

"There's nothing to showcase. The other associates are going to hate this." Alec slid his wet palms on the steering wheel, leaving a trail of moisture.

"You're the shiny new car," said Claire.

"What are they? Clunkers?"

"The firm spent more resources on getting a commitment from you. They want to show off what they bought. Prove to the naysayers that you're worth every penny."

"Who were the naysayers?"

"Same ones," said Claire. "They'll ask directed questions about your involvement with the case and assess your actions tonight. Who you talk to, who you don't talk to, how many drinks you have, what you drink. Scotch? Good scotch?"

"Damn, I should have spent more time on my speech."

"You'll be fine. It's a big show. More improv than major motion picture."

"Maybe it is a major motion picture," said Alec. "*Psycho*?"

"Ha. I don't think so. Maybe *Gone with the Wind*. You're the spitting image of a young Clark Gable."

"Frankly, my dear, I don't give a damn," Alec responded in Rhett Butler fashion.

Claire laughed at the impersonation as she checked her makeup in the visor mirror. Flickering lights of the parking lot appeared in the distance.

The country club was in high gear when Claire and Alec entered. The valet exchanged Alec's keys for a claim ticket, and they breezed through the entrance. Alec grabbed two champagne flutes from a tuxedoed waiter as coworkers approached with outstretched hands. He kept one glass and handed the other to Claire. She took a sip of the cold bubbles as Walter Blackman rushed toward them with exuberant pride. Alec braved the firm slap on the back without spilling onto his shoes.

"Nice job, young man."

"Thank you, sir."

Smelling of the same smoky vetiver and wood fragrance he always wore, Walter turned his attention to Claire with an outstretched open palm. He displayed fatherly pride as he cupped her hand between both of his.

"Impressive performance, my dear."

"Thank you. Our hard work paid off."

"Yes, it did," said Walter. "Now let's get into the party. People have been clamoring for the two of you."

With his arm wrapped around Claire's shoulders, Walter led Claire and Alec into the ballroom. Beneath shimmering chandeliers, elegant round tables were draped in white linen. In the center of each was a vase holding a single red rose. Buffet tables were adorned with silver covered pans emitting flumes of steam. The room portrayed a sophisticated charm.

Heads turned and conversations ceased as soon as the three entered the room. Spontaneous applause erupted. Walter squeezed Claire in closer. Since asking her to join the firm, Walter had taken a special interest in her success and a special pride in her accomplishments. Claire was unsure why she evoked this response but welcomed the professional benefits it offered.

"Let's raise our glasses to Claire Hewitt and Alec Marshall." David Bradford lifted his glass as cheers spread throughout the room.

Claire and Alec nodded and mouthed *thank you* while people devoured their drinks and waiters scurried around filling glasses. After every toast, conversations resumed until another toast was shouted above the rising noise.

"To the hard work and success of two of our best."

"To the bottom dollar. May it be ours."

It was an unending stream of congratulatory handshakes. Throughout dinner and after Claire and Alec's speeches, the toasts continued. They became more boisterous and the handshakes more rigorous as the waiters continued to pour. And before long, they had little to do with Claire and Alec.

"May we never go to hell, but always be on our way."

By eleven o'clock, most of the attorneys still in attendance were inebriated and little attention was paid to Claire and Alec. As a docile waiter refilled Claire's wine glass one last time, Claire caught Alec's attention and gave him the nod everyone recognizes after a certain hour. Alec finished his conversation and his drink before heading to the valet stand.

Within minutes, Claire had thanked the proper people and bid the necessary goodbyes. She paid special attention to Walter Blackman. He held her hand and her gaze longer than necessary. His affection was clear. After a final farewell to David Bradford, Claire darted out the front door and jumped into Alec's car.

She leaned her head against the headrest with closed eyes. Her hands were folded on her lap, and a smile graced her face.

"Why are you smiling?" asked Alec.

"I don't know."

"Yes, you do."

"I'm happy," said Claire. "I didn't sense the envy I thought would dominate. For the first time, I'm part of the ol' boys' club."

"Yeah, but that could've been the free booze."

"There is that." Claire laughed and sat upright. She turned

and glanced out the back window at the country club as it shrank out of view.

At half past midnight, Alec drove by Claire's building in search of a parking place. He scanned the lot beside the closed bank and pulled into a space at the end of the block. Claire's seat was reclined, and the smile remained on her face.

"Thought we'd finish the evening with a nightcap," said Alec.

"Great idea," said Claire as she sat up and jumped out of the car.

Although the entry lights were still bright, Norman had gone home for the evening. Claire spoke into the intercom, and a friendly voice allowed entry. She stepped inside and held the door for Alec. They both watched the numbers above the elevator door as they ascended to the top.

Claire kicked off her shoes the minute she walked into her apartment and shivered at the chill of the cool marble on her tired feet. She dropped her bag and scarf on the hallway bench.

"Hang your jacket on any of the hooks." Claire walked into the kitchen.

Alec draped his jacket on the first hook and followed Claire. She placed two Champagne flutes on the counter before reaching into a lower cabinet.

"We need to open something special." Claire knelt.

Alec admired the contemporary décor of the apartment while waiting. The ivory walls were in stunning contrast to the chocolate-brown furniture, and each wall was either adorned with exquisite artwork or revealed an uninterrupted Philadelphia skyline through floor-to-ceiling glass. The view was breathtaking.

With the ease of a French vintner, Claire released the cork on her expensive bottle of Dom Pérignon and poured two glasses. Alec's eyes grew wide when he noticed the label. Claire picked up her glass and slid Alec's closer to him. With a tender smile, he lifted his glass and tapped it to the edge of Claire's.

After enjoying the initial sip, Claire motioned for Alec to follow her into the main area. She sunk her toes into the plush carpet before collapsing onto her brown leather couch and redirecting her attention to the Champagne.

"This is a definite step up from what they were serving at the club," said Alec.

Claire grabbed the music remote and pointed it toward the black box on the shelf against the opposite wall. With the push of a button, mellow jazz drifted through the room.

"I hope you like Tommy Emmanuel," said Claire. "He's one of my favorites."

Claire and Alec listened to the smooth melody for several moments. Alec admired the apartment as Claire daydreamed out the window. It was a habit she took with her to work. There were no twinkling stars, but the moon disappeared and reappeared behind dark clouds.

"When do you think Landon will file the appeal?" Alec finished the last of his Champagne.

"He probably started this afternoon," said Claire. "But this time without Dana Massetti or Michelle Moss."

Claire sipped her Champagne and kept her gaze at the Philadelphia skyline.

The volume button didn't work, so she listened to the music as it was. Too loud and too fast. Clifford would be back any moment, and it wouldn't matter. Margo sunk deeper into the chaise lounge. She ran her hand across the smooth nap of the embossed velvet and watched the pattern change. Indigo became cobalt if rubbed in one direction, and navy became periwinkle when rubbed the opposite way. The shades of blue were exactly as the designer had claimed. Calming and soothing to the soul.

Margo gazed across the room. Not a speck of dust could be

seen on the bubinga shelves gracing the wall by the windows. The bright hue of the wood accented the dark spines of the classics that stood between the bookends. The glass in the picture frames had been cleaned and glistened under the warm lighting of the room. One photograph shone above the rest. It was the picture of a stunning girl with wild curls.

Tears filled Margo's eyes as she looked at that beautiful face. She lifted her hand to her mouth and whispered into her fist.

"Oh, sweet baby, I did my best. I did everything I could, but it didn't change a thing. I should have saved you."

Margo reached for her glass of Chablis as headlights shone through the windows and swept across the room. Moments later, the side door opened with its melodic chime, and footsteps trudged down the hallway to the den.

Clifford stood in the doorway with weary eyes and ruddy cheeks. Erect and stoic, he didn't move. His breathing wasn't visible, and his eyes didn't blink. He looked at Margo.

"You're going to be all right. I took care of everything."

Margo collapsed into her lap as tears flowed from her eyes. Her glass of Chablis slipped from her hand and lay on the chaise beside her thigh. The light liquid darkened the blue shades.

Clifford walked to his wife and returned the glass to the marbled table as he looked down at her pewter hair. He swept several strands behind her ear and turned her face toward him.

"We need to get rid of this."

Clifford lifted the pearl-handled revolver from beside the empty glass. He turned it in his hand and rubbed the monogram on the side. He then slipped it into his pocket, kissed Margo on her cheek, and said goodnight. She watched him leave through blurry eyes.

"I couldn't save you. But I made them pay, sweet baby girl."

Opioids:
What We Should Know

Opiates vs. opioids—the difference: Although often used interchangeably, opiates and opioids differ. Opiates are naturally occurring substances extracted from the poppy plant and manufactured into morphine, opium, codeine, and heroin. Opioids are the semisynthetic and synthetic chemical compounds produced in a laboratory that become oxycodone, hydrocodone, and fentanyl.
    cdc.gov-opioids-basics-terms
    merriam-webster.com

In 1980, a physician letter to the New England Journal of Medicine advocated for more liberal use of opioids in pain management. This letter is considered a key component in helping opioid manufacturers convince physicians that addiction was of no concern and has been cited repeatedly as the start of the opioid epidemic in America.
    nejm.org
    statnews.org

From 1990 to 1999, opioid prescriptions grew from 76 million to approximately 116 million, which led to them becoming the most prescribed class of medications in the United States.
    unodc.org

From 1999 to 2020, approximately 841,000 people died from drug overdoses. Prescription and illicit opioids were responsible for 500,000 of those deaths.
    cdc.gov. (March 19, 2020)

In 2015, there were 50,000 fatal overdoses, more deaths than by car accidents or guns.

> "*Opioids' Devastating Return*," Distillations 4 (August 23, 2018)
> abebooks.com

In 2017, the overdose death rate had risen to 70,237. Of those deaths, 47,600 involved an opioid.

> "*Drug & Opioid-Involved Overdose Deaths-United States. 2013-2017*," Morbidity and Mortality Weekly Report
> "*Drug Overdose Deaths in the United States, 1999-2017*," NCHS Data Brief (329)

In 2020, an average of 44 people died in the United States every day from overdoses involving prescription opioids. Prescription opioids were involved in almost 24% of all opioid deaths—a 16% increase in prescription opioid-occurring deaths from 2019.

> cdc.gov/opioids/data/index.html

In 2021, there were more than 106,000 overdose deaths, including both illicit drugs and prescription opioids. Over 80,000 overdoses were opioid related, and 88% of those deaths involved synthetic opioids such as fentanyl.

> nida.nih.gov
> cdc.gov/opioids/data/index.html

In 2022, there were an estimated 109,680 overdose deaths—more than a 2% increase from 2021.

> cdc.gov/opioids/data/index.html
> journalstar.com

Teens abuse prescription drugs more than any illicit drug except cannabis—more than cocaine, heroin and methamphetamine combined.

"Prescription for Danger: A Report on the Troubling Trend of Prescription and Over-the-Counter Drug Abuse Among the Nation's Teens"
US Office of National Drug Control Policy (February 23, 2019)

Non-medical prescription drug abuse has increased among teenagers with access to parents' medicine cabinets. Girls between the ages of 12 and 17 made up one-third of the new users of prescription drugs in 2006.
World Psychiatry 16 (1): 102-104 (February 2017)

In 2014, 6% of teenagers between the ages of 12 and 17 reported abusing prescription opioids.
"How Bad is the Opioid Epidemic?" Frontline. PBS (February 23, 2016)

Due to the increase in heroin supplies in the United States and the decrease in prices, heroin use doubled from 380,000 to 670,000 between 2005 and 2012. This inexpensive availability of a more concentrated alternative to expensive opioids is a factor in why 80% of heroin addicts today began their drug use with legal opioid prescriptions.
"Opioid Overdose Crisis" National Institute on Drug Abuse (June 1, 2017)

Opiates such as morphine have been used for pain relief in the United States since the 1800s and were frequently used during the Civil War for minor ailments. The pharmaceutical company, Bayer, began selling heroin as a pain reliever and cough suppressant in 1898. Physicians were unaware of its addictive nature until 1920; it became illegal with the Anti-Heroin Act of 1924.
"Frontline Pharmacies" Chemical Heritage Magazine (October 29, 2018)
"Opioids: From 'Wonder Drug' to Abuse Epidemic" CNN (April 11, 2017)

In 2013, the cost of prescription opioid overdoses and abuse in the United States was $78.5 billion due to healthcare costs, criminal justice expenses and lost productivity. This cost rose to $504 billion by 2015.

> *"The Economic burden of Prescription Opioid Overdose, Abuse, and Dependence in the United States, 2013"* Medical Care 54 (October 2016)
>
> *"The True Cost of Opioid Epidemic Tops 500 Billion, White House Says"* CNBC (November 20, 2017)

Opioid addiction and abuse have made hospitals and clinics among America's most dangerous workplaces. American healthcare workers have a 16 times greater risk of suffering workplace violence than workers in any other sectors and accounted for 73% of all nonfatal workplace violence injuries in 2018.

> abcnews.go.com/Health
> axios.com/2023/08/10/escalating-violence-americas-hospitals

Approximately 50% of healthcare workers will experience workplace violence during their careers.

> ncbi.nlm.nih.gov/pmc/articles

Due to the escalated threat of violence, 40 states have passed laws creating or increasing penalties for violence against healthcare workers, and numerous hospitals across the nation are arming security officers and establishing their own police forces.

> abcnews.go.com/Health

In the United States, fatal drug overdoses increased by 539% between 1999 and 2021. In response to this increase, elected officials have begun passing drug-induced-homicide laws to charge individuals with homicide when they supply drugs that result in a fatal overdose, even when there is no intent to kill.

> usatoday.com/story/opinion/policing/2022/08/02/drug
> -induced-homicide-cases

Acknowledgments

Nothing we do occurs in a vacuum. It's always the people around us who help make us who we are. The people with whom we share our lives lift us up to reach a little higher, challenge us to be a little better, and use their voices so that we may find ours. I want to thank all the people around me who helped my dream come true.

On the publishing side of things, I'd like to thank my publishing team at She Writes Press. These are the amazing people who believed in me and got me to where I am today. Thank you Brooke Warner, my publisher, for seeing potential in my story and having faith in me to bring it to life. Thank you Shannon Green, my project manager, for your continual patience with my never-ending list of questions and your expertise in guiding me in the right direction every time. Thank you to my editors, Krissa Lagos and Mikayla Butchart, for giving so much of your time to see all the details I missed. Thank you Julie Metz for the stunning front cover. And my deepest gratitude to Fauzia Burke, my publicist, and Cassidy Ault, my social media and website manager, for their invaluable guidance, insight, and energy in getting this book into the hands of readers everywhere.

Most notably, a huge thank-you to my wonderful husband, Phil, and my children, Patrick, Ann, and Madalyn. It was your continuous support and unremitting endurance in the reading of yet another "final draft" that kept me going. Thank you Phil for never questioning how I was spending my time and for trusting in me. It was your patience and quiet understanding that helped push me to the finish line. Thank you Patrick for your gentle nudges to pick up the pace and get it done. Thank you Ann for always diving into what I handed you and willingly accepting a new version again and again and again. And thank you Madalyn for always standing by me with that affirming smile and proverbial pat-on-the-back that told me what I was doing was worthwhile.

Without the support, and encouragement of those who stood with me in this process called writing, this story might not have been told. It is my hope that those who are living this nightmare will find comfort in knowing others see their suffering and that they are neither alone nor blamed. I also hope that those who feel they are distanced from the opioid crisis will read this story and realize opioids are right around the corner from all of us.

It is this hope that brings me to those of you who took the time to read *Side Effects Are Minimal*. Thank you for doing so. It's a privilege to write something that others choose to read. I feel honored that you spent your time and money reading this novel.

ABOUT THE AUTHOR

Laura Essay attended the University of Nebraska and obtained a law degree with honors from Creighton University School of Law. *Side Effects Are Minimal* is her debut novel. Her knowledge of the opioid crisis stems from her previous work as assistant attorney general and a driven desire to expose the truth about opioids in America. For over a decade, she has devoted thousands of hours to working for the underprivileged, providing food and shelter to the homeless and refugees relocating to Nebraska. She served as a court appointed special advocate for foster children and in 2016 launched a fundraiser that provided hundreds of car seats for infants in need. In her leisure time, Laura enjoys cooking, music, running, and travel. She lives in Lincoln, Nebraska, with her husband and Australian shepherd, Riley.

SELECTED TITLES FROM SHE WRITES PRESS

She Writes Press is an independent publishing company
founded to serve women writers everywhere.
Visit us at www.shewritespress.com.

Match by Amy S. Peele. $16.95, 978-1-64742-018-5. How does a San
Francisco transplant nurse who never takes drugs die of an opioid overdose in Miami? How does an eight-year-old boy avoid the ravages of
dialysis and get a kidney transplant fast, and what does a high-ranking
politician have to do with it? Best friends and nurses Sarah Golden and
Jackie Larsen are determined to find out.

Hold by Amy S. Peele. $17.95, 978-1-64742-245-5. The holy grail of
transplantation is Tolerance, which would allow patients' bodies to accept
their transplants with no need for drugs. Who would kill the four most
prominent immunologists in the world to prevent this life-saving medical
advance from being achieved? Friends and amateur sleuth nurses Sarah
and Jackie are determined to find out.

About the Carleton Sisters by Dian Greenwood. $17.95, 978-1-64742-440-
4. A mother's impending death forces her three alienated middle-aged
daughters—a diner waitress, a heartsick alcoholic, and a Las Vegas show-
girl whose career is on a sharp decline—to finally face each other and the
mystery of their father's disappearance.

On a Quiet Street: A Dr. Pepper Hunt Mystery by J. L. Doucette. $16.95,
978- 163152-537-7. A funeral takes the place of a wedding when a woman
is strangled just days before her wedding to a district attorney—and Pepper, whose former patient happens to be the brother of the victim, is soon
drawn into the investigation.

Provectus by M. L. Stover. $16.95, 978-1-63152-115-7. A science-based
thriller that explores the potential effects of climate change on human
evolution, *Provectus* asks a compelling question: What if human beings
were on the endangered species list—were, in fact, living right alongside
our replacements—but didn't know it yet?

Water On the Moon by Jean P. Moore. $16.95, 978-1-938314-61-2. When
her home is destroyed in a freak accident, Lidia Raven, a divorced mother
of two, is plunged into a mystery that involves her entire family.